D1274214

PUNK SAMURAI SLASH DOWN

Punk Samurai Slash Down

THAMES RIVER PRESS
An imprint of Wimbledon Publishing Company Limited (WPC)
Another imprint of WPC is Anthem Press (www.anthempress.com)
First published in the United Kingdom in 2014 by
THAMES RIVER PRESS
75–76 Blackfriars Road
London SE1 8HA

www.thamesriverpress.com

Original title: *Panku Zamurai Kirarete Sōrō*
Copyright © Kou Machida 2004
Originally published in Japan by Kadokawa Shoten Publishing Co. Ltd., Tokyo
English translation copyright © Wayne P. Lammers 2014

All rights reserved. No part of this publication may be reproduced
in any form or by any means without written permission of the publisher.

The moral rights of the author have been asserted in accordance
with the Copyright, Designs and Patents Act 1988.

All the characters and events described in this novel are imaginary
and any similarity with real people or events is purely coincidental.

Printed and bound in Sweden by ScandBook AB.

A CIP record for this book is available from the British Library.

ISBN 978-1-78308-127-1

This title is also available as an ebook.

This book has been selected by the Japanese Literature Publishing Project (JLPP),
an initiative of the Agency for Cultural Affairs of Japan.

PUNK SAMURAI SLASH DOWN

KOU MACHIDA

Translated by
Wayne P. Lammers

THAMES RIVER PRESS

The samurai, a masterless *ronin*, sat at the front of a wayside teahouse. It was a magnificent sunny day.

With teacup in hand, he absently watched travelers coming and going along the provincial highway. After a time, he set the cup down, rose to his feet, and marched briskly across the wide spot in front of the teahouse. A father and daughter in pilgrim's garb were resting on some large rocks in the shade of three scraggly pine trees on the far side.

The father appeared quite worn out already, and to judge from the way he grimaced as he pressed a hand to his hip, he was suffering from a touch of lumbago. His daughter, a pretty girl of perhaps seventeen or eighteen, appeared at a glance to be the very picture of health, but in spite of fussing over her father with considerable ado, she was having some difficulty attending to his needs because she was in fact blind.

An ailing father and his sightless daughter. Had the pair perhaps set off on this pilgrimage in the hope of gaining relief for their debilities?

The ronin halted in front of the two and gave them a smirk. Which was an odd thing to do. He could have smiled. That would have seemed natural. But this was unmistakably a smirk. Then, before either had time to wonder about the incongruity, in a single motion faster than the eye could see, he drew his sword over his head and, *slash*, brought it down in an angled stroke that cut the old man from right shoulder to left hip.

Unghh. The victim's right arm came up as he fell backward. His carotid artery had been severed, and blood sprayed from it like a fountain. The swordsman leapt back to avoid the splatter, and assumed a swaggering stance with his naked sword resting against his shoulder.

The man's body twitched as the blood continued to flow. It was all too obvious that nothing could be done to save him. His daughter had sensed the alarming movements, but unable to see what had taken place, could only cling to his sleeve and cry out for him to answer.

What manner of outrage could this be? Without the slightest provocation, a samurai viciously attacks an innocent father and daughter making a tour of holy sites. How could such a thing be allowed to pass?

There were a large number of people in the immediate vicinity. Not just the master of the teahouse, but laborers, itinerant peddlers, a lion-dance troupe, and a pair of samisen jongleurs—to name just a few. Men and women of every imaginable description from among the great masses. But no cry or shout arose from these witnesses at sight of the heinous deed. Nobody screamed in terror or began racing about in panic. They simply stood in shocked silence, their faces frozen.

Not a word broke through the hush. The ronin said nothing, the onlookers said nothing, and the proprietor, too, said nothing. The only sound that could be heard beneath the clear blue sky was the uninterrupted twittering of birds. Then a samurai strode out of the crowd to greet the swordsman with a nod.

"If I might beg your pardon, sir."

"Yes? What is it?"

"My name is Nagaoka Shume, retainer to Lord Kuroae, the daimyo of this domain. And you are?"

Responding in kind to the mild tone of his interlocutor, the ronin calmly sheathed his sword and said, "Kakari Jūnoshin at your service, formerly of Sakushū Province and now without master."

"Then if you don't mind my asking, Master Kakari."

"Yes?"

"What cause did you have for cutting this man down?" A sudden sharp edge had entered his voice, suggesting he was prepared to take summary action if the answer failed to meet his satisfaction.

But Kakari Jūnoshin remained unruffled. "You wish to know why I cut him down?"

"That is correct."

"Then I will tell you. These two pilgrims," he said with a glance in their direction, "were about to bring a terrible calamity upon this land, so I took it upon myself to make sure that did not happen."

Having apparently breathed his last, the man now lay utterly still. His daughter sat in a heap beside him, lost in a daze.

"Why do you say they were about to bring calamity? They hardly look like they could hurt a fly."

"*Ha ha ha*, true enough. But that's what makes them so dangerous. They sneak in looking completely harmless and the next thing you know they've brought the whole domain down."

"I'm afraid I don't follow."

"Which is entirely understandable, since you're in the dark about who these two really are. So let me enlighten you. They're members of the Bellyshaker Party."

"Bellyshaker Party?" Shume gaped. "What the blazes is that?"

"I'm not surprised you haven't heard of them," Kakari said. "I'll be happy to fill you in." And he launched into the following account.

"Just as the Five Pecks of Rice League took China by storm at the end of the Han Dynasty, strange religious movements have frequently found fertile ground in this country during periods of instability. Bellyshakerism is another such false creed that has swept like a virus through the domains and provinces of the realm, and its spread has reached epidemic proportions.

"It all started with a man named Sudō Ranrinsai in Gifu Hashima, who formed a group that he named the Bellyshaker Party, as if it were a political organization of some kind, but the group is unquestionably religious in nature. Their central belief is that our world is bouncing around inside the bowels of a gigantic tapeworm. They think everything that goes on in this world inside the tapeworm's gut has no meaning, and so they long to escape into what they consider the true world outside—the only way out being, in short, by way of the creature's butthole.

"Now, their doctrines preach a number of different ways to accomplish this messy business, but in every case it involves a good deal of belly shaking, which is essentially a kind of dance. You stand with your legs apart and your arms stretched wide, then drop your rear end a tad and start shaking your belly vigorously back and forth. While keeping this up, you also close your eyes and slide your head forward and backward and side to side, letting out a string of yelps and moans. When a whole crowd of people starts doing this all at once, of course it looks completely absurd and senseless, but for the believers, that seems to be precisely the point. Since the giant tapeworm has a violent aversion to stupid, meaningless things, the Bellyshakers' prancing and dancing soon has it twisting in agony.

"Which, as I say, is exactly what they want. The tapeworm thinks some kind of toxic substance is assailing its bowels, and tries to shit the Bellyshakers out. It's their greatest wish come true—to be ejected into the world outside. Not that any of it goes so easy. I mean, after all, when we get toxins inside us, it doesn't do us much good to just writhe around in pain, now, does it? Our body's immune system has to kick in and come to our rescue before we can hope to get better. So, sadly enough, for Bellyshakers and beast alike, no ordinary clamor or commotion is going to get the poisons to pass—except that, since the whole idea of a giant tapeworm's gut came out of thin air to begin with, and since, far from the silliness being penance, the participants seem to be having such fun, maybe it's not such an unhappy situation after all.

"Still, if they want to be discharged as feces, they have to keep the shaking going, so they shake in front of people's gates, they shake at all the merchants' shops, they shake in public meeting houses, they shake wherever and whenever they may care, hollering wildly all the while. In the early stages, the sight of the half-naked believers shimmying about, many a comely lass among them, draws out the oglers both curious and lewd. But it's funny how people react when they see things they don't understand. No matter how good a time the dancers seem to be having, the onlookers are soon yelling at them to stop with their stupid antics on other people's doorsteps, even offering them money if they'll just hurry up and move along. But the dancers aren't about to be sent on their way so easily, they only shake their little bellies all the harder, which riles the spectators even more, until finally they turn to force— trying to drive them off with punches and kicks and stones and sticks. Unfortunately, the faithful see this as a sign of the tapeworm's suffering, which to them is a good thing, so they kick up their wild gyrations yet another notch.

"Under the circumstances, it need be no surprise that fatalities occur from time to time. But—perverse as it may seem—far from acting as a damper, this fact only spurs the silliness further.

"*How could that be?* you may well wonder, and the answer is really quite simple. Although the highest ideal may be to exit by way of the tapeworm's rear, to die in the throes of shaking is regarded with special favor as well. This is known as spewing, and even though they soon end up back inside the bowels, they believe they briefly get to visit the true world outside first, so the spewee, as it were, is regarded with great reverence, and worshiped from that time forward as what they call a 'Spew Saint.'

"To mention just one example, a holy man named Nitta Gohachi gained that status after he quite shockingly broke into the mansion of a clan elder and found his way to the daughter's bedchamber, where he exposed himself and danced with abandon until he was cut down by a retainer, his head lopped clean off, and in fact continued to dance for another two hours even after that. The story goes that his head tumbled through the air and landed in an alcove, from where he watched his headless body dancing away with a big grin on his face. Afterwards, in the middle of the night, even though there were no other believers present, the master of the house began shrieking for them to stop and went on a rampage with his sword, going from room to room cutting down everybody in sight before hanging himself at a nearby shrine. Adherents accept every detail of this preposterous legend as absolute literal truth.

"There's an old saying about falsehoods: 'One dog barks, and a thousand dogs echo.' Beliefs of every kind spread like a contagion among the people, and this one's no exception. The membership keeps on swelling.

"Which is of course no small concern for the authorities. The more the population of these ignoramuses grows, the more tax collections drop and the budget gets thrown out of whack. When the shortfall has to be borrowed, interest costs bring new strains on the purse strings, resulting in reduced stipends for the vassals, cutbacks in spending, and whatever other austerity measures those in charge of finances can think of—but since the problem lies in dwindling revenue, their options are severely limited. Retrenchments make the lives of bottom-rung samurai exceedingly tenuous, and some of them begin joining the sect themselves, now spending their time shaking their bellies instead of going to work. Meanwhile, even among the higher-ranking families, the women and children start turning to the cult, which further upsets the normal order of things—adding to a vicious cycle that puts both politics and the economy in ever greater disarray.

"To head off a complete loss of control, the authorities have tried to clamp down, but since the belly shaking is essentially an act of desperation to begin with, repressive measures don't have much effect. All of which is to say, the Bellyshaker movement has gained enough steam that it can no longer be dismissed as just another insignificant new sect. When I saw it trying to stretch its nefarious reach to this domain as well, I knew right away it had to be nipped in the bud."

"*Hm-hmm*," said Nagaoka Shume gravely, as Jūnoshin wrapped up his lengthy discourse, "So these people are that dangerous, are they? And they're coming here? *Hm-hmm*… It doesn't sound like a threat we can afford to ignore. *Hm-hmm*."

"It's rather too late to be *hum-humm*ing about it now. They've already arrived."

"But I must say, this is an excellent turn of events!"

"Excellent? What are you talking about? There's nothing the least bit good about it."

"No, no, it is very good indeed. It would have been a disaster if this crackpot religion had had a chance to spread around, but you've cut them down before they could get a foothold…. Which reminds me. We still have the girl to get rid of," he said, reaching for his sword.

Jūnoshin held out a hand to stop him. "Wait."

"But if we don't hurry up and kill her, we'll soon have a contagion on our hands."

"Set your mind at ease. It doesn't spread through the air. It's best not to kill her yet."

"It is?"

"Yes, indeed. Trust me, you'll be better off taking my word on this."

"All right, then. But why?"

"We-e-ell, where to begin? Perhaps I'll start with your view that this is an excellent turn of events and all is now well."

"Proceed."

"In a nutshell, all is *not* well."

"Huh?"

"In fact, the situation is quite disastrously bad."

"Surely not. The domain has held the Bellyshakers off at the landing, so to speak, right on this very spot."

"Forgive me, but you are being far too optimistic. It's true that I cut this man down."

"There you go. It's all good."

"No, it's not all good."

"Why not?"

"With these Bellyshakers, if you see one, you have to assume at least twenty more are lurking somewhere nearby."

"Are you saying they may already have begun to multiply here?"

"There's a very high probability," Jūnoshin said, folding his arms.

"And how is that likely to affect the domain?"

"There's a good chance it's doomed."

"Y-you have to be kidding. What can we do to stop it?"

"Nothing, really. I suppose if you're lucky, the cult will find the ground here insufficiently fertile to take firm root, and it will naturally wither away, but if you're not so lucky, it'll spread like an invasive weed that can't be eradicated. I'm afraid that's the more likely scenario."

Jūnoshin's tone was matter-of-fact, but Shume flushed crimson. "A-are you serious?" he demanded, pressing closer.

But neither the sharpness of his tone nor his threatening body language had any noticeable effect on the ronin. "That's about that size of it," he said with an indifferent shrug, then added with a light wave of his hand, "Well, so long then." Turning his back on Shume and the still-dazed girl sitting nearby, he started to walk away.

Shume was taken aback. After all, the man had launched into a lengthy account of the new religious cult without even being asked, and then he'd stopped him from taking out the girl. Not only had he implied there was a good deal more to be said about the Bellyshakers, but he had yet to address the question of what to do about the girl. Instead, he was walking away.

"Wait! Hold on a sec," Shume called after him.

Jūnoshin turned. "Was there something else?"

"You can't just leave me hanging like this."

"What do you mean?"

"Isn't it obvious? First you ramble on and on, laying out all these alarming details, and then when I figure I'd better kill the girl, you tell me I shouldn't, sounding like you had good reason, so I'm waiting for you to explain why, but instead you declare the domain all but doomed and simply start walking away without offering the barest suggestion how we might forestall the calamity. You can't do that."

"I can't?"

"Absolutely not."

"I beg to differ."

"Why?"

"Think about it. It's not my fault that the Bellyshakers have infiltrated this domain, so it was strictly out of the kindness of my heart that I shared my knowledge of them with you. I could have left well enough alone and not said a peep. In other words, even if I've given you only one tiny morsel of information, you've still gained vital intelligence that you didn't have before. Yet now you're foaming at the mouth that I didn't give you enough. Basically, you're calling me a stingy bastard."

"Well, now that you put it that way…"

"That's the way it is no matter how I put it."

"But still…"

"But still what?"

"When I said I was going to kill the girl, you said I should take your word that it's not a good idea."

"Yes, I did."

"I could have sworn you were getting ready to say something more about why it's not such a good idea. Now, maybe it's just me, but that's definitely how it sounded. So I'm feeling like you've left me in the lurch, you know, like—"

"No, you're right, I won't deny it. At that particular point in time, I did intend to tell you more about the Bellyshakers, as well as what you should do about the girl."

"There you go. So, then, what made you change your mind? If I've offended you in some way, I apologize," he said bowing deeply. "I beg your forgiveness."

"Oh, none of that, now. It isn't becoming of a samurai. You haven't offended me at all."

"Then why?"

"I just don't feel like it anymore."

"Huh?"

"I was definitely considering it at first, but then I had a change of heart somehow, and I decided not to."

"What changed your mind?"

"It wasn't anything in particular. No rhyme or reason—it just suddenly seemed like too much bother to say anything more. Especially since I'm not under any obligation, and I was only speaking from kindness. I'm free to stop any time I want. So I'll be stepping on along now."

"Wait, wait."

"Was there something else?"

"I'm begging you. You have to tell me."

"Forget it."

Jūnoshin turned his back and started away again. The breeze rippled the back of his robe.

Until now, Shume had been standing there meekly with his head bowed, but in an abrupt change of attitude he now roared, "Hold it right there!"

"Give it up, will you? So long." The ronin didn't even turn his head.

"Halt, or else!" Shume bellowed after him.

"Or else what?"

"I'll kill you." Shume drew his sword and raised it in front of him.

"I don't think you really want to do that," the other man said coolly. He unsheathed his sword, too, but held it slack at his side, looking no more eager for a fight than he had sounded.

Shume raised his weapon above his head and began centering his energies with battle cries.

"*Hiyahh! Kiyahh!*"

"I mean, stop and think a minute," the ronin said as if growing weary of the whole thing. "You're trying to get some information out of me, right? How's that gonna work out for you if you slice me up?"

"It won't, but that's why I'm saying, if you value your life, you better help me out. And that's no idle threat. If you're not going to cooperate, then you're no more use to me alive than dead. I might as well kill you just because it'll feel good."

"Hardy har har har."

"Why the fake laugh?"

"You couldn't do it if you tried."

"That's what you think. Come on! Put 'er up!"

"I'm telling you, you really don't want to do this."

"Give me one good reason."

"I hadn't gotten around to mentioning it yet, but I'm actually a superhuman swordsman. I'm unbelievably, kick-ass good with this thing."

"Yeah, yeah, yeah, the same to you."

"I'm pretty sure we're in different leagues."

"You are, are you? Well, you might like to know that I have a certificate from the Ittō-ryū School."

"Ah, yes, yes, of course, I don't have anything like that. But I assure you, I'm really strong. Give it up, give it up," Jūnoshin said as he calmly returned his sword to its sheath.

"Enough of your games!" shouted Shume, as he stepped forward to slash at his opponent. The next instant, he found himself in a heap on the ground with his sword lying loose beside him.

As soon as he made his move, Jūnoshin had drawn faster than the eye could see and dealt a crushing blow to his wrist—turning the back of his blade down at the last possible instant before it struck.

Huddled in a heap with his other hand pressed tightly to the spot, Shume said nothing.

After putting his sword away again, Jūnoshin glanced about, looking embarrassed.

The girl still sat there as if in a stupor, unable to move.

In stark contrast to the tension surrounding the three motionless figures, the highway had regained its air of utter tranquility. The crowd of onlookers had long since melted away, tiring of the argument between the two men that seemed to be going nowhere. If they'd only stuck around a short while longer, they'd have witnessed the unfolding of a real-life showdown.

The cloudless sky was bluer than ever. The mooing of a cow could be heard now and then amidst the twitter of birds.

Before long these pastoral sounds were joined by a discordant *ah, ah, ah*, at first low but gradually growing louder, until the sound turned into a full-throated *wahh, wahhh, wahhhh*. The defeated man had broken into uncontrollable sobs.

A grown man in the prime of his life, bawling like a baby—it was a sorry sight to behold. Having gone inside when the crowd dispersed, the master of the teahouse now reemerged to see what the fuss was about.

The outburst made Jūnoshin feel awkward. "Since when does a samurai cry? Pull yourself together," he said, avoiding Shume's eyes.

"B-b-but…but…"

"There're no buts about it. Stop being such a wuss."

"But what am I supposed to do now?"

"You really are a piece of work, aren't you? Would you please stop that blubbering? Look, when I started out, I had every intention of telling you all sorts of other stuff. But then I got this vibe like, I don't know, like you thought you were entitled or something. Like you took my kindness for granted—*of course* I would tell you, what else was I going to do?—and it kind of pissed me off, so I decided to cut it short. But then what do you do? You go ballistic on me instead and come at me with your sword. Well, you can't expect me to just let you cut me down without a fight now, can you? So I strike back, and the next thing I know you're crying your eyes out, playing the victim. Are you kidding me?"

"*Wahhhh*, I'm sorry. Please don't hold it against me. I think I'm having some kind of panic attack."

"Panic attack, shmanic attack. I'm outta here. So long."

"*Wahhhhh*, no-o-o, wait! Please wait! If you go now, I have no idea what I'm supposed to do."

"That's not my problem. Get your hands off me. What the hell? Good grief! You're dripping snot all over."

"I wet myself a little, too."

"Now that's seriously gross. Come on, let go, I'm telling you! Look around, will you? We're drawing a crowd again. It's nothing, folks. Move along. Just move along."

"Please, I'm begging you."

Oh, man. Jūnoshin rolled his eyes to the sky as if he'd really reached the end of his rope, but then after taking a deep breath, mustered up a different tone.

"All right, fine. I'll tell you," he said.

"You will?"

"Yes, I will"

"M-much obliged, much obliged, I'll be most grateful." Shume bobbed his head obsequiously up and down.

"But!" he boomed, "I have one condition."

"Condition?"

"Yes."

"And what exactly might this condition be?" Shume asked with trepidation.

"Well, I originally thought I'd give you this information out of simple kindness. But then I started running up against all your attitude—the entitlement, the disrespect—after which you suddenly turned on me with your sword, and further after which you started bawling your head off, not to mention peeing yourself just to be nasty, so now I've just basically had it with you. I'm plain fed up. The kindness in me is gone, *poof*, plumb evaporated into thin air. But if you're still going to insist," he said, before taking a long pause.

"Yes? If I still insist?"

"Then it has to be a straight business proposition."

"Which means what?"

"That I come to it with selfish motives only, purely as a job, with no place for kindness. In other words, whether I open up or not depends entirely on the terms."

"By terms would you be referring to some sort of monetary consideration?" Shume asked apprehensively.

"Yes, you might say so. But actually, as I have indicated, I am masterless at the moment, and have been so for quite some time. I'm eager to find a position. So I'm thinking more along the lines of you putting in a good word for me with the clan for a post. Those are my terms."

"You wish to be hired as a retainer to Lord Kuroae?"

"Exactly."

"We-e-ell now," said Shume, "I daresay that goes beyond any authority I myself possess… The clan has certain procedures we're required to follow when bringing in new hires, you see, whereas if we're only talking about a sum of money, then something on the order of, say, ten *ryō* might be within the realm of…Or actually, maybe not. We have certain guidelines in place regarding remuneration for services, too, and in a case like this the range unfortunately tops out at one large gold piece, which I'm afraid isn't quite as much. That's the best we can do for you. Especially considering we don't actually know anything about you."

The moment Jūnoshin brought up the possibility of becoming a retainer, Shume had begun to hem and haw. Now Jūnoshin cut him off.

"You know," he said loudly, "I seem to recall that only a minute ago you were peeing your loincloth and bawling your head off. But now what? The second I lay out my terms, you're full of excuses why you can't do anything, there are certain procedures and guidelines to follow, you don't even know me. What kind of game do you think you're playing? Do you take me for a chump?"

"By no means."

"Then what the hell's going on here? Kicking up a fuss or scattering a few tears is cheap, so you're happy to put on a show, but once we're talking cold hard cash or a suitable stipend, it's just not possible?"

"I never said it wasn't possible. But times are hard, and we've already been going through the kind of cutbacks you mentioned, with everybody on reduced stipends, so under the circumstances, I couldn't help kind of, sort of, vaguely wondering if the idea of hiring someone new right now, at this particular moment, might, just may, possibly, perhaps be a bit of a tough sell, you know. That's all."

"Well, fine, if that's the way it is, I certainly won't insist. It's not as if I was bent on getting hired by hook or by crook. If you can't accept my terms, then we can just forget the whole thing. From my perspective, this isn't the only place that's got a Bellyshaker problem to deal with. And from yours, as you say, I'm an unknown quantity, so you're probably better off not taking me on anyway, right? Let the Bellyshakers run rampant and bring the clan down. All that means, *ha ha ha*, is that you'll soon be a ronin like me, wandering from domain to domain looking for work. Of course, even among ronin, specialists with my kind of expertise can find plenty of work, but what exactly was it that you do? Oh, never mind. Just forget we ever had this conversation. So long."

"Wait."

"What? You looking to try and cut me down again?"

"No, I'm over that. That was only because the blood rushed to my head when you said the clan was doomed. Sorry 'bout that."

"'Sorry 'bout that' is all you have to say for trying to cut my head off? Doesn't that sort of thing normally call for an expression of regret that carries a little more gravity?"

"You have my deepest apologies, including for the deficiency of my previous apology. Also…"

"Also?"

"With regard to that position, I will take the matter up with my superiors and do my utmost to bring about a favorable answer. Begging a thousand pardons," he said, dropping to his knees and pressing his forehead to the ground.

The sky overhead was so flawlessly blue it appeared to be a complete void.

Jūnoshin watched expressionlessly as Shume raced off toward the castle. The receding figure grew smaller and smaller, until finally it was no longer visible, at which point he contorted his face as if trying to dispel an itch in his nose, or perhaps as if remembering something very sad, and let out a single, clipped *Bwah!* After a brief pause he let out another lone *Bwah!* and then almost immediately followed that with an extended *Bwah hah hah hah, bwah hah hah hah hah hah hah.*

He was laughing with satisfaction at how he had sent Shume on his way.

"*Bwah hah hah.* Worked like a charm. I do believe I put enough of a fright in him that they won't go stingy on me. Once I've scared them some more and taken the cash, *heh heh heh,* I'll just cook up a likely excuse and make myself scarce. There's no way in hell they can stamp out the Bellyshakers. If there were, I wouldn't be here now, wandering from domain to domain without a master. *Nwah, nwah, nwa hah hah hah hah.*"

Ah, the villainy of it. Jūnoshin had been out to scam Shume and the clan from the get go. He pretended to know all about the Bellyshakers and how to stamp them out, when the truth was that he didn't have the first idea what to suggest or do, and once he'd frightened them into paying him a hefty fee, he intended to simply run off with the money and leave them to their ruin.

He hummed a little tune as he walked back to the old man's corpse.

"Once the Bellyshakers get in, the domain is finished. But I do need to make sure," he said, pulling the kimono open at the chest as if to check something. "Holy smokes!" he gasped, his eyes popping wide. "How can this be? I didn't doubt for a minute that he was a Bellyshaker, but he has no tattoo. Which means...*Ai-yi-yi.* It seems I've acted in haste."

He turned to look at the girl.

"So I suppose that means this chick isn't one of them either. Crap-a-doodle-doo-doo. Oh, but I'm not saying that to make a joke of it—it just popped out because it's something I say sometimes, when I'm talking to myself, and it doesn't mean, just because I said it now, that I was going for some kind of special effect, like to gloss over my feelings, but I probably can't deny that, somewhere deep down, I might have been sort of hoping a little—just a little mind you—that by saying crap-a-doodle-doo-doo I could sort of soften the fact that I killed the old man by mistake, sort of fake myself out, all of which is to say that in my heart of hearts I know I really did crap-a-doodle-doo-doo. Huh? Wait a minute. I said it again. So does that mean, maybe, that I'm actually sweating this more than I thought? Like I'm in an actual panic? The question now is this girl. If I let her go, I'll probably regret it later. There's no telling what kind of trouble she might make, so my best bet is to kill her on the spot. But I have a hard time being quite that ruthless—or rather, it's exactly because I wimp out at times like this that I've made so many missteps in life and wound up where I am. Talk about pathetic. But hey, so what? I doubt I can sink any lower than I am right now. Not to mention, even *I* have managed to do some pretty dastardly deeds over the years when my life was at stake. So I can be pretty sure I'm slated to go straight to hell when I die, but you know that story called 'The Spider's Thread'? After a life of murder and arson and a whole boatload of other bad stuff, the guy gets sent to hell to suffer for his sins, but then the Enlightened One takes mercy on him and decides to save him solely because he once spared a spider his life. It's really a very uplifting story. To take that example, letting this blind girl live could be considered a way of preserving my right to have the Enlightened One do the same for me. So, young lady," he said, turning to address her directly, "I'm not going to kill you. You're free to go. But I warn you to stay away from the vicinity of the castle. You showing up there could put a kink in my plans, so if I ever catch sight of you, I'll have to cut you down on the spot. Apart from that, you can go wherever you please—it's entirely up to you. Here's a little something to remember your father by," he said, tossing some coins at her feet and starting up the road toward the castle.

After he was gone, the girl twisted her lips in bitter disdain.

"Blow it out your ear. You're dead meat," she snarled, as she tore at a tuft of grass and got to her feet.

An hour later, Shume was kneeling before Lord Kuroae's chief councilor, Naitō Tatewaki, at his private residence.

When Shume finished his somewhat agitated report, Naitō acknowledged it with a small grunt but otherwise remained silent. He sat with tilted head, stroking the bottom of his teacup and gazing out at the landscaped garden beyond the veranda. Not surprisingly for a man of his caliber, he showed no sign of the consternation Shume had displayed upon hearing the alarming news.

After a time, he set his teacup down and asked, "What can you tell me about this ronin's background?"

"I'm afraid nothing, my lord. But he did strike me as a man of considerable reckoning."

"A man of considerable reckoning, is it? Well, isn't that something. These days the world seems to be chock-a-block with men of considerable reckoning, every which way you turn. Everybody's exceptional. The clan runneth over with men of considerable reckoning. I could even say without exaggeration that men of considerable reckoning are all we have. But this actually presents a problem. All these men of considerable reckoning are all of considerable importance so they all need to be given positions of considerable weight. But we have no such positions to offer. In fact, inconsiderable jobs of no consequence are all we've got. Of course, when enough jobs of no consequence come together you can accomplish things of great consequence, and that is in fact how it all works out, but our many men of considerable reckoning seem utterly oblivious to this fact. For example, the other day I asked a young fellow in the accounting section to draw up a document, and what do you suppose he does? He sneers at me and says, 'I didn't succeed to my father's post so I could do piddly stuff like that,' and he goes into a great big sulk. In the end, I had to take care of the job and deliver it myself. On another front, in view of the financial crunch we're having, I proposed a 'Learn from the People' initiative for the younger retainers to go out and spend some time in merchant houses around town, and what's the reaction? 'We've got our pride as samurai,' they tell me. 'There's no way we're doing that.' And as if that's not bad enough, they spout this off with a kind of swagger, like they think they're really somebody, all high on themselves for heroically standing up to a clan elder. Well, they're somebody all right, but not the kind of somebody they think they are. And then we have our big shots. Not that they really *are* big shots. The fact of the matter is they're a bunch of bozos. But organizations are funny that way—now and then you wind up with total nincompoops in positions of responsibility. The problem is, these good-for-nothings get it into their heads somehow that they rose to their posts not through some fluke of the personnel shuffle but through genuine talent, and this leads to all manner of foul-ups. Bozos being bozos, they're likely as not to misunderstand my instructions. If they don't understand what I told them, all they really need to do is come and ask, but since they think they're such bright lights themselves, they can't be bothered. They just take their wrongheaded notions and run with them. When I find out what they're doing, I can see disaster in the making, so I tell them to stop, but with their inflated sense of themselves, their whole attitude is *What? And ruin my whole brilliant plan? I can't do that. I'm the one who thought up this stupendous plan. What would the likes of you know about it? You're only the chief councilor.* They're so convinced of their own sheer genius that they forge adamantly ahead. Needless to say, I'd be neglecting the duties of my office if I didn't do something about it, so I call the offending party in and give him my strictest orders, but we're talking about a world-class moron with massive delusions of grandeur and a highly advanced defense mechanism that shuts his ears down cold the moment he hears anything that might threaten his perception of himself. The guy stops responding and sits there in a stupor, looking like that dumbass kid in *Osomatsu-kun* with a flag on his head. Or maybe he doesn't tune out completely, but every time you say something he scoffs and turns away, or he gapes at you wide-eyed as if to say, *What kind of crazy talk is this? I can't make head or tail of it—it's so totally surreal.* Of course, this doesn't mean he's actually surprised or confused about anything; it's all pretend—an act he puts on so he doesn't have to admit he's got no retort. Just having to put up with his cheap show is tiresome enough, but the real problem is still that he simply doesn't get it. So to break the impasse, I take my instructions directly to one of his underlings who's not so hopelessly dense, but that only serves to get the man riled up. He protests that I made him lose face and, showing a remarkable adeptness when it comes to trickery, he starts doing every underhanded thing he can think of to keep the project from moving forward according to plan. In that case, why not demote the blockhead and put somebody else in charge of the department, you may well wonder, but organizations like this are complicated, and that's far easier said than done. It was wearing me out to think about it, and then, just as I was gazing out at the garden over a cup of tea and taking a breather, you show up with another knotty problem to which the solution you say is to hire somebody named Kakari Jūnoshin we know nothing about, on top of which I've now been talking a blue streak for pages, which has tired me out even more, but I must agree that the appearance of these Bellyshakers within our borders is indeed a matter of grave concern. So even though I feel ready to drop, I suppose I'll have to meet the fellow and see what he has to say."

"Thank you, sir. I'm most grateful," Shume said, bowing to the floor.

Now, as it happened, even if it was also to save his own skin, Shume had approached Naitō with the best interests of the clan foremost. But the chief councilor was secretly turning a rather different concern over in his mind—to wit, how he might take advantage of this new disturbance to get the best of his longstanding archrival, Ōura Shuzen, and drive him from his position as the second-ranking councilor. But he was careful to maintain the appearance of complete calm, betraying no sign of the battle that had begun to rage within him, as Shume sat up again and mopped the sweat from his brow.

The bad blood that prevailed between Naitō Tatewaki and Ōura Shuzen was not of recent origin. Their families had served as senior retainers to the clan for generations, and since both of them were men of genuine intelligence, they could have brought great benefit to the domain if they had joined hands to work in cooperation.

But the two seemed utterly incapable of getting along. Naitō has recorded in his journal, *Stray Notes While Farting in a Mullet Pot*, that every time he sees Ōura it puts him in a foul mood for the rest of the day "because it makes me feel like my whole body is filled with some kind of repulsive slime." Ōura, for his part, has been heard saying of Naitō, "It always makes me want to punch him in the jaw when I see that know-it-all look on his face."

It's not unusual, of course, for best friends to be opposites—such as, for example, one being short-tempered while the other has all the patience in the world. Naitō and Ōura were just such opposites, with Naitō being fond of learning but not much of a swordsman, while Ōura was a master of martial arts but a complete nothing when it came to scholarship. Naitō favored European music, while Ōura enjoyed traditional Japanese. Naitō was a drinker, but Ōura preferred sweets. Naitō was large and corpulent, while Ōura was thin as a rail. If Naitō showered a novel with praise, Ōura would pan it mercilessly. Naitō liked red wine; Ōura drank white. When Naitō ordered eel, Ōura asked for weatherfish. Naitō would summon a Shinto priest, while Ōura called for a Buddhist monk. They were complete opposites both in character and in preference, and yet they could not get along.

They had been at odds with each other from a very young age.

Since they both came from samurai houses, they were of course schooled in the Four Books—*The Great Learning*, *The Doctrine of the Mean*, *The Analects of Confucius*, and *The Sayings of Mencius*—and the Five Classics—*The Book of Changes*, *The Book of Songs*, *The Book of Documents*, *The Spring and Autumn Annals*, and *The Book of Rites*. They began their studies in the traditional manner, sounding out the Chinese sentences character by character with little sense of what the words actually meant.

Naitō rose to this challenge with aplomb, but Ōura was nearly hopeless. Naitō would complete his passage without the slightest stumble, and then Ōura would begin sputtering out utter gibberish that bore no discernible relationship to what appeared on the page. Naitō would let out a deliberate snicker, *hyuk*, and all eyes would turn to Ōura. Flustered by the added attention, his gibberish would grow thicker. Unable to contain himself, Naitō would let out an unrestrained guffaw, *gwah hah hah*, and the entire class would explode with laughter. Ōura would grit his teeth in embarrassment.

But the tables were completely turned when it came to martial arts. Ōura displayed an easy mastery no matter what new moves the teacher threw at them, while Naitō was forever the clumsy bumbler. He'd have been better off to simply avoid such activities altogether if he could, but unfortunately for him the training was compulsory: every son of a Kuroae retainer was required to attend daily sessions at the Manabe Martial Arts Academy just outside the castle walls. You couldn't decide that you didn't like the classes and simply stop going. Pass by the place on any given morning and an uninterrupted series of ear-piercing shouts could be heard coming through the barred windows: *Hiyahh! Gahhh! Urgghh! Aiee! Yow! Kayahh!*

So Naitō was forced to attend just like everybody else. But he detested it, and not merely because Ōura cut such a wide swath there. Normally, students of Ōura's caliber didn't waste time with the likes of Naitō because their skills were too far apart, but whenever Naitō's turn came and he stood with his bamboo practice sword at the ready, Ōura would leap to his feet saying, "I'll take you on," and proceed to give him a relentless thrashing.

And on this particular occasion it was especially bad. During their Classics lesson the day before, when Ōura got stuck on one word in a seemingly endless loop while reading from *The Great Learning*—"con-con-conso-, console, consid-, consil-, con-con-con-con-consen-, con-con-console"—Naitō had called out, "It's 'conceal,' you cretin," and made such gleeful fun of him that Ōura had fainted in embarrassment and had to be fetched home by a servant.

With that incident fresh in his memory, Ōura naturally burned for revenge. He took his stance and began raising an intimidating string of battle cries.

"*Wagyahh! Shipooong! Kiyahhh!*"

This looks bad, thought Naitō, deciding the best strategy would be to let Ōura win his point and promptly concede.

"*Ryahh ryahh ryahh ryahh ryahh!*" he answered in the usual form, though without any great enthusiasm. He waggled his butt back and forth and flicked the tip of his weapon as if fishing for pond smelt, waiting for Ōura's move.

To Ōura, it looked as though Naitō was just horsing around to make fun of him, which naturally rubbed him the wrong way and got him even more riled up.

"*Wakyahhng!*"

With a furious shriek, he aimed his sword for Naitō's head. The bamboo flexed as it whipped through the air. Even resigned as he was, Naitō couldn't very well let himself be hit without offering any resistance at all, so he moved to parry the blow, but Ōura's strength was too much for him and his own sword came crunching down on his head beneath Ōura's.

"*Aiee!*"

This was the moment he'd intended to concede, but he was so stunned by the blow that all he could do was cry out in pain.

With Naitō thrown completely off balance, Ōura struck again, this time thrusting his sword like a spear.

"*Yashahhh!*" he shouted as he administered several quick jabs.

"*Ack!*" Naitō threw down his sword and fled, but Ōura quickly pursued him into a corner and continued thrashing away.

"Concede!" Naitō finally managed to get out. "I concede, I concede, you win!"

Unfortunately, since he shouted this while being subjected to a merciless attack, his enunciation wasn't as clear as it could have been. Ōura somehow heard it as "Conceal, it's conceal, you cretin!" and thought Naitō was repeating his ridicule of the day before. In a rising frenzy, he tossed his bamboo sword aside and, being an expert judoist as well, pounced on Naitō to execute a throw that sent him flying through the air and knocked him out cold. It looked as though Naitō might have sustained some minor injuries as well, but his family took care to hush that up lest their son be scorned as a weakling.

When Naitō was nineteen, his parents received a proposal of marriage for him. The prospective bride was Imaoka Hema, daughter of the clan's assistant treasury commissioner.

Hema was a peerless beauty. Wanting to get her settled, her father Iori had discussed her prospects with his boss, Commissioner Meguri Bunnojō, and they had decided the Naitōs would provide an appropriate match.

But there was just one small problem: she was at the same time being promised to another. As it happened, Iori was born the third son of Hanada Gen'emon, but had been adopted at the age of twelve as heir to the Imaoka family. His oldest brother Kazuma, Hema's uncle, had succeeded Gen'emon as head of the Hanada family, and he had seen fit to act on his niece's behalf in bringing a proposal of marriage to the Ōura family. The Ōuras had been overjoyed, and Shuzen himself was so ecstatic that he went around letting out random yelps and cries like those he raised at the martial arts academy.

"*Yashannng! Wakyakyahhng!*"

Iori and Kazuma and Bunnojō were all model samurai. How was it that three such fine stalwarts of the warrior class blundered into this double booking fiasco?

Well, in a way, you could blame it precisely on their being such exemplars, for it is the mark of a good samurai that he is a man of action rather than words. He does not make a habit, like the neighborhood gossips, of announcing to the whole world that he's going to do this, that, or the other before he does it. As a result, they had each moved unilaterally to action without consulting one another beforehand.

Of course, this is not a characteristic limited only to the military class. For example, any undistinguished, run-of-the-mill father is likely to waste great swathes of time flapping his lips:

"So, what do you think, everybody? What do you want to do? We've hit it right at mealtime, and the area doesn't have very many restaurants to begin with, so they've all got long lines waiting to get in. It's not often we get to have a family outing like this, and it seems like a shame to waste time waiting in line instead of having fun. I'm thinking maybe we should just pick up some sandwiches or something at a convenience store. What do you think, Mom? How about everyone else? A sandwich sounds good to me. What should I get you guys? Yakisoba rolls? You want sushi? Deli case sushi? Not a good idea, if you ask me. Take it from the voice of experience."

Yada yada yada. Then, when he finally goes off to find a store, he comes back empty handed, scratching his head awkwardly. "They were all sold out," he says. "Guess we have to wait in line after all."

Now contrast that with his exemplary counterpart: He wastes no time hemming and hawing or asking people's preferences; he simply steps right to action without a single word—and the next thing you know he's back, passing out rice balls and frozen cream puffs with no more than a "Here you go." Except it turns out that no one wants the food he bought because they were looking forward to eating at a restaurant even if it meant they had to wait—which is to say, even the consummate man of action can sometimes mess things up.

But the situation at hand involved something far more weighty than not being in the mood for frozen cream puffs. After a tremendous brouhaha that turned the whole castle upside down, several most excellent samurai were relieved of their duties or ordered to slit their bellies. Many others were placed under house arrest, and poor Hema herself shaved her head and went into a nunnery...

Be all that as it may, the years went by and the two rivals rose to become leading members of the governing council. Alas, they fought tooth and nail over every policy decision, and deliberations were forever being thrown into turmoil.

It may well be that a master of greater resource and sagacity could have deftly played the two antagonists off against each other to the benefit of the domain, but all that can be said with certainty of Lord Kuroae Naohito is that he was a man of most singular character.

In his *Stray Notes While Farting in a Mullet Pot*, Chief Councilor Naitō writes, "I have been told that even as a child, the young lord would point out and correct his teachers' errors," so it seems that he was born with quite an extraordinary native intelligence. But as he grew older, this was increasingly called into question.

It was not a matter of his turning to wine, women, and other untoward indulgences. In fact, the young lord, still known by his childhood name of Bennosuke at the time, was an exceedingly serious boy. That was precisely the trouble.

He was serious to a fault.

It is often said that excess is to be avoided in all things, but Bennosuke had a tendency to take things far too seriously. No matter what was at issue, he would stand on principle and refuse to budge a single step.

For example, he adhered to his tutor's teachings without compromise.

One day the lesson was: "He of honeyed tongue and fawning smile wants sincerity of heart." That is to say, if someone lays on the flattery and behaves obsequiously, he probably has ulterior motives.

Bennosuke took the saying to heart quite literally.

He was standing in the inner garden of the castle the next day when a guardsman named Igaki Zaru came his way.

"A very good day to you, Lord Bennosuke," he said, bending at the waist. "It's a pleasure to find you in such excellent spirits on this magnificent day."

He added every polite flourish the language had to offer as he spoke, which some might say was more self-deprecatory than necessary for an adult speaking to a child. But in light of the fact that the child in question was destined to be his future lord and master, it was more or less what one might expect. The boy, however, was annoyed.

"What's gotten into you, Igaki?" he said.

"I just wished to say what a fine day it is and how glad I am to see you looking well," he said more plainly.

Bennosuke appeared to be no happier with this response. "Igaki," he snapped.

"Yes, my lord?"

"Do you think I'm an idiot?"

"Oh, no, my lord, I would never."

"You'd never think such a thing?"

"Exactly so."

"Then let me ask you this. Why did you repeat the same thing twice?"

"I'm sorry?"

"Don't say the same thing twice. It's a waste of time."

"Forgive me."

"But that's actually not my point. What I mean, Igaki, is that you were going on just now about the magnificent day and my excellent spirits, but you're not the one who made it such a beautiful day, now, are you?"

"No, my lord."

"And how exactly would you know whether or not my spirits are excellent?"

"A thousand pardons."

"Don't say stuff you don't know. Stop wasting my time with useless niceties. That's what's known as flattery and fawning, and it comes from a lack of sincerity. 'He of honeyed tongue and fawning smile wants sincerity of heart.' The old saying sums it up nicely. It's because you don't understand that that you're always feeding me such blarney. You're a stupid blarney samurai, that's what you are. So, tell me, Igaki. Do you have sincerity in your heart, or don't you?"

"I have no words to answer."

He was forever calling up principle in this way, which gave those around him no end of aggravation and grief.

Over the years, as Bennosuke came of age, took the name Naohito, and in due course succeeded to the headship of the clan, everybody kept hoping that his overly precise tendencies might eventually ease, but as a matter of fact, they only seemed to grow worse—to the point that people started calling him Lord Literal behind his back. He was universally regarded as someone with whom you could not negotiate; who couldn't distinguish between principle and practice; whose vocabulary didn't include the word accommodation; who willfully acted on his own impulses without regard to what anybody else thought.

If to govern is to reconcile the many conflicting interests that vie with each other both inside and outside the domain and make them work in harmony, then few could be considered as unsuited to the task as Naohito. But being head of the clan meant it was impossible for him not to be involved, and so the affairs of the domain became increasingly unstable under his leadership. This owed in no small part to his utter disregard for both precedent and the facts on the ground—or rather, his utter inability to understand them.

When a spending report listed payments to shrines and temples whose purpose was unclear to him, he summoned the man in charge.

"What are these payments about?"

"They are customary payments that we make each year and must be continued."

"I mean what are they for, in nominal terms? What is their specific purpose?"

"Well, it's a little difficult to explain in nominal terms, but I suppose you could say the purpose is to serve as a kind of lubricant for better relations in this sector."

"I can't understand a word you're saying. Lubricant refers to substances you put on hard objects like cogwheels to reduce the friction between them. Are you saying the people involved here are grinding together like cogwheels and overheating?"

"You have a way with words, my lord."

"Very well then. I will go forthwith and lubricate them myself. Fetch me some oil... All right, you've brought me the oil, now show me the way."

And with that, Lord Naohito proceeded to visit each of the temples and shrines named in the report, where he poured oil on the officials, monks, priests, patrons, parishioners, and all other affiliated persons from head to foot. The result was a dramatic drop in unexplained expenditures, so perhaps Naohito's abilities as head of government were not to be sniffed at after all.

If figures of speech were lost on the man, so were subtleties of communication such as the telegraphing of unspoken understandings, reading or suggesting between the lines, letting one's eyes do the talking, and the use of reverse psychology. Excuses and dodges did not work with him, either. If you made a mistake or he caught you goofing off, he would ask bluntly, his eyes wide with bafflement: "Why did you flub this?" "Why are you loafing?" Every retainer in the clan lived in fear of what he might be asked.

With Lord Naohito behaving this way, the clan had split into two factions—those who threw their lot in with the Naitō family, and those pledging loyalty to the Ōuras.

These two factions were constantly at odds, forever trying to gain sole control of domain affairs. And there were times when this worked out for the better, as each faction strove to demonstrate its superiority by presenting the most progressive new ideas, and the group with the best plan was then given the lead in carrying it out.

But this was possible only so long as the older generation continued to keep an eye on things. Once the senior members of the families retired or passed on, and the younger generation succeeded them in their positions of responsibility, the situation rapidly deteriorated.

The two factions no longer vied with each other to present the best ideas. Instead, they directed all their energies to opposing and obstructing anything the other might suggest.

At Kuroae Castle, Lord Naohito sat on the dais in his audience chamber. Kneeling nearby, Deputy Chief Councilor Ōura Shuzen roared with laughter.

"*Bwoh ho ho ho ho!* Bellyshaker Party? Poppycock," he scoffed. "Are you serious?"

The man on the receiving end of this scorn, Kakari Jūnoshin, remained the very picture of cool. Cool in dress, cool in expression, cool in every aspect of his bearing. It was that particular look of cool that job seekers are known to self-consciously affect when going for their interviews—which is to say, a certain manufactured crispness adopted in the hope that the interviewer might say to himself, *Now here's a pleasant young fellow*, and decide to make an offer. To be sure, it is best to consider this species of crispness or coolness a lie, and, for example, when you sometimes find yourself wondering how a guy like *this* ever landed a job at a place like *that*, you can be quite sure it was by hoodwinking the human resources staff with the aforementioned deception. If a man like Jūnoshin, worn down by the dust of hardship and filth, anxiety and wretchedness that he'd experienced all too much of the time in his years as a ronin, were to behave without constraint in the manner most natural to him, he would come across as a nihilist and cynic who was a very long way from anything that could be called cool; but since on this occasion he held hopes of garnering both a reward and a stipend, he had given special attention to his attire and was taking care to speak politely, answering even the sneer in Shuzen's tone with a mild, yet crisp and unobsequious, "I am."

Beside him sat Nagaoka Shume. Alarmed at the brevity of Jūnoshin's reply, he hastily attempted an elaboration, but addressing such a high personage made the blood rush to his head.

"It's absolutely true, your excellency. I saw it with my own eyes. A Bellyshaker. He cut him down. The Bellyshaker, I mean. Cut down. And he did it. This man here, I mean. He cut him down."

"I can hardly make out what you're trying to say. Get a hold of yourself."

"Forgive me, your lordship. That is to say, I, I, I…"

"Enough, enough. You there. What was your name again?"

"Kakari Jūnoshin."

"All right, Kakari. You explain."

Jūnoshin now had his chance to hold forth not only on the calamitous effect the Bellyshakers could have on the domain but the vital importance of putting countermeasures in place without a moment's delay—along with his own indispensability in overseeing those measures. But he did no such thing. What he actually said was:

"You ask me to explain, your lordship, but I have already explained all there is to explain. Perhaps you wish me to simply repeat myself, but that, I daresay, is a waste of both our time. And yet, you did instruct me to explain again. Perhaps you failed to comprehend what I said because you're one of those dunderheads who can never grasp anything the first time, in which case I suppose I could take pity on you and run it by you again. But before I go to all that trouble, I feel compelled to ask: Are you in fact an idiot? A halfwit?"

As Jūnoshin finished this startling speech, Shume again spoke up. "I must beg your lordships' pardon and excuse myself a moment," he said, and withdrew from the room in a rather curious manner.

He had in fact peed himself. It had been too great a shock to hear such reckless words coming from the mouth of the man he'd brought here to recommend for employment.

What if it were to get out that he'd committed such an indignity in the presence of Lord Naohito? he fretted. It would be an unmitigated disaster. In fact, he would almost certainly be ordered to commit hara-kiri—and then what? Just thinking about it made his mind go white with terror, and he wet himself a little more.

In contrast to the fainthearted Shume, Jūnoshin remained a rock of composure, coolly casting his gaze out over the garden.

Ōura exploded in anger. "How dare you speak to me like that? A lowly ronin! The impudence!" He fixed Jūnoshin with a ferocious glare.

But the unruffled Jūnoshin simply picked up where he'd left off. "So it's true. You really *are* an idiot," he said loudly. "No man of your rank should be so quick to lose his temper."

Shuzen was livid. "I'll have your head! Prepare to die!" he shouted, leaping to his feet. A bolt of tension shot through the room.

Naitō Tatewaki had been observing the proceedings in silence up to this point, but he chose this moment to speak.

"Not so fast!" he boomed, and all eyes turned his way. "You forget yourself, Ōura. We are in the presence of Lord Naohito here."

"*Urgghhh*," grunted Ōura as he sank back to his knees.

"And you, Kakari, you have behaved poorly as well. Casting such outrageous insults at a high councilor is a serious breach of decorum. There must be no more of that."

Jūnoshin bent low in submission as if slapped down by the force of Naitō's words. "I am your humble servant, my lord."

"Now, if we can return to the question at hand, I must say that I find it difficult to dismiss the man's story as wholly preposterous. What say you to that, Ōura?"

"Anything a pissant like this tries to tell us has to be a lie. I don't believe for a minute that these so-called Bellyshaker types have infiltrated the domain."

Jūnoshin snickered, "*Heh heh heh.*"

"What's so funny?"

"Why should I think anything is funny?"

"Then what was that laugh about just now? I heard you go '*Heh heh heh.*' In fact, it sounded rather mocking. I don't think I like your tone," Shuzen said, with renewed fury. He turned to Naohito. "Even if it's true that he possesses some special expertise, it would be sheer folly to retain the services of anyone who shows such scandalous disrespect," he argued forcefully.

"I believe Ōura makes a legitimate point," declared the lord, and declined to offer Jūnoshin the employment he sought.

As he rode away from the castle in his palanquin, Ōura was still fuming. "*Grrr.* Where did that cocky little son-of-a-bitch get the idea he could talk to me like that? Pisses me off. I don't have to put up with the likes of him calling me a fool. I'm a senior member of the High Council, dammit! If he thinks he can get away with something like this, he's come along about a century too soon. I'll kill 'im. Hey, that's it! I'll get Manabe Gosenrō to rub him out. Except, *hmm,* I wonder if he's even still around. At any rate, there's no time like the present. Halt!" he shouted to his bearers and the entire procession came to a standstill. Lifting the blind, he called one of the escorts over and whispered in his ear.

When Ōura ordered the bearers to proceed a few moments later, a small, wiry man peeled away from the column and headed off in the opposite direction.

Nestled in a quiet bamboo grove at the foot of the mountains along the Takeda Highway, which was the main east-west route through the domain, stood a thatched house surrounded by a latticework fence and wrapped in complete darkness. It was the home of Manabe Gosenrō. There were no other houses nearby.

After having spent a great many years as a ronin without formal employment, Gosenrō's father Manabe Asesui became the Kuroae clan executioner when Gosenrō was fifteen years old. Asesui had begun instructing Gosenrō in fencing at a very young age, and the boy practiced with great zeal, tirelessly honing his skills. By the time he turned eleven, he was defeating full-grown men in training matches. Still striving to improve at seventeen, he began roving the hills and forests to harden his strike techniques on trees and rocks. He would disappear from home for days on end, fending off starvation by gathering nuts or tearing the flesh from animals he caught with his bare hands. With his untended hair left to grow wild and a piercing light in his eyes, he looked like a savage. He learned to sense the slightest disruption in the air, the tiniest twitch of a leaf, and instantly be on his guard. When villagers who came to gather firewood caught sight of him, they would often collapse in fright, and rumors circulated that demons had turned him into a long-nosed goblin. Asesui was understandably alarmed at the direction his son was taking and tried to steer him toward a path of scholarship, but his efforts fell on deaf ears; Gosenrō merely trained all the more fanatically in what appeared no longer to be the art of fencing but the art of total carnage.

On the very day Gosenrō turned twenty, his father abruptly keeled over and died. The young man immediately succeeded to his father's post, but it wasn't long before he submitted his resignation. Although he had made an effort to conduct himself more like a normal person after his father's death, his eccentric, misanthropic tendencies remained, and he found that he simply could not deal with the complex relationships involved in castle society.

This did not mean all his ties with the clan were severed, however. Since he had no qualms about killing, when there were criminals to be executed, he still answered the summons to carry out the beheadings, and when the powers that be wished to have someone assassinated now and again, he accepted those assignments as well.

As a matter of fact, such requests came with some frequency. A suspicious character who was exposed as a spy; a gambling boss who'd amassed so much power that even the authorities were forced to tread carefully; a wealthy merchant who had loaned the clan large sums of money; malcontents thought to be plotting an uprising—Gosenrō used his skills to eliminate them all. His fee was always 800 *monme* of silver per head, regardless of the target's social standing.

Disliking the home he had inherited in town with so many busybodies nearby, he decided to buy a farmhouse at the foot of the mountains some distance away, where he could live however he pleased. In the roughly ten years since, he'd come to view the world from the unique slant of a bystander, invariably taking a cynical, contrarian view of all that he observed. He adopted an outlaw mentality, telling himself that since he operated outside of society and all its trappings, he was free to do anything he wanted.

Across the room from him now, kneeling stiffly on the other side of the sunken hearth where a small fire flickered, was Ōura Shuzen's runner, Makubo Magobei, feeling the chill of Gosenrō's ill-natured gaze.

"So? What is it? What can I do for you?"

As he put on a show of courtesy, Gosenrō was cackling to himself with glee. A messenger from the councilor at this hour of night could mean only one thing: another hit job. He'd seen no need to help things along by broaching the subject himself— *Looking for me to knock somebody off?*—but the guy was certainly taking his time about getting to the point. He sat there acting shy and fidgeting, avoiding Gosenrō's eyes as if he were indeed waiting for his host to speak first.

It was starting to get on his nerves.

If he was sent to hire Gosenrō for a hit, then why didn't he come out and say so? Instead he just sat blushing and wriggling his shoulders like a woman trying to fend off unwanted advances.

Obviously, he was hoping that if he stuck it out long enough without saying anything, Gosenrō would obligingly save him the trouble. *What is it? A killing? Sure thing. I'll do it. Who'm I supposed to take out?*

Is he a total idiot? thought Gosenrō. *Sure, if a young samurai behaves this way when he first enters service, the older men with a fondness for boys might find it endearing and offer to show him the ropes. But this guy's hardly a spring chicken. When you see a man his age blushing and squirming and averting his eyes, all it does is make you cringe. Yet here he is, playing the helpless innocent, expecting to be indulged like a child. Well, no matter how cute he was as a boy so he had his elders wrapped around his little finger, he's not that boy anymore. Nobody gets to be indulged like that forever. In fact, he's at the age when he should be stepping in to take the younger ones under his wing himself. It's nothing short of a disgrace for a grown man like this to sit there simpering and shifting endlessly in his seat without speaking up!*

Gosenrō was incensed. Back when when was younger, if he got his hackles up like this, he'd have wasted no time giving the guy a piece of his mind. *Dammit, you're pissing me off, dude. This oughta teach you!* Then he'd have beat him senseless with his wooden practice sword and left him crippled for life PDQ. But the passage of years had turned him into the personification of pigheadedness, misanthropy, intolerance, prejudice, cynicism, and meanspiritedness. He intended to have some fun with his prey first. And it was in anticipation of the pleasure it would give him that he was secretly cackling to himself.

"Might I ask what brings you out to these parts at this late hour?" he prompted his visitor again.

"Uh, yes, as a matter of fact, what brings me is a request for your services."

"Oh, a request for my services," he boomed, goggling his eyes with exaggeration. "What sort of services might they be, I wonder? I simply cannot imagine."

Gosenrō's loud and mocking tone unnerved his weak-kneed visitor even further. Truth be told, it was this hopeless faintness of heart that had been responsible for the long gap between the middle of the day, when he had received his orders, and this late hour of the night. Dreading what might be in store for him once he arrived at Gosenrō's house, Magobei had dawdled hour after hour, wandering aimlessly about town for a time, stopping in at the temple for a lengthy chat with the sexton, and finding a variety of other matters that suddenly seemed more pressing to attend to; it hadn't been until after dark that he finally made up his mind to go, and even then it was only after he'd fortified himself with some dinner at an inviting eatery that he actually set out. Gosenrō's boisterous manner was nearly too much for a man of such shrinking disposition to bear.

"Well, um, I'm afraid it's a matter of some delicacy," he squeaked, barely louder than a mosquito.

"Delicacy? *Ha ha ha ha.* What are you talking about? There's no need for delicacy here. You must speak freely. It's not often I have someone drop in on me in the middle of the night without an appointment, but don't worry about it being an imposition or anything like that. Come, come, you mustn't hold back. Tell me what's on your mind. Chop chop. I'm a busy man, but you needn't worry about that either. If it's a lengthy matter, just take all the time you need—though there's certainly no harm in being brief if you can be. Since as I say, I'm a very busy man."

Cowed by Gosenrō's heavy sarcasm, Magobei merely stared at his knees, unable to speak. In the absence of a response, Gosenrō raised his voice even louder.

"Oh. I get it, I get it. You visited me at this ridiculous hour because, in a word, you want a one-on-one with me so I can show you a few things. I bet that's it. You're looking for a private lesson. Am I right?"

Magobei shuddered in fright. For Gosenrō to "show him a few things" would almost certainly mean to end up disabled for life.

"N–No, no, not at all," he said hastily. "By no means."

"That's okay, that's okay. I really don't mind—don't mind a bit. I'd be more than happy to do it."

"No, I mean it. That's really not what I'm here for."

"It's okay, I tell you. There's no need to be shy. Let me guess. I bet I know what happened. You got into a bit of a row with a friend today, and he made fun of you for not knowing how to use your sword—called you a desk jockey or nothing but a pickling stone or something of that nature. Insults are like water off a duck's back so long as they aren't true, but when they're actually not half wrong, they can really get under your skin, so you saw red and reached for your sword, but, *ha ha ha*, too bad so sad, it just so happens that he's right, you hardly know which end of your sword is up. Not to mention, you could get fired for being a hothead if you drew on your friend. So you thought you'd come to see me and pick up a few tips first, then go back to him after that, but not to summarily take your revenge—no, you figure you'll just challenge him to a friendly match on your day off or something, and get your jollies beating him to a pulp in front of everybody else. So, am I right or am I right? Sure thing, fella, sure thing. I'll take you on. Just come with me," he said, and got to his feet.

"No, no, it's nothing like that."

"Come, come, there's absolutely no need to be that way. It's no imposition at all. I'm happy to do it. But I'll be up front with you. You can't normally become an expert swordsman overnight. If you want to give it your best shot anyway, then what we'll have to do is practice with real steel. You're not going to gain much ground in just one day without losing an arm or two."

"Really, you've gotten the wrong idea. And use real swords? Are you kidding me?" he said with an awkward, put-upon smile, and Gosenrō's face was instantly transformed. Until that moment he had been saying *It's okay, it's fine* in what passed for a solicitous tone, but now the color drained from his face and his lips began to tremble. His cheeks twitched menacingly. He was of course putting on a deliberate act, toying with Magobei just to see how much he could scare him.

A gust of wind shook the trees outside. Then in a low voice bursting with barely contained anger Gosenrō squeezed out, "What did you say?"

Magobei stole a quick glance, but immediately averted his eyes again. Gosenrō had been frightening enough already, but now he was glowering at him in full fury.

A feeble "Huh?" was he could muster in response.

"I asked what you just said."

"Uh…nothing…"

"No, it wasn't nothing."

"Nothing I meant anything by."

"Don't lie to me. I heard you all right. 'Are you kidding me?' That's what you said."

"Huh?"

"You said, 'Are you kidding me?'"

"Huh?"

"I'm telling you that you said, 'Are you kidding me?' And don't you try to claim you didn't. You're pissing me off, you friggin' moron," he roared. "Here I am, offering to teach you a thing or two out of sheer kindness of heart—even though you're nobody I'd normally have anything to do with—and what do you say? 'Are you kidding me?' You put on a crooked grin and scratch your head and say, 'Are you kidding me?' That's what you say when you know the guy's an idiot and beneath you, way below your level in whatever it is you're talking about, not even close to being in your league, and yet he's totally oblivious to it. It's what Frank Zappa says when Sham 69 asks if he wants them to teach him how to shred. Not knowing where to even begin setting them straight, he just forces a smile and says, 'Are you kidding me?' In other words, it's a line that gets trotted out when you're looking down your nose at somebody. Man, does that get my goat. It gets my goat big time. Are you telling me you came all the way out here at this hour of the night just to look down your nose and snort at me? What's that about? Since when does a guy do that? I never heard of such a thing. At least not normally. So what am I supposed to do when I'm being dissed like that? Just sit here and take it? Isn't that asking a bit much? As a samurai, when somebody splashes mud on my face, I'm honor-bound to cut him down. So that's exactly what I'm going to do. And I could by rights tell you to just sit there and take it, but I'll give you a pass on that. You have my permission to fight back all you want. Draw your sword, Makubo Magobei!" he said with a ferocious glare.

Magobei had been listening to this tirade with his mouth wide and his eyes agog, when suddenly, without so much as an *Urk!* or *Ai-yi-yi!* he pitched forward like a toppling tree and landed with his face in his teacup. Then he fell completely still.

"What the hell?" his would-be executioner cried in surprise. "I haven't even done anything yet." He sheathed his sword and grabbed Magobei by the collar to lift him, but it was like picking up a floppy sheet of rubber.

He was out cold.

Gosenrō stood dumbfounded.

He'd been well enough aware of how soft the younger generation was these days, so ridiculously sensitive and fragile, but he'd never have expected one of them to simply keel over on his own.

Then again, if he thought about it, being constitutionally prone to passing out whenever you got yourself in trouble might have its advantages. In fact, how could you beat it? Suppose you made some devastating blunder and it meant major losses for the clan. Your boss naturally hits the roof and reads you the riot act. He demands to know how you intend to take responsibility. You promptly pass out. Nobody expects the person they're talking to to collapse right in front of their eyes, so your startled boss loses the head of steam he's been building up, and the question of responsibility gets tabled. Which is exactly what turkeys like this want. It's built into their immune system. They know that when they get themselves in a jam, they can get out of responsibility simply by going into suspended animation.

But the guy is after all a samurai. The world may happen to be at peace for the moment, but once war breaks out, he'll be expected to march off to battle and fight. What's he going to do then?

Oh, right, since his whole generation is just as wimpy as he is, it all winds up being mutual and perfectly fine. Both sides simply go *Eek!* and pass out at first sight of each other. Which means you have peace. The heaps of bodies you see strewn across the battlefield littered with weapons and armor and horse trappings are actually only passed out cold, not dead.

In other words, all those cannons and muskets they brought along are nothing but a joke, and what we actually have is a peace event—a massive pageant in which warriors don their armor and helmets, pick up their longbows and muskets and lances, and ride into battle, then lie down and take a snooze the moment they meet the enemy. Tall posts have been erected across the battlefield, with speakers mounted atop them playing "Imagine." When the samurai come to, they look around and see their enemy, also just waking up. Both of them quickly avert their gaze, scratching their heads in embarrassment. But when their eyes meet again, they have become friends. They smile warmly at each other. Some ganja comes around and they each take a toke, while up on the hill, a stage has appeared in the very spot where the general's command post stood until the farce of it all drove him back to the comfort of his castle, and Bob Marley and the Wailers are performing. *One love, one heart, let's get together and feel all right…* All hearts are united, and the warriors who've become friends sing *Wo wo-wo wo-wo* as they dance. A new kind of war for a new century…

Yeah, right. What a crock. Though it may not be entirely off the mark. Take Magobei, here, for example. Ask him if he's willing to sacrifice his life for his lord in battle, and the answer would almost certainly be no. Because the skill he's honed above all others is the self-preservational immune response he's demonstrating at this very moment in his state of suspended animation.

If there is a duality between name and substance, a samurai chooses the former over the latter. For example, by fighting heroically in battle. A townsman, on the other hand, chooses substance over name. In other words, while a samurai sees self-preservation in terms of protecting name—which is to say, position and honor—a merchant sees it in terms of protecting substance—which is to say, property and profits. Except the more naïve members of these classes are a bit different. What they try to protect is neither name nor substance, but something more along the lines of self-esteem or ego.

Suppose the big man orders one of these types to muster the troops and launch an attack. If he does as he's told and ends up getting routed, then he'll be remembered forever as a defeated general—a loser. Naturally, he doesn't want that. So he employs any means he can think of to get out of the assignment. "The thing is," he demurs, "my own personal take on the situation tells me that this really isn't the best time for a campaign. Since having the troops led by a person with such views is bound to have a negative impact on our side, and under the circumstances I simply don't feel up to that role yet at this point, my recommendation is to abandon the whole idea before we suffer a catastrophic defeat." He trots out a litany of convoluted objections and effectively refuses to deploy. In what has now become a three-way split between name, substance, and ego, he places the greatest weight on the last, and his foremost concern is allowing no harm to come to his sense of self. Whether it be defeat in battle or an affront far more trivial, such as being treated rudely on the phone by someone he cold-called, anything that might shake his self-esteem must be avoided by whatever means necessary; that is the modus operandi for men like him.

But wait, if old-school samurai sacrifice substance for the sake of name while merchants sacrifice name for the sake of substance, then what is this new breed sacrificing when they choose their own self-regard as paramount. Name? Substance? Both? It's a good question, and, surprisingly, the answer is neither—they protect their egos without sacrificing a thing. What they're asking for, in essence, is an eternal victory by default. They'll go to virtually any length to shield their self-esteem from threat, but not at the cost of either name or substance. Or to be more precise, coming as they do from relatively good families, the very notion that effort must be expended to preserve name or substance is alien to them, because these are things that simply exist, like the air we breathe. *I'm important,* they tell themselves, *so it goes without saying that I should get more than other people do. After all, this is me we're talking about.* It comes as naturally to them as thinking, *I am a man,* or

I am a woman—no deep contemplation or debate required. Basically, it never even occurs to them that refusing to obey the big man's command might put their name or substance at risk.

And why is this so? Because, having been born in an age of extended peace and coddled to no end not just by their parents but by everybody else around them, they believe without the tiniest shadow of a doubt that the silver spoon implanted in their mouth belongs right where it is. This gives rise to friction in every quarter, rotting the organs of government from within, and while each of them sits coolly guarding his own self-esteem, the administration falls into a muddle, clan finances collapse, and the domain meets its demise. They end up on the street as masterless samurai—and their bosses are right there with them. *Ha ha hahhh.* It's so hilarious.

At least it is to someone like me, who has marketable skills. I don't suppose this fellow here has ever contemplated such a dire end, let alone thought it would be funny. Part of me wishes I could be there when he finally realizes what's going on and flies into a blithering panic, but that's not going to happen for a while yet. The question is what to do about him now. Or to be more specific, what he'll do if I apply my resuscitation techniques and bring him out of his coma. Will he pretend nothing happened? Though I suppose since he's actually been dead to the world for a spell, it wouldn't be a pretense as far as he's concerned. Maybe he'll try some *Where is this? Who am I?* crap, hoping that can be the end of it, but if he thinks he can pull a gag like that on Manabe Gosenrō, he's got another think coming! On the other hand, with a guy like him, chances are he'll lay the apologies on thick like he does with his bosses after passing out on them, all but forcing me to show some sympathy, "Fine, fine, I'll bump the guy off, so here, have a drink of water and pull yourself together," and then once I've agreed to the job, he'll report back to the councilor that his mission was a success, "Everything's in order, your excellency. *Wo wo-wo wo-wo,*" and act like it was all a piece of cake, whereas if I turn him down, he'll spin some ridiculous lie to blame his failure on me, "The guy's a total nutcase. He demanded a fee of half a billion, not one copper less."

Damn! The crafty bastard.

Hmm. In that case, instead of resuscitating him, maybe I should just call a palanquin and send him on home the way he is. No, wait a minute. If I do that, there's a good chance he'll get his daylights back before he arrives, in which case he's guaranteed to lie through his teeth like I said before, so my better bet is to leave him be and just send a note to the councilor that one of his men is passed out at my place and someone needs to come fetch him. And then, *heh heh heh*, maybe I'll jack up my fee.

Going into the next room. Gosenrō sat down at his writing desk and drew the candlestick near.

The unconscious Magobei remained motionless on the floor.

Nagaoka Shume, who had been restlessly getting to his feet and sitting back down, getting to his feet and sitting back down for quite some time, now began pacing the dimly lit room in circles and speaking in a crisp, clear voice even though there was no one else present.

"So, I get this *boom boom boom* sound coming in, right? *Boom boom boom*, inside my head. And since I'm trying to come up with a name, I start wondering what somebody like Balzac does. Or other famous writers, for that matter—what do they do? *Boom boom boom*. It's basically a drumbeat. Tso. *Heh heh*. Not *so* but *tso*. Tso *boom boom boom*. Drumdrum Sashinpot. How's that sound? No, it's a rotten name. What would a sash be doing in a pot? More likely a snake. Hmm. *Boom boom boom*. Maybe Drumdrum Viperpot, then? How about that? Or just plain Snakepot? But people hate snakes like nothing else, except maybe scorpions, and it makes me picture a guy with a slimy pate and filmy, pin-hole eyes compulsively slithering his forked tongue in and out—*ai-yi-yi! Boom boom boom*. Not gonna be popular with the ladies, that's for sure. In which case, what? *Boom boom boom*. Go for broke and make it Viperius Spitpot? The slippery-slimy snake crawls out of its spittoon to coil itself around you. Oh no, oh no, oh no, not that. Just the thought of it gives me the willies. *Boom boom boom. Boom boom boom. Aaaaaaaaaaaaaaaaaaaaaaaaagh...* Crap, it's no use. I was hoping it might make me feel better if I really cut loose once, but I can't say it helped much. *Aaaaaaaaaaaaaaaaaaaaaaaaaaaaaaaaaaaaaa gh...* Known in common parlance as natural vegetable dyes."

As he began punctuating his increasingly heated monologue with the primal screams of a madman, he failed to notice Kakari Jūnoshin enter the room.

"Hey there, Nagaoka."

"*Boom boom boom*," he went on obliviously. "*Boom boom boom*, yeah. *Boom boom boom*, yeah. The slippery slimy snake coils itself about you, coils itself about you, and the tentacles of poverty stretch themselves around you. *A-hah! A-hah ha ha!* Are you really so attached to the stipend of a lowly cook? *A-hah!* Who did you say you were? Who? I haven't decided on a name yet. Because *boom boom boom*, yeah. *Boom boom boom*, yeah."

"What the hell're you running on about? Hey! Yo! Get ahold of yourself!"

"'Get ahold of yourself!' he says, lifting him by the shoulders. The battleship Ding Yuan refuses yet to sink. *Boom boom boom*, yeah."

"I can't make head or tail of what you're saying… Some crafty fox has latched onto him, I suppose. All right, then," said Jūnoshin, moving back a step. Calling on his training in martial arts, he looked Shume in the eye and, *Hiyahh!*, tapped him with a charge of energy.

"*Boom boom boom*, yeah. Ridiculo Monkeysol."

"Not giving up, are you? *Hiyahh!*"

"That Sabei man, he's rough around the edges. His daughter Sae, too, she's keeping her tail out of the teakettle. *Boom boom boom*, yeah. *Boom boom boom*, yeah."

"Snap out of it, I tell you! *Hiyah! Hiyah! Hiyah!*"

"Burning red as fire, because that's his temperature. The sea in summertime makes a holding tank for *koi*."

"He's still out of his mind no matter how many charges I give him. Must be one hell of a nasty fox that's got into him. In that case, I suppose I've got no choice. Better put him to rest before he does somebody harm," Jūnoshin said as he reached for his sword.

"*A ha, a ha ha ha*, sorry, sorry. I'll stop now," Shume said, abruptly reverting to his usual voice.

"When did you get your wits back?"

"I had them all along."

"You sure had me fooled."

"Once I got started babbling that way, it felt kinda good, you know, so…"

"So you thought you'd have some fun with me? You made a pretty sorry spectacle of yourself, you realize."

"I do apologize," Shume said, bowing low, but in his next breath he leapt to his feet and demanded, "But what I want to know is where you've been all this time."

"I wandered around town a bit and then stopped in at a tavern to nibble on some boiled beans and have a few drinks."

"As if you didn't have a care in the world. I don't suppose you have any idea what I've been going through in the meantime?"

"Of course I do. You were having a bang-up time here jabbering nonsense to yourself. Rambling on about slippery slimy snakes and such."

"Wrong, wrong, wrong."

"You don't say."

"Absolutely… Okay, fine, at the tail end there, I admit I was enjoying myself a little. But that was only after my mind went blank from the rush of realizing I'm hopelessly cornered. Before I got to that point, I was in enormous stress and turmoil. I still am now for that matter."

"Then do you mind if I ask you something?"

"Sure, go right ahead."

"What was all that '*Boom boom boom*, yeah' stuff about?"

"Oh, that. *Ta ta-ra rahh, ta ta-ra rahh, ta ta-ra rahh, chaka-chaka chaka-chaka chaka-chaka.*"

"Good grief. What's gotten into you now?"

"It's Jimmy Cliff. The intro to 'The Harder They Come.'"

"What's that got to do with anything?"

"The chorus goes, 'The harder they come, the harder they'll fall, one and all'—he's basically saying that life just keeps getting tougher."

"Is that right?"

"Uh-huh. And that sort of hits a chord with me right now, you know, 'cause I've got myself in a pretty big fix, but just singing the same old lyrics seemed kinda boring, so I figured I'd mix it up a bit, and that's what came out: *Boom boom boom*, yeah. *Boom boom boom*, yeah."

"I see. Okay, I think I get it, but what do you mean about being in a fix?"

Shume leapt to his feet and shouted, "You know exactly what I mean!"

"I do?"

"Don't give me that! Do you have any idea how I've been feeling?"

"Actually, it's because I don't that I asked."

"I can't believe I'm hearing this. No, I can't be hearing this. Give me a break, will you? *Boom boom boom*, yeah. *Boom boom boom*, yeah. Damn diddly damn, even my own Jimmy Cliff isn't any fun anymore. I just feel all the more cornered and sad."

"I don't get it? Is something wrong?"

"Of course something's wrong! Mind if I ask *you* something this time? Did it ever dawn on you what that Drumdrum Sashinpot and Viperpot and stuff might be about?"

"I haven't the foggiest."

"Names," he said. "Those were names."

"That much I gathered."

"I mean for me. Names for me."

"But your name is Nagaoka Shume."

"That's right, yes. But it's not exactly safe for me to use that name anymore, you see, so I was trying to come up with a new one."

"Why not?"

"Huh? Why not what?"

"Why isn't it safe for you to use that name anymore?"

"*Huh huh,*" he laughed weakly. "*Huh huh huh.* You, of all people, ask me that? Fine, I'll spell it out for you. Because of the way you talked to Councilor Ōura. *Duhhh.* Isn't it obvious? He's one of Lord Naohito's closest advisors. That means he's a very important person, in case you didn't know. And you spoke to that very important person in a very disrespectful manner. Is it any surprise that that very important person might have been very very angry? Now, you're an outsider, so it's no skin off your back, but somebody's going to have to take responsibility. And who do you suppose that somebody might be? Yours truly, of course. The man you're looking at. Because I'm the one who got scammed into recommending you. *Ha ha ha ha.* Which you can pretty well bet means I'm gonna be cut loose. Especially since the clan's on an austerity binge right now, and they're hell-bent on shrinking the payroll. So what happens then? I'll have to do whatever it takes to keep body and soul together. It might even mean stooping to some pretty lowdown things now and then. If I want to keep stuff like that from tarnishing my family's good name, I'd better start using an alias. Now do you see my problem? I wouldn't bet on *that,*" he said in what seemed like a single breath, and then he resumed his former babbling, "*Boom boom boom*, yeah. *Boom boom boom*, yeah. All right! It's getting to be fun again. Just let me stay crazy like this. *Aaaaaaaaaaaaaaaaaaaaaaaaaaaaaaaaaaaaaaaaaaaaaaa aagh!*" he screamed.

Jūnoshin nodded to himself as he watched the man's deranged antics. *I think I do see,* he thought to himself. A frog in a well never knows the sea. The man was born in the domain and always assumed he would die in the domain, so the thought that he might lose the place he's carved out for himself here must loom as a fate worse than death.

A wave of pity came over him.

"It's so sad, and it breaks my heart. It's so sad, and it breaks my heart."

"*Boom boom boom*, yeah. *Boom boom boom*, yeah. A-yeah, a-yeah, a-yeah-yeah-yeah."

"It's so sad, and it breaks my heart. It's so sad, and it breaks my heart."

"*Boom-ba-di boom boom*, going topsy-turvy, yeah. Oodles of boom-boom cakes, comin' right up, yeah."

"It's so sad, and it breaks my heart. It's so sad, and it breaks my heart."

"Ain't no ordinary boom-boom cakes, no sir, ain't just made of flour… Hey, wait a minute."

"It's so sad, and it breaks my heart. It's so sad, and it breaks my heart."

"What's that you're singing, Kakari?"

"It's so sad, and it breaks my heart. It's so sad, and it breaks my heart."

"Holy mackerel, now *you've* got the crazies. Come on, Kakari! Pull yourself together!"

"It's so sad, and it breaks my heart. It's so sad, and—huh?"

"What's with the broken record act?"

"Oh, sorry, sorry. I guess I got the tune stuck in my head somehow."

"That's not funny, dammit. I'm the one who got jobbed, so I *deserve* to go a little nuts, but why the hell should *you* get caught in an endless loop? Give me a break, will you?"

"My apologies. I assure you, I had no hidden motives."

"Hidden motives? Such as?"

"Actually, I wasn't thinking that far ahead."

"There you go again. That's exactly your problem. You don't think things through before you let fly. And then somebody else winds up paying the price—such as me getting the ax."

"No, no, you won't get the ax."

"Sure I will."

"Nope, not gonna happen. You might even come out of this with a promotion."

Shume momentarily brightened at the mention of advancement, but his face quickly clouded again with suspicion. A sarcastic smile tugged at his lips as he shook his head and scoffed, "Fat chance."

"I wouldn't be so sure."

"Yeah, right. You really expect me to believe I could be promoted after the guy I recommended badmouths a clan elder to his face? I still say fat chance. There's just no way. Or is there way? No, no, don't kid yourself. It's simply not possible. Though maybe…? Nah."

He looked at Jūnoshin with the eyes of a dog who's never gotten anything but the sorriest scraps suddenly being tossed a juicy bone.

"Say what you will, it's the truth. As I'm only now at liberty to reveal, I met secretly with the chief councilor before you took me to the castle, and the whole thing went exactly the way we planned. You can put your worries to rest."

"You're lying."

"What makes you say that?"

"I would've heard about it."

"And yet, it's an incontrovertible fact that I met with Lord Naitō before the audience."

"Likely story," Shume said, still refusing to believe him.

But Jūnoshin had indeed conferred with Naitō. They had met over tea in an outbuilding at Sondai-ji Temple.

"So, you're telling me that these Bellyshakers are a genuine menace?"

"Without a doubt, your lordship."

Naitō gave Jūnoshin a hard look, asking himself just how much credence he should lend to anything this dubious fellow had to say. He seemed self-assured to the point of cockiness, yet, for all that, appeared to be aware of the many finer considerations involved and was taking care to observe the proper decorum. At the same time, in spite of the grave tone he maintained throughout, there was something in his manner that suggested it might all be some kind of put-on.

In turbulent times past, men of his ilk might have held the fate of entire countries in their hands, thought Naitō. But in today's world, they're nothing but scam artists.

Still, if there was any truth to the threat these Bellyshakers posed, it needed to be reckoned with, so he listened carefully to what Jūnoshin had to say. He concluded it was probably true that the sect was spreading like wildfire, true also that the man had considerable knowledge of its nature and activities, but probably untrue that he possessed any special expertise for dealing with them.

An idea came to him.

"I wonder what your view might be of the commonly held perception that politicians are wily and unscrupulous characters full of schemes and tricks," he said, speaking at a leisurely pace and laying on several polite flourishes in his speech. Men of his rank and age did not normally use such exalted speech to address their juniors, and most young men would have been thrown quite off balance by such treatment, growing flustered and stumbling over their response, but Jūnoshin remained completely composed.

"I would agree. I have long believed it to be true," Jūnoshin said without a moment's hesitation.

Naitō started to click his tongue, but he restrained himself and continued in the same polite manner. "Then perhaps you will be interested to know that it is not necessarily so. Take myself, for example. I've never once resorted to any kind of scheming or trickery. The truth is, I'm lazy to the bone. Schemes and tricks are just too much trouble. So I've always made it my policy to shoot straight, and say exactly what I think. Have you ever read the novel called *I Am a Cat* by Natsume Sōseki?"

"I'm afraid I haven't had the pleasure."

"No, I wouldn't have thought so. There's this character named Také that everybody treats as the town idiot, and I was going to tell you his story, but now that I think of it, it's too much bother. See. There you have it. I say exactly what I think—straight face, no mincing words. That's the kind of man I am. And when I tell you that, it has to make you wonder about something, doesn't it? A certain question comes to mind? What is it?"

Now, the ability to read instantly what a powerful man wants and respond with exactly the question he's looking for—it indeed being a question he has asked for in this case, not an answer—is the mark of a master sycophant, and that is exactly what allowed Jūnoshin to ingratiate himself with so many movers and shakers. It was something that required a particular quickness of mind, and was certainly far beyond the capabilities of anyone like Shume.

"Perhaps you refer to the question of whether it's possible to survive the ruthless push and pull at the top by always revealing exactly what is on your mind."

It greatly improved Naitō's humor to receive the response he expected. The polite flourishes of his earlier speech were now gone, having disappeared in the course of his last few sentences.

"Yes, that's the obvious concern, isn't it. And you may be surprised to learn that it is indeed possible. What you have is everybody else plotting their schemes and tricks, weaving first one way and then another, quoting Latin phrases to boost their case, saying the opposite of what they really mean as a ploy in reverse psychology, launching trial balloons just to see if they'll fly, all sorts of other shenanigans. Meanwhile, I take the shortest, straightest route to where I want to go, cutting to the chase in plain and simple Japanese. And what happens? It becomes immediately apparent that everybody else's attempts to bend the outcome their way are bucketfuls of crap, and things proceed exactly the way I wanted. I can't deny, though, that it's a big drag to have Ōura Shuzen forever cooking up twisted schemes to throw roadblocks in my way because he's so completely clueless about the direct approach."

"I can imagine."

"So anyway, to hurl my usual straight, fast one at you, I'm guessing that all this time I've been giving you my spiel about how well things work out for me, you've been sitting there kicking yourself for getting stuck listening to a sermonizing old geezer blow hot air. Am I right?"

"By no means."

"Good. Right answer. If you were fool enough to take everything I said about straight talk at face value and told me it was true, then I wouldn't be able to work with you. So, very good. And in that case, I've got another straight, fast one for you."

"Indeed, sir. What might it be?"

"It's a lie that you know how to stamp out the Bellyshakers, isn't it?" he said, his voice cloyingly sweet all of a sudden.

"*Urg.*" Jūnoshin was caught short for words.

It was indeed untrue that he could offer any clear strategy, any muscular proposals, for containing the group's spread. He did have a first-hand knowledge of their practices, since he had worked as a kind of consultant for another daimyo out west just as the Bellyshakers were extending their influence across that domain, and he had seen them in action there. But that didn't mean he had picked up any particularly valuable tips about effective countermeasures to enact.

To press the point further, as an outsider in that instance too, his views had played no direct role in determining clan policies. By the same token, he had not generally been in the loop on information arriving from around the domain, so most of what he knew had been gleaned purely from the realm of rumor.

Which is to say, in a word, this was all a good old-fashioned hustle.

Now Naitō had called his bluff, and even Jūnoshin, with his nerves of steel—or was it mere bravado?—who made it a point not to panic or take things too seriously no matter what the circumstances, found himself unable to speak.

"Aha. Yes. To judge from that choking sound I hear, I seem to have hit the nail on its head," said Naitō, still throwing fastballs.

"Oh, not at all, sir."

"Uh-huh, uh-huh. Out comes the obligatory denial, of course, in a last-ditch attempt to gloss things over. But if you expect me to buy that and just say, 'Fine. My mistake,' then, well, that's not the way I work. You see, I'm not one of those seniors who have some compelling inner need for approval from the younger set. Men like that, they're basically running scared from the rude awakening of finding themselves over the hill. They're trying desperately to validate themselves by showing how much they can still identify with you young upstarts. Once their type get into positions of leadership, the domain in doomed. Business performance goes into free fall. We have way too many managers like that these days, who can't bring themselves to get tough with their workers, and they give me nothing but headaches. So don't expect any sympathy from me. I'm not letting you off the hook until I get a straight answer. You might as well get that into your head."

Jūnoshin fumbled for what to say. "Of course…I mean…that is…"

"And I might add that I have no truck for guys who try to sweet-talk me. One hears tell of these 'granddaddy charmers,' who turn on the gay vibes to cozy up to some powerful elder, and for some reason—Hah! 'For some reason,' I say. What a hoot! Whether consciously or unconsciously, it's totally calculated—we soon see the charmer advancing far beyond his abilities, but just so you know, I don't fall for that sort of thing. You'll never make yourself my special pet and magically find things going your way."

He's read me like a book, Jūnoshin thought. *Nothing works on this geezer. I suppose I might as well come clean.*

But when it hit him that he could end up getting killed, he quickly reconsidered.

What's to say he won't milk me for what I know, then turn around and kill me? he asked himself.

Damn, this is looking bad. When I ran into him on the grounds earlier, it seemed like the perfect chance. If I could make good on it and get his ear, I'd be home free. But it seems to have backfired. So now what do I do? Stick to my story and insist I know how to handle the Bellyshakers? But he's made it pretty clear he's already onto me about that, so I might be better off candidly admitting the truth and apologizing. Except he also warned me that that won't do any good. Which reminds me, my tried and true way of jogging my mind loose at times like this, so I can cool down and maybe see things in a different light, is to say to myself, "Looks like Little Miss Pickle's come to play"—as if the whole thing is actually someone else's problem. But I can't very well do that here—not when I'm sitting face-to-face with the old codger. Oh, what the hell. Maybe I'll just let it fly anyway.

"Looks like Little Miss Pickle's come to play."

"What's that?"

"Damn, it's no good. I don't feel anything loosening up at all."

"What're you muttering about?"

"Nothing, I mean, all I said was, it looks like Little Miss Pickle's come to play."

"Who the hell is Little Miss Pickle?"

"Um, well, actually, there's Little Miss Peaches and Little Miss Pickle, you see, with Little Miss Peaches responsible for all things good, and Little Miss Pickle for all things bad. As you might imagine from her name, Little Miss Peaches is always happy and pleasant and smiling sweetly, while Little Miss Pickle, also as her name might suggest, wears a sour face with shifty eyes that glare with discontent. Now, to explain how this might come up at this particular moment, it's kind of become a habit with me when I find myself in an awkward situation to say to myself, 'Looks like Little Miss Pickle's come to play,' and that's what happened a minute ago—just popped out without my even thinking. Terribly rude of me. You have my sincere apologies."

Taking Naitō's question as his opportunity to buy some time, Jūnoshin deliberately stretched his explanation out as long as he could.

"I see. So, in a nutshell, you're saying you find yourself in one of those awkward moments right now. And I wager it's because the claim that you know how to deal with the Bellyshakers has been exposed as a lie. That's what's awkward for you, is it not?" Naitō said, bringing the conversation back to his original question.

"Oh, no no no no no no no no," Jūnoshin hastened to deny. He had momentarily started to relax, but all at once was on full alert again.

"Now, why would you think you needed to repeat that eight whole times, I wonder? Because I'm right?"

"No no no no no no no no. Whoops, I did it again. But seriously, that's not how it is. It's like this. I said it looks like Little Miss Pickle's come to play, you see, because the very fact that my word is being questioned puts me in an awkward situation, not because what I said is a lie or anything."

"Did I miss something? If it isn't a lie, then what's to feel awkward about? All you have to do is assure me of your absolute confidence in knowing how to handle the Bellyshakers."

"Yes, of course, but that's not what I'm trying to say. I'm saying that when you think that way about me, if that's what you believe, then I have to explain that that's not true, and I have to convince you of that—I mean, convince you that that thing that you believe isn't true—that."

"Does this sudden torrent of demonstrative pronouns and mangled grammar tell me you're not really so sure of yourself perhaps?"

"See. There you go. That's exactly what I'm talking about. You say that sort of thing to make it difficult for me. That's all I'm saying. That and … well … shall I put it plainly? Yes, I shall lay it all out plainly. You are, if I'm not mistaken, completely convinced that I'm lying, and you want to me admit it, because if I do, then you intend, in short, to do me in. Isn't that right? You intend to kill me?"

"I suppose that's about the size of it. I've got enough other problems already, without having another potential source of trouble running loose around the domain."

"There. What did I tell you? You're planning to get rid of me. So let me ask you this: Is there anybody who finds out he's a marked man and *doesn't* think he's in a pickle? And yet you take even *that* as reason to doubt me. Oh, hold on, I'm not supposed to use demonstrative pronouns. When I say 'even that,' I mean even my saying it looks like Little Miss Pickle's come to play—that's what I'm referring to. Whoops, there it is again. The forbidden pronoun. That's what you're saying, right? No demonstratives? Talk about a pickle. I'm history already. You've already decided to rub me out. You never intended to listen to anything I had to say. No matter how I explain, you're just gonna use it to kill me, aren't you? If you're not going to believe me anyway, then what's the point of even trying? All I'm doing is wasting my breath—if that's how it is. Ooh, another demonstrative pronoun. Is it a capital offense? What a load of crap," said Jūnoshin as he turned aside in a sulk, and just at that moment the temple bell sounded.

Gonnng. Gonnng. Gonnng.

Three profoundly deep tones carrying a philosophical resonance that seemed capable of restructuring life itself rang out across the sky and slowly faded to nothing. Something gave way, and a chill went through his gut. "So," Jūnoshin said, about to go on, but at the same moment Naitō spoke up.

"Fine, I get it."

"Oka–a–ay… Get what exactly?"

"I get that you have no intention of answering my question. So never mind. But one thing needs to be perfectly clear. You've got yourself in a snit and turned all sideways over this, but I'll have you know this was never about me giving you the second degree and demanding answers; it was about offering you a chance to defend yourself. You chose not to do that, and worked yourself into a fit a pique about my questions. Well, enough's enough. I'm human, too. I can get ticked off just like you. Besides which, we're not conducting an objective debate here, about who's right and who's wrong. Because you and I aren't equals. All I have to do is give the word, and the guards listening behind those doors will leap out to grab you. And here's a little tip for you. They tell me you're supposed to be some sort of superhuman swordsman, but I wouldn't recommend that you resist. We've all seen those shows where a lone swordsman cuts down droves of attackers, but that doesn't happen in real life. So best not to resist. Now then, I suppose it's about time to give the signal."

"Wait!" Jūnoshin cried.

He had no plan—the word had leapt out of his mouth on its own accord when he realized he was actually on the verge of being killed.

"What is it?" Naitō asked with a withering stare.

"Please don't kill me," Jūnoshin blurted.

"What did you say?"

"Please don't kill me," he repeated, this time taking care to enunciate his words distinctly.

"Aha," said Naitō with some surprise, his gaze still fixed on Jūnoshin. This man had obviously gotten where he was in life by making impertinence his stock in trade, and when it became so depressingly, laughably clear that he intended to use the same routine with Naitō, he'd tried to head him off by signaling it was no use. For the longest time, the fellow had seemed oblivious to these hints and continued to fight back, but now, suddenly, it appeared he was ready to cave.

"Aha, I see," he repeated. "I take it you've finally decided to come clean. If I heard you right, you're now begging me to spare your life. Ve-e-ery interesting. I had you pegged as a bit more pigheaded, or maybe I should say more of a nihilist, which suggested to me that if I said I'd kill you, you'd simply scoff, *Fine, so you're going to kill me. I'll just go have myself a peek at the afterlife,* and laugh indifferently in my face before going calmly to your fate, but I guess I was giving you too much credit. I sure didn't expect you to turn meek on me the moment you knew you'd be killed."

They were baiting words, intended to provoke the recklessness of youth into lashing back, but Jūnoshin refused to even nibble.

"Indeed, sir, you could not be more correct. All I ask is that you not kill me."

"Uh-huh. The picture gets clearer all the time. I intend to kill you, and you beg me not to. In other words, there's a gap between our two positions that somehow needs to be closed. But as it happens, you've already brushed aside the helping hand I extended from my side, which must mean that you intend to erase that gap entirely on your own. So, what've you got?"

"I'm not sure I understand."

"Helloooo? Am I talking to an airhead? Did I catch you napping? Are out to lunch? If you're going to insist on doing this the hard way, maybe I'll save myself the trouble and just kill you quick after all," Naitō said, as if nothing would put him out more than to have to repeat what he'd just said.

"Sorry sorry sorry sorry."

"Sorry for what, exactly?"

"Uh, right, that is, I believe you meant that it's up to me to state my case."

"Correct. It's entirely on your shoulders to make me not want to kill you. That's what I'm saying."

His back was to the wall. He had been focused solely on what he might be able to get out of Naitō, which is to say, the benefits that would come his way, and he'd never given any serious thought to what he could offer in return, which is to say, what might be in it for Naitō. Of course, Jūnoshin had deliberately hinted at certain things, and Naitō had made certain assumptions on his own. But the conclusions he reached were the ones Jūnoshin wanted him to reach, and any genuine benefit to Naitō had not been part of the equation.

"Well, let me think… The question is why you're better off not to kill me, and I suppose, in the end, it basically boils down to how useful I can be to you if you let me live."

"Except the part about knowing how to handle the Bellyshakers is a lie. Correct?"

Jūnoshin realized there was no sense in trying to dodge the question any longer, so he replied forthrightly, "That is correct."

"Then that leaves me no choice but to kill you."

"Wait, not so fast."

"What?"

"Even if I have no ready action plan to offer, there's still the fact that I was right there on the ground, right? So, I don't know, it's like they say, *You have to have been there*: there are certain kinds of data you simply can't get any other way, and I have that data, now, don't I? That's the key, from my perspective—that's what we need to focus on: that I might be able to provide you with valuable information of such a nature, and that this might become the basis for some mutually agreeable arrangement under which I can be of service, of which we can explore the possibilities, if we could perhaps approach it with open minds that allow us to think about our mutual benefit in those terms, that would be my hope."

"You're showing your true colors again."

"What colors might you be referring to?"

"The colors of a con artist. In spite of all I've said, the first chance you get, you go right back to spouting gobbledygook and trying to shift responsibility away from yourself. This is not a mutual exploration of possibilities. *You*, by yourself, are making a pitch. Is that understood? I'm not going to repeat myself a third time."

"I'm terribly sorry, your lordship."

"So, to distill what you've said so far, you're claiming that you possess a body of knowledge regarding the Bellyshakers that I will find useful. Do I have that right?"

"Yes, your lordship. That's exactly right."

"I notice that you've started gussying up your language again all of a sudden. *Hah hah hah.* Well, whatever. You won't fool me with empty courtesies. In any case, the scenario you're suggesting doesn't really have much appeal for me. I mean, let me ask you this, young man. Were you actually in charge of Bellyshaker affairs when you used to work for that other clan?"

Jūnoshin opened his mouth to speak, but Naitō cut him off before he could utter a word. "No more lies, now," he said sharply. "If I catch you at that again, you're dead."

There was a pause before Jūnoshin reluctantly admitted, "No, I wasn't in charge of anything. I was only a general consultant."

"I guessed as much."

"B-but I hasten to add, as I said before, that what I have to offer as someone who was right there on the scene, rubbing elbows with those affected by the events, should be very valuable."

"*Hah hah hah.* You see yourself as representing the voice of the victims, I suppose. Those idiot reporters who specialize in rambling pieces that pull on the heartstrings must be hounding you for interviews. But we don't generally need that sort of man-in-the-street details when we're making policy decisions. And when we do, we can get all we want simply by inquiring through appropriate channels. In other words, it's too insignificant a payback for the risk of letting an alien element have his run of the domain. Long story short, what you know about the Bellyshakers can't save you. *Hah hah hah.* So, shall we get on with it? The killing part?"

"W-w-w-wait! Um…that is…um…if I may be so bold…"

"You have something else?"

"I am a superhuman swordsman."

"Yes, as already noted. And I should care about that because?"

"My skills with the sword might come in handy to you."

"How so?"

"I mean as a bodyguard or something. I could fight off anyone who tries to cut you down."

"*Hah hah hah*, I think I'll pass."

"May I ask why?"

"Think about it. You're supposed to be unequaled with your sword. But what if that sword turns against me?"

"On my life, I would never!"

"Oh, but I have to wonder about that, don't I? At the moment, we sit here blandly discussing the potential merits to us both of entering into a contractual relationship. But what's to say you won't turn coat on me the minute you find a better offer? Especially since it's a relationship built on suspicion and desperation. In addition to which, people sometimes simply go bonkers all of a sudden."

"*Urk.*"

Hee hee hee, thought Naitō, as he watched Jūnoshin squirming in his seat. The guy's turning tamer by the minute.

Jūnoshin noticed the smug grin spreading across the councilor's face. "*Ai-yi-yi!*" he said, "From the way you're smiling, it's obvious you've made up your mind to kill me, and you're probably already picturing the grotesque and embarrassing spectacle you think I'll make of myself. Oh, brother. The jig is up for me. I'm going to die. How will I stand it? I'm so scared." He was trembling.

With his eyes still fixed on Jūnoshin, Naitō mumbled as if to himself, "The man's actually got a pretty good head on his shoulders."

"Huh? Did you say something?"

"I was noting that you had a pretty good head on your shoulders."

"That's very kind of you to say, sir—except you're still going to kill me, right? You make me feel proud by telling me I've got a good head, and then you just chop it off. In fact, the way you said it, it almost sounded like you were reminiscing about somebody who's already dead."

"Ye-e-es, I think he might just fit in after all," Naitō mumbled as if to himself again.

"Fit in where? Are you fretting about the size of my coffin or something? That's really not necessary, you know. You can just take my body out in the wild somewhere and dump it. Though if you insist, I supposed I'd like one of those hexagonal jobs like Dracula has."

"Why that style?"

"Plain old spite, really. *Ha ha ha.* To leave the impression that I might rise again for revenge. Oh, I might as well tell you, I'll definitely be coming back to haunt you. Maybe I'll show up as a half-decayed zombie. *Ha ha ha.* I've seen the light. The way of the samurai is the way of dying. Man, I don't even know what I'm saying anymore."

"Well, even to be able to say that you don't know what you're saying is to your credit. But never mind that. It's your claim about being a superhuman swordsman that I'm getting at."

"What about it?"

"What I was really observing is that you seem remarkably intelligent for a man of surpassing skill with the sword. Of course, a man can be smart in many different ways, but I was thinking you seem smart in an anti-superhuman-swordsmanlike way. Now, normally, when I make a statement like that, I'd expect to be asked why. Weren't you going to ask me that?"

"Why?"

"Very good. I like a quick study. When we first started talking, you'd probably have gotten your back up and demanded, *Why should I have to ask why?* Or if you didn't say it, you'd at least have been thinking it. But to answer your question, you talked a while ago about presenting a grotesque and comical spectacle when you died and thought I would be amused by it; then, when I told you

you had a good head on your shoulders, you said you were going to be killed anyway so it made no difference. What this tells me is that you're able, at least to a degree, to look at yourself from an objective point of view. In my experience, that's not something most superhuman swordsmen can do."

"Is that right?"

"No mistake about it. The problem with sword adepts is that they seem to think they're the be-all and end-all, and they have trouble seeing things from anyone's perspective but their own. It's ridiculous, for example, how one of them will come to you with a straight face and demand 100 ryō, and when you're surprised and ask him why you should have to give him such a princely sum, he's even more surprised and wants to know whyever not? Well, if you delve into his psyche a bit, you find out he's thinking, *I am me, the one and only, so for you to even think of not giving me this money is a complete outrage*, which is to say, he lacks any conception that other people think of him as *you* or *him* rather than *me*; he thinks that since he regards himself as *me*, everybody else must regard him as *me* as well. He attributes no separate emotion or will to the other person because he's never learned to make a distinction between self and other. In essence, he's like the baby whose entire world is his mother: he sees the entire world as his mother."

"Do you really encounter people like that?"

"A lot more than you'd think. Especially among superhuman swordsmen, since they have the self-righteous tendency to believe that they can ultimately resolve anything and everything by simply cutting someone down. It's also quite common among musicians and film directors, who are prone to this I-am-me syndrome for some reason even though their occupations require a certain degree of talent and intelligence. They're both used to having whole entourages who see to their every need, so maybe that's where they get on the wrong foot."

"Well, I am...er...that is, yours truly is an unemployed ronin who's been through many hard times, so..."

"Oh, but it's not uniformly a matter of how well off the person has been. A surprising number of men in much straitened circumstances fall into the I-am-me thing without realizing it."

"Is that right?"

"Yes. But the difference with you is that, although you may be something of a con man, always looking to take advantage, you're also quick as a whistle, and you do have a clear sense of distinction between self and other."

"I see. It's gratifying to hear. But I'll soon be dead anyway."

"So, that's when it hit me that you might actually fit in. Especially since you seem to have learned you need to be straight with me."

"Meaning…?"

"Meaning I started thinking I just might take you on."

"Seriously?" Jūnoshin cried out. "I don't have to die after all?"

"Possibly. But I don't know. Maybe it's not such a good idea. With that con-man thing going, how could I ever trust you, really? It's a tough choice. Do I want to hire you…or kill you? I guess I'd rather hire, but…hmm…what's to say you wouldn't turn on me?"

"Never, your lordship," Jūnoshin said like a corporate salesman whose only redeeming quality is his earnestness. "Absolutely not."

"So you say, but talk is cheap," Naitō responded, in the manner of a petty merchant who can never bring himself to trust anybody.

"I had a little sister," Jūnoshin said. "I mean when I was a boy. One day our mother gave us each a pork bun. I started eating mine right away, but for some reason my sister didn't. She waited for me to finish my last bite, and only then did she slowly begin eating hers. Why? Because she wanted to flaunt it, the rotten devil. Anyway, she starts in on her pork bun, savoring every bite. I felt totally bereft, as if I hadn't eaten a thing. So I said, 'Hey, sis, how about a bite for your big brother.' She said, 'Would you really take food from your baby sister's mouth? What kind of big brother are you?' That pissed me off, so I said, 'Shut up. Gimme.' Then my sister goes into this singsong voice and says, 'Maybe I will … or maybe I won't.' Every time she said, *Maybe I will*, I'd get my hopes up, but then she'd say, *Or maybe I won't*, and my hopes would be dashed. I was like a dog that's eager for a walk, giving its master those pleading eyes. All this time, the pork bun kept shrinking, and soon it was down to the last bite. The little twerp still wouldn't give it a rest. *Maybe I will…or maybe I won't*. 'Have a heart,' I said. 'Show some pity for your poor brother, sitting here like a neglected dog. How can you deprive me, when you know how badly I want it? Don't you feel sorry for your miserable, forlorn brother?' But she only taunted, 'Not the tiniest bit, dummy,' before popping the last morsel into her mouth and dashing away. But even my mean sister's a proper married woman now, taking care of her in-laws and doing just fine."

When he was finished, Jūnoshin looked up at Naitō with moist, puppy-dog eyes.

The councilor frowned. "What exactly is your point? I'm a busy man, in case you didn't know," he said. His ill humor was quite plain.

"Oh, oh, oh, um, um, um, I'm terribly sorry, my deepest apologies," he answered in a fluster. "I actually had two reasons for telling you this story. First, by recounting to you such an embarrassing incident from my past, which I've never in my life told to anyone else, I'm demonstrating that I place my complete confidence in you, and am prepared to share freely and openly, without holding back, any and all information I possess. And second, I'm sure you will have observed as you listened, that I could in fact have beat my sister up and stolen her pork bun at any time. That is what most big brothers would do. But my own approach, down to the bitter end, was to seek a resolution through negotiations, and I hope you'll see from this that I'm a man of integrity who acts in good faith. That's what I wanted to say."

"Very well. I think I get the gist. All right, then, that's what we'll do. At least for the time being, I'll spare your life."

"Oh, wow, do you mean it? Thank you, thank you, thank you. I'm most grateful indeed. I've been saved. I promise to serve you faithfully and diligently. I will conduct myself with scrupulous honesty." He prostrated himself.

"I'll expect your very best. And as for the scrupulous honesty part, that can be just between you and me. I have plenty of enemies within the clan government. There's no need for you to be honest with my associates or other members of the inner circle."

"I understand completely, my lord. From this moment on, I am your vassal. Your wish is my command."

"Of course, it will be best if no one else knows about this. You should continue conducting yourself as if unattached. Now, here's what I want you to do. Come closer." He waited while Jūnoshin shuffled forward on all fours like a dog. "All right, I'm now going to give you your first assignment. It's a simple matter, but be sure to listen carefully. If you have any questions, save them for afterwards. You may not take notes. I will not repeat myself, so take care not to miss anything."

"At your service, my lord."

"Very well. Here are your orders. Tomorrow, at the castle, I will recommend you to Lord Kuroae as a new special investigator for religious affairs."

"So, I am to…wait until after you are finished to ask my question, if you will please proceed."

"You're testing my patience already, but very well, I will continue. I take it you remembered my instructions in the nick of time. Anyway, when I recommend you, the second councilor, the man named Ōura Shuzen I mentioned earlier, can be counted on to object: *Is that really necessary, I don't think it's a good idea, blah blah blah.* When he does that, I want you to give him a taste of that impertinent, contemptuous attitude you so enjoy dishing out to your elders. Say something mocking that makes him look like a fool. Those are your orders."

"Um…"

"What is it?"

"May I ask my questions now?"

"Yes, you may. But be brief."

"In that case, if I may dispense with the usual niceties and go directly to the point, first, I would expect Lord Ōura to react in some way when I make him look like a fool, so how do you wish me to react to that reaction, and second, what is your purpose for having me do this? Those are my questions."

"Excellently done. I will be most pleased if you continue to exercise such exemplary efficiency in all matters. Speech has a tendency to become bloated with long-winded circumlocutions and seasonal greetings and other conventional turns that waste everybody's time. I actually counted once, and discovered that in the case of a telephone conversation, formal greetings and other formulaic phrases made up a full ninety percent of the words spoken. I did the same for face-to-face meetings, after first asking my interlocutor if it was all right for me to record the conversation of course, and found the proportion to be somewhat lower, at seventy-five percent of the words spoken—which I would speculate is because being able to see the other person's face puts the parties more at ease. By contrast, the same figure for fax messages is twenty-seven percent, and for email, seven percent, so in essence, an exchange of information that requires one minute by email can be expected to take approximately ten minutes over the phone. It's a frightful waste of time. Of course in the case of email or fax, the parties do have to spend time beforehand gathering their thoughts and putting them into words, which is why some people think it's too much of a hassle and decide to just ring me up quick on the phone instead, but that's what I call a real nuisance. What they're basically doing is gathering their thoughts after they already have me on the line, which is to say, they're using my brain to accomplish half of what they should have used their own brain for to begin with. In a word, it's time robbery, brainwave robbery—that's what I think. Now, let's see, what was I saying?"

"I believe you were commending me for my brevity."

"Ah, yes. Yes indeed. It was excellent. That much was excellent. But the rest is a different story. You wanted to know how Ōura might react when you ridicule him, along with how you should respond, but that simply won't do. The problem is that you're looking to just follow orders, which is the worst possible attitude you can bring to your duties. After all, since I am not Ōura, I have no way of knowing how he might react until we are there. Nor do you. So your job is to stay in character as the outrageously rude upstart I asked you to play, and to determine for yourself in real time what your response needs to be. Any idiot can follow instructions. I don't need a man who faithfully does just what he's told. I need someone who can think for himself and act on it, and then take responsibility for the consequences. If that's not who you are, then you're no use to me. I might as well kill you."

"I apologize, my lord. It was a foolish question. I retract it."

"Very well. Next, you asked me what my purpose might be for having you do this, but that's not something you need to know.

You are a soldier. A soldier is but a game piece on the board. If every game piece made a habit of asking why he should carry out an attack, and the general always had to answer to everyone's satisfaction before the troops could move, the battle could never get started. All a soldier needs is to advance when he's told to advance. A lot of the spoiled brats coming up these days want to know it's for a good cause before they'll get down to work, but that sort of warm-and-fuzzy, 1970s folksong mentality doesn't cut it in the corporate world. Because business is war. Harp too much on warm-and-fuzzy and the company goes belly up, throwing you out on the street. Then what're you going to do? Complain angrily that you never got a satisfactory answer? Who do you expect to be complaining *to*? The corporation's not your mommy and daddy. It can't afford to be forever making allowances for you. The ones who don't have what it takes get restructured out of a job. You will, too, of course, if your performance isn't up to snuff. Though in your case, we can dispense with the tangle of red tape that normally has to be followed. I can just kill you, and that'll be that. Any more questions?"

"I beg your most gracious pardon. I will do exactly as you said."

"Then I expect to see you at the castle in the morning," Naitō said, and started to rise.

"A moment. Just one moment, if I may."

"Was there something else?"

"I'd like to confirm, I believe, that I am now under your employ. Is that correct?"

"Indeed, though in a strictly private capacity."

"Then, although I do not wish to be rude, might I be permitted one small inquiry?"

"Permission granted."

"What sort of remuneration can I expect to receive for my services?"

"Hmph. You simply can't stop disappointing me, can you?"

"A thousand pardons."

"Well, I could simply tell you that your remuneration is getting to come out of this alive, but I've already wasted far too much time here, and this final question you raise essentially removes the last shred of interest I had in you as a person. I suppose by forcing me to address such a mundane concern, you feel like you've somehow managed to get in a lick, but you have to realize that I hold the purse strings of an entire domain in my hand. The sum you'll be paid for your efforts is a matter of vanishingly trivial concern, yet I see that just asking me about it is making you hyperventilate. *Hah!* Cracks me up. What a joke. So tell me. How much were you looking to get?"

"A sum of perhaps 800 *monme* silver would make me most grateful indeed."

"Eight hundred silver? Isn't that rather a reach? Am I walking into some kind of shakedown? Maybe I should kill you after all. You're turning out to be a regular pain in the ass. Come to think of it, when I was a kid we had a cheeky maidservant who insisted on being paid beyond her due, and the steward used to grouse over what a headache she was. But let me ask you this. Why eight hundred? How'd you come up with that particular number?"

"Well, I've been depending on the hospitality of Nagaoka Shume ever since arriving in town, and I'd like to repay the kindness he's shown me—especially since he's in very tight circumstances himself at the moment and quite pressed for funds, what with one thing and another."

"Ah, yes, that fellow. He had his stipend cut in half in the restructuring, didn't he. It's certainly a fine sentiment, wishing to repay your debt to someone who's offered you a helping hand, so I don't suppose I can quibble. Fine, I'll pay you the eight hundred you ask, except it'll be the equivalent sum in copper."

"Thank you, my lord. Perhaps I could have it then?"

"Good grief, it's not as if I carry that kind of money around with me. You'll have to pick it up later."

"Would that be at your mansion?"

"No, stay away from my place. There's an agency in town called Bishū-ya. You can go there."

"Will I need to submit a written voucher of some sort?"

"That won't be necessary. I'll arrange it so they know what to do."

"I'm much obliged."

"Very well. You may go now."

"My lord."

Jūnoshin bowed to the floor and kept his head down as he edged backward, rising to a crouch only as he exited the room.

From the above complete transcript, Jūnoshin related only the high points to Shume, taking care to omit anything that might put himself in a poor light.

When he was done, Shume said, "So you're telling me that the business at the castle was all a charade?"

"That's right. The whole thing was set up beforehand and proceeded exactly according to script."

"Wow, I can hardly believe it!" Shume said, making no effort to hide his surprise. As a blinding flash of white exploded in his head before fading to silently falling snow on a winter mindscape, he asked with the innocence and candor of a small child, "But why?"

"Good question. I had no idea at first either, but the more I thought about it," he said, then stopped short for a moment before going on. "Actually, I was about to let you in on my current thinking, but..." He paused again and leaned conspiratorially toward Shume with a gleam in his eye.

"What?"

"Being cooped up in the house like this is depressing. How about we adjourn to a suitable place in town to continue our conversation over drinks?"

"That'd be nice, but I regret to say the coffers are empty."

"*Bwah hah hah hah.* Don't you worry about that. I've got all the money we need."

"Huh? How's that?"

"Haven't you been listening? I just told you that Lord Naitō hired me as his operative and was going to pay me."

"Oh. You mean you already...?"

"Exactly. I stopped in to collect at Bishū-ya on my way back from the castle. See, look at this," Jūnoshin said, as he took a money pouch from the bosom of his kimono and tossed it on the floor. Shume hurried over to pick it up and felt its heft in his hand.

"So it was all true?"

"Did you think I was spinning yarns?"

"Well, knowing you…"

"Give me some credit, will you? What would I gain by lying to you? Not one red copper."

"What will you do with it?"

"That's just what I'm saying. As a start, I thought we could go into town to continue our exchange of views on recent developments, but since merely exchanging views sounds kind of dry, I thought we could lubricate things with a drink or two. Except just having a drink or two still doesn't have a whole lot of pizzazz, so maybe we can liven things up by calling in some girls who do a little bit of this, and some more who do a little bit of that, and have ourselves a grand old time singing and dancing, *hey hey, ho ho, clap clap, shaky shake.*"

"I don't think that's such a good idea."

"Why not? I'm not talking about causing anybody trouble, I'm just looking to spend my hard-earned money on some good old-fashioned *hey hey, ho ho, clap clap, shaky shake.* What's wrong with that?"

"Oh, absolutely, absolutely, nothing wrong at all. But unfortunately, thanks to the financial crunch, we're under a sumptuary edict, and any lavish spending of that kind is sure to draw the disapproval of the authorities."

"Aha," Jūnoshin nodded thoughtfully. "I see what you're saying. And if they decided to investigate how I got so flush, my employment with Lord Naitō might come to light. Damn. I suppose we'll have to forget the lavish stuff, and settle for one of those tired old sit-down joints you see in samurai movies on TV, where the ronin or somebody walks in and self-importantly shouts, 'Hey pops! Bring me rice and saké.' You know, with the torn paper lantern hanging from the eaves, and a waist-up shoji-screen door that has the word EATS scrawled across it. Come to think of which, there's something I've always wondered about: what exactly do you get when you call for rice and saké like that? Under the circumstances, *rice* obviously means *food* as opposed to *drink*, so I suppose you can expect it to come with a side or two—some pork-and-vegetable soup and a few pickles, maybe. But the thing is, afterwards, when they slap a few coins on the table and say, 'I'm leaving the money here,' it never looks like they're putting down more than five or six *mon*—ten at most. These days, if you go looking for a meal like that anywhere around here, you're likely to pay fifteen just for the soup, plus, I don't know, probably at least another ten for the pickles, though it might depend on the shop. Figure five for the rice, and the saké's got to be at least twenty, so what's that come to? We're already at fifty mon. It never seems like they're leaving anywhere near that much."

"Hello?"

"So what gives? Are they shorting the check? Do they figure the shop's too scared of ronin to complain?"

"Hello?"

"But, of course, if it were anything like that... Huh? Wait a minute. What was I talking about?"

"You were doing sums of some kind."

"Oh, sorry, sorry. Umm, let's see, where were we? Ah, right, right, right. So we'll just go get something to eat."

"That's still not such a good idea."

"What's wrong with it? I already said we'd skip the conspicuous consumption."

"Right, but there's the separate matter of the not inconsiderable expenses I've been covering for you since the other day. I need you to square up with me on that first."

"Oh, don't even mention it. That can be anytime."

"You've got it backwards: that's for me to say, not you. The fact is, I'm at rock bottom here. Not only am I out the cost of the formal wear you needed for your audience at the castle, but I'm sitting on a number of other debts, and I might also draw your attention to something else," he said, lifting an arm with his forefinger extended. "Do you see that?"

"Of course."

"What do you see?"

"A finger."

"No. I meant there," he said, giving his finger a shake.

"Dirt under your fingernail?"

"Are you trying to get your face bashed in? I'm telling you to look over there, where I'm pointing," he said, shaking his finger again. "That empty space against the wall."

"Sorry. I was just messing with you. I knew that's what you meant all along. Anyway… Oh! That's where that magnificent family altar of yours used to stand. What'd you do with it?"

"I was all out of money so I had to sell it. My poor ancestors— how will I ever make it up to them? That's why I need you to pay me back."

"How much are we talking about?"

"Three ryō."

"That's…that's highway robbery."

"There's no robbery involved. It's exactly what you owe me. So it's reckoning time. Let's see the money," Shume pressed.

But he was no match for Jūnoshin in negotiations of this kind.

"Now now now now now," said Jūnoshin, "there's no need for you to get worked up about this. That's all part of what I'm suggesting we can discuss over drinks. All in good time, all in good time, off we go, off we go, off we go."

Jūnoshin practically carried Shume out the door, and the two fell in step on the road to town.

"Ah, this looks like just the place," said Jūnoshin, coming to a halt.

They were standing in front of a shop with the word EATS written in large characters on its waist-up shoji door and a paper lantern hanging under its eaves.

"It's places like this that have some of the best food."

"I wouldn't be so sure."

"Oh, come on. You never know," Jūnoshin said as he slid the door open and led the way inside.

A large wooden table was surrounded by stools made of empty saké barrels topped with straw mats. On the near side sat an elderly man engaged in conversation with two younger fellows—to judge by their appearance, a shopkeeper and two tradesmen. Across the way, several construction-worker types were drinking shōchū from thick earthenware cups.

Jūnoshin took his sword from his sash and with a loud "Pardon!" made his way to the back of the room, where there was additional seating on a raised tatami floor. Shume followed. There was a word of acknowledgement from behind a partition at the back, where the kitchen appeared to be, and a moment later the owner emerged.

"Welcome."

"Hey there, pops. Rice and saké."

"Certainly, sir."

After the man had gone, Jūnoshin smiled at Shume and said, "I've always wanted to do that."

"Huh?"

"Like I was saying before, you know. I've had this burning question as to what asking for rice and saké actually gets you in one of these—"

He was interrupted by the proprietor's return. "Here you go," he said, as he set two bowls of rice, one saké ewer, and a pair of small cups on the table.

"What's this?"

"I believe you asked for rice and saké."

"And this is really all we get?"

"Yes, sir. Your rice, and your saké," he motioned.

"Well, damn, in that case, let's see, is this the menu here? Um, all right, in that case, let's have cod roe in ponzu sauce, some chicken meatballs, sea bream sashimi, and *hmm*…what else?"

"That already sounds like an awful lot of food," Shume put in.

"It's fine, it's fine. So, what else, what else? Oh, the well-boiled daikon."

"I'll be back with those items shortly, sir."

When the proprietor was gone, Jūnoshin lifted the saké ewer and poured Shume a cup before doing the same for himself and promptly tossing it back.

"So, what do you think?" he said, eyeing Shume. "Your verdict from that first slug. It's really quite good, isn't it?"

"If you say so."

"Yes, indeed. It's a very good saké. From the looks of this place, I can't say I had particularly high hopes, but wine is complicated and you just never know."

"If you say so."

"Indeed, indeed. Very complicated indeed. The subtlest little differences in flavor can offer your palate whole new experiences.

You just don't get that with beer, which all tends to taste the same. Though the ones from the Southern Barbarians do seem to be quite a bit more distinctive."

"If you say so."

"What's all this 'If you say so. If you say so' business—as if you couldn't care less? Is something the matter?"

"What do you expect?" Shume shot back. "Have you forgotten what we came here for? It was to discuss Lord Naitō's intentions. Yet all you do is prattle on about how good the saké is, beer's just not the same, and meanwhile I get left on tenterhooks about whether I'm going to get the sack. You'll have to forgive me if I'm not especially in the mood for chitchat!"

This rare burst of unfettered indignation from the usually diffident man took Jūnoshin by surprise, and he responded with an equally rare turn of seriousness. "Ah, indeed, how insensitive of me. I must apologize."

But at that very moment, the food arrived, and he reverted immediately to form. "*Ohh hoh hoh hoh hoh.* Look what we have here! Ah, yes, yes indeedy, where the saké's good, you can count on the noshes to be ... Oh, I don't suppose you're familiar with that usage, are you? Up at the capital—and the whole of Kamigata, really—that's the 'in' term these days for all these sorts of accompaniments to drink. But whoops, you're probably getting ready to blow your stack again if I keep on like this, aren't you?"

"Not really, but—"

"Fine, fine, so all right, from this moment forward we shall make no special note of these mouth-watering treats staring us in the face, and furthermore, without regard to how surpassingly delectable we may find each tasty morsel heretofore consumed, we shall refrain from alluding to that fact and remain focused solely and strictly on the crucial matter of business we came here to discuss. Does that meet with your satisfaction?"

"What're you blathering about now?"

"I'm simply saying that the presence of the food is of no interest to us, or rather, I don't suppose I should lump us together like that, since I myself would in fact be happy as a clam to talk about the food with you, while it is you who are interested only in discussing your employment situation. Which in fact goes to show just how obsessed those of you in stipendiary positions are with office politics, as in the story I once heard about a man who went to a party, and when the party was breaking up, a number of those present called for an after-party, so they all divided up into several conveyances to go to the next venue, and he happened to be thrown together with a office worker, who went on endlessly about the politics in his workplace, even though his companion was a ronin and had absolutely no interest in any of the intrigues he was describing in such detail, of which I could in fact give you an example, but see, there you go, my mere mention of the possibility made you cringe, because personnel politics play such a huge role in your life. Except that in this case, even though the story is about a subject so dear to your heart, you don't actually have any interest in it, because it doesn't involve you personally. Which does make sense, when you think of the nearly fanatical hold personal stories can exert on people, and the same for things like the Olympics and J-League Soccer. The basic principle seems to be that when you have a web of direct relationships involving a complex of small zero-sum moves combining with a simple, archetypal story it makes people go a little crazy and lose themselves as if they were in a drunken stupor. Meanwhile, it's the people who can't get into that story who go off and join the Bellyshakers... But I guess this is still the kind of talk you're objecting to, isn't it?"

"Exactly so."

"Okay, I get it, I really will pack it in this time. So, where should I start? What do you want to hear?"

"I want to know exactly what Naitō said about me."

"You certainly get straight to the point."

"For me, it all boils down to that one question."

"That may be so, but you have to understand that the chief councilor has the entire clan to think about. He can't be concerning himself with your personal situation."

"Then what's going to happen to me?" His voice cracked, as all the nerve he'd built up seemed suddenly to give way, and he returned to his usual timorous self,

"That depends on how things develop as a whole."

"So, how do you expect them to develop?"

"Who knows? But since we've cast our lot in with Lord Naitō, it's the moves he makes that concern us most."

"I see. In that case, what do you suppose his thinking is?"

"So we finally come round to that. The question you're really asking is what his motive was for arranging with me ahead of time to behave like I did at the castle."

"Oh, yes, that's right, that's right. I'd forgotten that part."

"That's your downfall. You're too worried about saving your own skin to see the big picture. So, are you ready? Pay attention. Lord Naitō argued that the clan needed a program for dealing with the influx of Bellyshakers and proposed hiring an expert in the field, namely me. Are you with me so far?"

"Exactly, exactly. But then you behaved so scandalously that the whole thing fell apart, and that means the one who originally recommended you to Naitō, namely me, has to be held accountable."

"Except that's not going to happen."

"Why not?"

"Because at this point there's no question of accountability yet. It's only after something bad happens that the finger pointing can begin. All we have so far is an impertinent son-of-a-bitch who acted abominably and got sent away. End of story. There've been no negative consequences."

"But it was a serious breach of decorum inside the castle. Isn't that a problem?"

"It might be if we lived in times of peace and prosperity. But that hardly describes the present state of the domain, now, does it? The treasury is on the verge of collapse, and clan government is swirling with intrigue. Everybody's too busy dealing with their own pressing affairs to worry about some nobody from outside who behaved badly. I suspect Lord Ōura's the only one who can work up any steam about it."

"But to anger one of the clan elders is political suicide."

"Don't you believe it. Remember, we're in the Naitō camp. It's true we can't afford to get on his bad side, but Ōura can fume all he wants and it doesn't touch us."

"You're sure about that?"

"Absolutely. Naitō and Ōura are born enemies. There's no way they'll ever stand together."

"Now that you mention, I don't know much about it, but I've often heard they have differences of opinion."

"My point exactly. You're really not very with it, are you? Even an outsider like me picked up on that right away. But leaving all that aside for now, the more important point is that the true blame game is still up ahead."

"M-meaning that I'll get let go after all?"

"Relax. This isn't about anything on your level. Here's what's going to happen. First we'll get more and more of these Bellyshakers coming into the domain and spreading their doctrines. Pretty soon, everybody's spending their time shaking instead of working. And not only that, these are people who believe the whole world is trapped inside a giant tapeworm, and they have a sense of right and wrong that's totally upside down and backwards, so they commit break-ins, they torch houses, they force themselves on young girls— or they do even crazier stuff like chopping their own arm off or setting their hair on fire with a big smile on their face. And thanks to budget cutbacks, there aren't enough police anymore to preserve public order, so things just keep getting more and more out of hand. That's when the blame game begins. Suddenly everybody's demanding an answer for why something wasn't done sooner."

"I see."

"So who do you think gets the blame at that point? You think it'll be Naitō, the man who said I should be hired?"

"That wouldn't make any sense. He said that before anything happened."

"Then will it be the person who brought me to Naitō—which is to say, you?"

"Why should I get the blame? The whole reason I recommended you was so none of that would happen. Because you duped me with your scare-talk about the clan being doomed."

"Now, hold on, that doesn't sound very nice. I didn't dupe you. If any of it happens, the clan really could be threatened. So who does that leave? Who gets the blame?"

"I suppose it'd have to be the man who sent you away—Ōura."

"You think? So what's the result? The entire Ōura camp gets swept aside, and the chief councilor gains sole control of the government."

"Wow, so that's how far ahead he was thinking," Shume exclaimed.

He folded his arms and looked up at the ceiling for all of about two seconds before unfolding them again to pop a bite of the roe into his mouth and take a drink of saké.

"Hey, you're right," he said airily. "This food *is* good."

What a sorry fellow this man was, to change his tune just like that the moment he knew his position was secure.

Shume went on, "All things considered, then, you're welcome to go on staying at my place until you hear further."

"I believe I'll do that," Jūnoshin said, and tossed back another cup of saké.

A few days later, Jūnoshin was whiling away the early-afternoon tedium at Shume's house stretched out on the tatami, gazing blankly up at the ceiling with his left arm for a pillow, slicing his legs open and closed now and then, or bending his knees up and waggling them back and forth. Every so often he would hear a clatter or rustle somewhere outside. Then suddenly there was a woman's voice at the door, calling, "Hello? Anybody home?"

"*Oo la la,*" he said, leaping to his feet and heading excitedly toward the front of the house.

The woman was standing just inside the open doorway. She appeared to be from the pleasure district.

"What can I do for you?" he said drearily.

"I'm sorry to bother you, but some guy, he gave me this, and asked me to bring it to you?" she said, raising the end of each phrase like a question. She thrust a letter into Jūnoshin's hand and promptly disappeared.

An odd smell reminiscent of a fart lingered in the air after she was gone.

When he broke the seal, the letter was short and to the point, with none of the usual salutations or seasonal references: "Kindly take the first left after Matsuman-ya and come to the riding ground you'll find just before you reach the woods. See you there."

That was all.

He decided without hesitation that he would go. It could be some kind of trap, of course. But what did that matter? He was a superhuman swordsman. If things went sour, he would simply cut the man down, and besides, it could turn out to be something profitable. He had heard how the famous founder of a certain well-known firm always made time for anybody who wanted to see him, even after his company had become one of the world's leading corporations. The idea was to bet on possibility. It was foolish to pretend you're busy when you're not, or to play the big shot and refuse to see people.

Besides, I'm really not the least bit busy at the moment, Jūnoshin thought. *Nor am I running a big business.*

A pair of geta with red toe-straps had been left in the entryway, so he slipped them on and started out, listening to the gentle scrape and clack of the wooden risers against the ground as he walked.

Beyond the edge of town, as he neared the woods, he came to a field where a large circle had been cut in the grass to make a training ring for horses. Stopping a little left of its center, he stood and looked around. There was no one in sight.

"What is this—some kind of prank?" he muttered to himself.

Just then, two samurai emerged from the shadows among the trees and came striding toward him. One was short and thin and fidgety. The other was ordinary to look at, but he carried an unusual air about him somehow. The men approached in silence and came to a halt about six feet away, where they simply stood looking at him, still not saying a word.

After waiting for several moments, Jūnoshin grew impatient. "I take it you're the ones who requested my presence here?"

They stood mutely with their arms clasped inside their kimono sleeves in lordly composure. But as he continued to study them, he wondered if he saw some quavering. His blood rose.

"What's with the silent treatment? You're starting to piss me off. It's like when somebody calls me on the phone and says 'This is Tanaka,' then just clams up and doesn't say anything more. Speak up!" he said, his voice rising to a shout.

"You die!" bellowed the man on the left, drawing his sword with blinding speed and mowing it across Jūnoshin's legs, *fwoosh!*

Any ordinary opponent would surely have found himself on the ground with his legs cut out from under him, but Jūnoshin was a superhuman swordsman. In the split second before the blade could strike, he had leapt eight feet backward, then had quietly drawn his sword and raised it in front of him, prepared to parry his assailant's next move.

"You obviously know who I am to attack me like this, but no honorable man strikes without warning. Name yourself!" he roared. His voice was deep and resonant, but he was secretly wishing to himself that he'd stayed home.

The man began to laugh. "*Heh, heh-heh, heh heh heh heh heh heh.* Hoooo boy. That took something out of me. But I have to admit I'm impressed. You dodged my secret move, 'Winnie-the-Pooh Gets Badass Drunk and Grumbles in His Cups.' Since you've shown yourself to be a worthy opponent, I shall be happy to give you my name. I am Manabe Gosenrō. It's a pleasure to make your acquaintance."

"Manabe Gosenrō, is it? *Heh heh.* Nobody's had me this pumped up in a good long while. I'll give you a taste of your own medicine soon enough, but I'd like to know first who that fellow stretched out beside you is," Jūnoshin said, motioning the hilt of his sword toward the second fellow, who was now laid out flat on the ground, not looking too chipper.

"Him? He's Makubo Magobei."

"What's he lying down like that for? Is he sick?"

"He has a habit of passing out cold whenever things start to get dicey for him."

"Sounds like an unusual sort of guy. What's dicey for him now?"

"I suppose the fact that if this turns into a real fight, he won't be able to just stand by and watch. But enough about him. I'm here to kill you, so I believe I'll get on with it."

"*Eee heee heee heee.* We'll have to see about that. This time I'll take the lead. Are you ready? You may have 'Winnie-the-Pooh Gets Badass Drunk and Grumbles in His Cups' or whatever, but let's see what you make of my 'Pug-nosed Reception Girl Without a Lick of Makeup.' *Gwaiyahhh!*"

Clack clack clack!

He rushed at his attacker with a ferocious scowl and equally ferocious cry.

Swisshh!

Dodging the blow by the skin of his teeth, Gosenrō said, "Well, well. You really do have moves. Now let's see how you handle my 'Hutch the Honeybee has Plumb-Crazy Eyes.'"

"Sticking with the kiddie-tale theme, are you? Show me what you've got!"

They battled each other in this way for the better part of half an hour. It was a contest of skill against skill and wits against wits. They each used every technique in their arsenals: the Full-Face Rosette; the Stealth Sandal Flip; the Dreaded Human Firepan; Ebi'ichi's Lantern Slash; Fox Rolls the Family Jewels. They were both bleeding from minor cuts sustained when they'd failed to dodge quite completely. And they'd both begun to feel that special bond of men who've fought each other to the hilt and come to respect the other's strength.

Pant pant pant.

Wheeze wheeze wheeze.

"You're good."

"Same to you."

Leaning hard on their swords to hold themselves upright, they exchanged a smile. But the contest would not end until one of them collapsed.

Their legs wobbled precariously beneath them as they resumed their fighting stance.

"*Kiyahhh!*"

With a piercing shout, Jūnoshin surged forward, only to be met by an unexpected cry.

"Stigger?"

"Huh?" Caught by surprise, Jūnoshin froze in his tracks. "Stigger?" he repeated, mostly to himself. "The only ones who ever called me that were my parents, and Auntie Yagi, and … who else? They pretty much all have to be dead by now. Oh, except Shōko, who was my own age, not to mention…holy smokes!"

In his astonishment, his knees nearly buckled under him. The assassin sent to kill him was one of his childhood friends!

"Is that really you, Grub? It's sure been a while."

"No kidding."

"How long do you figure?"

"Must be twenty years."

"Man, could it be that long already? It's hard to believe. Sure does take me back, though. What're you up to these days?"

"Just puttering around, mostly. But it can get boring with nothing to do, so I hire out as a hit man now and then. On commission, you know."

"A hit man? You don't say."

"Whoops, that's right."

They both jumped back at the same time—a good six feet each.

They faced off with their swords at the ready again.

But neither could feel the fire coming back.

"Hell, I'm not gonna do this," said Gosenrō.

"Huh? What do you mean?"

"My heart's not in it anymore—now that I know you're stinking old Stigger. I keep thinking about that play we were in together when we were something like three years old. I played Yoshitsune after he was grown up, and you played when he was still the kid Ushiwakamaru. Remember that?"

Somewhat tentatively, Jūnoshin lowered his sword. "You bet. I was jealous 'cause you got to wear a cool samurai costume. All I got was some wimpy court kimono and a dumb old flute. And it was a stage flute to boot, so it didn't even make any sound."

"Man, does this bring back memories. Do you remember how you and Shōko came to my rescue afterwards?"

"We did?"

"Yeah, you did. After it was over, I was standing in a field by myself, and these kids who said they'd seen the play came up. There were five of them. They said I pissed them off so they were going to teach me a lesson. On closer inspection, I recognized the guy who was the cow's head in the play, and also a kid who played a servant. I guess they didn't like that I'd gotten the lead. They meant to beat me up, and I saw right away that I couldn't figure on getting off easy just because they were kids. Most of them weren't any special threat, but I knew one of them was going to be real trouble—an older kid named Saomu, probably around eight at the time. His ronin father was a meth addict, and the kid was already hooked on the stuff, too, which meant there was no telling what he might do. I was scared out of my wits, and all I had to defend myself with was the flimsy little bow Yoshitsune got to carry in the play. Then you and Shōko came along with your flute and fan, both made of good solid wood, and the two of you started whacking at the five guys with those. That's what saved me. I remember when you were thumping Saomu with your flute, a syringe fell from his cloak and shattered on the ground. His little brother, who was around our age, burst into tears, and that's when I first became aware that the world was filled with sadness. The setting sun had dyed the fields red, and its backlighting made the woods in the distance look dark and eerie. All of a sudden I felt like the sky was closing in on me and I couldn't breathe. Next thing I knew I was bawling like a baby. Even though you guys had saved me. And while I went on blubbering, you two made sure I got home safely. I can't very well kill somebody who did that for me, now, can I?"

"I suppose not. And if you're not going to kill me, then I've got no cause to fight you either. I mean, I can't say I'm happy about being lured out here to get slashed at, but once I know it's just my old friend the Grubster, I can shrug it off easily enough. Whadda ya say we forget it ever happened and go back to the way we used be? What're Saomu and the others up these days anyway—all the kids we used to know?"

"I'm with you, I'm with you. Except I have no idea what anybody else's doing, either. My family moved here pretty soon after you left, and I haven't been back since. How about you? What've you been up to?"

Jūnoshin averted his eyes for a moment, then looked up again and gave him a sad smile.

"Oh, different stuff," he said. "A whole lot of different stuff."

Sensing from Jūnoshin's tone that it hadn't been all smooth sailing for him, Gosenrō decided not to press him for details. He just smiled thinly back.

There was a brief silence before Jūnoshin spoke again. "If you don't mind my asking," he said, "why exactly were you trying to assassinate me?"

"Ouch. I was sort of hoping you might just let that slide, but basically, I was hired."

"By who? This guy here?" Jūnoshin said, indicating the man lying unconscious on the ground at their feet.

"No, he's just a gofer. By his boss."

"You mean Ōura Shuzen? He hired you?"

"That's right."

"Then isn't this going to get you in trouble? Quitting on him, I mean."

"No worries there. I don't belong to any of the clan factions, nor am I beholden to them. I only kill for cold hard cash."

"I guess you should be all right, then."

"Yep," he said, as Magobei started to stir and let out a groan.

"Shut up. I almost killed my old buddy because of you," Gosenrō said, jabbing him hard in the pit of his stomach with his scabbard.

"*Urgh.*"

Gosenrō watched as he turned the whites of his eyes and slipped back into unconsciousness.

"So long as I give you back your money," he said, pulling a pouch from the folds of his robe, "I don't owe you a thing." He loosened the string and began pouring out the 800 monme of silver atop the senseless man. "There," he said when he was done, "That felt good. Now, how about it? We've got a lot of catching up to do. What say we go find a drink somewhere?"

"My sentiments exactly. And by the way, it's a good thing you didn't go through with your mission for Ōura."

"Oh? Why's that?"

"He's gonna be history any day now."

"You don't say. How do you know?"

"I'll fill you in along the way," Jūnoshin said, as they fell in step together on the road back to town.

Once the two men had moved out of view, another figure emerged from the woods behind the riding ground. The man's skin was deeply darkened by the sun, and the foul odor he carried about his person served as a measure of how long it had been since his last bath. He was a refugee from the neighboring domain.

Unable to pay his taxes, he had fled his village and taken to the mountains, where for a time he'd survived on nuts and shoots, but with the supply of even that sustenance running out, he had come down into the hills near Kuroae looking for other sources of food. That was how bad conditions had become in his domain. Thankfully, Kuroae territory had not yet fallen into such dire straits. But it was anybody's guess how long the population here would be able to continue in their state of relative comfort. The crisis could come at any moment.

The man first made a careful survey of his surroundings, then, with movements as nimble as a monkey, gathered up every last piece of silver scattered atop Magobei's belly and disappeared back among the trees.

Poor Magobei. What would be in store for him now? First his hit man bails, and then he's out the money as well. Lord Ōura's vituperation was sure to be savage.

But he would of course go into his usual fainting spell to muddle things up. Happy-go-lucky fellow!

Meanwhile, unaware of what had transpired at the riding ground after their departure, Gosenrō and Jūnoshin continued on their way into town.

"Here we are. Around this corner and we're in the castle district, I believe. Whoa, what's that godawful smell? Oh, it's this crowd of beggars. Man, look how many there are."

"Yeah, they've been on the rise lately. I think they're refugees from the next province."

"Why doesn't the clan do something to keep them out?"

"Nobody has time to think about such things because they're too busy jockeying for power."

"Which is exactly where I come in. Would you care to guess what brings me to this domain?"

"No idea. But from the looks of you, I'd guess you must be a ronin."

"And you'd be right, but more specifically … well, let me ask you this. Have you ever heard of something called the Bellyshaker Party?"

"Not that I recall."

"It never ceases to amaze me how out of touch you people are around here. That's who's responsible for this sudden influx of refugees. They're this crazy religious sect who think they can get to a better place just by shaking their bellies back and forth all the time, to the point that they even give up food and drink. Their movement spread like wildfire through the western provinces a while back and brought quite a few clans to ruin. When they realized the seriousness of the threat, the other clans decided to clamp down hard, and for a while the group seemed to have gone into a fatal decline. Watch out for that puddle. But we're talking about total fanatics here. The fire appeared to be spent, but not all the embers had gone out. About six months ago, some diehard elements got things going again, this time here in the east, and the movement caught hold among the peasants in the next province. Now everybody's so busy shaking their bellies, there's no one left to bring in the harvest."

"You mean the famines we've been hearing about next door aren't from drought or floods?"

"Exactly. And I'm telling you that that has everything to do with the impending fall of Ōura Shuzen."

"How so?"

Jūnoshin recounted the entire story for his friend—how Chief Councilor Naitō had warned Lord Kuroae that the influx of Bellyshaker elements spelled potential doom for the clan so he needed to hire an expert, namely Kakari Jūnoshin, to deal with the matter; how Naitō had arranged ahead of time to have Jūnoshin deliberately insult Second Councilor Ōura during the audience so that Ōura would object to his hiring; and how this assured that blame would fall on Ōura when the Bellyshakers began to wreak their havoc, with the result that he would be summarily dismissed.

"So that's why I say it's a good thing you didn't complete your mission. Ah, perfect timing. Let's go in here," Jūnoshin said, entering the eatery he'd recently discovered with Shume. While he was still working his way to the back, he called out, "Hey, pops, bring us some saké and an assortment of starters—chef's choice! And make it snappy. I'm not fond of having to wait. Oh, and one more thing.

Be sure not to overheat the saké. Not that I want it to be lukewarm, either, but it's got to be just right—a little bit hot, but not hot hot. Now, where was I? Right, I was saying what with all that, we know Ōura's going down, so believe me, you're definitely better off not killing me."

As he heard the words coming out of his mouth, he wondered if they didn't sound more like a veiled threat—that Gosenrō would come to rue the day if he went through with the assassination— than a word to the wise offered with his best interests at heart. Might his friend take his kindness as nothing more than a pretense and see his true intent as intimidation? He wished he had chosen his words more carefully.

"Ah, here comes the food! Yes, indeed! All right, man, drink up, drink up. How many years do you suppose it's been?" he said effusively as he poured the saké, then promptly found himself worrying again about sounding insincere and arousing suspicion of his motives. The more he worried about it, the more he seemed to do exactly what he was worried about, with gushy phrases like "Man, oh, man!" and "Isn't that a hoot?" and such peppering his speech, each one making him want to kick himself all over again.

Across the table from him, Gosenrō sipped on his lukewarm saké, trying to think of where he might be able to buy some apricot kernel water.

Nearby sat a man watching the two of them and thinking, *Egads!*

He had a decidedly odd look about him.

His silken kimono, white split-toed socks, and leather-soled sandals, together with the way he was perpetually flipping a fan open and closed, might have prompted the guess that he was an entertainer of some kind, or perhaps the young master of a prominent family. But this foppish dress and manner seemed completely out of keeping with his clean-shaven head and the thickset muscles that bulged like the Deva kings on a frame that must have measured no less than six foot nine at full height.

His name was Egere no Konji, and he was in fact a secret agent in Chief Councilor Naitō's employ.

Which raises the question of what such a man might be doing in this modest neighborhood eatery, drinking all by himself.

The answer is simply that he was enjoying a few drinks.

Even secret agents will imbibe a drink or two on their days off. And even secret agents have days with nothing in particular to do, or when they're feeling vaguely depressed and can't get in the mood to work.

This being one of those days when nothing special needed to be investigated, Konji had decided to while away an hour or two over some saké and roasted smelt. But then had come the surprise.

He'd spotted this most unexpected pair engaged in a tête-à-tête.

Huh? Huh? Huh? What the hell? That's Manabe Gosenrō with his back to me. And the one facing this way and doing most of the talking is that guy Nagaoka Shume's been palling around with lately—name was Kakari Jūnoshin, if I recall. What could that pair have to talk about? I just can't imagine. I absolutely cannot imagine.

With the answer eluding him no matter how hard he wracked his brains, he ordered some more saké and perked up his ears.

"*Eeyahhhhh!*"

An hour later, a giant of a man could be seen racing furiously through the bamboo grove at the edge of town, screaming at the top of his lungs. It was Egere no Konji. He was feeling bitterly humiliated, consumed by a sense of defeat. He'd started on an aimless tear just to run off some steam because he could no longer bear to sit still. And he was beating up on himself as he ran.

"I'm a spy. I gather information for a living. And yet I listened to those two guys talk for an entire hour without learning a thing. Who the hell is Grub? Who the hell is Stigger? What's Shōko to them? Grub threw the tricycle in the creek and Stigger waded in with white rain boots to fish it out? What kind of code is that supposed be? I can't make head or tail of it. I don't have a clue, damn it! They have to be up to something no good, but what? I feel so wounded. I mean, I'm a sensitive guy. It hurts my feelings. It undermines the pride I have in my work. *Eeyahhhhh!*

Why do they have to put everything in terms I can't understand? *Eeyahhhhhh!"*

As a matter of fact, this was not the first time Konji had had one of these fits. Which is to say he probably wasn't cut out to be a spy.

Sometimes he would compensate by turning uncharacteristically talkative—like the entertainer who tries to humor everyone he meets. But this left him feeling almost as miserable as before. It seemed to be a defense mechanism that kicked in willy-nilly, lest his spirit be wounded for life. And it was when even this failed to protect him that he flew into a frenzy like now.

To tell the real, whole, honest, unadulterated truth, it may have been more suited to Konji's inborn nature—not to mention made him much happier in life—if he had stayed away from the exciting world of undercover intrigue and stuck to being an ordinary tradesman of some kind.

Seeing Konji, passing villagers called to each other that there was a mad fiend dashing helter-skelter in the bamboo grove, and hurried uneasily away.

Sondai-ji was the biggest temple in town, and the surrounding lands it owned were covered with some seven thousand Yoshino cherry trees. At the height of spring, the blossoms came into full bloom and turned the entire hillside into a veritable dreamscape. People from all around gathered with food and drink to picnic under the glorious display. It was a scene of great calm.

Two men gazed out across this vista from within the temple precincts. The first was Naitō Tatewaki, and the other Kakari Jūnoshin. The chief councilor had asked Jūnoshin to accompany him on a visit to a grave, from which they were now returning.

"It's really quite stunning how peaceful it is, is it not?" Naitō observed.

"Do you think so, sir?"

"I certainly do. Just take a look. The commoners and peasants are out in full force with their fish cakes and rolled omelets and roasted calamari and shrimp on the half-shell, eating and drinking to their hearts' content under the flowers. Some are even composing verse. I can't think of any better word for it than peaceful."

"Indeed, sir. It's truly a blessing."

"What was that? I'm not sure I heard you right."

"Um, well, you mentioned how peaceful it is, so I simply said it was a blessing."

"So you're telling me that you think it's a good thing?"

"Well, yes, I believe people everywhere pray for peace as being preferable to war."

"I see. So I gather that you are of the pacifist persuasion."

"My apologies, sir."

"There's no need to apologize, but perhaps you could remind me then: when was it, exactly, that you and I first met?"

"Around the beginning of the Second Month, I believe."

"And we are now already in the season of cherry blossoms."

"As they often say, time flies like an arrow. Days turn into months before you know it."

"They certainly do. It's already been over a month. Yet during that time, nothing notable has taken place. I wonder what the problem could be?"

"Problem, sir?"

"Don't try to play dumb with me, Kakari," Naitō said, abandoning his mild tone. "Mess with me too much and you know I'll kill you."

Jūnoshin flinched. He did know, of course, exactly what Naitō was talking about. The Bellyshakers. An entire month had gone by with no sign of their predicted arrival anywhere in Kuroae territory. Quite the contrary, in fact—even the refugees who once filled the streets had melted almost completely away.

"Might you be referring to the Bellyshakers?" he said with some reluctance.

"You're damn right I am," Naitō snapped. "You talked as if the Bellyshakers would start causing trouble any time, But here it is a whole month later and we haven't heard a peep from them. You need to understand. I've been sticking my neck out every day at the castle, beating the drum about what a threat these people pose. Just yesterday I was bending Beren Taisuke's ear about how we faced certain disaster if we failed to develop an anti-Bellyshaker plan, no matter what Ōura said. I'm even being called 'Lord Bellyshaker' behind my back. If these people turn out to be a no-show, I'll get laughed out of town. So what the hell is going on? When are they going to arrive?"

The question put Jūnoshin on the spot.

He had been collecting a stipend from Naitō in the name of investigative services for over a month now, but the only investigating he had done was in the pleasure quarters, where he'd been spending his time at a brothel named Bizen-ya with a girl named Koteru—a comely lass with dimples in her smile. He would lie with his head in her lap, munching on beans, pulling on his nose hairs, and thinking how long it had been since he'd been able to take it so easy. Thinking, *Ahh, the good life. What I'd give for it to go on forever!*

Now, in desperation, he spoke as if through a stifled a yawn. "Whaarll? Hehhh hahhh whoo heeey."

"I can't make out a word you're saying. You told me these people were running amok in the domain next door, but the number of transients coming across our borders has actually declined. Explain to me what's going on. I need a straight answer."

Jūnoshin knew he couldn't go on muffling his words forever. "Well, that is, I mean," he stammered, "the refugees, as I said, came here to get away from the Bellyshakers. But now their numbers have dwindled, as you note, and this might seem, at least at first glance, to suggest the Bellyshakers are gone, but as a matter of fact, that is far from being the case, and in actuality it represents the calm before the storm, which is to say, a sign of their impending arrival. What's that? You want to know why? Well, you're putting me on the spot here, but you see … it's … as I say … it's actually quite obvious. The people who came here to get away because they wanted nothing to do with them have gone home, right? That means—stay with me here—that must mean that they no longer want nothing to do with them, which in turn must mean that they've all gone over to become Bellyshakers. See what I'm saying? It's the only logical conclusion. So then you want to know when they're going to be here, but it's not exactly easy to say, I mean, when you're dealing with people who are, to put it plainly, people who are, if I may be blunt—may

I be blunt?—completely out of their minds. To put it plainly, as I say. So when we're talking about people like that, about when they might decide to show up, well, I mean, there's just no way to predict it with any certainty. Not me, not anybody. That's right. We just can't say."

"I see." Naitō folded his arms.

"I'm glad you understand," Jūnoshin said, hurrying to drive the point home.

"What I see," Naitō said, "is that I don't understand one bit of it. I suppose I'll have to send somebody over there to do a little poking around. Otherwise, we might never get anywhere."

"In that case, I'll be on my way directly."

"Who said anything about you? You probably figure you'll just keep on going and never come back. I'm not falling for that."

Jūnoshin's spirits sagged. The big man had seen right through him.

Naitō chose Egere no Konji for the mission to the neighboring province, and summoned him so that he could issue instructions in person.

"*Eh-heh eh-heh eh-heh*. I'll be right on my way," said Konji, managing to sound both eager to please and unsettlingly creepy at the same time, then hurried off.

"*Tee hee hee*," Naitō chuckled as he sipped the tea his steward, Sugawara Yōichi, brought him after Konji was gone. When Sugawara asked him what prompted his amusement, he merely said, "Oh, nothing," and chuckled again, "*Tee hee hee*."

He was in a good humor because his longstanding efforts to get Ōura Shuzen removed from office had finally succeeded.

Two days before, in a private audience with Lord Kuroae, Naitō had once again underscored his grave concern over the dangers posed by the Bellyshakers.

Since the daimyo as always took what he was told at face value, without suspecting the slightest ulterior motive, he raised his voice in anger. "If such a harmful religious sect has become active, why hasn't the council taken steps to clamp down? It's inexcusable."

"*A ha ha*. Indeed, my lord. The need for countermeasures has been of great concern to me for quite some time. You may recall an audience in which I had a young man named Kakari Jūnoshin introduced to you."

"Ah, yes. The fellow that Ōura rebuked for impertinence."

"That's correct, my lord. It had come to my attention that he was extremely well-informed regarding the Bellyshakers, and that his expertise would be indispensable in formulating effective plans for fighting off their menace. Unfortunately, Ōura allowed a personal grudge to cloud his judgment and made certain that the fellow would be kept far away from any deliberations on the matter by the council. That has led directly to the present crisis."

Lord Kuroae made a troubled sound. "Can this be true?" he asked Naitō. Needless to say, it accomplished nothing for him to ask such a question of the very man who'd brought him the shocking information of uncertain veracity that he wished to verify. It was no better than when young people exclaim "Really?" or "Are you serious?" or "You're shitting me!" But Lord Kuroae was asking a serious question, and he expected an honest answer.

"No, I was actually lying. To tell the truth, it was all a scheme I cooked up to oust Ōura from his post," would have been that honest answer—except, of course, nothing could have induced Naitō to utter it. Instead, putting on an air of great importance, he said, "I regret to say, it is indeed so."

The daimyo exploded with rage. "That low-down dirty son-of-a-bitch—doing whatever he pleases. Is he trying to make a mockery of me? I am seriously pissed off about this. Summon him at once."

"Might I ask what you intend to do?"

"That goes without saying. I'll order him to slit his belly. No, wait, that's too good for him. I won't permit it. A man like that deserves no better than crucifixion. Crucify him and chop off his head to be displayed at the prison gates!"

This talk of execution made Naitō a little queasy.

His clever scheme could actually get Ōura killed. He wasn't so sure he liked that.

Not that he hadn't killed anyone before. But it had always been strictly out of necessity, like brushing away sparks to keep his clothes from catching on fire: he was attacked first, and defending himself had required the use of lethal force. This was a little different. For one thing, there was the longstanding friction between himself and Ōura. For another, he could not escape a twinge of guilt that one of his first thoughts when Shume brought Jūnoshin to him had been, *This is my chance!* Did letting something like that bother him mean he was losing his edge in his old age? On the other hand, none of that changed the fact that he hated Ōura's guts. *I know! Kwah hah hah hah. I'll put him through a wringer worse than death. That way, I can live in satisfaction that he got what he deserved, instead of having to nurse my conscience for killing him. Let me think, now. Ah, yes*, he said to himself as an idea came to him. *The monkeys...*

"But, if I may, my lord."

"What is it? I don't want to hear you pleading for his life. I won't have that."

"I understand completely, my lord, but at the moment, between our fiscal predicament and the threat of the Bellyshakers, we are faced with a crisis in which the clan's very survival is at stake. It is not a time when we can afford to lose valuable personnel. Contemptible as he may be, Ōura's abilities as an administrator are considerable. I fear we would sorely miss those skills if we were to be deprived of them at this juncture."

"Very well. What do you suggest?"

"As it happens, the domain's only monkey trainer, a man by the name of Shōsuke living in Hedaka Village, died of a sudden stroke last month. Sadly, this means neither the members of your household nor your subjects will be able to enjoy monkey shows anymore. So my suggestion would be to appoint Ōura as monkey commissioner and put him in charge of training the monkeys. I have no doubt he will acquit himself most respectably in the post."

"An interesting idea. But what good will that do? Are monkey shows really so important?"

"Absolutely, my lord. Having a hearty laugh boosts morale and lets the peasants and townsfolk go out to till their fields or conduct their trade in good cheer again the next day. Without monkey shows, the world would be a very dark place indeed."

"I see. In that case, I'll do as you suggest. I hereby appoint Ōura to the office of monkey commissioner."

"A most excellent decision, my lord. I recommend not assigning any deputies or other staff to the office. It would be best for the commissioner to train and handle the monkeys himself."

"Arrange it as you see fit."

And so Ōura Shuzen had been made the domain's official monkey trainer.

"*Bwa hah!*"

No longer able to contain his mirth, Naitō erupted in a guffaw as he recalled his exchange with Lord Kuroae and conjured up an image of Ōura stumbling over himself trying to teach his monkeys a new trick.

"*Bwah hah hah hah hah hah hah hah!*"

Laughing boisterously now, he decided someday soon to visit the newly christened Bureau of Monkey Affairs in Hedaka, so he could see for himself how the man was faring in his changed circumstances.

As a matter of fact, at that very moment, Ōura was hard at work training one of his charges to dash across the floor to where he stood, clamber up the front of his cloak, execute a neat little flip over his head, and land upright on his shoulder.

"All right, Tarō, let's try that again. Ready? Go."

At the signal, Tarō showed no hesitation as he came scampering toward Ōura and right on up his front—only to somehow miss his timing on the flip so that he lost his balance in the air and landed on Ōura's head instead of his shoulder.

"*Ai-yi-yi!*" Ōura cried out.

And it wasn't only from the pain. Owing to the stress of losing his beloved master, Tarō was having digestive troubles. He had lost control of his bowels in mid-flip as well, causing splatters of diarrhea to rain down on Ōura.

Looking at himself covered in monkey shit, Ōura shouted in frustration. "Why is this happening to me? I'm a clan elder!"

He was feeling desperately sorry for himself at being on the losing end of the power struggle. But better this than death, he told himself. Since he'd been left to live and suffer this indignity, he would persevere through any hardship, no matter what it took, until he could redeem his name and topple Naitō from his perch.

With this vow, Ōura got to his feet and called for Tarō again. The monkey was cowering behind the woodpile, trembling in fear of his terrifying new trainer.

It had been three days since Konji's departure for the neighboring province, and Naitō remained in a very good humor.

"*Tee hee hee hee hee.*"

He was yet again chortling to himself over tea in his sitting room, when he heard someone calling at the back door.

"Hello? Anybody home?"

"Now, who could that be, out of the blue?" his steward Sugawara mumbled as he headed for the door. Moments later he returned with a letter in his hand and sat down in front of Naitō.

"Who is it? Ōura come to beg for mercy?"

"No, your lordship."

"Then what?"

"A runner with a report from Egere no Konji."

"Aha, he sent something in writing ahead of his return, did he? That's good of him. He's an efficient fellow. What you might call an interim report, I suppose. It looks very thorough. So, is the runner still out back? There's no need to stand on ceremony. Show him directly into the garden."

Sugawara retraced his steps and found the courier crouched down near the back door, poking a stick at a parade of ants and sending them into a tizzy. The man was wearing a wilted old kimono with the back tucked up, and looked none the worse for wear in spite of the long journey.

"Hey, you."

"Yes?"

"Come with me."

"Yes, sir."

Sugawara led him around to the garden. "Wait right here," he said. "His lordship will give you something for your trouble."

"Y-y-yes, sir," the man stammered. He seemed quite bewildered as he knelt formally with his hands on his thighs and looked about the garden.

"The man appears to be a halfwit, sir."

"Never mind that. I'm going to read the report now. Just have him wait."

Naitō unrolled a section of the letter and held it up in front of him. It was a lengthy document. It began with the simple title, "REPORT," written in a surprisingly accomplished hand. At first he responded periodically to what he was reading with *Hmm*s and *Uh-huh*s and *Ai-yi-yi!*s and *Urk!*s, but in time he fell silent and the scroll began to shake in his hands.

REPORT

To: Naitō Tatewaki, Chief Councilor
From: Konji of Sakana-chō, Peasant

As I prepare to report on what I have learned about the strength of the Bellyshaker movement in neighboring Ushichiku Domain, it occurs to me that in all the time I have served as your agent, I have always delivered my reports to you in person, and this will be the first I present in written form, so please overlook my poor writing and poor hand. As a matter of fact, I feel quite at sea over what sort of style to adopt, and I'm kicking myself for not having read a novel or two along the way so I might be better prepared. But bemoaning such things will only keep me from the task I sat down to do, I suppose, so I shall proceed without further ado to my report.

I arrived in the domain on a magnificent spring day that suggested summer must be just around the corner. The trees were such a deep, verdant green and the breeze so refreshing, I set aside my mission for a time and stopped to soak my feet in a stream running beside the road. "This is heaven!" I exclaimed. A pastoral landscape spread out in front of me. "Flowers paint the meadows / I'll pick them all for you!" Before I knew it, I had broken into song. Other travelers were giving me strange looks as they hurried on by. Uh-oh, can't have people noticing me, I thought. I'm supposed to be under cover. Better switch gears.

Coolly, I lift my feet from the water and take in my surroundings. I'm glad to see only peasants. A sly grin tugs at my lips as I reach inside my cloak. The touch of cold steel. One of the best daggers in the world, forged by the peerless swordsmith Komatsu Gorō Yoshikane, served as the model for this replica. My one true friend. Definitely a splurge for a low-end snoop like me, but I'm not one to stint on the tools of my trade.

Continuing down the road, I soon come to a barrier gate. No need to panic. I cross back and forth between the provinces often enough that I know the man in charge. He thinks I'm in the dried sardines business. Cracks me up. Ah, my dear, dear man, Tanaka Tahei. I'll have to remember to send you some flowers next week. I'm afraid the big grimy city is more my style.

But having got myself across the barrier, I'm thinking I'll never finish the report if I keep this up. Looks like I'd better switch gears again. The part I've written so far seems too full of airs, you might say, and mostly untrue, as if the content is bending to the form, which might be fine if this were literature, but being an investigative report, it's not really appropriate, so I promise to stick to just the facts from here on out, except that in my several attempts, I can't seem to avoid getting caught up in stylistic considerations when I write, and that pulls me away from the real task at hand, which is to report my findings, so now I'm thinking that what I need to do is banish the whole writing thing from my mind like this and just pretend I'm talking and taking down the words, if I might respectfully beg your indulgence, but oops, I seem to have lapsed right back into letterspeak, and oops again, I really need to stop being so self-conscious about the way I'm writing. No more. My apologies.

So, to get to my report, Ushichiku is quiet. Master Kakari claimed the Bellyshakers have taken over and brought the domain to ruin, but I've seen no sign of that. When I arrived three days ago, the winter wheat was in full grain and all appearances were of a tranquil and prosperous domain. A far cry from Kuroae! Just kidding, just kidding.

I kept wondering if this could really be such a hotbed of Bellyshakers as I continued on my way to the castle town, where I decided to stay at an inn called Mochi-ya. I had no special reason for choosing it over anywhere else. A runner from the place came up to me as I walked into town and said if I hadn't already made arrangements, he knew a nice inn, then plied me with such flattery that I started to feel obliged. That's all; nothing more. Especially since it wasn't particularly fancy.

Forgive me, I seem to be rambling again. Actually, since I'm such a poor writer, I suppose what I should really do is summarize just the most important points as quickly as possible, but I have a problem with everything getting mixed up in my head if I don't go one step at a time in order like this. If I try to force it any other way, as you saw earlier, it comes out like one of those impressionistic celebrity essays that leave you wondering what's the point, or like a hardboiled mystery with a narcissist hero who can do no wrong, so, sorry, but I need to stick to the course of events like I've been doing so far, if you'll please indulge me.

The manager of Mochi-ya is an affable man named Iyazō. He asked whether I'd prefer the main building or one of the cottages, so I asked for a cottage. The main building is just rows of tatami rooms separated by sliding doors, but the cottages are all self-contained units, each with its own front entrance and everything, and I thought that would be better for me. It does set me back a little more—with two meals included, I'm paying one ryō per night for the cottage, compared with only a quarter of that for a room in the main building—but as you know, I'm kind of sensitive, and I have a hard time sleeping when I hear strange movements and noises around me. Also, being so big and tall, I tend to get a lot of stares when I'm eating in company, not to mention all sorts of tiresome comments about how a big man like me must eat a lot, or I must be quite a drinker, and so on, and although I've learned to grit my teeth and put up with it, the truth is, it really drives me crazy. If stuff like that got in the way of my work, there'd be no point in my even being here, so that's why I decided on a cottage.

Anyway, after showing me to my room, Iyazō came back with the guest register, so I gave my name as Matsuo and put down my occupation as a moneylender's rep. While I was writing that down, I offhandedly asked, "What's this I hear about some strange group called the Bellyshakers causing trouble around here?" He just said "Huh?" and gave me a puzzled look. I wondered at first if he was playing dumb, but I'm a seasoned investigator after all, I figure I can usually tell the difference between a guy who's playing dumb and a guy who really doesn't know, and he really didn't seem to know. But to make sure, I asked him again. This time he raised his voice as if suddenly remembering, "Oh, yes, yes, there *was* a bit of a stink for a while, as I recall," and then just laughed and went away.

It was too late to do anything more that day, so I settled in for a hearty dinner. The food was actually surprisingly good. The seasoning was what you'd call Kamigata style, which I understand is all the rage even in Edo these days. The secret's in the stock. They use kelp along with the usual bonito, which gives it extra body. That's what makes Kamigata cuisine so much tastier. In any case, if anybody's looking for lodgings in Ushichiku, Mochi-ya gets my highest recommendation. The first day I just went straight to bed after that.

I began my intelligence gathering activities bright and early the next morning, asking everybody I came across what they might know. First was a man from Echigo staying in the cottage next door. He said he's been traveling around the country since retiring as a wholesaler of crepe fabric. Then I asked a maid named Onui. She's the cute, sweet-tempered girl I was so happy to get for dinner the night before, only to be disappointed when partway through she switched off with another girl named Oshige. But Onui came again in the morning when I asked for some tobacco. Next was Rosaku, the old man who takes care of the garden. He told me he was born the heir to a thriving seafood business in Kamigata, but got disowned for too much fast living, and spent most of his life as a drifter before winding up at Mochi-ya.

I decided to see what I could find out around town and talked to all kinds. I met a rather beguiling yet plain-spoken girl named Ogin, who said she was an accredited teacher for a school of Southern Barbarian dance called "ballet." Then I talked to a gambler named Yashichi. Also a ronin named Matsudaira Chōshichirō. He talked like he had a bad case of nasal congestion. After that there was a woman doctor named Beni-no-Suke and a plainclothesman named Shingo.

I've covered a lot of ground since then. A tavern called Tanuki-ya, the public bath house—there's a gambler who goes by the name of Goldie who always seems to be there no matter when I drop in. A playhouse, a newssheet publisher, a run-down tenement house, an employment agency—the agent was a square-jawed man who spoke in Kamigata dialect and… well, well, look what we have here. Sorry, but Onui just came in with my dinner, so I'll have to wrap this up quickly.

Long story short, the Bellyshakers are history. The people here have practically forgotten they even existed.

I guess the last gasp came when local authorities nabbed the founder Sudō Ranrinsai. But from everything I hear, the movement was already fading fast anyway. Ever since some other domains decided to clamp down on the sect a year and a half ago and let it be known that its teachings were a hoax, members had begun to drift away. In the western provinces, bounties were being offered for the apprehension of Sudō and other sect leaders.

This prompted them to take to the highway, fleeing eastward, and they eventually landed in Ushichiku. Since word of the sect's misdeeds had yet to reach these parts, they saw the uninformed population as fertile ground for spreading their doctrine and set right to work. Bellyshakerism spread rapidly, and for a time the domain was on the verge of ruin. That was probably when all those starving refugees started swamping Kuroae.

But I have to give the clan leaders credit. They called a meeting at that point and issued an edict proclaiming death without trial for anybody who joined the group. That scared most people into going right back to their Buddhist denominations. Basically, all the dancing turned out to be no more than a catchy rhythm thing. What a bunch of simpletons, is what I say.

There were some diehards, but they were rounded up and brutally slaughtered. I guess it was pretty horrific. People getting cut down with swords or run through with spears while they went on smiling and dancing right down to the bitter end. If they were tied up with ropes, then just their fingers or their heads would go on bobbing to the rhythm. The story is that they seemed completely happy to be killed. When I pressed for an explanation, I got some garbage about how dying early lets them escape this world of suffering because a giant tapeworm spits them up, and although they ultimately have to come back, they're venerated and worshiped after their deaths as something called "Spew Saints." I couldn't make any sense of it at all.

But naturally, the founder and elders were only in it for the money, so they weren't about to martyr themselves. They split up the cash they had on hand at Bellyshaker Party Headquarters and hightailed it every which way.

Sudō was eventually surrounded and captured by bounty hunters while taking a nap in the home of some sweet young peasant girl he'd made his lover. He definitely got his just deserts. By all accounts, he had been behaving quite wantonly .

He clubbed a cow to death and roasted the meat in a marinade of soy, cooking wine, sesame seeds, honey, wild shallots, and chives, and called it Korean barbecue, dipping it in more of the same sauce as he chowed down. The smell of the beef carried for miles around, and everybody nearby had to hold their noses as they came and went along the road.

Not only that, but eating the beef really got his blood running, and he went on a rampage through the neighborhood, raping every woman he laid eyes on—young, married, or widowed, whatever her age. People were really getting up in arms, so sect elders arrived with stashes of money and went from house to house smoothing things over, but there were still a number of suicides. Sudō then had the gall to call the suicide victims "Spew Saints," and their young husbands apparently knocked him around pretty good for it.

Some of what he did wasn't just incomprehensible but creepy.

For example, he would wrap himself in garlands of buttercups and launch into loud, off-key singing—shouting, really, with no recognizable melody, so you just wanted to cover your ears.

Alas, we have come to our doom,
But even in doom can we find
Seeds of hope to bring us solace,
That we have done what we could;
In appreciation of our efforts,
Those seeds of hope guard and protect us;
So are the things we did yesterday
Forgiven and forgotten,
And the things we'll do tomorrow,
Filled with Divine Blessing.

He would work himself into such a state belting this out that he'd plunge into a cesspool and go right on singing, and then when he saw somebody coming his way, he'd leap out to throw his arms around them, raising his voice even higher. With this going on day after day, the villagers were at their wits' end. It was too disgusting even to be angry. And the cesspool was clogged with flowers to boot.

The sect's other leaders behaved in much the same way. They engaged in scandalous displays of decadence and depravity—eating four-footed animals, giving themselves over to debauchery, some of them falling into the clutches of gambling as well.

Such conduct could not escape official notice for long. The village leaders got together to inform the authorities, and soon after that Sudō and his confederates were taken into custody.

The families they'd been staying with were also arrested, and anybody else who'd associated with them was rounded up as well. Nearly all were executed. It was a very nasty business.

Sudō confessed everything at trial.

He'd given various fanciful stories about his origins before this—he had simply materialized out of thin air, or he was descended from imperial stock going back thirty-three generations to Prince Atsumi, and so forth—but now he revealed that he was the illegitimate son of a sawyer named Isami and a widow named Esun who lived in Etchū Province, and his real name was Taichi.

He was apprenticed to an apothecary in Kamigata at age twelve, and by the time he turned fourteen he was a hardened miscreant. Although he behaved himself when he was in the shop, behind the scenes he associated with gangsters and burglars, mixed narcotics for sale on the side, engaged in thievery himself, and generally got up to no good.

But as they say, "A good deed goes unknown outside your gate; a misdeed is trumpeted a thousand miles." When Taichi was twenty-seven, the apothecary found out what he'd been up to on the side and gave him the ax. Even as he carried on his secret life of crime, the young man had by then become the third-ranking clerk, and he'd been looking forward to having a branch of his own to manage someday, but now this was not to be. Embittered over his ruined dreams, he set fire to the shop and, with the flames rising around him, murdered his former employer and wife, raped their daughter, and decided once and for all to pursue a life of crime.

For a number of years after that, he adopted the guise of a medicine peddler and went about the country committing theft, murder, and rape. When he grew tired of this routine in his mid-thirties, he made his way to the imperial capital and invested his ill-gotten gains in a small drugstore called Pilgrim's Aid Pharmacy. The business thrived, and in due course he purchased the shops on both sides to expand. It was also around this time that an intermediary came to him with a proposal of marriage, and he took a wife. As he reached the age of forty, he was finally settling down.

But barely a year later, he was investigated on suspicion of dealing in illegal substances, and when he got slapped with a hefty fine, his fortunes went into rapid decline. That same year, he became involved with a religious sect called Afterlife, founded by a priest named Sōke in Bushū Province. The main rites centered on members taking intoxicants and engaging in sexual orgies. This is probably where the basic principles of Bellyshakerism had their roots. I suspect Sudō's original connection with the group came through his illicit drug sales.

As he became more deeply absorbed in the activities of Afterlife, Sudō decided to close up his shop. Also about then, his wife became ill and died. Or it's quite possible he killed her.

The sect was eventually exposed as a fraud and dissolved, but in the meantime he had traveled much of the country quietly spreading its teachings. People say there are still quite a few hidden believers keeping the sect's practices alive in parts of Mino, Etchū, and Toyama.

Some years later, Sudō entered serfdom in Gifu Hashima. His circumstances had become so desperate that he was forced to bind himself over as a slave. The landowner turned out to have a heart of stone. He refused to call Sudō by name, instead subjecting him to an endless barrage of "Slave, do this, slave, do that." The disgruntled Sudō decided to start a new religion. This is what ultimately became the Bellyshaker Party. He worked out the tenets by escaping into his own private daydreams while laboring in the fields under his hard-driving master. Drawing on the methods he'd developed while proselytizing for Afterlife, he converted the maid and manservant, then the landowner's wife, and then his daughter. Before long the only one in the household not shaking his belly was the landowner himself. They locked him in a shed, where he soon went mad and died.

After that it was full speed ahead. The new faith spread like a prairie fire, seeming to know no bounds.

Sudō went on to describe the sumptuous living that followed—giving free rein to his desires, indulging in every imaginable extravagance, feasting to his heart's content. He also admitted that the teachings of the faith were entirely made-up.

When he was done, the court sentenced him to die. He became distraught the moment he heard the verdict.

"But the jailer said if I honestly told the truth I'd be spared," he protested, "And I believed him—that's why I confessed. Now you're telling me I have to die anyway? That's not fair! You were supposed to let me live if I talked. That's the only reason I decided to cooperate. You can't do this. It's not fair. After I told you everything."

They say he went on and on whining and whimpering like that, refusing to accept his fate to the very end.

He made a terrible scene again when the time came for him to be beheaded—kicking and screaming, twisting and squirming, wetting and soiling himself, even passing out. With all the carrying on, the executioner said he couldn't do his job, so four or five guardsmen had to hold the doomed man down while he applied the sword to his neck like a thread-cutting lathe.

And the clan leaders were really smart. Not only had they made him a public spectacle, they then published his story in a quickie book that included a full transcript of his confession.

The tale of the fallen icon became a huge hit among readers. An ample dose of sex and violence didn't hurt. Sales shot right through the roof. The publisher Bokuseidō Press was able to buy a tract of land and put up a big new building. They were raking it in hand over fist. Lucky bastards.

Anyway, after all this fuss and folderol, the Bellyshakers are now gone without a trace. The former believers destroyed all their objects of worship and went back to being the hard-working subjects they always were, and the land is prospering again. But I figure any group's got to have its determined true believers, and I ought to be able to find remnants somewhere if I stick around and dig a little deeper, so that's what I thought I'd do next. Or do you want me to just come on home now?

Also, I'm getting low on funds. I'd be much obliged if you could send me another fifty ryō or so. Cash or money order, either is fine. Without it, I'll be forced to move into the main building. As I say, I'd be much obliged.

That about does it. This concludes my report. A thousand prostrations.

P.S. I rambled on so much that Onui's long since gone. The sacrifices one makes for the cause!

Your humble servant,

Egere no Konji,

From Ushichiku with love.

When he finished reading the report, Naitō looked up at Sugawara and snapped, "Go get Kakari Jūnoshin."

"As you wish, my lord. But what exactly did the letter say?"

"I told you to go get Kakari."

"Indeed, sir. With all due haste."

"Then get moving."

"Certainly, certainly. But could I first know what the letter said?"

"Never mind that now. All in good time. Just go find Kakari and bring him here."

"Yes, sir, I'll do that, but why can't you tell me what it said? Please? Pretty please?"

"That's enough! I said get going!"

"Fine. I'll be on my way. But if you don't mind my asking, does this mean I'm beneath Kakari?" Sugawara said, punctuating his words with several sniffs. Then he quickly withdrew from the room before Naitō could respond.

What's he getting his loincloth in a bunch for at a time like this? Naitō wondered for two brief seconds, staring off into space, but quickly came to himself again and began skimming back over the report.

The courier kneeling in the garden was swaying his body back and forth as if in time to some tune.

As he entered, Jūnoshin greeted Naitō like a laid-back showman. "Hey, there, how's it hangin'?" It seemed clear enough that Sugawara had not tipped him off.

Until that moment, the chief councilor had been preparing a whole catalog of choice phrases for chewing Jūnoshin out, but the man's happy-go-lucky manner took the wind from his sails, and he suddenly found himself at a loss where to begin.

"I got a letter from Egere no Konji," he said plainly. "His word is that the Bellyshakers have been wiped out. What do you have to say to that?"

Damn! he thought, as soon as the words were out of his mouth. He'd intended to sound off a bit, make the man feel some heat, blow up on him at the top of his lungs, then rake him over the coals some more in barely more than a whisper, gradually ratcheting up the pressure to drive him into a psychological corner; but instead he'd blurted out the question just like that. He'd hardly even sounded angry!

While Naitō was berating himself for this blunder, however, the news of the Bellyshakers demise had come as a severe blow to Jūnoshin. He appeared quite shaken as he tried to respond.

"S-s-s-so you're saying, um, um, in other words, in other words, in other words, you're saying the Bellyshakers have gone belly up? Th-they've gone belly up? Bellyshakers belly up?"

"What're you stuttering and babbling about? That's exactly what I'm saying. The Bellyshakers have gone belly up."

"And what, what, what does that mean exactly?"

"Not a thing. Except that *I*, who have been talking up the threat these people pose every chance I get at the castle, will now be disgraced and driven from office. And *you*…well, you'll probably be executed. By the way, whatever happened to that other fellow, what's his face, Shume or something?"

"He's now assisting Lord Ōura."

"He works for the monkey commissioner?"

"Yes."

"How in the world did that come about?"

"My guess is that certain people had it in for him."

There could be little doubt about that. When he formally appointed Ōura as monkey commissioner, Lord Naohito agreed to let him have just one aide. But no one from the disgraced councilor's faction was willing to volunteer for the assignment.

"Why don't *you* go?"

"No way. I'm a samurai. I'd sooner kill myself than stoop to training monkeys."

"I know what you mean. But you have to feel kinda sorry for his lordship."

"Then *you* go, if that's how you feel."

"No way."

"So what do we do?"

As they were all trying to get someone else to accept the onerous task, one astute fellow pointed out that the whole thing went back to when that guy named Nagaoka Shume said the clan should hire Kakari Jūnoshin. Without his big mouth, they wouldn't be in this fix, so they should make him pay for it by fobbing the job off on him. A heated debate ensued, with the upshot that Shume soon became Ōura's deputy.

Although Jūnoshin himself was deeply implicated in the sequence of events as well, he related all this to Naitō as if it had nothing to do with him.

As a matter of fact, Shume was finding life at the Bureau of Monkey Affairs very much to his liking. For one thing, although it entailed no additional stipend, the deputy commissioner post was a promotion in rank. And more importantly, he'd always known that he wasn't really cut out to be a bureaucrat, but he discovered that he was remarkably good at training monkeys.

You could even say he had a genius for it.

The wildest monkeys brought down from the mountains only yesterday grew instantly tame under Shume's touch. To his simian charges, he was father, mother, sovereign master, and divine lord all at once. He was ruler of their domain and they were like putty in his hands as he led them seamlessly through their repertoire of side-splitting routines—magic tricks, acrobatics, musical performances, the fish-scooping dance, celebrity impressions, and the like.

Never before had he had so much fun from one day to the next.

And it had become the same for Ōura.

In the early going, to be sure, he had exploded in fits of fury every time he got scratched or shat upon by the monkeys. But as the days went by and he continued to practice under Shume's patient guidance, he'd gradually started to get the hang of things, until finally, he, too, came to experience genuine enjoyment in putting the monkeys through their paces. Without any prompting from Shume, he could now be seen working with the monkeys from the crack of dawn to late at night, helping them hone their ball-balancing or other skills.

When Shume sometimes watched from behind a door, he would itch to step in and say, *No, not like that. Like this.* But he bit his tongue, knowing it was better to keep quiet and let Ōura work things out for himself.

As they poured saké for each other by the hearth in the evening, Ōura would often reminisce.

"When I sit here like this, it's hard to believe I used to spend my days at the castle jockeying for position at the top. All that seems like a dream now. But you know what, Shume? I don't have the tiniest shred of regret. My whole life now is with the monkeys—rising with them in the morning, spending my day with them, getting ready for bed with them at night—but I've come to realize just how precious each day is. The stuff at the castle was actually a nightmare. I feel like coming here has taught me for the first time how a person really ought to live. Know what I mean?"

Overcome with emotion, all Shume could bring himself to say was, "My lord."

"Now, now, let's not have any more of this 'My lord' business. I'm not a high councilor anymore, I'm plain old Ōura Shuzen. Just call me Shuzie," he said, and burst out laughing.

But the ambition for power had not deserted him altogether. Once he got a little more in his cups, he would sometimes blurt out, "That son-of-a-bitch Naitō. I swear I'll kill him," or he would grumble one thing and another about the monkeys…

Be all that as it may, Jūnoshin found himself in a quandary. Depending on how things played out, Ōura could be restored to the council while Naitō was sent away to train monkeys, and Jūnoshin himself could end up minus a head.

"S-so, how does this change things?" he asked, his voice trembling.

"It doesn't," Naitō said quietly.

"What are you saying?"

"I'm saying it doesn't change anything. The Bellyshakers still exist, and they'll still be coming to this domain. That's what I'm saying."

Jūnoshin was confused. He said before that the Bellyshakers had been wiped out, but they were going to come after all? How was that possible? What could this old geezer be thinking? Had he gone nuts?

"Uhh, I'm not sure I understand," he finally said. And as he listened to Naitō's response, he realized just how crafty a man he was dealing with; Jūnoshin was obviously no match.

"As I told you, Egere no Konji said the Bellyshakers were no more," he began. "But so what? Whether they exist or not, their impending arrival on our soil is an established fact. If their demise means they can't come after all, then we just have to make it happen ourselves. There's nothing to it. Spread a little money around, get some people to shake their bellies, and voilà! We have Bellyshakers. What's that you say? Fraud? What difference does that make? They were a total fraud to begin with. For that matter, you're a fraud, and I'm a fraud, and the whole clan is a fraud. As I know all too well from my years on the High Council, the clan's been both financially and morally bankrupt for a good long while already. We've just been dolling things up by slathering on plenty of pancake to hide the blemishes. In fact, the domain is politically bankrupt, too—the whole administrative structure has gone to pot. Which ought to mean, of course, that everybody pulls together and gets busy figuring out how to make things function properly again. But I guess that's just too much trouble, so instead, they all sit around telling each other 'I'm okay, you're okay,' letting each other off the hook. The thing is, you can only keep that up for so long. It's starting to dawn on them that they're living in a painted-picture world. Compared to that, cooking up a few fake Bellyshakers is hardly anything to get excited about. Stop sounding like such a sissy. You're the one who lives by this sort of thing.

If flimflammery got dressed up in a kimono and stuck a sword in its sash, nobody could tell you apart. Pull yourself together, kid. Whatever it takes to survive—that's what you need to focus on. Otherwise, one pop and it's all over for someone like you. For example, at the moment, these hands still hold the power, so cross me and you're finished. Whew, I must be talking too much. I'm all worn out."

"Who'll be getting the honors, then?"

"What's that?"

"I wondered who was going to be in charge of getting this fake Bellyshaker thing going. Just out of curiosity."

"Why would you even need to ask? You, of course."

"That's pretty much what I figured. Except it also occurred to me I might be wrong, so … Anyway, in that case, I'll be on my way."

"Wait. I can't have you going alone. I'll need to send somebody else along to keep an eye on you, at least until you meet up with Konji. And I've got some instructions to write down for Konji, too. So just sit tight for a bit."

As Naitō was telling Jūnoshin to wait, Sugawara entered looking blue in the face.

"You're not going to believe this, your lordship."

"What's the matter? You look peaked."

"It's about the messenger Egere no Konji sent."

"Ah, yes, the simpleton. What about him?"

"Well, actually, um, it's kind of hard to explain…I mean, if I don't put this just right, you might think I've totally flipped out, so, um, where to start…?"

"Hmph! Get to the point! I'm in the middle of some important business here."

Sugawara flushed. "Very well, sir. I understand. I'm just a no-count steward, after all. I'm sorry to have bothered you. In that case, I don't believe I'll even try to explain. If you'll please come with me, you can see for yourself," he said, and immediately started away.

"Good grief, Sugawara, what's gotten into you today?" Naitō said as he rose to follow, and Jūnoshin fell in step behind him.

The steward led the way to the kitchen, where the man in question was squatted on his haunches in his threadbare kimono, tucking into a sizeable ball of rice. He was so intent on his eating that he failed to notice the men come in.

"What is it? Why'd you bring me here?" Naitō demanded. "What am I supposed to see?"

Sugawara ignored him and called to the man.

"Hey, you."

The man didn't respond. He went on stuffing his face.

"Hey, you," Sugawara repeated, raising his voice a little.

Still no response.

"Yo! You there!" he said, his voice now a full shout. "Answer me!"

The man finally noticed he was being spoken to.

"I, I, I, I, um, um, um…"

Stuttering incoherently, he rose to his feet in such a fluster that it was painful to watch. He stood there with the half-finished rice ball in his hand, his forearms spread, both palms up, eyes darting back and forth and looking over his shoulder, teetering like someone who'd just gotten out of bed, even stumbling a time or two. Sticky grains of cooked rice dotted his face.

"This is his lordship. You need to show him the proper respect," Sugawara admonished.

The man's eyes widened and he grew even more flustered. He puffed his cheeks like a dove and said, "Um, I, um, um, um, I was just, just, just, um, I'm sorry, I was just, just, e-e-eat-eating, um, eating this rice ball. Um, I, um, I'm sorry. You gave, um, you gave, you gave it to me."

In spite of his strenuous efforts, nobody could make out what he was trying to say. But there was, in fact, an explanation for his inordinate agitation.

A short while before this, Sugawara had showed the man into the kitchen to see about getting him something to eat. A maid was just then making some rice balls for one of the menservants, so Sugawara simply took one of those and gave it to the messenger. She was then called away to another part of the house, and when Sugawara followed her out, the man was left in the kitchen by himself. He devoured the rice ball in next to no time at all. Right in front of him on the counter were three more of them sitting neatly in a row on a bamboo leaf.

Knowing he shouldn't, but unable to resist the temptation, he reached for one, then another, and had just taken his first bite out of the third when Sugawara returned. He thought he was about to catch hell for it, and that was why he'd worked himself into such a state.

But no daimyo's chief councilor or anyone in his employ was going to bawl a man out over three measly rice balls. The courier's fears were utterly unfounded.

"You're babbling nonsense again," said Sugawara sharply. "Hurry up and offer his lordship your respects."

The man's eyebrows shot up and he stood speechless for several moments. Then he said, "Re-re-re-respects? Um, I, I don't, um, um, I mean wh-wh-what, wh-what, no, h-h-how do you mean, respects?"

"For crying out loud, don't you even know that much? Just say your name and bow."

"Oh, ohhh, ri-ri-ri-ri-right. Um, I, I, I'm Osamu, Osamu," he said, then jerked his head down and up like some kind of mechanical puppet.

Naitō had been quietly watching Osamu throughout this exchange, but was growing impatient with Sugawara.

"What's this all about, Sugawara?" he demanded sharply. "You said you wanted me to see something."

The steward remained calm. "Yes, sir," he said, then turned again to the messenger, who still seemed to think he was in for a tongue-lashing. "All right, Osamu. Now show his lordship that thing you did."

"Wh-what th-th-thing would that be, sir?"

"The trick you showed me in the garden. Do that trick again."

"Oh. A-a-all right, I, I, I can do that. But, um, um, um, with what?"

"Well, let's see. How about that bucket over there? Show us with that."

"A-a-all right."

Seeming to relax for the first time, he smiled and lifted his arm toward a wooden bucket sitting in the corner of the dirt-floored part of the kitchen.

"What's he going to do?" Naitō asked, and then suddenly couldn't believe his eyes.

Without anybody laying a finger on it, the bucket had risen about three feet into the air. After hovering in place for several moments, flames flickered up to engulf it, and before long it had burned to nothing.

Nobody uttered a word. The temperature in the room had gone up, and a bead of sweat trickled down Jūnoshin's cheek. Naitō smelled scorched wood. The trees could be heard rustling in the wind outside. Osamu stood tall in the dirt area, still seeming to teeter from his great height.

Several long moments went by before Naitō and Jūnoshin both spoke at once. "What the hell was that?"

Sugawara offered the following explanation.

"When I left the room a while ago, I remembered that Konji's man was still waiting in the garden and decided I'd better go check on him. I found him just standing there staring vacantly up at the sky. I thought, man, he sure is tall. I mean, because he looks like such a doofus in that whirlpool kimono that's so ridiculously short for him, you know. But then I thought how even a guy like him has a mother and a father and his own special place in the world, and it seemed kind of heartbreaking and sad.

"So anyway, I called to him, and he practically jumped out of his skin and started looking wildly about. It turns out that's more or less how he reacts to anything—no matter what I said or told him to do, he'd give a little jump and look like he was scared stiff. It's basically because being so dumb, he almost always messes things up even when it's the simplest little thing, so he's gotten so used to being chewed out that he automatically assumes he's going to get it even before he's done anything, and it puts him in a panic.

"After calming him down, I asked him his name, and he tells me it's Osamu, so I say, 'Okie-doke, Osamu, I'll be needing you later, so I want you to just sit tight for now. Don't go wandering off anywhere.' I figured you'd have a reply for Egere no Konji. He says okay, so I push open the garden wicket and step into the path leading to the back gate. But before going any farther

I happen to glance over my shoulder, and I see him standing with his arm stretched forward, moving it up and down—like some idiot practicing to be a surveyor or something. Naturally, I wondered what he was doing, so I turned back around for a better look, and I was literally floored. I don't mean I literally fell to the floor, of course—I'm only speaking figuratively. It's my way of saying how flabbergasted I was. When I looked where he was pointing, over by the well, I saw a garden rock big enough to fill your arms hovering in midair, rising and falling with his movements. For a little while, he keeps shifting his arm up and down, but then he lifts it a little higher than his head and stops. The rock rises with it to about the top of a pine tree and then it stops, too. At that point, he lightly closes his fingers into a fist and flicks them open again like he's shaking off some water or something, and the rock shatters into a million pieces. Without making the slightest sound.

"It was totally mind-boggling, but he just stood there like it was nothing, like it was the most natural thing for him to do. I thought I was going to pee myself, I was so stunned. But it wasn't the sort of thing you could just pretend never happened, so I walked as nonchalantly as possible back to where he stood and said, though I have to admit my voice was quivering a bit, 'What's that you're doing there?'

"He goes into a tizzy again and says, 'I'm sorry, I'm sorry, I'm sorry,' like he's ready to burst into tears, but I managed to calm him down and ask him some questions. The gist of it is that he has these amazing powers to lift things off the ground and set them on fire and whatnot without ever touching them. He's known about it since he was little, but every time he tried something, the grownups would yell at him, 'Stop your messing around. Don't you know it's rude. Maybe this'll teach ya,' and give him a savage scolding and beating, so he learned pretty quick that he couldn't let anybody see. After that he kept it all a secret, and when the urge to exercise his powers got too strong, he'd go off into the mountains by himself and amuse himself moving boulders around or setting the forest on fire. Makes me shudder just to think. Anyway, when he realized I'd seen him, he was terrified what I might do.

"I told him not to worry and asked him to show me again. So he lifts another big rock into the air and makes it shatter into bits like the first one. I tipped him a few coppers for his trouble, and he starts thanking me profusely and calling me 'boss.' Just for that, he seems to think he's forever in my debt somehow, and I get the feeling he'll do pretty much anything I say. I guess until now he's been keeping body and soul together by wandering the streets of Ushichiku and pushing freight carts or picking up other odd jobs in exchange for food or small change. To look at him, you wouldn't think he's much over twenty, but he says he turned thirty-five this year.

"So that's his story," Sugawara said in conclusion. "What do you want me to tell him?"

"*Tee hee hee*," Naitō chortled up his sleeve. "This guy's going to come in handy."

Kakari Jūnoshin, Sugawara Yōichi, and Egere no Konji were gathered in one of the cottages at the upscale Mochi-ya Inn in Ushichiku, drinking together.

In front of each was a tray table laden with the remnants of a feast on which they had gorged themselves to the gills. The soup bowls were tipped, the chopsticks crossed, and the trays themselves pushed askew.

They sat in a bloated haze, too stuffed to speak.

They had eaten to their hearts' content and then some.

The mood should have been one of supreme satisfaction, but the room was filled with a profound sense of desolation and emptiness.

Finally, unable to bear this feeling any longer, Jūnoshin opened his mouth. "But it really does go to show, doesn't it?"

"What goes to show what?" said Sugawara.

"Oh, I don't know. I got tired of sitting here with nobody saying anything, and it seemed like something to say, but then I realized I didn't have anything to follow with."

"You're a real devil-may-care sort of guy, aren't you."

"Call me devil-may-care if you want, but at least you have to give me credit for my commitment to keeping the conversation rolling. On that score, what's your problem, Konji? What happened to your 'Chatty Konji' reputation? I thought you were selling yourself as the undercover agent who can outtalk anybody. It's not like you to be sitting there all clammed up."

. "*Heh heh*, selling myself as an undercover agent—that's a good one. But what can I say? For the last I-don't-know-how-long, we've been stuffing our faces, focused only on satisfying our appetites. And we've achieved total gratification. But that's kind of sad, don't you think? I mean, we were all feeling kind of down in the mouth, and we figured something good to eat might make us feel better, so we asked Iyazō to fix us up something really tasty. And lo and behold, that's exactly what he does. He brings us this spread that's simply out of this world. That's what I think's so sad—that we said what we wanted, and he gave us exactly what we asked. When he goes and does that, it doesn't leave us any room for debate. I mean, if he'd brought a bunch of stuff that wasn't any good, we could talk about that. *What is this shit? The guy can't cook worth beans. This inn reeks.* Or if we'd expected the food to be horrid but it turned out to be great, we'd have something to talk about then, too—we'd be thanking our lucky stars. But when he just brings us what we told him to bring, and then, well, that's it—there's nothing more to say. At that point, all we can do is go head-to-head with the hunger in our bellies, each of us on his own. And once the sheer pleasure of gorging ourselves is over, we're left with this dreary sense of emptiness."

"I have no idea what you're trying to say," Jūnoshin said.

"You don't follow?"

"Not a word of it. And besides, I doubt the discomfort we're feeling comes from anything so blasted complicated. It's just that we don't actually know each other very well—that's all. You always have to expect a certain amount of awkwardness when three virtual strangers sit down to eat and drink together."

He had a point. Except for Naitō's orders, three men of such widely divergent origins, careers, and character would never have found themselves sharing a meal.

The chief councilor had immediately set his eyes on Osamu's special powers as the perfect means for keeping tabs on Jūnoshin during his mission to Ushichiku. If Jūnoshin tried to run off, Osamu could simply eliminate him.

Not only that, those same powers would be handy for helping concoct the fake Bellyshaker revival. Miracles were an indispensable tool when it came to launching new religious movements. Dress up Osamu's gifts in those terms, and people'd soon be joining up in droves.

But he couldn't simply send Osamu along with orders to do these things. The man was too stupid for that. Even if Naitō patiently fed him his instructions in small morsels, like a mother chewing food for her child, it would still be in one ear and out the other. Nor was the answer to have Jūnoshin relay Osamu's orders. Jūnoshin couldn't be expected to tell Osamu to keep an eye on him or to burn him to death if he tried to hightail it.

So, in the end, he fixed on the solution of sending Sugawara along as well, since Osamu seemed so grateful and devoted to him for his kindnesses and had even taken to calling him "boss."

Sugawara had politely objected at first, saying it would be the height of presumption for the likes of him, a mere household steward, to think he could serve in a matter of state, but he had ultimately allowed Naitō to prevail on him, with the result that he and Jūnoshin and Osamu had soon departed Kuroae together, smuggled themselves into Ushichiku, and joined up with Egere no Konji already staying undercover at the Mochi-ya Inn.

"That may be true," Sugawara said. "But in my experience, it's pretty much always like this, no matter who you go out to dinner with. At least among us ordinary folk. Though I don't suppose you have much opportunity for such things when you're a ronin."

Jūnoshin bristled. The steward had addressed him with the informal *you*, disregarding his samurai status. But if he said anything, it could easily escalate into a fight, so he suppressed his irritation and answered mildly, "Well, I'm sure you're right. Come to think of it, though, Osamu has it nice on that score, doesn't he? He can use the same casual language no matter who he's with and get away with it. Nobody ever gets mad at him. Which reminds me, *Master* Sugawara," he said pointedly, "you put Osamu up alone in the main building. Is it really safe to leave him there on his own? Aren't you worried at all?"

"About what?"

"He could run away, or simply wander off."

"I'm sure there's no concern of that. I told him to stay put, so he won't be going anywhere. He's devoted to me."

"That does seem apparent, but the man's a halfwit, after all. Don't you think he could forget?"

"I'm really not worried. Besides, there's no reason we should have to pay a whole ryō a night for him."

"You'll get no argument from me there. So, then, is everything in order for tomorrow?"

"I believe so."

"We'll start by looking up that fellow who used to be one of the Bellyshaker big shots."

"Excellent idea, excellent idea."

"I suppose it's time to call it a night, then."

"You're going straight to bed?" Konji put in.

"What do you mean? Did you have something else in mind?"

"*E heh heh heh.* There's a tasty little dish I've taken to visiting at a house near here. I'm her secret lover."

"Why, you dirty devil," said Jūnoshin. "I believe I'll tag along, too. How about you Sugawara? You figure on just dousing the lamps and getting into your lonely bed?"

"You're going to the pleasure quarters? *Hmph.* Scandalous!"

"So you won't be going, then?"

"Maybe I'll just have a little peek, too."

"Oh. You *are* going."

And so to further savor that emptiness of satiety, the three men set out with eager anticipation for a hot night in the brothel district.

The following morning, three grumpy men and a cheerful fourth could be seen hurrying through town at a near trot.

"Any chance we could take it a bit slower, Konji?" said Sugawara. "I don't know if it was bad wine or what last night, but my head is pounding."

"Same here, same here. It may be fine for you because you're a hardened spy, but we're definitely feeling the effects."

"Don't give me that. I had no more luck with the ladies than you two, so I filled the time drinking just as much. But we've got to get to this place ASAP, or the guy's going to be hopping mad. We're already hours late."

"Have a heart, Konji," Sugawara said woefully. "I turned down my girl's offer of breakfast trying to look macho, so now I'm famished. Let's find some hospitable place to catch our breath and order up some tea-rice or something."

"Forget it. We have an appointment."

"I know, but I've actually been thinking about that."

"Yeah?"

"If you ask me, this is definitely a situation that calls for us to fortify ourselves first. Sure, I understand that normally you'd think time was of the essence. Here we are, getting ready to show up way, way late, so it should be a matter of common courtesy that we hurry over as fast as we can."

"Exactly. That's why I say we need to keep moving."

"But that's in fact the wrong way to think about it."

"How so?"'

"Well, basically, we're running on empty. And that inevitably means that we're not at our best. It'd be rude to arrive at less than our best when we're meeting somebody for the first time. The proper thing to do, therefore, is to stop and fill up, so we can be at our best and our brightest when we appear before our host."

Jūnoshin saw it for what it was—a purely self-serving argument—but he was hungry too, so he held his tongue.

Konji decided he'd had enough of arguing with the determined Sugawara. "All right," he said. "How about this place?" He stepped to one side of the street and ducked through a white-on-indigo shop curtain that read, "The Loosened Belt."

Osamu bent his tall frame and peered into Sugawara's face. "W-w-w-we're stopping to e-e-e-eat? To eat?"

The little eatery was bustling, and the four men were soon enjoying a breakfast of rice, coddled tofu, and saké with great gusto.

The inclination to tarry came from the essentially backward nature of what these men had been sent to do.

No matter what a man's work might be, he'd like to feel that he's doing something genuinely worthwhile and making a meaningful contribution. But Naitō's assignment for these men was to reconstruct a religion that had gone defunct after being exposed as an unmitigated fraud—a sorry task if there ever was one. Faking the revival of something that was false to begin with was like creating a knockoff of a knockoff, and felt about as noble as robbing a children's bank—hardly the sort of thing that got one's juices going.

This was what had Sugawara and Jūnoshin dragging their feet, but Konji found the job distasteful as well. He couldn't stop stewing over the fact that he was an investigator, not an events planner, and something like this was quite simply outside his expertise.

Osamu alone never stopped smiling. He sat there seemingly without a care, his bare shanks sticking from the hem of his undersized kimono, chewing on his nails as he gazed out idly at passing dogs and dragonflies.

So they lingered over their so-called breakfast of saké and tofu and rice, then relaxed for a time with toothpicks in their mouths and their kimono chests bared before finally putting the restaurant behind them and resuming their journey to the home of former Bellyshaker leader, Chayama Hanrō.

As they neared their destination, the tension began to mount.

By Konji's account, the top brass of the Bellyshakers had all been half mad, with a reputation for brutality and viciousness, but Chayama had been by far the most brutal and vicious of all. He was a shockingly diabolical figure, noted for his extreme right-wing take on the sect's doctrines as well.

He regarded every evil as good.

This view derived from the premise that we all live in an illusory world floating inside the bowels of a gigantic, cosmic-scale tapeworm, and any act of evil or deviltry has a poisonous effect on the creature, resulting in a disruption of its digestive system that aids in the excretion of people as feces into the true world outside. It followed, therefore, that all such deeds should be considered praiseworthy.

Invoking this principle, Chayama exercised his perverse instincts to the fullest.

He killed people at the slightest provocation—or even purely on a whim. Other members of the sect applauded him for it, saying that dying in this world meant the victims would be spit up by the tapeworm and get to see the true world outside—never mind that they would eventually have to come back to this illusory world again, which made it a distant second best to being shat out into the true world for all eternity as excrement.

They still didn't want death for themselves, of course, but it was fine for others. Or perhaps they merely thought Chayama might kill them if they offered any objection.

Chayama also introduced the practice of using human heads in a sacramental food eaten at holy feasts. First a sacrificial victim's head was cut off and its contents scooped out to be fed to swine. The cavity of the scull was then filled with well-washed uncooked rice and an equal amount of water, vegetables, clams, saffron, salt, and soy sauce, and buried in a pit along with superheated rocks to bake up as a casserole of sorts.

The thought of eating such a horrifying dish turned people's stomachs. To judge from the way he never took any for himself but was always urging it on his guests, Chayama presumably felt the same.

"You must have some of this," he said. "It's holy sustenance from the body of a saint."

"How about you? Aren't you having any?" someone would often ask.

"As a party leader, I am not permitted to partake of such exalted food," he replied. "A leader must always serve in a spirit of self-sacrifice. One of the sacrifices I make for all of you is to eat the meat of the animals that have become tainted by being fed the unclean parts you must not consume."

He then dug into a sumptuous, mouth-watering spread of ham, sausage, and Dongpo's pork belly.

If he didn't want to eat it himself, then he hardly needed to concoct such a grisly dish to begin with, but that was what he'd done.

This perversity was but one illustration of the man's twisted character. Another was the incongruously soft-spoken and polite manner with which he carried out his brutalities. Before killing the faithful, he would bow to them and say, "If I may have your kind cooperation, I will now elevate you to Spewdom."

Perhaps the single most striking expression of Chayama's perversity was his face.

His natural features had once been quite ordinary, but nobody could look at him anymore without bursting into peals of laughter. A bizarre collection of tattoos covered his entire face—two sharp peaks replacing his eyebrows, wild kabuki-esque swirls around his eyes and mouth, and silly red discs on each cheek—making him look like a cross between a scarecrow and a clown.

The sound of such earnest and polite language coming from a person of his appearance was simply too hilarious to bear. As the listener erupted in laughter, Chayama would pretend to have not the slightest inkling why. "Is there something funny about my face?" he would ask, and when the listener failed to reply for laughing too hard, he'd continue, "Fits of laughter are among the things the devilish tapeworm most detests. You are blessed. I will now elevate you to Spewdom," and slaughter the person on the spot.

It is difficult to imagine anything crueler than deliberately making people laugh, then summarily killing them for it. Yet Chayama had covered his face with outlandish tattoos precisely for that purpose—which says a great deal about what an impenetrable and monstrous man he was.

Since this was who the four men were on their way to meet, it is easy to see why they might be growing nervous. Even if this former Bellyshaker heavyweight had been living a quiet, inconspicuous life since turning informer to save his skin, there was no telling what he might do if one of them started laughing. They did have both a telekineticist and a superhuman swordsman among their number, so they probably didn't need to fear the worst, but with a man like this, no one could predict how things might play out.

They came to the edge of town. A tranquil, pastoral landscape spread out before them. Jūnoshin turned to Konji.

"So this Chayama Hanrō guy lives out in the country?"

"That's right. He's supposed to have a farmhouse a ways on up ahead."

"Does he live alone?"

"Apparently."

"What does he do about cooking and cleaning and that sort of stuff?"

"Word is that he pays one of the neighboring farmwives to come in and see to things."

"I see," said Jūnoshin, sinking into thought.

He was having trouble deciding how best to approach the man. The story was that he lived under the alias of a retired gambler and kept his history with the Bellyshakers strictly under wraps. This suggested a certain amount of tact might be called for in broaching the purpose of their visit.

First and foremost, there was Chayama's reputation for wanton brutality to think of. If he didn't like talking about the Bellyshakers and Jūnoshin happened to hit a sore spot, it could set him on a rampage. Even short of that, the man could summarily refuse to cooperate if he took the slightest offense. Yet, there was little question that without his help their fake Bellyshaker revival would be doomed to fail.

And if it fails, what happens to me? Jūnoshin fretted. *Lord Naitō will go ballistic and pass the word to Sugawara, and Sugawara will pass the word to Osamu, and Osamu will then lift me off my feet and set me on fire. Which of course means I'll die, and that, naturally, is something I'd like to avoid. So my primary objective has to be to make sure none of that happens, but I'll be damned if I know how.*

Seeing the troubled look on his face, Sugawara spoke up.

"What's the matter, Kakari? What're you thinking so hard about?"

"I'm trying to figure out the best way to bring up our business with Chayama."

"Oh, is that all?"

"What do you mean, 'Is that all?' You make it sound like it should be easy. Got some bright idea?"

"Not really, but I could do the talking if you'd like."

"Are you sure? You only came along to be my watchdog."

"Sure, why not? I'll be glad to."

"Thanks, that'd be great." Jūnoshin said, thinking that this brought Sugawara up a bit in his estimation. He had formed a low opinion of the fellow from the peevish way he'd whimpered about being just a steward in one breath, only to turn around and address Jūnoshin like an inferior in the next, but he had obviously misjudged him. He was turning out to be a very sensible, open-hearted, likable guy. Jūnoshin inwardly folded his hands and bowed his head in gratitude.

It was a gorgeous day. Skylarks sang overhead.

It had been on just such a day that Jūnoshin cut down the blind girl's father. He thought what a sad thing he'd done.

Across the open fields ahead, a white plaster wall came into view. They could see that it was a large farm compound fronted by a wall of storehouses with an imposing gate in the middle. No other homes stood nearby. Its lone presence asserted itself in the middle of the countryside as mountains rose beyond.

"That's the place, folks," Konji said. "Now, let me remind you again, we can't afford to have anybody laugh when we see him. I think Osamu in particular needs to be careful, since he seems easily affected."

"Right," said Sugawara. "I'll make sure he understands."

"Considering the danger, should we maybe have him wait outside?"

"No, no, we want him with us, just in case. If Chayama happens to go berserk, we'll need him to save the day. Just don't anybody laugh. No matter how hilarious the guy looks."

And with that, Sugawara briskly led the way through the gate.

Urp.

Jūnoshin pressed a hand to his lips as he doubled over. His shoulders were shaking and tears squeezed from his eyes.

He was determined not to laugh. But it was proving to be a tall order. Chayama's face was just that comical.

He'd been amply forewarned about the outlandish artwork that combined a scarecrow with a clown and joker on top of a goddess of joy. And it might not have been so bad if all that had been applied to a face whose features were more endearing to begin with.

But Chayama had once been a man of rugged countenance, with a prominent forehead, piercing eyes, and a tall straight nose lending him an appearance of forbidding gravity. Each and every crease testified to the hard-fought battles of a powerful intellect.

It was onto this craggy face that two silly red discs had been inked, along with teepees for eyebrows and a crazy quilt of other graffiti-like flourishes. The shading around his eyes was droopy, while the border around his mouth broke upward like a smiling cat, adding to the freakish effect.

If he'd already looked like a fool beneath it all, none of this would have seemed so comical. But when overlaid on a seemingly intelligent and sensible visage, the result was uncontrollably hysterical.

Mustn't laugh, mustn't laugh! The more Jūnoshin admonished himself, the more difficult it seemed to become. He'd kept his eyes averted after only the briefest glimpse, but, *bo-yo-yoing*, the hilarious face insisted on popping back into his head and spinning around in circles or sticking its tongue out at him. It was so funny, his mind was in a haze. Tears spilled from his eyes, and irrepressible waves of silent laughter rippled across his back.

Konji was no longer with them. Upon catching sight of Chayama, he had clapped a hand over his mouth to stifle a guffaw and raced out the door in a crouch like a man about to hurl.

In his befogged hilarity, Jūnoshin wished he had done the same. But it was too late now, so he concentrated on keeping his head down, while his body continued to shake.

Osamu, for his part, appeared completely unfazed. He was obviously missing the reflex that prompts a person to laugh when witnessing something comical. The condition is far more common than most would ever guess, even among people of much greater intelligence than Osamu. And of course, since these folks don't see themselves as stupid, they generally consider themselves qualified to deride sophisticated turns of wit as unfunny—though, come to think of it, you'll sometimes catch them rolling on the ground with tears in their eyes over mere pratfalls and mooning and other juvenile gags.

Sugawara had shown no sign of cracking up, either, but in his case it could best be attributed to his occupational conditioning. A samurai's steward cannot be laughing or crying over every little thing if he is to effectively manage the household. He had therefore learned to hold his feelings in check, and he could maintain the impassivity of a Noh mask at will. Which is not to say he was a cold fish, for he experienced the same emotions anybody else did; he simply kept those personal sentiments locked deeply within. The trapped feelings sputtered in protest inside their prison. But the mask of his face did not break down as he broached the purpose of their present visit.

"We've come from Kuroae, Master Chōbei, with the hope of seeking your help in a certain endeavor."

Chayama remained silent, his eyes shifting among his visitors with an expression of mild amusement. In his new identity as a retired gambler he was known as Chōbei of Kameyama.

Ignoring the look, Sugawara pressed ahead. "Our inquiries tell us that you're not in fact a former gambler named Chōbei, as you falsely claim to be; you're Chayama Hanrō, a prime mover of the defunct Bellyshaker Party, who managed to escape death and go into hiding in this remote place through what might be considered a kind of plea-bargaining arrangement. And that's exactly why we've come to see you. We want you to close up house here and return with us to Kuroae. I'm not at liberty to divulge why, except to say that we're preparing to launch a Neo-Bellyshaker movement in our domain and require your assistance in connection with that. The obvious reason being that we lack sufficient knowledge of the teachings. You, on the other hand, are well acquainted with those teachings since, as I say, you may be going around announcing yourself as a one-time gambler named Chōbei, but that happens to be a bald-faced lie. Don't try to deny it. I assure you we've investigated the matter thoroughly, and we know you used to be one of the top Bellyshakers. Which is why, if you don't mind, we need you to come with us. Now, to be perfectly candid, I should tell you that you can't expect there to be any money in this for you. It's not entirely impossible, I suppose, but as you're no doubt aware, our domain is undergoing grave financial difficulties at present, so although I'll certainly bring the question up with my superiors to see if there's anything we can do, your remuneration will most likely be zip. But even with that knowledge, we hope you'll be amenable to helping with this important venture. What do you say?"

As he listened to Sugawara giving this little spiel, Jūnoshin felt a chill spreading into every corner of his body, and the fits of laughter he'd been struggling to contain abruptly subsided.

He'd been had.

In a show of kindness, the steward had offered to do the talking, but then what does he do? He takes the blunt approach, giving no care to politeness and even being outright rude, deliberately trying to provoke Chayama. What possible reason could he have for doing this? *He's trying to make trouble for me*, Jūnoshin thought. *For some reason, he must have it in for me. That's why he's playing this dirty trick. He thinks it'll be funny if I fail and get killed, the twisted bastard.*

Jūnoshin lifted his head to look at Sugawara out of the corner of his eye. The steward was calmly awaiting Chayama's reply, his lips slightly pursed.

Was this the correct reading of the situation? As a matter of fact, no. Sugawara was not being deliberately rude in order to provoke Chayama; he actually thought he was being polite. But how can this be said of a speech that could be expected to spark indignation in practically anyone?

It had to do with Sugawara's position as steward to a man of near-supreme power within the domain.

Since Lord Naitō had no wife or child, his household was entirely in Sugawara's charge. Purchases of charcoal, rice, produce, seafood, fabric, prepared foods, and the like were all under his sole discretion. He determined how much of what to buy, and from whom. This understandably meant that vendors vied with each other to flatter him and go the extra mile in responding to his needs, in effect treating him as if he were one of the nobility himself.

Similarly, given Naitō's standing as Lord Kuroae's chief councilor, all manner of visitors appeared on his doorstep. They came, of course, to ask for his influence. As his steward, Sugawara was their first contact, and nobody was allowed inside without his say-so, while at the same time, even those who gained entry could spend endless hours waiting their turn if he put them at the end of the line. So those of lower rank bowed and scraped obsequiously for his favor, while even persons of considerable stature plied him with ingratiating pleasantries.

Which is to say, he held a measure of genuine power in his hands.

But in all these circumstances, it was because the other person was asking favors that Sugawara could speak however he pleased and no one dared raise a stink. This time Sugawara was the supplicant, and yet it was almost as though he were saying, *If you'd like, I'll do you the favor of asking for your help. What do you say? Are you interested?*

Must be nice, having a proper job, thought Jūnoshin. *If any of us freelancers talked like that, we'd get squashed like bugs. The guy thinks nothing of his listener's interests, only of his own needs, yet sees no reason to lower his head in the slightest, and if anything, puts on superior airs.*

Jūnoshin racked his brain for a way to smooth things over, but he could think of nothing that might temper the message Sugawara had already delivered: *We know you're a criminal. Cooperate or else. You won't get paid. Deal with it.*

A butterfly fluttered in through the open door.

Chayama still said nothing, and the tattoos covering his face made it impossible to read his thoughts. Sugawara waited with his lips set in a firm line, as if to declare that, having said his piece, he wasn't going to utter another word until Chayama spoke up. The butterfly had caught Osamu's attention, and he was following its movements with his mouth hanging open.

Jūnoshin's stomach clenched tighter as the silence lengthened.

The dirt-floored entrance area where they'd come in was dim except for the rectangle of light formed by the open door. The darkness inside. The brightness outside.

After a wait that felt like forever to Jūnoshin—though the interval might actually have been quite brief—Chayama finally opened his mouth to speak.

"So you folks have come from Kuroae, have you?"

The voice was very soft—nearly inaudible.

"Yes."

Sugawara's simple, clipped answer seemed inadequate to Jūnoshin, so he hastily added, "Indeed, that is correct, sir. We have come from Kuroae." After he had said it, he thought what an idiot he was.

"And your business with me is that you wish me to start preaching the word again?"

"Yes."

"Indeed, that is correct, sir. We'd like you to spread the teachings again."

"I see." He closed his eyes. Since each of his lids was tattooed with the image of an eye, his eyes appeared to be open even when they were closed. It looked utterly absurd, but Jūnoshin no longer felt any impulse to laugh. Sugawara did not laugh either. Osamu merely wriggled in his seat, still without the slightest peep.

"I have one question," Chayama said, opening his eyes again. He looked just as ridiculous with his eyes open. "Are you undertaking this effort sincerely, or as some kind of ruse? Cut right to the chase for me, if you would."

He fixed Sugawara sharply in the eye.

Sugawara replied without hesitation. "As a ruse, of course."

Jūnoshin frantically contradicted him. "No, no, no, no, no, no, no. He doesn't mean that. He's lost his head from the excitement of seeing you. It's not a ruse at all. We're completely sincere and serious about this. If I may speak plainly, that is, to be perfectly plain about it, my very life is at stake here. Unless the faith can be revived, I will die. It's that simple. How can I not be serious about that? I certainly *am* serious. Dead serious."

Sugawara seemed taken aback by this sudden torrent of words from Jūnoshin, but Chayama's expression did not change—or rather, since his absurdly idiotic expression was unalterable to begin with, he gave no visible sign of his feelings as he responded in the same measured voice as before—like a philosopher grown weary of intellectual pursuits, or a prophet saddened by the people's stubborn heedlessness to his warnings.

"So one of you says it's a ruse, while another says it's serious. No doubt you are both telling the truth. As a matter of fact, either answer is perfectly fine with me. The question is what kind of reaction you might have been looking for as you gave your answer. I was observing the drannar of your desires solely from the standpoint of Egubo. Around a crystal clear moon-drop twines a spinning wheel of aloes. Isn't that what life is about? The song of annihilation should be sung at the lowest point of man and home. I will go with you to Kuroae. I believe that is the will of Egubo."

"Um, sorry if I couldn't quite follow most of that," Jūnoshin said with trepidation, "but did I hear correctly that you will come with us?"

"Is that not exactly what I said?" Chayama replied curtly. "When by Egubo's divine guidance any should seek the word, I shall betake to the very ends of the earth. I remain in this place only because no one has come to me since the darkening of the light. To have received this visit fills me with the greatest of joy."

Jūnoshin felt on pretty shaky ground with the mannered religio-speak and specialized industry jargon, and it occurred to him that the man might simply be out of his gourd, but at least he had confirmed his intention to go with them to Kuroae. That was what mattered.

Now we just need to get moving before he changes his mind, he thought. But that face is going to attract attention. I'd better send Konji to get him one of those wrap-around hoods.

Relieved that their mission appeared to be a success, Jūnoshin's thoughts turned immediately to practical matters. But then he noticed Chayama eyeing him rather pointedly.

"If I may," he said, and Jūnoshin's heart leapt into his throat. He half-expected the next words out of the man's mouth to be, *I will now elevate you to Spewdom.* He threw a furtive glance toward Osamu as he confirmed the touch of his sword guard against his knee.

But what Chayama said next was an even greater surprise than if he'd abruptly declared Jūnoshin bound for sainthood.

"Would you by any chance be Stigger?"

"What? First Manabe, and now you? Nobody's called me that since I was a boy. How do you know that name? Who are you?"

"Well, how about that. Long time no see, Stigger. We used to be neighbors when we were kids. I'm Saomu."

Saomu. His skin crawled just to hear the name.

The boy had been the worst of the worst. He had no mother and lived with his father, a gaunt, moody ronin who terrorized the kids in the neighborhood with his fits of temper. The man was a meth addict, and his idea of doting fatherhood was to tell Saomu what a good boy he was and get him hooked, too—by around the time he was eight.

This gave Saomu a perverse sort of self-confidence that made him turn increasingly violent. He killed pet dogs with a sharpened bamboo spear, then skinned them and threw their carcasses into holy precincts—a shocking act of desecration. If he failed to get his way, he would follow the offending person around until he had him where he wanted and poke him in the eyes or squirt glue up his butthole. Once, when a sumo wrestler slapped him down for making fun of him, he bore such a grudge that he set fire to the inn where the touring strongmen were staying, and all twenty of them were burned to death. He was only eleven years old at the time.

The faint of heart would wet themselves at the mere sight of the boy. Even full-grown adults trembled at the thought of what he might graduate to in years to come if he was already up to such frightful things at barely more than ten, and it was as if those very fears had come true when he began brutally cutting people down as one of the Bellyshaker bosses.

To learn that Chayama was Saomu put Jūnoshin instantly on high alert again, wary of what he might do. Say the wrong thing and it could trigger an outburst. But to say nothing at all might provoke the man just as much, so he couldn't simply keep his mouth shut. He needed to choose his words carefully.

"Is that right? So you're Saomu, are you?" he started in blandly. "Wow, you've changed so much, I really didn't recognize you. Oh, but I don't mean that in a funny way or anything, just—how should I put it?—just that it never ceases to amaze me, you know, how the years leave their marks on us—no, no, I'm not talking about on a superficial level, like the tattoos and stuff, no, not that at all, but on a deeper level, you know, about how the years have been kind to you as a person, and that really comes out on your face. But man, oh, man, I can hardly believe it. This sure does bring back memories. Speaking for myself, I've certainly had my share of ups and downs, but… hey, that reminds me, do you remember a kid from the old neighborhood we used to call Grub? I found out he lives in Kuroae now. That's right. I hadn't seen him in ages either, until by happy coincidence he came to kill me the other day. It's a long story, but we wound up going out and getting drunk instead, you know. Is that right, is that right? So you're Saomu. Tell me, then, Saomu. How the hell have you been since whenever it was? Been keeping healthy?"

Chayama responded in the same gentle manner as before, like someone lost in a dream and out of touch with reality, doling his words out into the space between them in an almost meditative tone.

"So I've changed, have I? You're speaking of my tattoos, of course. Please pay them no heed. And I'd appreciate it, too, if you didn't mention them again. I had them done in Gifu. That's a fact. That's the absolute truth. Are you asking me to tell you about the journeys of my soul? Perhaps I'll check with Egubo about that sometime. On some night when the drannar of sadness is feeding nectar to my soul. I was already bonkers when I was but a boy. Then I went even more bonkers when I got to be fifteen. In the apothecary warehouse, the energy charger busted up the teathic. Do you have any idea what teathic is? It's a mash-up of *tea* and *ethic*. Egubo's divine dog. I got caught up in all that when I was fifteen, and I've been through untold experiences in the time since. I tasted human brains; I indulged in the most profligate of carnal ecstasies; I copulated with the devil and sang the anthem of unity at the crossroads. Houses are built and houses are torn down. The multitudes must keep that more firmly in mind. I'll be right back with some tea. It will do you good to drink it. Experience the teathic."

He stood and stepped down to the ground, then disappeared down a passage leading to the back of the building. Jūnoshin whispered to Sugawara.

"Are you getting any of this?"

"Hardly. But at least he seems to have agreed to come with us."

"He said he's bringing us tea."

"Uh-huh."

"Best not drink it."

"Why not?"

"It could be poisoned."

"I doubt that."

"Don't bet on it. I knew this guy when I was kid."

"So I gathered. It's quite the coincidence. Stranger than fiction, as they say."

"Yeah, it kind of blows me away. But I'm telling you, he's a dangerous man."

"As I'm quite aware."

"Sure, but I'm talking about what I saw up close. The evil in this guy must have been full grown before he even came out of the womb. When I think of that, it's hard to imagine the tea *not* being poisoned."

"But you heard that business about the ethic of tea. Sounds to me like he's probably a real stickler about form. It could look bad if we leave it sitting."

"Except there's no doubt in my mind that the stuff's going to be poisoned. Oh, here's an idea. We'll let Osamu go first."

"Go first?"

"Right. We'll get him to take a drink first, and if he doesn't keel over, then we know it's safe."

"Aha. Excellent idea. That's what we'll do."

A short while later, Chayama returned with cups of tea on a tray and placed one in front of each of them.

"There you go, Osamu," said Jūnoshin. "Our kind host has brought us some tea. There's no need to be shy now. Go ahead and have a drink."

In his usual fashion, Osamu thought he was being scolded and immediately grew flustered.

"Huh? Me?… Um… A-a-a-am I okay? Wh-wh-what? Wh-wh-what did I…? I-I-I didn't…" he said, his eyes darting anxiously about the room.

"He's not scolding you," Sugawara reassured him. "He's just urging you to have a drink of your tea."

"Oh, t-t-t-tea. A d-d-drink? All right. Yes," he said, reaching for his cup.

He drank it in a single gulp and exploded in a violent fit of coughing. "*Ghack ghack ghack, khoff khoff, urp, wheeze, wheeze, wheeze.*"

"Are you all right?"

"*Wheeze,* y-yes, w*heeze, wheeze.*"

"It obviously went down the wrong way, but otherwise he seems none the worse for it."

"Better wait a little longer. It could be slow-acting."

"But if we go on stalling too long, he might get suspicious."

"I'll say something to tide us over," Jūnoshin said. "Ah, Master Chayama, apologies for the embarrassing display. I'm afraid Osamu here is a bit of a goose. Just take a gander at his eyes. Nothing but goose eggs, you see? About all you can do is throw them in some soup for dinner. He has the mind of a child, really, so I hope you'll make allowances."

"That's straight out of a classic comedian's routine."

"Ah, you recognized the allusion. I'm much obliged."

"But never mind that. Please. You two must take some refreshment, too. There's no need to be polite. All creation will crumble."

"I only made things worse," Kakari hissed to Sugawara under his breath. "Now what do we do?"

"How's Osamu doing?"

Osamu had survived his coughing fit, but he was opening and closing his mouth as if trying to cool a burned tongue. He looked like some fool practicing for a bun eating contest. He was also rapidly blinking his eyes.

"He seems to be okay."

"I suppose we have no choice. Shall we go for it?"

"Yeah, I guess so. It could be worse not to."

They steeled themselves and gulped the tea down as if swallowing bitter medicine, only to immediately sit up in surprise. It was sublimely delicious.

The sweetness of nectar filled their mouths as the liquid flowed across their tongues and down their throats, leaving behind an aftertaste so refreshing and crisp it made them want to burst into song. A thin membrane of tingling wrapped about their heads beneath their scalps and felt utterly wonderful.

"*Lying in this state / on a bed of thriving grass / among black bamboo / the young deer of springtime come / has a bellyache, it seems.*"

"*Be that as it may / in the crane's upper garden / the great door is split / and all is torn asunder / a belly of lithe bamboo.*"

As he watched Jūnoshin and Sugawara exchange these nonsensical verses, Chayama allowed a faint smile to play across his lips.

"*Tee hee hee,*" he chortled. "There were four of you at first, but now you are only three. Where do you suppose the other fellow went? The three of you here have begun to suffer your egos on the border between reason and annihilation. Trapped in the depths of illusion, you have begun crying for help. Shall we give your missing companion some tea later on, too? I really do wonder where he could have gone to."

The "other fellow," who with a single glimpse of Chayama's face had clapped a hand over his mouth and rushed out the door like a man about to lose his breakfast, was at that moment standing in the walled yard between the gatehouse and the farmhouse.

The space was filled with a soft light that made Egere no Konji feel as if his very soul were being washed clean.

Its gentle glow fell alike on the tall gatehouse framing the entrance and on the tiny blades of grass creeping forth along the ground in the far corner, and everything it illumined in between seemed to exist in a state of grace.

A young woman stood before him.

He felt a tide of warmth rising in his chest merely from being in her presence.

Upon first emerging from the house, he had tumbled to the ground in convulsions as he tried desperately not to laugh. He knew he didn't dare let loose even after getting outside.

As he lay writhing in comic anguish, someone had approached from behind and said, "Are you ill?" It was the voice of a young woman.

Realizing that the truth might be awkward, he pretended he had indeed been feeling sick, but quickly got to his feet. "I'm feeling much better now," he said.

When he lifted his head after dusting himself off, he gaped in wonder.

She was the most beautiful woman he had ever seen.

In his work as a secret agent, Konji had in fact encountered a great many members of the opposite sex, and more than a few of them had been women of striking beauty. But once he got to know them a little, he would almost invariably discover that they were quite ordinary women who held no interest for him.

There was something elementally different about this woman.

So much more beautiful was she that it frightened him to think such beauty could even exist. Most men coming face to face with such beauty would surely wonder if it was a trick of the gods—or perhaps some kind of divine trial.

For any who did not experience such doubts, the woman's beauty was a gift of purest grace.

Merely to have laid eyes on her made Konji feel gloriously happy.

He asked to know her name, and she answered without the slightest reserve that it was Ron. She explained that she lived with Chayama and looked after his domestic needs.

Konji stood in the soft light of the courtyard in a state of perfect bliss.

His only wish was that he might go on talking with this beautiful woman forever.

He was like a child.

Makeshift huts crowded the levees all up and down the riverbed. Their numbers were growing rapidly as summer neared, inhabited by a new population of homeless that came from within the domain itself.

Last winter the town had been overrun by refugees from neighboring Ushichiku, but between the turn of the year and the beginning of spring, their ranks dwindled dramatically. In fact, the exodus of these refugees was initially swollen by Kuroae residents going to beg in Ushichiku. The authorities there moved quickly to clamp down on alien arrivals, however, and the Kuroae homeless had been turned back to drift about within their own domain.

These vagrants were quite the miserable sight, barely keeping up a human appearance while living an animal existence. Their hair was matted in disarray, and their clothing could have been mistaken for strips of kelp held to their bodies with a length of straw rope. Most suffered from skin afflictions of various kinds; flies could be seen crowding about open red sores on their swollen and blackened feet. Some wandered endlessly from one part of town to another with no identifiable purpose; others sat spiritlessly at the roadside, lost in a daze.

At one particular street corner where transients of this ilk plodded constantly by, a group of four men and women were squatting against an earthen wall over which a large pine bough stretched from the garden within. They were the most colorful Chayama Hanrō, the amazing telekineticist Osamu, the peerless beauty Ron, and one other man. The time was mid-morning, approaching the end of the Hour of the Snake.

The four were dressed in matching black kimonos tied with black sashes, their legs wrapped in black puttees over navy blue split-toed socks and straw sandals—which unfortunately could only be the color of straw. The sight of four people dressed all in black gathered in a silent huddle was itself unusual enough to draw curious stares from idle passersby, but Chayama's outlandish tattoos caused even shop assistants in an obvious hurry to stop and gape for a moment before coming to their senses and hastening on.

On the other side of the street crossing stood a restaurant called "House of a Different Flour." In spite of its unconventional name, the place had longstanding roots in the community, having been established two generations ago by a man named Hyōemon, who developed a unique menu of dishes featuring freshwater fish and vegetables. Helped also by reasonable prices, it had quickly become a hit among the dining public, and to this day it enjoyed a reputation as the best eatery in town.

On the second floor of this establishment was a private room looking out over the intersection, where three men at the window were observing the four figures in black. The men were none other than Kakari Jūnoshin, Sugawara Yōichi, and Egere no Konji.

"Is this really going to work with Chayama looking like that?" Sugawara said.

"Yeah, actually, I had the same question," said Jūnoshin. "Won't everybody know right away exactly who he is? In which case, won't the Ushichiku authorities raise a stink? So I asked him about it. He assured me I had absolutely nothing to worry about as far as Ushichiku was concerned."

"All right, then. I suppose I should stop fretting."

"Except for the fact that he's a total loon."

"So you say, but he seems normal enough if you ask me. A perfectly affable fellow. Except sometimes I can't figure out what he's trying to say."

"That's because you don't really know the guy. I've known him since he and I were kids—all too well, I'm afraid."

"Yeah?"

"You better believe it. Why else do you think I suggested we get him one of those wrap-around hoods that hide your face? He said no thanks, he preferred the simple scarf type, so I sent Konji to buy one of those, only to have him nix it as too garish, not the sort of thing he could ever wear. Which is how he ended up not covering his face at all."

"Uh-huh. And that's exactly why I'm standing here wondering if this is really going to work. Can he really get the Bellyshakers going again? And that other guy—what was his name?"

"Jōji," said Konji. "He's supposedly a carpenter."

"With that silly grin that never goes away, he looks like some kind of halfwit."

"Could well be."

"Certainly doesn't inspire confidence. Chayama's the one who brought him in, right?"

"Yep."

"It's hard to believe a guy like that'll be any use in spreading the word."

"I guess he fits into Chayama's system somehow or other," Jūnoshin said, then cracked a silly grin himself. "And then there's that chick Ron. She's quite the looker, isn't she?"

"She's a beauty, all right."

"How about you, Konji? You think so, too?"

"Mmm," said Konji, averting his eyes.

"Do you suppose she's Chayama's squeeze?"

"Hard to say, but it doesn't seem unlikely."

Konji was about to exclaim, *No way!* when the four black-clad figures huddled against the earthen wall stood up as one.

"Looks like it's show time," Jūnoshin said.

Konji held his tongue and directed his attention out the window.

Jōji stepped forward with a stick in his hand and scratched a circle in the ground around the group. When he was done, he hefted a rock about the size of a pickling stone in his two hands and began chanting some unintelligible mumbo-jumbo in a deeply solemn manner—first turning his eyes to the sky, then looking down at the rock, then up again, back and forth.

The group had been drawing many passing stares even before this, but with this new bit of drama several people stopped to see what might follow.

"What are you doing?" one of them eventually called out.

"The providential forces of the universe are coming into alignment," Jōji replied, "and this stone will soon rise out of my hands into the air."

"What's going on?" asked a latecomer.

"He says that stone's going to float."

"Yeah, right."

"I'm just telling you what he said."

"I'll believe it when I see it."

Even as they spoke, more gawkers were coming up behind them.

"What's up?"

"We're not really sure, yet."

"Hey, let's see what it's about."

In a matter of moments, the crowd close by had ballooned to nearly thirty people, while many others were casting curious eyes from farther away. When he judged the time to be ripe, Chayama climbed onto a box Osamu had brought along for the purpose.

At the sight of his face, gasps of horror rose from some while laughter and back-slapping came from others, but he seemed completely oblivious to these reactions as he launched into a speech.

"Is there anybody here who does not bear suffering in his or her heart? If there is, then please just move on by, be on your way. But I dare say none of you will see fit to leave us. Why? Because you do, in fact, have suffering in your heart—every one of you. *Tee hee hee hee.* It's so hilarious. *Die, you turdhead!* So why is it that you suffer so? That is what I am about to explain to you. You did not come into this world to suffer; you came into this world to enjoy every imaginable pleasure and to laugh to your heart's content. Why oh why, then, must you always feel so miserable? The answer can be found in how this world came into being."

In the background, Jōji had gently begun beating a drum. *Boom. Boom. Boom. Boom.* Single beats at leisurely intervals, unvarying in strength. *Boom. Boom. Boom. Boom.*

Chayama went on. "This world was created by Egubo. She originally envisioned a world shaped like a nose. That is to say, she wanted a nicely mounded hillock that had two burrow holes in its side, with cute little bunnies and prairie dogs poking their heads out of those burrows. That's the kind of world she pictured. But a clueless old wet fish named Donbora had to step in her way. He was adamant that the world should be in the shape of a *menko* card. That's right—like in the kids' game. So you could slap it down hard and flip any other world nearby on its backside. Egubo thought this would be appalling. In a world like that, all the people would get blown away. Donbora gave a smirk. 'That's exactly why it'd be so cool,' he said, to which Egubo replied, 'Your heart is made of stone,' and stabbed him in the chest with a bamboo spatula. He was furious. 'You're gonna pay for this,' he growled. As he glared at her in anger, another man named Fukuoka appeared and said, 'Now, now, there's no need to be going at each other like that. Let me mediate.' But he only complicated things when he added, 'I think a nice compromise would be a world shaped like a Chinese spoon.' Then, with it already turned into a three-way argument, yet another man named Gerumu appeared and argued that the world should be like shaved kelp, a mass of tiny threads that turn to mush when it rains, tangling things up even more."

Boom. Boom. Boom. Boom. The intervals gradually shortened as he spoke. Moving in time with the beat, Ron and Osamu spread their feet a little, raised their forearms to shoulder height with their hands loosely balled, and began shaking their hips and bellies back and forth. *Boom. Boom. Boom. Boom.* It was hard to tell whether they were just doing as the spirit moved, or faithfully following some prescribed routine. With her wavy tresses jouncing about her head and the bare flesh of her legs flashing at her loosened hem, Ron's movements carried an alluring sensuality.

As half the crowd exchanged quizzical looks, wondering what kind of silliness it could be, the other half decided it looked like fun and promptly joined in.

Chayama never paused. "The debate dragged on for quite some time. As the discussion moved farther and farther away from the simple and adorable world-like-a-nose concept she'd begun with, Egubo became fed up; she quietly dropped out of the conversation and slipped away. Donbora, Fukuoka, and Gerumu proceeded to create a world with the features the three of them could agree on. When Egubo later saw their handiwork, she hit the roof. 'I can't imagine anything more convoluted and ridiculous!' she exclaimed. Stabbing herself in the arm with her spatula, she drew some blood and boiled it down into a giant tapeworm. Then she hurled the tapeworm into space and called after it, 'O thou great tapeworm! As a precipitate anomaly within the vastness of the void, you must parasitically consume this false new world by swallowing it down whole.' The tapeworm did just that, and that's how our world came to its present state. In other words, not only was our world shaped by the misguided notions of Donbora and company to begin with, it was then subjected to the indignities of a tapeworm's digestive track. Is it any wonder we're all tormented by suffering and delusion?"

Boom boom boom boom boom boom boom boom. The tempo of the drum increased some more, and Ron and Osamu moved faster and faster to keep time with it.

"So what are we to do? Are we to try, somehow, to rebuild this world for the better? Are we to strive to lead lives of virtue by performing kindnesses to others in the world as it is? The answer in both cases is no. Absolutely positively not. It wouldn't do one whit of good. Why not a whit of good? Because Egubo pays no attention to such things. She doesn't even recognize the legitimacy of this world. Any attempt to better this world or to live virtuously in it would imply the world has legitimacy, which goes against the will of Egubo, who was supposed to be the true creator of our world. Does that mean, then, that we should respond with violence and destroy this world? The answer is again no. And the reason is much the same. The Great Mother Goddess Egubo does not recognize this world, and nothing meaningful can come from tearing apart something she does not recognize. So to ask the question once again: what are we to do? We must escape from this sham of a world to strike down its three creators—Donbora, Fukuoka, and Gerumu, who live on the outside—and we must then take their severed heads and escape that outside world, too, to deliver them as an offering to Egubo in the world outside the world outside this world, and beseech her once again to create a simple and lovable little nose-like world where we can all live in happiness."

Bom bom bom bom bom bom bom bom bom bom bom bom bom bom bom bom bom bom bom bom bom bom bom bom bom bom bom bom bom bom bom bom bom bom. The drumming continued to pick up speed, and so did the bellyshaking.

"And this, of course, leads us to the next question: how do we go about escaping from this world, from this corrupt and fraudulent world, into the true world outside? We do it, quite literally, by becoming shit. The tapeworm, too, is a living creature. Like any other living thing, it must eliminate its waste. So we must all become turdheads. And what do I mean by this? Think about what happens when you eat or drink something that's gone bad. You'll either throw up or get the runs. It is the same with the tapeworm. You must all become the most stinking, rotten idiots you can. The more stinking and rotten you become, the bigger bellyache you'll give the tapeworm, and the sooner it will pass you out into the world beyond. So how do you become such a superlatively rotten idiot? That's right, you guessed it. All you need to do is look at the two dancers to my rear. Have you ever seen anything quite so idiotic?"

Chayama broke off. Behind him, Ron and Osamu shook their bellies as if in a trance, with their eyes glazed over and droplets of spittle dribbling from their lips. After several moments of silence, Chayama, too, began slowly twisting his belly back and forth.

His movements were much slower, and had an almost menacing quality about them.

On the one hand was the vigorous shaking of the hulking Osamu; on the other, the sensual motions of the vivacious and lovely Ron, flinging her hair about. And at the apex of the triangle out front swayed the outlandish Chayama, whose countenance and bearing made him the very picture of sublime idiocy.

The sight of the three figures dancing hypnotically to the beat seemed to embody all the pain and sorrow, all the tragedy and comedy of living in this world, and it struck some hearts with deep pity, while triggering violent anger in others.

"Get lost!" shouted a man belonging to the latter group as he sent a stone flying.

The projectile hit Chayama in the forehead and broke the skin. A trickle of blood descended over the artwork on his face.

"*Bwah hah hah ha ha ha ha ha ha ha ha*," he roared, and went on swiveling his torso about, not the least bit perturbed. He looked as if he could be the Lord of Hell himself.

"Too bad we can't hear what he's saying," Jūnoshin said as he watched the proceedings from the second floor of the restaurant.

Neither he nor his companions could make out a word of Chayama's speech, so they had no way of knowing what was really going on. But when Chayama began shaking his belly, they each reacted quite differently to what they saw.

"It makes me feel sad," said Konji.

"Looks like fun," chirped Jūnoshin.

"It's outrageous!" fumed Sugawara.

They stood watching in silence for a time. Then Sugawara burst out, "Hey! Someone in the crowd is shaking his belly, too!"

"Probably a shill," Konji said.

"A shill? What's that?"

"Somebody you pay to act like a stranger and get the buying started. The rest of the people see him buying and decide they want in on the action, too."

"So a decoy?"

"Yeah, pretty much."

Sugawara turned to Jūnoshin. "Did Chayama hire somebody like that?"

"Not that I know of."

"But you wouldn't think just seeing a little bit of that sort of thing would make anybody want to shake their belly. Hey, wait a minute. I actually know that guy. He's one of Ōura Shuzen's men. Makubo Magobei. What the hell's *he* doing here?"

Sugawara was right. The man shaking his belly in the crowd was indeed Makubo Magobei. But he was so changed in appearance as to be almost unrecognizable. As the proud employee of one of the most powerful men in the clan, he'd been wont to strut about town in fine kimonos with nary a hair out of place, holding his nose high and scattering silent farts like a pampered child well past the age of thirty. Now he looked like a fallen man, a bare shadow of his former self. His kimono was badly faded, held together with no more than a length of crude rope, and he wore crumbling straw sandals on his feet. His hair hung like a tangle of seaweed around his head, his ribs protruded sharply from his chest, and his skin was covered with untold layers of grime.

How could this have happened?

It was, in fact, entirely his own doing. He had made his way through life regarding every personal obligation, every personal responsibility, as something to be dodged. To what end? To protect his naïve and easily wounded ego from the buffeting of the outside world. His most constant fear in life was the threat of injury to his ego. In the name of preventing any such damage, he lied without qualm and stooped to all manner of despicable deeds. If others suffered great misery or even went to their ruin as a result, so be it—he did not allow the slightest twinge of conscience to torment him. After all, there could be no substitute for himself, and he believed that the world would be devoid of meaning if it were to be deprived of his consciousness.

Whenever things began to go badly for him, he would simply faint. But the world is made up of a great many people interacting with each other in the course of time. Just because one man checks out for a while doesn't mean everything else in this world of flux also grinds to a halt.

Or to put it another way, since Magobei's associates had no means of placing the progress of surrounding events on hold during his temporary unavailability, they were forced to deal with the immediate problem in his stead. By the time he came to again in a fuzzy-headed haze, as if waking from a deep sleep and completely unaware of what had transpired, the threat that originally unhinged him would have been largely laid to rest, neatly sparing him from having to expend any effort of his own toward resolving the issue— and saving him also from any potential blowback to his ego that this might have entailed.

Those who got sucked into these little dramas were never very happy about it, but their ire was no match for Magobei's prodigious gifts in self-preservation, his rhetorical slight of hand, or his deftly acted charades. As a result, he had convinced himself that he could make it through his entire life in this manner, evading responsibility and protecting his delicate ego from any harm.

But one eventuality he had not accounted for was the downfall of his patron, Ōura Shuzen.

When the long-time high councilor was driven from office, Magobei promptly began seeking a new position. To his dismay, every prospective employer he approached gave him the cold shoulder. At one time or another, they had all been victims of his trick for evading responsibility.

One merchant saw no point in mincing words. "My dear sir," he said, "you are an incompetent, irresponsible phony. I can't imagine any situation in which I would ever consider hiring you, and you certainly won't get a recommendation from me either."

Deeply wounded, Magobei promptly passed out.

When he regained consciousness a short while later, he carefully slit open his eyes to look about him. He saw that he'd been moved out of the way into a corner. The shop clerks were busily taking care of a large delivery that had just arrived, and nobody was paying the least bit of attention to him. He lay as he was for a time, wondering if somebody would eventually come to check on him, but when nobody did, he simply got to his feet and slipped out the door. Hearing a slight commotion behind him as he stepped into the street, he turned to find someone scattering salt in his tracks to purify the premises, and he keeled over again.

Fainting here, fainting there, his search for new employment continued, but to no avail. And so he had sunk to his present condition. He lived in a state of semi-derangement, with the wounds sustained by his ego constantly letting blood.

His fear had been that if he were to take responsibility for anything, it could later come back to bite him, but after having successfully dodged this threat for so long, he now found himself being called to account as never before. He racked his brains to understand how it could have happened, but remained ever at a loss. To find the answer, he would have had to tear down the massive walls he'd built around himself over so many years, and that, quite simply, was not something he was capable of doing.

So at this juncture in Magobei's life, Chayama's speech came like manna from heaven. The message that this was a false world, a world created in error, not even worth the trouble of destroying, and that since the bodies and souls that resided here were but fleeting figments in a place that should never have existed to begin with, nobody needed to take any responsibility—in fact you were better off just shaking your belly and acting the complete fool—could hardly have been more welcome.

So that's what it's all about! he thought, and was already swiveling his torso to the beat.

As he settled into the motions, words like responsibility, despair, remorse, regret, contrition, shame, and meal ticket vanished one after another from his consciousness, *poof, poof, poof,* and an ineffable cloud of well-being rose to envelope him.

This is a real kick! he exclaimed to himself as he found his groove.

Then with Magobei effectively filling the role of a shill, others in the crowd loosened up as well, and began following his lead. Though their movements were self-conscious and awkward at first, it was really only a matter of rotating their bellies left and right, so it wasn't long before they were swinging about as smoothly as Osamu and Ron. They soon lost themselves in the beat.

"I don't get it," said a man whose companion had swung into motion. "Why would you want to do that?"

"I can't explain it, but try it and you'll see. When you get going with the rhythm like this, you just feel incredibly happy. It's fun."

"Then I suppose I'll have to give it a try," the first man said as he began shaking, too.

In a matter of minutes, twenty onlookers had joined the action. Among them were two apprentices, two salesclerks, an itinerant peddler, a pilgrim, six other drifters like Magobei, two peasants, two food-peddler tarts, a samisen jongleur, a Buddhist nun, and a housewife.

Including the three who'd started it all off, there were now twenty-three bellies twisting and turning to the beat. *Bom bom bom bom bom bom bom bom bom bom bom bom bom bom bom bom bom bom, bom bom bom bom bom bom bom bom bom bom bom bom bom bom bom bom, bom bom bom bom bom bom bom bom bom bom bom bom bom bom bom bom bom, bom bom bom bom bom bom bom bom bom bom bom bom bom bom bom bom.* It was quite the spectacle, and they certainly did seem to be having great fun. The women danced with sensuous abandon, tossing their hair wildly about and flashing bare shins beneath fluttering kimono hems.

Jōji went among the shakers placing a bite-sized piece of something resembling bread in each person's mouth. "This is the shit of Egubo, meathic for the bowels," he told them.

Chayama called out, "When you shake your bellies, you too become part of the divine shit. That is your path to true freedom, for each and every one of you. Take of the meathic." After a brief pause he went on, "When people cast stones, it is a sign of the tapeworm's suffering. Fear not this sign. If a stone strikes and kills you, you may fail to become divine shit, but you will become a Spew Saint." Still shaking his belly, he raised his voice again.

"Everything in this world is an illusion. Escape to the true world outside!"

Someone had apparently reported the commotion to the authorities. Two policemen came rushing up.

The ranking officer was a constable named Ebe Sōjirō, a man with a reputation for being particularly callous and cold-blooded. His kimono was made of high quality silk crepe, worn in the long style and topped with a fine haori cloak. On his feet were leather-soled sandals, and he had two swords, long and short, thrust carelessly into his belt. He approached the crowd with a big grin on his face, the very picture of composure. The other man was his young assistant.

In the upstairs room, Kakari clicked his tongue. "Damn. Just when things were getting good, that asshole has to show up."

Ebe waded into the crowd and said, "Where do you think you are? This is a public right of way. We can't have this kind of nonsense going on."

He did not raise his voice, and he never lost his grin—which some of the shakers found unsettling. Several of them quickly gave up their movements.

"No sense in getting myself hauled in," one of them muttered.

Ebe stepped up to him. "Excellent, excellent. That's the right idea. Just so long as you understand. Now, who started all this hullabaloo, anyway," he said, turning about. "Was it you?"

Ebe's eyes had landed on an apprentice from a seafood wholesaler named Hodon-ya. The boy was returning from an errand when he'd seen the crowd and got caught up in the spirit of the moment. Afraid he might be let go if his master found out, the boy went blue in the face and shook his head with a shudder.

"Not at all, sir!"

"Then who was it?"

He pointed at Chayama.

Ebe turned to look. Chayama looked straight back. Their eyes locked.

Still grinning, Ebe strode up to Chayama. "So you're the one who started this ruckus, are you?" He gave a little snicker.

Chayama said nothing. But his movements had stopped.

Nearly everybody else took their cue from him and halted their shaking as well. The only ones still in motion were Osamu and Ron.

A few in the crowd quickly slipped away, fearing potential repercussions, but most remained where they were, curious to see what would happen.

"How'm I supposed to find out anything if you're going to clam up? Well, never mind that. All in good time. Count on it, I'll soon have you spilling your guts with tears running down your face. Speaking of which, that's really quite the mug you've got there. But if you think you can intimidate me with it, you better think again."

"So you're making fun of my face, are you? Well, be my guest— say whatever you want. It won't bother me in the least. Because when all's said and done, your gray matter's going to burn. That's the nub of it. I got these tattoos in Gifu."

"What're you blathering about? Did you think you could go around stirring up trouble and just get away with it?"

"This is not merely my own doing. It was Egubo's will that all root crops put out large, magnificent blooms to color the ground. The canals of time are what hinder this. What is it that runs amok? It need not be stopped. The drannar of sadness coils itself around the old-timers. Unloose them. He who is of humblest origin should ascend the throne. Those of highest birth will sing in the lowest places. When the time comes to stand up, their knees will remain buckled. You minion! You dog! Leave this place at once!"

"*Ohh hoh hoh hoh.* Did you actually call me a dog? That's quite the insult. I'm shocked! *Oh hoh hoh hoh. Ah hah hah hah.* But I wager you'll soon change your tune. Before I'm done with you, you'll be bawling your head off and begging for mercy. Now come with me."

He grabbed Chayama by the collar and raised his hooked truncheon in front of his face.

"If you try to resist, you'll feel the brunt of this."

"Unhand me, you infidel! I'll not say it again. Filthy dog, unfit even for food. Begone!"

Sensing his authority ebbing among the crowd in the face of Chayama's rebuke, Ebe roared with anger. "Don't you call me a dog, you freak-faced crackpot!" He brought the flat side of his truncheon down on Chayama's forehead with all his might. *Wham!*

The small break in the skin from the flying stone now split wide open, and blood poured over his face like sappan dye from a bucket.

As Ebe momentarily froze at the ghastly sight, Chayama said, "My hearty congratulations! You have made an opening in my head. The body is a closed system. There was a famous author who believed the truest form of self-expression lay in tearing that closed system open and allowing its insides to spill forth, and he staked his all on that act. Why did he have to stake his all? Because opening up the body and allowing the insides to come out turns the world on its back. In precisely that sense, you have now created a fissure in this world—though it may still be only a tiny start. In recognition of your meritorious deed," he said, making a brief pause before going on, "you will now be elevated to Spewdom."

Ebe had no idea what the man was talking about. "Enough of your babbling! Move it!" he barked, and started to drag him away.

"All right, Osamu," said Chayama. "Make this man a Spew Saint."

"A Spew Saint? Yes, sir."

Answering with uncharacteristic self-possession, Osamu halted his bellyshaking and stepped forward. Ebe was a bit unnerved when he saw the man's size, but he kept up his bold front with that same grin still pasted on his face.

"What's your problem? You askin' to be hauled in, too?" he said.

Osamu silently extended his arms toward the constable with his palms down, and very slowly began lifting them toward the sky.

Ebe's body rose gently into the air.

The grin vanished and his face went deathly white. He began flailing his legs wildly about. "Help, Ginji!" he cried.

But his sidekick's legs had buckled out from under him and he could not move.

By the time Osamu's hands reached the level of his eyes, Ebe had been lofted higher than the men watching from the second floor of House of a Different Flour—higher even than the roof.

"Help! Let me down!" he wailed, no longer making any effort to preserve his dignity as tears streaked his face.

But his desperate pleas fell on deaf ears. Osamu merely curled his fingers into fists and flicked them open again as if shaking off some water. To the insipid sound of a poorly struck hand drum, *pok*, Ebe's body exploded into a million little pieces and scattered in every direction.

The crowd watched stupefied as a fine mist of blood descended over them. *Boom. Boom. Boom. Boom. Boom. Boom. Boom.* Jōji returned to beating the drum at a more leisurely pace, and Chayama's voice rang out again.

"A vessel of corruption has been transformed into a Spew Saint. Let us all rejoice!"

"Woo-hooo!" A cheer of approval erupted from the crowd. They'd had no more love for Ebe than they had for snakes and scorpions, and they were delighted to be rid of him.

"Do you tremble in fear before the powerful?" Chayama asked. "Set your minds at ease. No longer need you fear the persecution of your feudal lord, your priest, your husband, your magistrate, your landlord, your village headman, your boss, your group leader. Any who lowers the iron fist of oppression upon you will be disgorged into the void as a Spew Saint. Rejoice! Shake your bellies!"

"All ri-i-ight!" the crowd roared again, as the drumbeat abruptly took on a new urgency. *Boom boom boom boom boom boom boom boom. Boom boom boom boom boom boom boom boom.* The people shook their bellies as if possessed.

Nothing could stop the fledgling movement now.

The crowd continued to swell with hand-to-mouthers barely eking out an existence from day to day with no better hopes for the future; with disgruntled workers still feeling the sting of a dressing down from the boss; with social climbers whose ambitions exceeded their abilities and who believed they weren't getting their due; with congenital ditherers who couldn't make up their minds what to do with themselves; with gamblers wallowing in the depths of despair after blowing every last copper to their name; with laborers unable to find work; with the destitute; with perennially neglected courtesans relegated to grinding tea; with vagabonds drifting aimlessly from province to province—in short order ballooning to more than a hundred strong. The streets became clogged with shaking and tumult, making the cross streets impassable.

Many of the shakers joined in the drumbeat, pounding on pans and woodblocks and whatever else they could find for making noise. Out came gongs and fish blocks, wood-clappers and hand drums, raising an ever more fevered beat that pulsed through the air.

"The midday hour is upon us. Let those who are hungry, break open the restaurants! Let those who are thirsty, break open the wine shops!" shouted Chayama. "Know that to break open any part of this false world and release what it holds within is of the same merit as cracking open your bowels and letting them spill forth."

In other words, since it was a phony world to begin with, to plunder it was merely to lay bare its intrinsic falseness, and no one need feel any twinges of conscience for it. The hungry and thirsty could break into whatever restaurants and wine shops they came upon without the slightest qualm.

Though couched in reason, it amounted to a thinly veiled incitement to riot, and that was exactly the effect it had. The negative energy pent up in the crowd erupted in three resounding cheers, and the Bellyshakers spread out toward nearby restaurants like sumo wrestlers running shuffle-foot drills, gyrating their torsos with arms outstretched and hips bent low.

Being closest to where the whole rumpus began, House of a Different Flour was the first to be hit.

"Sounds like all hell's broken loose downstairs," said Konji. "What do you figure we should do?"

"It might not be safe to stick around."

"I'll go have a look."

While they waited, Sugawara and Jūnoshin could hear wood splitting, dishes crashing, and sundry other bangs, thuds, and cracks, punctuated by cries of *No! Stop! Aaack!*

Konji had not been gone long when he returned badly scraped up and missing a kimono sleeve. His topknot had come undone and his hair hung loose.

"'Might not be safe' is an understatement," he said. "We need to get our asses outta here!"

With normal perceptions of right and wrong swept away by Chayama's words, the crowd was running completely amok. They stuffed their mouths with whatever food they found, and if anybody tried to stop them, he got his head bashed in with the nearest scrap of wood. Bellowing *It's a phony world, and I'm busting its belly open!* they poured wine down their throats, flipped the tatami over, tore apart the furniture, and smashed every dish they found. Here and there men were trying to get under the maids' kimonos. And in the middle of it all stood Osamu, laughing hilariously as he lifted people into the air and blew them to smithereens.

"But if it's really that bad, we could get our own heads bashed in," Sugawara said uneasily.

"Maybe I should just cut them all down," suggested Jūnoshin. "I mean, seeing as how I'm a superhuman swordsman, a handful of rioters shouldn't give me too much trouble."

"Don't even think of it," Konji shot back. "The sight of blood is the last thing we want to give this crowd right now. They're definitely not normal. I don't know what they might have eaten, but it's like they're high on something—blasted totally out of their minds. Our best option is to sneak out the window here and crawl along the eaves to the house next door."

"But our sandals are downstairs…"

"Forget 'em. No sense in getting your head split open over some piddly pair of sandals."

"But we have our honor to uphold. A samurai can't go creeping barefoot out of an upstairs window. If word got out, we'd never hear the end of it."

Sugawara was still hemming and hawing when the rioters came stomping up the stairs and began tearing apart the neighboring room. *Bang! Thud! Crack!* The bone-jarring noises were getting too close for comfort.

"Fine," snapped Konji. "You can go on downstairs and leave by the front door wearing your honorable sandals. But I'm an undercover agent, so the window works perfectly well for me. Which'll it be for you, Kakari?"

"I'm freelance and don't really have to worry about honor, so I believe I'll take the window, too. See you later, Master Sugawara. Except, actually, I guess we probably won't see you."

"Wait! I'm coming, too."

The three men slipped out the window as if they were adulterers or thieves stealing away from the scene of their crime.

The mob of Bellyshakers seemed to be working themselves into an ever greater frenzy. Their pounding percussion throbbed across the bright blue sky.

"We need to report this to his lordship right away."

Having escaped by the skin of their teeth, the three men turned their steps toward Lord Naitō's mansion. As they moved away from the restaurant crossing, the streets quickly returned to their normal tranquility. It felt like any ordinary afternoon.

"It's hard to believe how quiet it is just this far away," Konji said.

At that moment several young men came rushing toward them from around the corner. They excitedly pointed past the three men, and quickly raced off in that direction with their eyes flashing.

The three reached the Naitō residence only to find it deserted. Sugawara immediately sensed something ominous in the air. Nothing appeared to be out of place, and yet the house felt fundamentally different somehow.

Whether the sensation came merely from a breakdown within his own psyche, or from the normal equilibrium of the place actually being disrupted, he couldn't say. But he felt a deep sense of foreboding.

"Maybe the councilor got an unexpected summons," he said. "I'll run up to the castle and see." He changed into his formal clothes in a great flurry and departed.

Jūnoshin and Konji were left by themselves.

The storm doors and windows were all open, allowing a fresh early summer breeze to move through the house.

Daylight from the garden filtered in across the veranda and partway into the sitting room, leaving its innermost reaches in shadows. The two men sat facing the garden about halfway back.

"It's so peaceful," Konji said.

"It sure is."

"It's like all that uproar never even happened."

"Exactly, exactly."

"What do you suppose the term is for this?"

"The term?"

"Uh-huh. How would you describe this feeling? This moment."

"Well, I suppose you might call it a lull in the action."

"Mmm. I'm not sure that quite does it justice. I mean, sitting here in an empty house, of an afternoon, doing nothing, just staring off into space: it's like I've somehow slipped out of the whole framework of my existence; like all my gears have disengaged, and this special moment could go on forever. That's what it feels like. That kind of moment."

"Sounds to me like the sort of thing a Bellyshaker might say."

"It does?"

"Definitely. This stuff about slipping out of the framework and a moment lasting forever—doesn't that sound pretty Bellyshaker-esque?"

"Really? You think? Seems totally different to me," Konji said. "And since it kind of gets on my nerves to hear you say that, how about we change the subject? What did you think of the response we got today?"

"Looked like a success to me. There must have been at least a hundred of them shaking their bellies in the end, and they tore that restaurant completely to pieces, so it puts Lord Naitō in the perfect position to say I told you so."

"Right. The only question is whether we need to keep it spreading some more or if that was enough."

"Uh-huh."

"But there's one thing I really don't get. Why would all those people start shaking their bellies just like that? I mean, you wouldn't normally expect them to be taken in so easily. The guy's got con-man written all over his face, literally, and none of what he says makes the least bit of sense. Yet in next to no time at all, everybody's shaking it up. That's what I don't get."

"I figure it's because they don't know how to think for themselves anymore. So when somebody says, 'I'm hot stuff,' they

take him at his word and think, *Wow, this guy's really something.*
Basically, they have no critical eye. That place today is actually the
perfect example—House of a Different Flour. It's nothing special,
right? But their sign says 'The best food in town since before your
granddaddy was born,' so people assume it's true and line up in
droves. Same thing when somebody tells them so-and-so's a bad
egg, and they just take it on faith. They're simpletons. That's what
it boils down to."

"But isn't this some kind of new low? I mean, sure, some
people are like that, but I always figured they were exceptions—a
few crazies here and there, or guys who've simply thrown up their
hands, like Makubo Magobei. But that was a pretty big chunk of
people shaking it up in today's crowd. Perfectly normal-looking
people. Wholly respectable shop clerks and housewives. That's what
surprised me. That even people like that were falling for it. So
many of them. I mean, when a guy tries to tell you that the world's
floating around inside the bowels of a giant tapeworm, it's just such
obvious hogwash. No normal person's actually going to believe
anything like that, right?"

"That's where you're wrong," Jūnoshin said. "They don't
believe it because it makes any sense. They believe it because it
appeals to them. If somebody came along to tell them that because
they're idiots, they all have to slave without pay for the rest of their
lives, you can bet they wouldn't accept that so quickly. But this guy
said everybody's actually supposed to have an easy life, and it's only
because the world's messed up that they have to suffer, so of course
they're going to believe him. Especially when it rolls off that velvet
tongue of his dressed up in the same sort of fairy tale they've heard
all their lives. *Boom.* It's all over in a single go. Easy win. Because
they're such morons."

"I guess I hadn't thought of it that way," Konji said with a sigh,
then silently gazed out at the garden for a time. There was a nandina
bush with a large spider web glistening between its branches. A
butterfly was struggling to free itself.

"So, what do you figure you'll do next?" he asked Jūnoshin.

"Depends on what Master Sugawara finds out."

"No, I didn't mean right now so much as after this is all over."

"How about you?"

"Me? Well, actually, that's exactly what I'm asking myself. It's hard to get excited about carrying on as a secret agent around here, you know. I've been wondering about maybe getting into a bit of trade."

"I figure I'm pretty much finished around here, too. Especially since I'm not getting paid any more right now. I suspect it's time to make the break and move on—wouldn't want to outstay my welcome. But even for that, I'll need some traveling money."

"Are you married or anything?"

"I was once."

"Think you'll ever get hitched again?"

"Maybe. If the right woman comes along. Speaking of which, I can't get over how pretty that Ron girl is. Do you figure she's Chayama's woman? I suppose that's what we have to assume."

"I wouldn't be so sure."

"If I can find a way to get another payday out of Lord Naitō, maybe I'll ask her to marry me and we can find someplace better off than here to open a little shop or something."

"You don't say," Konji responded a bit testily, even though he was the one who'd asked the question to begin with.

It was at that moment that Sugawara returned.

"Here you are," he said as he came into the sitting room.

"Ah, you're back. What did you find out?"

"We've got trouble."

"Trouble?"

"The whole town's been turned upside down."

By Sugawara's account, the town had descended into complete chaos. In the space of only an hour or two, the number of Bellyshakers had grown to more than five hundred. They were roving wildly through neighborhoods, breaking down doors and looting wantonly, even setting some of the homes ablaze. Driven to despair, many of the victims burst into maniacal laughter and began shaking their bellies, too—swelling the rabble further.

A base of operations for the growing movement had been set up in the dry bed of the Yōrei River. Tall scaffolds had gone up, atop which massive drums were constantly sounding the Bellyshaker beat. At tents nearby, a kitchen detail was boiling cauldrons of rice gruel to feed the hungry, and plundered casks of saké had been broken open and equipped with dippers so everybody could help themselves to drink.

From this party headquarters, platoons of Bellyshakers were fanning out across town to shake their bellies and carry on their pillaging. When a police detective hurried to one such scene with a squad of deputies, they were all surrounded and pelted with stones; they quickly took to their heels with tears streaming and noses running. The lawless mobs were effectively left to do as they pleased.

"Okay, we get the picture," said Jūnoshin when Sugawara finished his account. "But being chief councilor and all, isn't Lord Naitō the one who's ultimately in charge of restoring public order? What'd he have to say about the situation?"

It was of course a perfectly reasonable question, but Sugawara could barely muster an answer.

"He wasn't there," he said weakly.

"He wasn't at the castle?"

"He's apparently in Hedaka."

"Hedaka? What's he doing way out in the boondocks at a time like this? The others must be furious."

"No, not at all."

"Whyever not? I certainly would be, under the circumstances."

"At any rate, they're not."

"Why not?"

"Because everybody else is in Hedaka, too, including Lord Naohito."

"Oh," Jūnoshin said. "Really?"

"Yes, really."

"What for?"

"To see a monkey show."

Right about the time Chayama and his cohorts appeared across the street from House of a Different Flour, an assistant whispered in Lord Naitō's ear at the castle. Word was, he said, that Ōura Shuzen had made himself into quite the accomplished monkey trainer since taking up his new post.

Naitō chortled with glee. *Tee hee hee.*

Then he got to thinking: It cracks me up to hear it, but why should something so hilarious end with me chuckling under my breath only to myself? Imagine how much more fun it'd be if we all went out there together and had a good laugh watching the man sweat it out with the monkeys.

He promptly requested an audience with Lord Naohito and was soon admitted into his presence.

"My lord."

"What is it, Naitō? I understand you have a matter of business to discuss. Speak."

"Indeed, my lord. It's about Ōura."

"What about him?"

"Well, sir, you will recall that you appointed him to be monkey commissioner some time ago. As it happens, I received word today that his hard work has paid off, and he has learned to handle his charges with great competence."

"That's all well and good, Naitō. Buy why should you need to ask for an audience just to tell me that? Are you an idiot?"

"Most humble apologies, my lord. But my request for this audience was not merely to inform you of this fact. I wished to bring up a related matter."

"Fine. What is it? Get to the point."

"Indeed, my lord. With Bellyshaker concerns and so many other pressing matters to attend to of late, it has been weighing on my mind that you, my lord, have been unable to find a moment's rest. Now, by timely coincidence, it comes to my ear that your new monkey commissioner, Ōura Shuzen, has turned himself into quite the respectable monkey handler. Such being the case, I wondered if you might wish to order up a command performance on some suitable date."

"What?" Lord Kuroae snapped, drilling Naitō with his eyes. "Are you suggesting that I should actually see one of these monkey shows?"

"Forgive me. At a time of so many other urgent demands, it was a foolish idea. I must beg your pardon."

"No, no, no, you needn't apologize in the least. I believe your point is that when a person is busy, it is easy to become overly fatigued. To prevent this, it's important to take breaks and relax from time to time, and to carry the point a step further, there is no better break for its salutary effect on the human psyche than taking in a rib-tickling show put on by performing monkeys. That's what you're saying, is it not? You make an excellent point. Let us go."

"Ah, I'm much relieved, my lord. I feared I was about to receive your ire. In that case, when would you like to schedule this diversion?"

"When? Why, right now, of course."

"Huh? Right now? L-l-let us not be hasty, my lord. That is to say, it is all well and good, but there are a variety of arrangements that must be—"

"Are you telling me you just popped this off the top of your head without getting anything ready first?"

"Oh, not at all, my lord, but—"

"Then what's the problem? Come. Let us go. In fact, come to think of it, I'm sure I'm not the only one around here who could use a little R&R. So long as we're going, let's make it an official clan affair and take the whole household along."

"The whole household?" Naitō exclaimed, but Lord Naohito was already on his feet and headed out the door.

"This was certainly a surprise."

"No kidding. Ordering the whole clan to a monkey show right out of the blue. What could Lord Naohito be thinking? I've been working on a proposal that's due by the end of the day, and it's likely to be bad news if it doesn't get done."

"I'm in pretty much the same boat myself. I was supposed to meet with the folks at Izutsu-ya this afternoon. They kept claiming they were too busy and wouldn't agree to a time, and it was a royal hassle just to get it on the calendar, but now I'm off to some stupid monkey show instead."

"Then again, this could turn out to be a real treat, seeing Lord Ōura, of all people, yukking it up with a bunch of monkeys. I have a feeling we'll be glad we didn't stay hunkered down at the castle—even if it does involve a certain amount of collateral grief."

"True enough, true enough. I can hardly wait to see what kind of face he makes when he's up there on stage with his monkeys."

Shortly after midday, some fifty members of the Kuroae household—all but a token handful left behind to hold down the fort—were parading along the country road toward the Bureau of Monkey Affairs in Hedaka. While complaining about the precipitate manner in which Lord Naohito had forced them to change their plans, the retainers' chatter was also filled with eager anticipation of the planned entertainment.

They went merrily on their way, little knowing that the town behind them was at that very moment being turned upside down. A shimmering of heat could be seen rising here and there over the fields and paddies on either side of the road, signaling the arrival of summer.

Lord Kuroae's surprise decision had set off quite a scramble at the castle, and word of the clan's impending arrival caught those at the Bureau of Monkey Affairs equally off guard. But since in this case it was a matter of two monkey trainers and their elderly cook, the effect was considerably more subdued.

"We can just put the monkeys through their usual paces."

"Right. I practiced with Hentarō and Shii today, so their balance ball and coin toss tricks are probably the best place to start."

"Should we include one of their skits?"

"Ah, yes, a skit. It'll mean quite a bit more prep work for you, but since the lord himself is coming, I suppose we should."

Ōura and Shume put their heads together to come up with a program for Lord Naohito and the clan.

"I'd better start getting things ready right away," Shume said, rising to his feet.

The Bureau of Monkey Affairs housed only three men but a far greater population of monkeys. Yet, the annual budget provided by the clan was a mere one and a half ryō, which was woefully inadequate to cover costs. In fact, the outlays for feed alone came to some three ryō a month. Ōura and Shume had been offsetting this and other expenses by taking the monkeys on tour around the domain to generate income. When they weren't on the road, they offered regular performances for nearby residents right there in the compound, and they'd constructed both a stage and tiered seating for this purpose.

As you entered the gate, there was a short passageway between the ends of two longhouses that extended along the front wall of the compound on either side. The monkeys lived in the structure to the left, and the men occupied the one to the right. Both buildings were of very cheap construction. In the passage between them were several posts, which often had monkeys chained to them.

After the two longhouses came descending tiers of box seating on either side, constructed of rough-hewn timber and facing a simple, two-foot-high platform that was open to the sky directly ahead. The box seats were furnished with rush mats to sit on, and nearby farm families would come bearing picnic lunches and saké to nibble and sip on as they enjoyed the monkeys' acrobatics; today the usual mats were replaced with carpets because the great lord himself would be attending.

All of this filled the area that would normally be the front courtyard of a walled compound, with the main dwelling located beyond where the stage stood, but in this case no proper residence had been built in that spot, only another longhouse. In spite of the inexpensive pine lumber used in their construction, the houses by the gate were still relatively new and large enough to hold as many as a hundred monkeys, giving them a certain stateliness. By contrast, the single-story building behind the stage was small, old, and forlorn. It served as a dressing room for the monkeys who were waiting to go on stage.

The stage itself had not been equipped with any of the commonly seen special features, such as a raised walkway jutting out into the audience, but a large camphor tree stood at stage left, and to the right was a small pond.

It was mid-afternoon by the time Lord Naohito arrived with his retinue. There being nowhere else for him to go to rest up from the journey, he was shown directly to the tiered seating. Several farm maidens from the vicinity arrived with tea, fruit, and a tobacco tray.

After a brief interval, Ōura came out and knelt on the ground in front of the stage to greet his august visitor.

"Welcome, my lord. It is truly a great pleasure to see you again."

He was wearing the traditional monkey handler's outfit of tight-sleeved cloak and pantaloons, with a tam on his head. The visitors peered down at his curious figure from their elevated boxes.

"Are you keeping well, Ōura?" Lord Naohito responded directly rather than through an intermediary.

"Indeed I am, my lord. Thank you."

"I'm glad to hear it. Now, be quick and show us these monkeys of yours."

"As you wish, my lord."

He briefly withdrew to the dressing room, then reappeared and stepped onto the stage with a single monkey in tow. In his right hand he held a short switch. Shume stood by in the wings to assist.

"I will be entertaining you today," Ōura declaimed, "with the amazing talents of my performing monkeys. My name is Ōura Shuzen, once upon a time a member of our good Lord Naohito's high council, and—"

Nearly everyone in the audience burst out laughing, as Naitō felt a secret tingle of glee. It was so irresistibly comical to see the one-time clan elder introducing his monkey act in the theatrical tones of a showman. The man had even learned how to poke fun at himself as a way of making his audience laugh.

But Lord Naohito stared at the stage without showing the slightest hint of a smile.

Ōura continued. "First to join me on the stage is Hentarō, a male who has this year attained the age of seven. Now, where are your manners, Hentarō? Offer the lord a greeting," he said, rapping the floor with his switch.

The audience waited in anticipation, expecting the monkey to bow to the lord. Instead, he stood looking oblivious to what was going on, his eyes wandering off in an entirely different direction as he scratched himself on the hindquarters.

"Didn't you hear me, Hentarō? What're you sticking your nose in the air and scratching your behind for? I told you to offer the lord a greeting. He's come all this way to see you. You mustn't be rude."

But the admonishment appeared to fall on deaf ears. Continuing his inattentive act, the monkey toddled about the stage obliviously for several moments before turning his back to the audience and lowering himself on his haunches.

Ōura grew flustered. "What in the world's gotten into you, Hentarō?" he said in consternation. "Why are you being such a bad boy?"

He scurried over to where the monkey sat and slapped the floor several times with his switch, but Hentarō only seemed to grow more perturbed with each stroke. Then all of a sudden he lashed out with a flying kick, which sent his master tumbling in an exaggerated fall.

The audience roared with laughter. But the all important Lord Naohito, who'd been following these events with an increasingly sour look on his face, had apparently run out of patience.

"Ōura!" he called down to the stage. He spoke in a strong voice that projected well.

Now quite apart from how competent or incompetent a particular performance might be, the events unfolding on a stage belong to their own discrete dimension, removed from the normal flow of time, and it generally requires more than a little nerve to reach across that divide and interrupt their progress. But having been born to privilege as a daimyo's heir, Lord Naohito was able to do this without the slightest hesitation.

"What's going on here, Ōura? Why won't the creature greet me properly? It's outrageous."

"I'm utterly mortified, my lord."

"There's no need for you to be mortified. All I'm asking is why the creature doesn't show me the proper respect. What is the reason? If it's simply that he lacks the intelligence, then fine, but if he's being insubordinate, then he needs to be disciplined. So which is it? Answer me."

Ōura prostrated himself on stage.

"If I may be so bold, my lord, please allow me to explain. What you have just witnessed is a performance. It is part of the monkey's act."

"Refusing to greet me is his act?"

"Exactly so, my lord. The sight of a person, which is to say myself, being flummoxed and mocked by a beast, which is to say the monkey, was intended to be humorous and comical, but I can see in retrospect that it succeeds only in being rude, as you have so aptly pointed out. Please accept my deepest apologies for having presented you with such a disrespectful performance."

He pressed his forehead to the floor in abject apology. Meanwhile, Hentarō had seated himself in a formal position next to Ōura and he, too, prostrated himself with his forehead to the floor. The grave, even sorrowful, expression on his face attested to the deep concern he had for his master, and it pulled on the heartstrings. Even Lord Naohito appeared to be moved.

"Fine, fine. Just so you understand," he said. "Now then, you may continue."

"Thank you, my lord. With your permission, we shall move directly to our next act," Ōura said, cutting short the warm-up portion of Hentarō's routine to proceed to his showcase—the balance-ball feat.

Shume came on stage with the ball and set it in place.

Ōura slapped his switch on the floor and Hentarō obediently leapt up onto the ball. It was of course in the nature of the ball to roll out from under him, but the monkey was able to keep it from doing this by indiscernibly adjusting the pressure he exerted on the ball with his feet. He simply stood there holding the ball steady, and that was all. A sense of desolation fell over the stage and crowd, and not a sound could be heard.

There was nothing the slightest bit entertaining about it. Which only stands to reason, of course, since the appeal of performing monkeys is not in their raw skill, but in how they start out by making various little blunders and going into a funk or otherwise refusing to do as they're told, in such a way that the supposedly inferior beasts even seem to get the upper hand over their human masters at times, only to eventually come around, taking the repeated admonishments to heart and mending their ways to perform each step properly. The sight of them finally getting it right is so completely endearing that the audience erupts spontaneously in applause.

That is to say, the fun of monkey shows rests in a repeated pattern of rank inversion. But being of literal mind and a stickler for form, Lord Naohito had effectively forbidden any deviations from normative behavior. There could be no humor in a monkey show that had been deprived of such playfulness.

To judge from the troubled glances he threw Ōura's way as he shifted his weight atop the ball, even Hentarō had sensed the awkwardness in the air. Feeling sorry for him, Ōura commanded him to dismount, and he dropped to the stage.

There'd been nothing to signal that the act was over, so Ōura declared, "You have just witnessed the balance-ball feat," and bowed low to the ground.

Silence. Not a soul clapped or said a word.

After a brief pause, Lord Naohito spoke. "All right. I get it. You call it the balance-ball feat because the monkey balances on a ball. There's certainly no mistake there. That's exactly what it was. So, then. What's next?"

Ōura felt utterly drained, but since the lord was asking for more, he had no choice but to go on.

"Next on the program is the coin fetch," he said weakly.

The entire audience seemed to flinch at the prospect of more of the same. Ōura could muster no enthusiasm, either, and even the new monkey being led on stage seemed weary. Lord Naohito alone looked on in eager anticipation.

The routine was supposed to begin with the monkey behaving in a sulky manner and refusing to introduce himself. He would then clamber up onto Ōura's shoulder, leap into the air to do a flip, and land upright on his master's bent knees. But these warm-up bits would clearly be wasted on the lord, so Ōura decided to skip them. In fact, the whole thing seemed so silly that he found himself launching into a lengthy explanation instead.

"This trick will be performed by the monkey Shii. Although I call it a trick, it's really nothing special. Shii goes to fetch a coin I toss—and that's all. I normally offer some commentary along the way to make the audience laugh—'Oh, my! I never knew monkeys were such grasping creatures,' and that sort of thing—but of course it's not true. He doesn't have a clue about the coin's value; he's only doing what he's been trained to do. He knows I'll shower him with approval and give him a piece of fruit when he does what I say."

Ōura didn't customarily let the audience in on the tricks of his trade like this, of course, and it gave him a certain thrill to do it now. Once he'd spilled the beans, the monkey show would never be the same again. The thought gripped him like a spell.

When this is all over, I imagine I'll go back to the cheery smiles and silly banter that have always livened our routines. But it won't ever be as free and easy as it used to be. Not after what I said just now.

He tossed a coin into the pond and slapped the stage with his switch. "All right, Shii," he said. "Go fetch the coin like we practiced."

After staring uncertainly at Ōura for several moments, the monkey plunged into the water with a look of resignation, dove to the bottom to retrieve the coin, and scrambled back out to hand it to Ōura, trembling with chill.

"And that was the trick known as the coin fetch," Ōura said quietly, turning to face Lord Naohito.

An uncomfortable silence filled the air. One might even have called it menacing.

The crux of the problem no doubt lay in the fact that Ōura had switched jobs only recently. If he'd been a career entertainer, he'd have long since learned that he couldn't let anything affect the way he ran his act no matter how dimwitted Lord Naohito might be.

Naitō was grinning ear to ear at the sight of his once high-and-mighty rival reduced to playing with monkeys, but as he felt the menace thickening in the air he became alarmed that Lord Naohito might lose his temper.

"Perhaps we should call for an intermission at this point, my lord," he said. "I think we could all do with a little break."

"A break? Nonsense. I'm already on a break. That's what this entire trip is supposed to be. Why would I want to take a break from my break?"

"Indeed, my lord, we have all come here for a break, but it occurred to me that taking a break from that break might trigger a multiplier effect that would make it even more of a break."

"What kind of nonsense is that? I should think taking a break from a break would mean going back to work."

"Forgive me, my lord, what I'm trying to say is—"

At that moment two figures rushed into the aisle between the seating tiers and hissed, "If we might have a moment, your lordship!" Naitō turned to find Sugawara and Jūnoshin looking up at him. Konji had come with them as well, but he was hanging back by the longhouses.

"Oh, it's you fellows," Naitō said. "Lord Naohito is busy with a monkey show at the moment. I don't know what you want, but whatever it is, it'll have to wait."

"It's a matter of great urgency, sir."

"What is it, Naitō? What's going on?" the lord demanded.

"My steward is asking to speak with me."

"Your steward? Fine, fine. By all means, go find someplace where you can talk. In which case, I suppose we might as well take that break from the break you were proposing."

"Indeed, my lord, I believe you will find it most agreeable."

"Very well, then. Let it be so."

The entire clan breathed a sigh of relief. Ōura and Shume did as well—and so did the monkeys.

There was no ready accommodation to which the daimyo could retire for the intermission, so with the help of the lord's retinue, Ōura's longhouse was tidied up in a great hurry and a place was prepared for him there. Since this ruled out that location for their own conference, Naitō and his men remained behind in the otherwise deserted box seats. A monkey chained to one of the posts in the aisle was staring into a vat of water.

"Aha!" Naitō exclaimed with delight when he heard Sugawara's news. "So the bellyshaking has begun! Excellent work! I can stop worrying about ending up with mud on my face."

"But the thing is," the steward added nervously, "I'm concerned that the situation may have gotten a little bit out of hand."

"Why should you be concerned about that? The leaders are in our pocket, are they not?"

"Yes, but the crowd's gotten itself so worked up that we have a virtual riot on our hands."

"No worries, no worries. Just bring down the iron fist and the foolishness will stop. Isn't that right, Kakari?"

"Indeed, sir. Except, as a matter of fact, it's turned into a rather large crowd."

"Large crowd? Like what? Twenty? Thirty?"

"A few more than that, I'm afraid."

"Relax, relax. Even with forty or fifty, it's nothing but a bunch of peasants and townfolk we're talking about. The mere sight of spears and muskets will have them quivering like leaves and scattering to the winds."

"Actually, it's even more than that."

"What? Are you telling me they're pushing a hundred in just one day?"

"No, as I say—"

"Well, how many *is* it then?"

"Our latest estimate is about eight hundred, but the number could easily keep on growing. The whole town's been turned upside down. Roving bands are going from house to house breaking down doors, helping themselves to whatever they please, and torching what's left. In many cases the homeowners are so traumatized that they simply snap, erupting in wild peals of laughter as they start shaking their bellies, too, and it just keeps snowballing. They've established a base of operations in the riverbed, where they put up tents and scaffolds and have great big drums pounding out the Bellyshaker beat. When the police tried to step in, they were pelted with rocks from every side and driven away in tears. With no one to restore order, it's become extremely dangerous to go anywhere near town."

When Jūnoshin finally paused for breath, Naitō exploded in anger.

"How could you let this happen? Don't you realize how limited our forces are right now? For fully commissioned samurai, all we've got are the fifty odd men who came with us here today. It's them plus a handful of foot soldiers. We used to have as many as a hundred, but without any wars going on it seemed like a waste, so I downsized to just twenty. And even those twenty haven't had a lick of training. I've mostly had them doing clerical stuff and other odd jobs. That means the biggest force the clan can muster, including every over-the-hill veteran and wet-behind-the-ears greenhorn we've got, is a grand total of seventy. How're we supposed to put down a mob of a thousand with no more men than that? Well, at any rate, the first thing we need to do is get back to the castle."

"That might not be such a good idea," Sugawara said.

"Why not?"

"The area is teeming with lawless rioters. They're likely to attack when they see the lord's retinue coming."

"I shudder to think what Lord Naohito's going to say to this… Man, this could be tricky. If I'm not careful how I bring it up, he'll have me in knots. Maybe we can buy some time with the monkey show while we see if we can get things under control. What do you think, Kakari? Is there anything we can do?"

"Well, when it comes right down to it, the whole thing's nothing but a put-on. A staged event. So we just need to get hold of Chayama, and we can make it go away."

"Right, right. Come to think of it, it's not really a question of our strength, is it? Which means our only real concern is his lordship. We simply have to make sure he doesn't insist on rushing back to the castle."

"Exactly," said Jūnoshin. "And for that, I think our best bet is for you to be completely up front with him. Give it to him straight just how much trouble the Bellyshakers are causing. All the better that the man who spoke out against hiring me is sitting right there. Point out that if it weren't for his naysaying, we wouldn't be in this fix of having to stay away from the castle, and then grandly declare that you're now sending me to put an end to the mess. It's just what the doctor ordered."

"Sounds good. But are you sure you can pull it off?"

"Not to worry. We brought Chayama in ourselves, and his money's coming from the clan, so I'll just go talk to him. But it does mean Lord Naohito and his men will have to remain here tonight. Are you okay with that?"

"As I said, I'm a little worried how he'll react, but I think I can persuade him. It hadn't really clicked with me until recently, but sugarcoating and beating around the bush doesn't work with that man. He responds much better when you approach directly and give him the straight pitch."

"That's the plan then," said Jūnoshin. He and Konji promptly headed back to town, while Naitō and Sugawara stepped into the longhouse where Lord Naohito had gone to rest.

Inside was a single open room big enough to serve as a practice space for martial arts. Having been tidied up in haste, there was still a certain mount of detritus lying about here and there. The section farthest from the door had been partitioned off with a folding screen in order to offer the lord a measure of privacy.

Naitō knelt at the edge the screen and bowed to the floor.

"I have received some alarming news, my lord," he said in a voice loud enough for everyone in the room to hear.

"What is it? Speak."

"The activities of the Bellyshakers I've spoken of before have suddenly spilled into the open, and they have apparently set off a considerable disturbance in town. I'm told there is rioting in the streets."

"That's intolerable. Clamp down at once. I must return to the castle."

"That is not advisable, my lord."

"Why not? It's vital that I be in my castle at times like this."

"I'm afraid it is simply too dangerous. Rioters being rioters, there's no telling what they might do. That's why it's called rioting."

"I see. But then what am I supposed to do? Sit idly by with my arms folded?"

"Not at all, my lord. There is a man named Kakari Jūnoshin. He is well-versed on the Bellyshakers and what to do about them."

"Yes, I remember. I was going to hire the fellow but Ōura raised a stink. I rewarded his impertinence by demoting him to monkey commissioner."

"Exactly so, my lord. That's the fellow. I have already dispatched him to take care of the matter. Everything should be back to normal by morning. With apologies for the discomfort, my advice is for you to remain in this place overnight and return to the castle on the morrow, after order has been restored. That is my recommendation as your chief councilor."

"Very well. The discomforts will be nothing if I think of it as encamping for battle."

"So good of you, my lord. By your leave, I must now go to speak with the monkey commissioner."

Naitō withdrew, leaving Sugawara behind to fill the retainers in on the particulars. They were clustered in small groups around the room, drinking tea and chatting casually. Some stepped out front to play with the monkeys chained to the posts in the passageway. Happy-go-lucky fellows.

"I guess it's been a while, Ōura," Naitō said, approaching the monkey commissioner with a broad grin stretching across his face.

"Yes, it has," returned Ōura, surprising himself by how calmly he was able to say it.

Naitō's grin was of course his way of saying, *Tee hee hee, serves you right*, and the same sentiment had been expressed quite plainly in the laughter that had burst from the other clan members during the performance. Had Ōura still been living and working in close quarters with Naitō and the others, it would probably have stung far worse. But he was now in a different place, and refreshingly immune to such nastiness. What's more, the events on stage earlier had given Ōura a new sense of distance even from his role as a performer, and this had rendered him quite fearless.

"I know you came here to mock me," he said. "You dragged the whole clan out here to make me your laughingstock. Well, you wasted your time. Because, to put it bluntly, I've realized that whether you're a monkey commissioner or a high councilor, you're both just as wretched as the other. I may feel sorry for myself, but I feel just as sorry for you and the rest, too.

"Aren't you funny. *You* feel sorry for *me*? Fine, pity me all you want. But that's what you call a retrograde position. It's sour grapes. You let yourself get carried away by your emotions and, in a word, you blew it. All my alarms have now been vindicated. The Bellyshakers showed up just as I said they would, and they're running amok all over town. None of us can get back to the castle."

"You sound rather pleased about it."

"In some ways, I suppose I am. But it's not because my counsel was accepted. I'm just glad to finally have it demonstrated once and for all that you were wrong. And I'm a little bit relieved, too, because, as a matter of fact, I was actually feeling a twinge or two of conscience earlier as I watched you on stage with your monkeys, knowing I was the one who put you there. But then all of a sudden the Bellyshakers really did appear, which tells me that if you'd had your way, we'd have been caught completely flatfooted, powerless to respond—and that means you got exactly what you deserved. That's what pleases me."

"Listen to you. I suppose you actually believe your own lies. I've figured all along that if the Bellyshakers showed up like you said, it'd be because you made it happen."

"What could possibly give you that idea?"

"I've traveled around the country with my show. I know perfectly well that the Bellyshakers were wiped out."

"And I suppose you plan to inform Lord Naohito of that fact?"

"No. I like the monkeys. I enjoy practicing and performing with them. Though I pity myself a little for feeling that way."

"But you pity me, too."

"That's right. I pity you, too."

As it happens, this was not the conversation that anyone standing nearby would have overheard. The actual words the two men exchanged were limited the following:

"The Bellyshakers have come to town."

"Interesting. After all this time?"

"That's right. After all this time, the Bellyshakers have arrived."

"So what're you going to do about it?"

"At the moment, it's much too dangerous to go anywhere near town. We'll all need to stay here tonight."

"That's fine. I'll cancel the rest of the monkey show."

But beneath their painted grins, they were both busily probing between the lines to read each other's true inner thoughts, so that it was as if the foregoing conversation had silently taken place between them. They had, in a way, reached an understanding—if only the understanding that there would never be any genuine understanding between them.

They stood looking at each other for quite some time, wrapped in the smell of animals that still lingered over the stage.

Jūnoshin and Konji made their way back to town. The day was coming to an end, but far from losing steam, the Bellyshakers' rampages still seemed to be on the upswing. Storefront after storefront had been broken into and ransacked. Personal items from the living quarters—grinding pestles and cutting boards, washbasins and garden ornaments—were scattered about the shops, while business items—cashiers' grates, abacuses, and ledgers—littered the back rooms. No doubt it had been done deliberately, in accordance with the Bellyshaker teaching that the proper positions of things should be inverted. Needless to say, the looters had made off with anything of value. Every drawer, desk, wardrobe, and storeroom had been rifled through in the process, and their unwanted contents were strewn everywhere. In many of the houses they could see upended braziers billowing great clouds of ash and steam.

On the other hand, they also passed shops where the owners had opened their doors and set out trays of rice balls along with a saké cask and dipper. The idea was apparently to ingratiate themselves with the looters in the hope that they might go a little easier on them. As a rule, these places had the tatami turned over as well, to accommodate muddy feet. But there was no discernible sign that the measures had done any good. The Bellyshakers had been quite impartial in their destructiveness. Besides the astonishing disarray everywhere, some of what they'd left in their wake seemed utterly without rhyme or reason. A chamber pot had been plopped down in the middle of the road. A neat row of six Jizō statues had been lifted onto somebody's rooftop.

Bellyshakers were coming and going or standing about in groups all up and down the street. Everybody they passed seemed to be caught under the same spell; those who were still in their right minds had presumably thought it best to get out of town. Barely half a day had gone by since the shaking began, and yet already their clothes were filthy, their skin blackened with grime, and their hair in wild tangles.

To do as the spirit moved appeared to be the rule of the day. Men were sprawled out at the roadside gorging on the food and drink they'd helped themselves to. Somebody walking along would let out a sudden whoop and shake like there was no tomorrow for several steps before falling back into his former gait. Here a whole crowd formed into a circle to shake it up together; there a lone figure stood in the shadows facing a wall, absorbed in his solitary gyrations.

Also roaming the streets were bands of drummers and samisen players, whipping up the throngs with their constant frenzied beat. Word of something going on had spread to the countryside, and me-too types from nearby villages were gathering in droves to join the shaking and looting without the first idea what it was about.

Jūnoshin and Konji could hear people talking about the Bellyshakers as they passed.

"There's just such an amazing feeling of togetherness, you know? I'm so grateful for all the wonderful new people I've met!"

"Thank you, Bellyshakers! I was starving, so the rice gruel down by the river really hit the spot. It blew me away. Thank you, Brother Osamu, Brother Jōji, Sister Ron. My happy belly started shaking like crazy. Everybody around me was whooping."

"I wish stuff like this happened every day."

"What a blast! You really can't beat it! All these free and easy folks finding each other."

"A teetering farmer was coming on to this cute chick. I thought he was trying to shake his belly with her, but it turned out he was just drunk."

"This's so much fun. I wish I'd known about it sooner."

"Bellyshaking's the best! Though there's still room for improvement. It's a problem that you can't eat and shake at the same time."

"Those guys in front of House of a Different Flour doing that weird finger-pointing bellyshake just amongst themselves can all go to hell as far as I'm concerned."

"It's hard to believe that some people actually don't want to shake."

"All the trash and sludge and road apples strewn everywhere sure are a bummer, though. They keep me from really getting into the groove."

"Brother Chayama and his hard-working staff deserve a big hand. Thank you, thank you, it's been such a blast. I can't remember the last time I felt this good."

They saw Bellyshakers everywhere they went, but the samurai quarter was noticeably quieter than the merchant district. It owed in part, no doubt, to the houses there offering less in the way of money and fine objects to steal, but even so gates stood ajar, and they could see clear signs of looting. Whether because they'd hidden or fled, or because they'd been taken away—perhaps even killed?—there were no women or children in sight.

As they walked side by side down a quiet street lined with samurai residences, Jūnoshin and Konji passed a home where a half-crazed woman was stumbling about in a state of undress that suggested she'd been raped. She was obviously a woman of rank.

"This is bad," said Jūnoshin, averting his eyes.

"No kidding."

"Every last house has been tossed."

"So it seems. At this rate, we pretty much have to expect the worst at Lord Naitō's place, too."

"It's probably been turned completely upside down."

"Did you leave any valuables there?"

"No, I'm safe on that score. But will you just look at this place— what a mess! Every tree and shrub in the garden's been yanked out of the ground. Can you imagine the strength that would take?"

"Sort of makes you want to have a look inside, doesn't it," said Konji.

"Yeah, it does. People's houses are weird that way. They're unexplored worlds that are always right there. Not to mention, a naked expression of the owner's personality."

"Exactly. And when the owner isn't there anymore, it suddenly becomes a totally different place—like an old museum that's falling to pieces. Care to stop for a peek?"

"Better not. We've got other things to worry about."

"Like what?"

"Like if we run into some Bellyshakers and they realize we're not with them, they might pound us to a pulp."

"Nobody's given us any trouble so far."

"But we've gotten some pretty strange looks. Like they had half a mind to punch us in the face."

"Now that you mention it, I suppose you're right. Once we get on through here, it's only a hop and a skip to the levee, and the nearer we get, the more of them we're likely to run into, so I suppose we'd better be prepared to shake our bellies a bit."

"Except I can't really say I know how."

"Can't say I do either."

"It might pay to practice a bit before we get any closer."

"Good idea."

Stepping to the side of the street, they attempted to move their bellies in time with the drumbeat in the distance.

"Is this about right, do you think?"

"I'm not sure. Maybe drop your butt lower and bow your legs more, like this."

"But then my swords get in the way and I can't shake as much."

"I see what you mean. Makes me feel like I'm gonna fart, too."

"Then let's try bringing our butts back up a bit."

As the two were still working out the kinks in their style, some men came into view up the street, shaking their bellies and raising a chorus of high-pitched cries and yelps as they approached. All six of them had frizzy, sun-bleached hair tied in clumsy topknots, and wore cheap, unlined kimonos printed with a bizarre spiral pattern that instantly marked them as country bumpkins. As a matter of fact, the men themselves were all too painfully aware that people regarded them as hicks and stumblebums, and they had long since given up on hitting it off with the ladies. But joining the Bellyshakers today had freed them from their normally depressing opinion of themselves.

Stumblebum, my ass. Once you get shaking, what difference does it make whether you're hunky or frumpy? When your robe falls open and your hem hikes up, you're just as big a slob no matter what you've got on. Covered all in dust. Wading through filth. There's no such thing as a bumpkin when it gets like this; you just shake it up with everything you've got, and nothing else matters in the whole wide world. It's liberation day for all us country hicks.

Convinced that the tables had turned, they were shaking in jubilation.

But they didn't stop at rejoicing. Their pent-up resentment also surfaced in bursts of aggression. When they saw a natty dresser, they tore at him from all sides and left his kimono in shreds; when they came to a fancy shop, they thronged inside and laid it to waste. Having become Bellyshakers, they were bent on dragging the rest of the world down to their own level of cloddishness. If you tried to resist, you were killed on the spot. And all the while they kept big silly grins plastered across their faces.

"They're coming this way. What should we do?"

"It's not like we have much choice. Try to go with the flow."

Jūnoshin and Konji did their best to mimic the men's movements as they noisily drew closer. *Ha-yahh! This's the tops! O-hoh o-hoh o-hoh!* Their style of shaking was a bit different. Keeping their feet together, they spread their arms wide and waggled their torsos back and forth in tiny rapid jerks. It ought to have worn them out, but their youth seemed to be giving them the energy to keep it up. Making pointy-lipped clown faces, they thrust their oscillating bellies in front of them as they bore steadily up the street.

It was all too comical, and Jūnoshin had just about decided he'd had enough, when something caught his eye and he went back to shaking with everything he had.

Dangling from the man's outstretched hand was the freshly severed head of a beautiful woman, still dripping blood.

The blood scattered every which way as the head bounced about, and several drops hit Konji and Jūnoshin in the face. They looked at each other's spotted cheeks and let out a weak laugh, then promptly echoed the men's high-pitched shouts.

"*Ha-yahh! O-hoh! Wa-oh!*"

Huge crowds jammed the riverbed as if for a grand festival. The sun had long since sunk beyond the horizon, but faces were lit up in the bright red glow of bonfires.

The clouds of dust being stirred up had blackened every face with grime, but nobody seemed to notice. People moved about the riverbed with expressions of utter placidity on their faces, as if they'd been released from every last source of stress in their lives.

Not everybody was shaking his belly. A good number sat motionless on the ground, looking lost to the world, and the crowd gathered around the cauldrons of rice gruel were busy tucking into their bowls, their eyes fixed blankly on some distant point in space.

Two towers of scaffolding had been erected to the north and south. Next to the southern tower stood two large tents.

Jūnoshin and Konji took it all in without a word as they made their way through the crowds, both of them feeling decidedly out of place.

Konji was the first to speak. "Can you believe the size of this crowd?"

"It's something else all right. That and this incredible dust. I can feel the grit in my teeth."

"Not to mention in my hair. How can these people stand it? They seem completely oblivious."

"Yeah, well, probably because they're a bunch of airheads."

"From the looks of things here, I guess you don't necessarily have to be shaking all the time."

"Right. In fact, most of them are just hanging out. I don't think we need to worry about drawing attention. What I don't get, though, is how they can stand to eat and drink when they're choking in all this damned dust."

"Being airheads probably helps on that score, too."

"I suppose. So, any ideas about where we might find Chayama and his team?"

"Shall I look for somebody to ask?"

"Yeah, why don't you do that, if you don't mind."

"All right. I'll be right back."

Konji moved away through the crowd, peering into passing faces for someone who looked like he might have his head screwed on relatively straight.

"This could be tricky," he muttered to himself. "How do I decide who to ask? Once you start taking a closer look, they all look like they're missing something upstairs. Though that may be how I look, too, for all I know. Aha, that guy over there concentrating on his bowl of gruel seems like a laid back sort. Maybe I'll try him… Excuse me?"

The man looked up at Konji with large beady eyes. The innocent eyes of a deer.

"Sorry to bother you, but would you happen to know where I can find Chayama Hanrō?"

"You want a mountain of tea?"

"No, no, it's a person's name—Chayama Hanrō."

"Well, if it's tea you want to know about, I'm actually the grandson of Okakura Tenshin, who wrote *The Book of Tea*. Or was it that he's *my* grandson. Anyway, I once recorded a song I wrote called the 'Okakura Tenshin Blues.'"

"You'll have to excuse me."

"Any luck? What'd you find out?"

"It's no use. They're all impossible dolts."

"Mmm. So, what do you suggest next?"

"Well, there're those tents over there. How about we try them? Since Chayama's the leader, it might make sense for him to be in one of those."

"All right. Let's see what we find."

Making their way to the nearest tent, they lifted the flap and entered. Jūnoshin promptly took a hard elbow in his side and let out a groan, while Konji bashed heads with somebody and saw stars.

It was hardly a wonder. The place was surprisingly roomy inside for a tent, but it was still only a tent and probably couldn't hold more than about thirty people with any degree of comfort. Yet there must have been upwards of seventy gyrating bodies crammed inside, and with musicians on top of that pounding out a feverish beat and whipping them into a frenzied dance, a certain amount of elbow-jabbing and head-knocking was inevitable.

It was extremely hot. And heated. As the musicians kept up their wild thumping, some of the dancers were crying *ahh, ahh, ahh, ahh* in quarter notes, while others were belting out *hey-ey, hey-ey, hey-ey, hey-ey* in eighths, and in the background still others were shouting *oh-hoh, oh-hoh, oh-hoh, oh-hoh.* The din was deafening; it felt as if they'd entered the *Great Shrieking Realm of Hell!*

"You all right?" Konji screamed into Jūnoshin's ear.

"Are you kidding me? It hurts like the dickens! *Ai-yi-yi.*"

"It's pandemonium in here."

"Man, oh, man. The pain could drive me mad."

"Think maybe we should do some shaking, too?"

"Good idea. We're less likely to get walloped if we're moving with everybody else."

"All right, then. Here goes. *Oh-hoh, oh-hoh, oh-hoh…*"

"*Oh-gyoh, oh-gyoh…*"

"*Ha ha ha ha ha.* This is actually kind of fun."

"Not bad at all."

"*Oh-gyoh, oh-gyoh, oh-gyoh, oh-gyoh…*"

"*Oh-doh, oh-doh, oh-doh, oh-doh…*"

As expected, once they got to shaking, they were spared the pain of getting bumped and bashed by their neighbors.

The movement inside the tent was more like the writhing of a single primitive organism than a jumble of separate Bellyshakers. When they first entered, Jūnoshin and Konji were like foreign bodies invading a cell, so they had naturally taken their knocks. But once they'd been assimilated into their new environment, they no longer had to contend with such battering. At least that was how Konji explained it to himself as he danced.

Alas, the comfort he took proved to be a short-lived delusion, for soon somebody was picking a fight with Jūnoshin—which is to say, the two newcomers had not managed to shed their foreign-body status after all.

The challenge came from a young farmer shaking his belly in front of Jūnoshin. At first he had simply been minding his own business, but then he noticed Jūnoshin and began staring at him as he danced. Was it somebody he should know? Jūnoshin wondered, but try as he might he could not place the face. His puzzlement only grew when the man halted all his movements and just stood there glaring at him.

Several moments went by. Then, suddenly, he demanded, "What the hell do you think you're doing here?"

Now, as previously noted, Jūnoshin was a superhuman swordsman. He could have cut the man down in the blink of an eye. But this was hardly the place to draw a sword. He pretended to be so absorbed in his shaking that he hadn't heard, and tried to edge inconspicuously away.

But the man wasn't about to be ignored. "Answer me, you asshole!" he said.

Jūnoshin decided to play dumb. "I'm just having fun shaking my belly like everybody else."

"Aha! Your true colors emerge. Did you really think we're shaking our bellies for the fun of it? *Yo!*" he roared. "Stop the music! Stop the music!"

Jūnoshin had been figuring the guy for some two-bit rowdy who was off his gourd, but when the music promptly ceased he realized he might be dealing with someone who had some actual clout. The muffled boom of drums could still be heard coming from outside. Black shadows lurked in the corners of the tent.

"Listen up, everybody," the man shouted. "We've got imposters here! Donbora or Gerumu spies, no doubt! I caught some unnatural shaking, so I decided to keep an eye on them, and now I'm sure of it. No way are these guys belly brethren. Kill them! Send them to Spewdom!"

Instantly, the air became charged with hostility. In every shadow there seemed to lurk a viscid savagery.

"Looks like we blew it, Konji. They're onto us."

"What'll we do?"

"We've got no easy escape. I'll have to carve a path with my sword and see if we can fight our way out. You're a big man, so I assume you can take care of yourself. With those muscles, you must have quite a punch."

"Actually, I only look that way."

"Only look it? Well, damn. In that case, fall in behind me and try to stay close. They're only a bunch of peasants and townsfolk, so we should be fine."

"But we're so outnumbered."

"Numbers aren't what count in a fight; what counts is making the right first impression. Just watch how I slice this guy up."

But when he tried to lower his center of balance to draw his sword, he discovered he was too hemmed in by the press of bodies around him to drop his hips even the slightest bit.

"Sure does cramp my style," he muttered to himself, but suddenly the whole crowd was pouncing on him, so to hell with lowering his center of balance, he swiftly pulled his sword, *shinnng*, and in the same motion cut through the arm of the man standing next to him, *chok*, sending a forearm tumbling through the air as blood spurted from the stump it had been separated from.

With the spray hitting him in the face, Jūnoshin shouted, "Bring it on, you morons!"

The Bellyshakers fell back, stunned by the sight of the severed limb from one of their own. But Jūnoshin's challenger was already exhorting the crowd again.

"Well, bully for him—he can lop off a man's arm. How about we do the same to his head? Rip it right off with our bare hands! Are you with me, folks? What're you so afraid of spewing for, you spineless cowards!" he bellowed, and the throng was closing in again when a woman's voice rang out from the back of the tent.

"Stop!"

There was authority in the voice. Not only did it halt the crowd in its tracks, but it made Jūnoshin lower his sword. The tent fell silent as the woman strode forward to face Jūnoshin.

It was Ron.

She obviously held great sway here—no doubt because of her connection with head honcho Chayama. The man who'd been denouncing Jūnoshin offered a polite "Sister Ron!" and then said no more; the rest of the crowd stood in mute silence, as if struck with awe.

But on second thought, nothing he'd seen so far suggested this group had any real discipline. *Could it be,* he wondered, *that the authority she appeared to command came not from her proximity to power but from her own peerless, even sublime, beauty?*

At any rate, such was her beauty as to give rise to this thought in Jūnoshin's mind: the incomparable sheen of her hair; the long, slender stretch of her limbs; the glow she seemed to cast on everything around her.

He could scarcely believe that he'd thought her a mere child when he first set eyes on her in Ushichiku.

Her dazzling countenance held him rapt for several long moments before he realized that he needed to say something.

"Much obliged, Ron," he said, and then mentally kicked himself. *Am I a doofus or what?*

But Ron didn't seem to think any the worse of him for it. "Come with me," she said, taking his hand and leading him toward the back of the tent. Konji followed.

The crowd shifted to let them pass. Jūnoshin watched Ron out of the corner of his eye as they went.

When they reached the back wall, Ron lifted a flap and stepped on through. Since it was like the flap by which he and Konji had first entered, Jūnoshin expected it to lead back outside, but instead he found himself in a room about the size of ten tatami mats. What's going on here? he wondered. The ceiling was vaulted, the walls were plastered, and water dripping from above suggested they might actually be underground. Come to think of it, when Ron was leading him through the tent, it had felt as though they were walking slightly downhill.

In the middle of the room stood a large table with a clumsily-made bud vase in the middle holding two forlorn-looking flowers—a chrysanthemum and a cockscomb. Chayama sat on the far side with his arms folded across his chest. A glass bowl with a lighted candle in it hung from the ceiling nearby. Shadows played across Chayama's eccentric face in its flickering yellow light.

Ron proceded around the table and sat down next to him. Osamu was already standing motionless behind him.

Not quite sure what the appropriate greeting should be under the circumstances, Jūnoshin half-hoped Konji might say something first and threw a glance his way, but the big man stood staring into space like a brainless oaf.

I suppose he figures he can have his head in the clouds because I'll do all the talking, he thought to himself in a fit of annoyance. But then again, the man was only an agent. If they had drawn up an organizational chart for their little cabal, it would show the chain of command running from Naitō at the top, to Sugawara, to himself, and then to Konji at the bottom, so as the ranking member present, it was only natural that Jūnoshin should take the lead. There was simply no getting around it.

"Good evening, Master Chayama," he said, finally accepting the inevitable. "You appear to have a rousing success on your hands—with all these Bellyshakers."

His attempt at being affable seemed lost on Chayama, however, as the man continued to sit there mutely with his arms folded. *Say something, you friggin' freakface!* Jūnoshin fumed, but knowing he'd only be asking for trouble if he were to say it aloud, he held his tongue. On the other hand, he wasn't about to let the likes of Chayama intimidate him either, so he decided to dispense with any further formalities and get right down to business.

"You will be pleased to know, sir, that we regard the Bellyshaker endeavor as having fully achieved its objectives. We see no need for any additional expansion. As a matter of fact, in certain respects, things have already gone a bit too far. From our perspective, we were looking for a disturbance that would involve perhaps a hundred people. But what did we get? A thousand or more airheads running wild all over town. So first thing tomorrow, we need you to move toward shutting it down. In the meantime, the clan is mustering its troops, so you'll want to tell all those halfwits out there not to oppose them. Also to get rid of anything they might have in the way of weapons. The attack will begin at, well, let me think—let's say two in the afternoon. That should give you ample time to spread the word about throwing down weapons and not fighting back. Meanwhile, I'll let the troops know not to hit this tent, so be sure to stay in here during the assault. At exactly four, the troops will pull back. I imagine the better part of the crowd will have either dispersed or been killed by that point, but if there's anybody still left, you need to declare the party officially over. Two *ri* directly east of here is a mountain called Mt. Tokugo, part way up which you'll find a Buddhist temple called Geran-ji. Wait until dark and make your way there. At dawn the following morning, the clan will commence a search-and-destroy operation to mop up any lingering elements, so you don't want to be anywhere near town by then. If anybody tries to follow you to Geran-ji, tell Osamu to vaporize them. And as for you, Ron, we'd like you to come with us for the time being, to avoid a replay of what happened a minute ago. After returning to Hedaka tonight, we'll take you to Geran-ji before the attack tomorrow. Once the others join you there, we'll make sure you all get safely back to Ushichiku. Did you get all that?"

Jūnoshin kept a careful eye on Chayama as he detailed these instructions—most particularly because he had no intention of delivering the man back to Ushichiku. His real plan was to set fire to the tent during tomorrow's attack and burn him to death. But try as he might, he could glean no hint of what Chayama might be thinking beneath his lurid, weepy-smiley tattoos.

After sitting quietly for several moments, Chayama unfolded his arms.

"Stigger?"

"Yes?"

"And the other fellow—Konji was it?"

"Yes."

"Could I perhaps offer you two some head soup?"

Without waiting for a reply, he directed Ron and Osamu to go and get some soup for their guests. They disappeared through the tent flap and returned a few moments later, each bearing a steaming bowl and pair of chopsticks. Ron placed the bowl she carried on the table in front of Jūnoshin, and Osamu placed his in front of Konji.

The bowls held a clear soup, with pieces of something golden yellow, rather like sea urchin, floating in it. Jūnoshin sipped the broth, which was salty and slightly bitter—not the least bit tasty. Seeing him cock his head dubiously, Chayama spoke up again.

"It's not a question of how good or bad it may taste, nor of attainment or failure. It is purely a question of sin."

"A question of sin?"

"Yes, sin. Look closely at the soup. See how clear it is? With the heads of sinners, the broth becomes cloudy. When the heads are free of sin, the soup is clear. The difference is manifest. It is a form of trial by ordeal."

"I'm afraid I don't follow."

"Naturally, no one is without sin. Merely to exist in this false world is a sin. And yet that soup is clear. It is because I made it specially for you myself. The explanation is quite simple. At the moment I sever the head, that person's soul is spewed into the true world beyond. The head itself becomes an empty shell, like sloughed off skin, so it is no longer filled with sin. It makes better stock that way."

"Huh?"

Jūnoshin and Konji looked at each other in horror. For several long seconds, neither of them could move, but then Jūnoshin abruptly got to his feet.

"Excuse me while I go throw up," he said, and hurried out of the room. He returned a short while later, all color drained from his face. Likewise for Konji, who excused himself moments after Jūnoshin.

"Did you see that?" Jūnoshin hissed when Konji got back.

"See what?"

"If you have to ask, then never mind. Better you don't know."

As he hurried past the great cauldron on his way through the tent, Jūnoshin had seen human heads bubbling in the boiling broth. Locks of hair swirled about the surface like strands of seaweed. Detached eyeballs and ears and a swatch of skin with a nose protruding from it bobbed up and down. It was the first time he'd come face to face with the true savagery of the Bellyshaker Party.

What a fool he'd been to think they were just staging an event. In great dismay, he realized that it had taken on a life of its own and was no longer in their control. As he sat in stunned silence, Chayama spoke again.

"Why wait until tomorrow?" he said. "It's silly. Go tell the troops to attack without delay. The weather has already begun to move in reverse. Though only slowly at first, it will gradually build momentum and pick up speed. Then time will become untied. I told you before, you must always keep in mind that houses are built and houses are torn down. Have you been heeding that? Would you have us repair to the castle and burn it to the ground?"

"Excuse me?"

"I hope you'll never ask me to repeat myself again. The dwellings that people build in this world must all be leveled in the end. To demonstrate this in both the representational realm and the phenomenal realm, would you have me burn down the castle? For although I have burned a great many things in my time, what's most in need of burning right now is the castle."

It finally sank in that Chayama was serious about destroying Lord Kurae's stronghold.

"That wasn't the deal!" he shrieked, his voice rising to a hysterical pitch. "You weren't supposed to bring back the Bellyshakers for real! All we asked for was a small disturbance. What you've given us is total chaos. I mean, what do you expect me to do now? I can hardly show my face back in Hedaka with things as they are. So would you have me decamp? *Heh heh heh*, I thought I'd give that funny locution you've been using a spin, but it didn't come out quite the same, did it—like you're foisting responsibility on the other person? It sounded more like I was asking myself an unwelcome question. Well, to hell with it. I'm still owed money, but I think I'd probably better make myself scarce."

"That is not Egubo's will. You must go back to report on our activities. Let me remind you that I received these tattoos in Gifu. The world regains its entropy when the messiah's flowering heart spins back to its lowest point. This begets harmony. And harmony is the all-encompassing. You must not be so concerned about an appearance of harmony that you neglect true harmony. Return to your employer. Report back to him and tell him what you have seen and heard here."

Listening to Chayama's gibberish, Jūnoshin wondered if he shouldn't just pull out his sword and cut the man down. His main worry was that Ron might get angry with him.

But hell, he thought, *who cares if she gets mad? I should do him in anyway. That'll leave Jōji and Osamu... Whoa, whoa, whoa, what am I—a total idiot? Why should I have to bloody my own hands when I've got Osamu? Just lift Chayama into the air, and ka-boom. Use your head, man, use your head! The one catch is he'll only listen to Sugawara or Konji.*

"If you don't mind," he said to Chayama, "I need to speak with Konji a minute." Grabbing Konji's sleeve, he led the way through the flap into the tent.

The great cauldron was practically right under their noses. Trying not to look that way, he hissed, "I forgot about Osamu. He's our man."

"What're you talking about?" Konji said remotely.

"We can get Osamu to do his thing on Chayama and blow him to bits. I tell you, I had absolutely no idea how stark raving mad this guy was."

Still all Konji offered was a tepid, "Oh. Uh-huh."

He had a good reason for being in something of a funk.

The name of that reason was Ron.

As a matter of fact, he harbored an excruciating crush on the woman. But when she'd come to their rescue in the midst the Bellyshaker mob, she'd only seemed to notice Jūnoshin, and hadn't given Konji so much as a glance. Then on top of that, she'd actually taken Jūnoshin's hand as she led them through the crowd, and she'd been giving him eyes all through their meeting with Chayama. The only reasonable conclusion he could reach was that Ron loved Jūnoshin, and this had been a far greater jolt to him than the contents of the roiling cauldron. It was driving him out of his mind to think of it, and yet now, the detestable man who'd stolen Ron's heart was blithely talking to him about blowing Chayama up. He really couldn't bear it. He knew perfectly well that he was being jealous, and that he shouldn't allow personal feelings to affect his job performance, so he was trying to maintain a professional attitude, but the best he could muster when they put their heads together was a halfhearted *Oh* and *Uh-huh*.

Unaware of Konji's inner turmoil, and never having anticipated any need for discussion to begin with, Jūnoshin barely even waited for his response. "Good. I'll go get him then," he said. Stepping back to the flap, he stuck his head through. "Could we see you out here a minute, Osamu?"

A few moments later, Osamu came through the flap smiling cheerfully.

"Here's the deal," Jūnoshin said in a whisper. "Chayama's got to go. We want you to use that power of yours to blow him up."

But instead of obediently doing as he was told, Osamu started to hem and haw.

"Huh? B-blow him up? I-I-I don't know… B-blow him up? That doesn't seem… I-I mean, I don't think… I-I-I don't think I should do that."

For all his considerable size, the man had given no sign of having a will of his own before this, so the pushback came as a surprise to Jūnoshin. But he had little doubt he could argue him into submission.

"It's not a question of what you think. It's a question of obligation. You haven't forgotten how good Master Sugawara was to you?"

"No."

"And Konji here was very good to you as well?"

"Yes."

"Well, there you have it. This isn't coming from me. It's coming from Master Sugawara and Konji. They're the ones asking you to do it. Isn't that right, Konji?"

"Uh-huh," he grunted, though without looking either of them in the eye.

"See. What'd I tell you? When somebody does you a favor and then later asks you for a favor in return, don't you have an obligation to do it?"

"Yes, sir."

"Then you need to go and repay the favor."

"Yes, sir."

"We'll wait for you here. Bring Miss Ron back with you when you're done. We'll all go together to find Master Sugawara. There'll even be monkeys there for you to play with. I bet you like monkeys, don't you?"

"Yes, sir."

"All right, then. Time's a wasting. What's keeping you? Chop chop."

But in spite of Jūnoshin's repeated urging, Osamu didn't budge. He stood looking quite ill at ease for several moments, until finally he looked up and said, "I-I-I can't. I-I-I just can't do, do, do it."

Jūnoshin was furious. Who did he think he was, talking back like that? But he knew Chayama would hear if he raised his voice, so he held his anger in check.

"Why the hell not?" he squeezed out between gritted teeth.

Osamu seemed taken aback by the sudden menace in Jūnoshin's tone, and a bead of sweat trickled from his brow, but he stood his ground.

"Well, um, Master Chayama has been very good to me, too. Very, very good."

Jūnoshin was opening his mouth to ratchet up the pressure, when Chayama poked his face through the tent flap.

"Hello there."

Jūnoshin thought his heart would pop right out of his chest.

"Whew, you startled me. Boy, did you startle me. I wish you wouldn't startle me like that," he prattled as he tried to regain his composure. "In case you wondered, we're planning a birthday party for Osamu. It's his birthday tomorrow, you see."

"Never mind the lies. I can pretty well guess that you were plotting to get rid of me."

"Oh, absolutely not, sir."

"But you're wasting your time. Osamu is now my raging soul. My flying sash ornament. Though that's not to say that Ron is my placid soul. Can you come here, Ron?"

"What is it?"

"I'm about to offend your ears with stipulations for after the darkening of the light, so I need you to listen to me carelessly. You and Osamu are to go with the two men now in our presence, and in a company of four with the two men now in our presence, repair to the place where the employer of the two men now in our presence awaits their return. There you are to abide and recover your harmony. Jōji and I will see to the burning of this place and the castle. We will burn them to the ground."

"Yes, sir."

"And if Stigger here should try to make a break for it, tell Osamu to send him to Spewdom. You'll find a lantern over there. Take it with you."

"Yes, sir."

The moment Ron assented, Jūnoshin knew his only choice was to go peacefully back to Hedaka. He would worry about what came next after he got there.

They crossed the now-empty tent and emerged into the open. The bellyshaking was continuing all up and down the riverbed, and the drumbeat from the tower was at a fever pitch. Hundreds of bodies jostled about in the light of the many bonfires, and it appeared to Jūnoshin like something out of a dream.

The river itself was a black streak in the darkness, its face glittering with light. Some of the crowd had waded in, and were shaking their bellies as they stood shin-deep in the water.

One over-exuberant fellow leapt from the middle of Genga Bridge as he shook. The river was only about a foot deep in that spot, running over a solid bed of rocks. He broke his neck and died on impact.

As unabated anarchy reigned, the company of four slipped quietly out of town to make their way toward Hedaka by way of the Takeda Highway. The road took a winding path along the foot of the mountains. Dense growths of bamboo climbed the hillside to the left and stretched to the edge of a drop-off on the right, beneath which they could hear the rush of a river.

Walking in the lead with the light, Osamu let out a gasp and stopped short. When he lifted his lantern, its dim pool of light lit up a fallen samurai with naked sword in hand, surrounded by several limbless bodies. To the left of the road stood a gate topped with a roof of fine hinoki bark, and a narrow path could be seen leading into the bamboo forest beyond.

"The one is obviously a samurai," said Jūnoshin, "and I imagine the others are Bellyshakers. Go check them out, will you, Konji?"

"Huh? Me?"

"Yeah. Could you go check them out?"

"Right, I got that. It's just that it doesn't seem right."

"What doesn't seem right?"

"Actually, it's been bothering me from before how you seem to think you can tell me what to do. Except you're not really my boss, right? I mean, I'm only working for Lord Naitō, so far as I'm aware. And that's who you're working for, too. Which should make us equals, seems to me. So where do you get the idea you can boss me around all the time? I don't get it."

He had raced through this little speech without stopping, glancing repeatedly in Ron's direction and becoming more and more worked up as he went. Now it took him a moment to catch his breath.

Good grief, thought Jūnoshin wearily. *Why does he have to choose this particular moment to raise such an awkward subject? It's not as if I'm hanging out with him because I love his company. We were thrown together purely by chance. And now I'm supposed to listen to him bleating on and on with his eyebrows shooting in peaks? Sheesh! But I don't dare argue with him because it'll only put him in a worse tizzy and make our messy little situation here even messier, so I guess I better let him have his way on this one.*

"In that case," he said, turning to Osamu, "could you accompany me with the lantern?" As he started toward the fallen figures, he muttered under his breath, "What a royal pain in the ass. Who does he think he is, anyway? At any rate, I don't like this. It's hardly good news to discover that Bellyshakers have made it this far out already. But the guy they tangled with was obviously no slouch, either. Just look at all the arms and legs he sliced off. Hello? Is he still breathing?"

Jūnoshin stepped over a severed forearm with a sickle in its grip and looked down at the fallen man's face.

"Holy cow!"

It was none other than Manabe Gosenrō—superhuman swordsman, fencing instructor, and assassin for hire. Jūnoshin's very own childhood friend.

"Hey, Grub!" he shouted, squatting down next to him. "You all right? Can you hear me?"

Watching from a distance, Konji and Ron could see that Jūnoshin had recognized the victim. They came hurrying up.

"You know him?"

"Yeah, he's an old friend. Name's Manabe Gosenrō. He's actually an old friend of Chayama's, too."

"You don't say," Konji said, his tone thick with sarcasm.

What's his problem this time? thought Jūnoshin, having just about had it with the man's attitude. But it seemed too much trouble to explain so he simply said, "That's right."

"Uh-huh. You don't say," Konji repeated, and then almost immediately went on. "It just so happens that I once saw you meeting secretly with this man at a local tavern."

"Ah, so the master sleuth has been at work. In that case, I guess you already know everything, so I don't need to fill you in."

"That's about the size of it," Konji said smugly, but beneath the surface he was roiling, for although he had indeed witnessed Jūnoshin and Manabe talking over drinks, the truth was that his professional pride still stung from having come away without a clue about their connection. And since he'd been out of the room when Chayama revealed he was Jūnoshin's boyhood neighbor Saomu—first rolling on the ground in the courtyard trying not to laugh, and then mesmerized by Ron's incomparable beauty—he knew nothing about that side of the story either. What he didn't know about the three of them was eating him up.

He could feel his stomach tightening into a knot. He wanted to scream, but the fact that Ron was there held him back. He felt like he was being driven deeper and deeper into a corner.

The attack at Manabe's home had taken place approximately one hour earlier.

Unaware of the events in town, the eccentric loner was passing a solitary evening at home—drinking saké, plucking on his samisen, and belting out some of his favorite tunes. Such were his oddball pleasures.

By unhappy coincidence, just as he was reaching top form, the six Bellyshaker bumpkins came along the stretch of road out front.

There were no other houses in the vicinity, so the bamboo grove was serenely quiet. But then the sound of Manabe singing at the top of his lungs reached them, and they gleefully smashed through the gate, broke down his door, and thronged inside to shake their bellies.

The fiercely independent man who jealously guarded his privacy and had no use for company saw his home being invaded by a band of strangers. Right when he had on a nice buzz to boot. It was unforgivable. He reached for his sword and leapt to his feet.

"I'll teach you to trespass on my property!" he yelled.

Now normally, given his superhuman mastery of the sword, he would have dispatched a mere six men in a trice. But on those nights when he took out his samisen to play, he had a habit of drinking himself quite blind, and the advanced state of his inebriation rendered him barely able to stand.

Even so, once his sword was out, it seemed to have a bracing effect, and he managed to take one man down. But the others were too hopped up on shaking their bellies to be intimidated. One of them picked up a scrap of wood and swung it at Manabe's head.

Thanks to his extensive training, he was able to dodge a direct hit, but with alcohol to slow his reflexes, the blow caught him on the shoulder and knocked him to a knee. At that, the Bellyshakers seemed to lose interest and turned to go, raising a string of scornful hoots as they tore and smashed their way back out of the house and down the path to the road. But powered by a surge of rage, Manabe staggered back to his feet and followed, overtaking them just as they reached the road, where *chok! chokk! chokkk!*—in very short order he'd scattered sixteen limbs on the ground. His only mistake had been to lose count and let down his guard after finishing off the fourth man. When he paused to catch his breath, his head began to swim, and he sank to the ground—which gave the last fellow a chance to sneak up from behind and bash him in the head with a hefty stone.

The blow cracked open his skull and knocked him senseless, but as he fell, his sword swept sideways and sliced the man clean in two.

It was an instantaneous reflex. Only a true master of the sword's deepest secrets could have carried out such a feat even after his brain had been crushed.

And so it was that Manabe came to be lying on the brink of death in the middle of the road.

"At any rate, there's nothing we can do for him here. We'll need to take him with us to Hedaka. Konji, go grab a storm shutter for a stretcher, will you? Or rather, let me rephrase that, since I wouldn't want you to grouse about me bossing you around again. My dear Konji, I wonder if you'd be so kind as to retrieve a storm shutter from the house?"

"So it's still just Konji, is it? Still no 'Master'? Uh-huh. Well, I suppose I can let it slide this time. I shall be back shortly."

Jūnoshin watched Konji disappear through the gate and heaved a weary sigh. "The next question's obviously going to be who gets to carry it. He's bound to make a stink if I ask him to, so I suppose it'll have to be Osamu and me. What a pain," he muttered.

"Master Kakari, look," Ron said.

"What?"

"The sky is red."

He looked the way she was pointing, and sure enough, the sky to the west was lit up with color even though darkness had long since fallen. Chayama had set the castle afire.

"Wow, you're right. Red as can be," he said, as he stood gaping at the sky.

Nagaoka Shume cocked his head uncertainly as he went about assembling items for the monkey show backstage.

The troupe's dramatic repertoire had always been limited to either "The Soga Brothers" or "The Subscription List," and he needed no special consultations with Ōura to get the necessary props and costumes ready for those shows. The items themselves were all quite minimalist, of course, given that they were to be worn or handled by monkeys. There was never any question about the cast, either, since the actors were always the same—"The Soga Brothers" being performed by Lulu, Tarō, and Torué; "The Subscription List" by Hedemo, Hentarō, and Shii.

But Ōura had told him they would be performing "The Egret's Song" today. This was an original one-act that he had written himself, and he had once let Shume see the script.

The story begins with a scene where several young egrets are roughing up one of their elders. A man happens by (it is in fact the great Buddhist holy man Kūkai), and his heart goes out to the victim of the abuse. "Stop that right away," he admonishes the youngsters. "That's no way to treat your elders."

"He's only getting what he deserves," the youngsters protest, and together they explain why. The old fellow had come into the tavern they operated and downed three cups of shōchū along with a plate of fenneled broad beans and three grilled skewers, then started to walk out without paying. When they blocked his path and demanded to know what he thought he was doing, he'd blithely shrugged that he didn't have any money.

After listening to their account, the man (in fact the great Kūkai) says, "Under the circumstances, I can certainly see why you would feel wronged. But perhaps the fellow has some circumstances of his own. Let us also hear his side of the story."

With some urging, the old egret begins telling his unhappy tale. Once upon a time he had served as chamberlain to a great lord, administering wisely and commanding the respect of all who knew him near and far. But among his colleagues was a man with a twisted mind and heart as black as night, whose vicious slanders ultimately caused him to be driven from office. As he drifted from place to place, his eyesight began to fail, as did his ability to fly, and since he could no longer forage for himself, he had fallen prey to want and ordered food and drink for which he had no means of paying.

By the time the egret finishes his lengthy tale of woe, the man (in fact the great Kūkai) has quite lost patience with the heavy doses of self-pity it contained, but given his established reputation as a holy man, he doesn't feel he can simply walk away. "He deserves sympathy for what he's had to go through," he tells the youngsters. "You should forgive him."

But they won't hear of it. "I don't see how that's any kind of excuse," one of them says.

Their unwillingness infuriates the man (in fact the great Kūkai). "Well, if you're that devoid of compassion, then you're beyond the pale," he fumes. "You might be interested to know that I am the legendary Kūkai. Let's see what you think of this," he says, and promptly turns them all into weatherfish.

"There," he says, turning to the old egret. "I imagine you're still pretty hungry. Help yourself to some fresh fish."

The egret replies, "They may be weatherfish now, but they were my own kind before. When I think of their sad plight, I couldn't possibly eat them. I appreciate the gesture, but no thanks."

Kūkai is deeply moved. "I must commend you. You have a noble heart. As a reward, I will transform you into a monkey."

And with that, he turns the elderly egret into a monkey, and restores the weatherfish to their former state as young egrets.

In a flood of joyful tears, the new monkey and the rehabilitated egrets thank Kūkai over and over. They vow to each other that they will always hold compassion in their hearts from this day forward, and come to the aid of any monkeys or egrets they see in distress.

Kūkai looks on with a smile as they fall into a circle to sing and dance in celebration. Then, before anybody knows it, he is gone. Their joyful singing goes on and on, echoing high into the sky.

It was obvious to Shume from the start that it was not the sort of thing that could actually be performed on stage.

Even apart from its content, the simple fact that it was a wholly new work presented a major hurdle. Monkey shows are defined by parody: their humor rests in seeing animals who cannot possibly perform like humans attempting nevertheless to do exactly that; the audience is entertained by how far their performance falls short of the original. But for this to work, the audience must already be familiar with the underlying story, and that is not possible when the script is an original work.

To compensate for this shortcoming, Ōura had woven the well-known figure of Kūkai into the story and had him perform a miracle in accordance with his legend, which everybody could be expected to know. But the story's center of gravity remained elsewhere, in the hard-luck laments of the elderly egret that comprised by far the greatest bulk of the performance in terms of both dialogue and event—none of which the audience could be acquainted with beforehand.

The idea of monkeys playing egrets was also problematic. Playing Kūkai was acceptable because it fit within the normal methods of parody, but outside those parameters, it was basically impossible to see the monkeys on stage as anything but monkeys, and to expect the audience to believe a monkey was an egret was simply asking too much—not to mention, those egrets then had to be transformed into weatherfish for a brief spell before being restored as egrets, and even the odd one out had to play an egret who has suddenly found himself turned into a monkey. Even with the natural gifts Shume brought to the task, he couldn't be expected to coax such complex nuances out of the performers, and no matter what kind of clever twists he might come up with for staging the events, the audience was bound to end up thoroughly confused. As a matter of fact, even an experienced cast of human actors would have difficulties with this script.

"Hoo boy," he murmured as he finished reading, trying to hide his dismay behind a watery smile.

Since Ōura had said nothing more about it after that, Shume assumed he had decided to scrap the whole thing. But then today, out of the blue, Ōura had announced that he wanted to perform the play for Lord Naohito.

You'll never take the high councilor out of this man, thought Shume. *He may say, 'I'm a plain old monkey trainer now, just call me Shuzie,' but inside, where he really lives, he still sees himself as the big shot he used to be, and he expects me to hop to when he expresses his wishes. Peh. High and mighty to the end.*

Then, as Shume was already gritting his teeth at his boss's fiat, Ōura threw him another curve: he ordered him to prepare Deusu Nobu'uzu for the role of Kūkai.

Deusu Nobu'uzu was not a monkey to be trifled with. Even Shume, with his demonstrated gifts as a trainer, found himself at a loss when it came to this creature.

Most incredibly, the monkey had somehow learned to speak human language.

He was, in effect, a volunteer, who had come down from the mountains of his own accord to live at the Bureau of Monkey Affairs not long after it was first established. His unusually large frame prompted a quip that he was built like a rice mortar, so they decided to call him Deusu, meaning "big mortar." Deeming him too old to learn new tricks, Shume mostly left him to his own devices instead of trying to train him, but one day, when he was cleaning the box seats, he got the odd feeling that he was being watched and turned to see Deusu standing behind him, looking very much as if he had something to say.

He smiled. "What's up, Deusu?" he said playfully. "Did you have something you wanted to tell me?"

The monkey shook his head as if to say no before turning on his heels and walking off toward his quarters.

Shume felt a chill go down his spine. The monkey's mannerisms and bearing were just like those of a human.

He told himself he was imagining things, but when it happened again, and then again, it became increasingly difficult to dismiss it as his mind playing tricks on him, or as some other fluke.

For a time, he still kept it to himself, mulling it over privately. But when the pregnant looks continued, and Deusu even gave him a thumbs-up with a smile, he decided he'd better mention it to his boss. Ōura initially had the same response, attributing it to Shume's overactive imagination, but once he began paying closer attention, he too could see the signs suggesting that Deusu understood human language. He realized there was a serious question that needed to be addressed.

"I suppose we could try asking him," he said.

"How, exactly?"

"Just ask him point blank, 'Can you understand what I'm saying?'"

"All right. But…?" Shume trailed off.

"But what?"

"Do you really think he'll give us a straight answer?"

"There's only one way to find out. Go find him and bring him here."

This had been Ōura's standard operating procedure during his many long years as one of Lord Kuroae's top advisors: to summon the individuals involved and question them. Even so, it felt decidedly odd to be doing that with a monkey.

The interview took place in one of the box seats. As Shume led Deusu in, he displayed none of the squirreliness so typical of monkeys, carrying himself instead in a poised and attentive manner that seemed to say: *What is it? I understand you have something to ask me.*

The oddity of the situation hit Ōura a second time as he watched Deusu sit down in front of him. He perched on the railing with his legs crossed, sitting erect with his chest thrust forward and both hands on his knees. It was a pose reminscent of some hotshot impresario.

In working with monkeys, Ōura had become fond of the way their short legs swelled in the middle and tapered sharply to the ankles. He thought it was cute. But Deusu's legs showed none of this typical form.

He momentarily found himself uncertain how to proceed. Should he address Deusu as he would a person, or did he need to stick to his usual way with the monkeys? Still wavering, he decided he'd simply have to plunge in.

"Look here, Deusu. There's something I wanted to ask you. Don't worry, it's nothing particularly difficult, okay? Are you listening to me, Deusu? Good. Now, I'm going to ask you a question, and if your answer is yes, I want you to raise your right hand, okay? Got that? For yes, raise your right hand, and for no, raise your left hand. Are you ready?"

He watched Deusu for a response. The monkey had been nodding his head up and down as he listened, but instead of raising either hand, he just stared back at Ōura with eyes that seemed to say: *Well? Fire away.*

Ōura took care to speak slowly. "Do you understand the language we speak?"

Deusu said nothing, nor did he raise a hand. He merely stuck a finger in his ear and scratched.

Ōura tried again. "I'm asking if you understand our language, Deusu. Raise your right hand if you do."

Deusu still failed to raise his hand, but his answer was as good as if he had.

"Do you mind if I just skip the rigamarole and answer this way instead?" he said.

"I think I'm going out of my mind," Shume gasped.

Ōura felt much the same way as the enormity of what he had just witnessed sent a shudder through him, but his curiosity soon overcame the shock and he was able to go on.

"How is it that you can speak?" he asked.

"Well, how is it that *you* can speak?" he shot back, and continued to offer similar responses in the exchange that followed—deftly deflecting Ōura's most burning question about what had led a monkey to gain the power of speech. But he did volunteer a number of other bits of information.

"You call me Deusu, but my real name is Nobu'uzu," he said. "I don't mind, though. I also like the name you gave me."

"You keep feeding us chestnuts and acorns, but to be honest, they're really not to our taste. We're generally partial to white rice."

"I'm perfectly well aware that I'm still just a monkey. I suppose you could say I'm biding my time right now, waiting for opportunity to knock. In the meantime, I do rather like it here. It's like living in a sanitarium, or in some secluded utopian community."

And so on.

Deusu's first words, spoken so matter-of-factly, had sent penetrating chills up and down their spines, but as Ōura and Shume went about their routines from one day to the next, exchanging good-mornings and good-nights with him and chatting about whatever happened to come up, the monkey's ability to speak soon came to seem like the most natural thing in the world. Not only that, but it gave the trainers an avenue for insight into aspects of simian psychology previously inaccessible to any human being. For example, it came out that monkeys have no problem at all jumping up onto a square pedestal, but for some reason they find triangular ones terrifying; also that they dislike wobbly foods, like blocks of *konnyaku* jelly or anything made with agar. Deusu had quickly come to fill a crucial intermediary function between the humans and the monkeys, listening to what each side had to say and communicating it to the other.

But they never selected him to take a role on stage.

Although a number of different reasons could be cited for this, first among them was the concern that it would simply be too overwhelming for the audience if he were to come out in front of them and begin reciting lines. Hearing a monkey speak for the first time had given Ōura and Shume a tremendous jolt even though they had already suspected he might be capable of speech. They truly wondered if they could be losing their minds. What effect would such an event have on peasants and townsfolk without the slightest inkling? Who knew how many of them might really go mad?

And even for those who didn't *go* mad, you had to expect they would *get* plenty mad. When people encounter something they don't understand, they have one of two responses: they either accept it without much thought, or they see red. Once provoked, the audience could turn into a rioting mob, or they might report to the authorities that the monkey commissioner was doing things that suggested ties to banned Christian sorcery—neither of which development Ōura or Shume wished to risk.

But the more significant reason rested in Deusu himself. From his physical bearing, to the way he spoke, and to the entire aura he projected, he simply didn't have the *je ne sais quoi* of an actor, and for him to actually appear on stage seemed about as improbable as James Brown singing a Kiyomoto ballad to the accompaniment of a samisen. He projected a certain dignified air, which acted as a barrier to any thought of asking if he might be interested in performing—though this is not to suggest that Deusu behaved in a particularly self-important manner.

And yet today, Ōura was tapping Deusu to take the lead in "The Egret's Song," of all things, and had ordered Shume to prepare the necessary props and costumes.

"What could he possibly be thinking?" Shume muttered aloud as he went about his assigned task. "If he weren't the boss, I'd give him a good rap on the head with my fan,"

Just then the door slid open with a sharp rattle and Ōura stepped into the room, sending Shume into a panic.

"Oh, oh, um, um, I, I—"

"What're you getting in a dither about?"

"Right, that is, um, it's the egret's costume, sir. I can't find anything like what the script calls for, and I'm at wits' end."

"In that case, you can stop worrying. The play's been canceled."

"Canceled? Whew, that's a relief."

"No, it's not a relief at all," Ōura said.

Shume shot to his feet. "My deepest apologies, sir!" he said. "I didn't mean it's a relief that your play won't be performed."

"I'm not talking about the play."

Ōura briefly filled him in on what was happening with the Bellyshakers in town.

"I'm sorry to hear that," Shume said, feeling all his worries melting away. It ought to have been of much greater concern to him that the clan on which his livelihood depended was facing an existential crisis, but he was just happy to have "The Egret's Song" out of his hair. Though now a monkey trainer, his mind still worked like that of a low-ranking functionary or salaryman.

"Everybody's gathered in the longhouse," Ōura said. "You should come, too."

"As soon as I get things cleaned up here," Shume said, and let out a quiet little *hyuk*.

In the longhouse, an informal debate was underway. The majority were clamoring for all-out war.

"Bellyshaker Party? What a laugh! Who cares how many there are—they're nothing but a common rabble. I'll personally boot every last one of them into the next province," boomed one retainer, with cheeks puffed and eyes slits as he jerked his head from side to side.

"A volley or two from the musket corps, and the idiots'll go crying home to their mommies. *Ah hah hah hah hah, hack hack hack, ghurk*," another burst out boisterously, before choking on his own excess of enthusiasm.

"*Hmph*. So the guy behind it all is some twerp named Chayama Hanrō? Who does he think he is? I'll slice him up in one quick flash of this," blustered another would-be hero, slapping the hilt of his sword with a ferocious glare.

In short, the troops were eagerly thumping their chests.

Suddenly there was a loud pounding at the front of the building. *Bam bam bam bam bam.* The man closest to the door called out, "Who's there?"

"Open up!" came the answering shout. "It's me! Kakari Jūnoshin!"

The man pulled the door aside. Behind Jūnoshin stood Konji and Osamu, bearing a bloodied figure on a storm shutter. Ron brought up the rear.

"We have a wounded man. Lay out a futon!" Jūnoshin said, his voice still raised with urgency.

The surprised retainers peered down at the stretcher and immediately recognized Manabe Gosenrō. But there was no doctor in Hedaka, and summoning one from town was out of the question. They gave him some shōchū with egg as a restorative, and did what they could to patch up his wounds with a few scraps of cloth they managed to scrounge up.

While keeping one eye on the first-aid being rendered, Jūnoshin turned to the man who'd opened the door. "I need to speak with Lord Naitō," he said.

Naitō was going over options with Naohito on the other side of the folding screen when the doorman came to relay Jūnoshin's request.

"It seems Kakari Jūnoshin is back, my lord," Naitō informed Naohito.

"Is that right?"

"He will have the latest word. If you'll excuse me, I'll go see what he has to report."

"There's no need to excuse yourself. Have him shown in and take his report right here."

"It would be unfitting for a man of such low rank to address you directly, my lord,"

"It's fine. I don't mind in the least."

"But I'm afraid it's quite unheard of to—"

"I'm saying it's fine, so let it go," Naohito snapped, out of patience with Naito's repeated objections. Once the lord had made up his mind, he brooked no further argument.

For his part, Naitō had been maneuvering to hear Jūnoshin's account in private, so that he could decide what his master would actually hear—coloring things to his own advantage and omitting anything that might be to his detriment.

"Besides," Naohito added, "we are now effectively at war. It's no time to be quibbling about proper protocol. Show him in at once. No wait. On second thought, once we've heard his report, the next step will obviously be to call a meeting of the whole, so why waste time, let's just go straight to the meeting. Everybody can hear what the fellow has to say, then we'll throw the floor open for discussion. Make it so."

He had given the order, and his order was law. A council of war was promptly convened with Naitō presiding over the proceedings.

Lord Naohito sat facing his retainers at the front of the room. Ōura and Shume were in attendance as well. Ron, Osamu, and Konji withdrew to the monkey house.

"All right, Kakari," Naitō said to the ronin. "Perhaps you can start things off by giving us the latest on developments in town."

It was not without some trepidation that he set the ball rolling. Reasonable and proper as it was for Lord Naohito to order this meeting, there were times when doing what was reasonable and proper could lead to all manner of complications and invite nothing but trouble.

Meanwhile, Jūnoshin found himself in a quandary. What exactly was he supposed to tell the lord here? When he departed for town earlier in the day, he had promised to bring the disturbance under control, but things hadn't exactly worked out the way he planned, or to put it more plainly—though no one else in the room could possibly know it yet—the castle had been torched! To candidly relate this fact here might well prompt his immediate demise. *You claimed to be an expert, but you didn't have a clue, you dirty fraud. Off with your head!* And yet, what else could he do? Concoct a lie? It would be only a matter of time before the truth came out anyway. Considering and dismissing a variety of options in the space of little more than an instant, he concluded his best course was to make a clean breast of it.

His decision was based in large part on the sense he had gained of Naohito's character. He knew the lord was a man of principle who tolerated no nonsense. Far from being a threat to him, this ought to mean that, so long as Jūnoshin didn't attempt to obfuscate, Naohito would accept the report for what it was, regardless of what he had accomplished or failed to accomplish in town. Instincts he had cultivated through many long years of freelancing told Jūnoshin that his best bet for negotiating his way through this tight spot was straight talk.

So he laid out the facts as he had witnessed them: The badly wounded man they'd hauled in on a stretcher was fencing instructor Manabe Gosenrō. The town was teeming with Bellyshakers as if a grand festival was in progress; it was also being systematically destroyed by them. Arson, robbery, rape, and murder were rampant. The largest assembly of the fanatics was in the dry bed of the Yōrei River, where they were dancing up a dust storm. Many of them appeared to have lost their senses. Chayama Hanrō had brazenly defied Jūnoshin's instructions and declared his intent to set fire to the castle. Then he had made good on the threat. The castle was burning even now.

Jūnoshin offered only the facts, unadulterated by any subjective assessments.

As anticipated, Lord Naohito erupted with rage.

"We must march for town at once to put down these brigands! The castle is the ultimate symbol of peace and order in our domain. How dare they set it afire? It's an outrage we cannot let pass! Round them all up, tear them limb from limb, and stuff their parts in field latrines with a *So there!* My horse! Bring me my horse!"

But Naitō caught hold of Naohito's robe as he started to rise.

"I must beg you to remain seated, my lord."

"You expect me to sit still while my castle is burning? Unhand me, Naitō!"

"We must not be hasty, my lord. This is war. We will be courting defeat if we rush into action without a well-considered plan. To lash out blindly in the heat of the moment may feel bold, but it is not true courage. The true measure of courage is in bearing patiently while the necessary preparations are made, and then to crush the enemy decisively when the time has ripened."

The principle was sound, and Lord Naohito could not naysay it.

"*Hrumph.* I suppose I have no choice. I don't like it, but I'll just have to grit my teeth," he said as he sank back onto his cushion.

With a sigh of relief, Naitō turned to face the gathering and urged, "If you have any thoughts on the matter, now is the time to speak. This needs to be a candid discussion. You should feel free to state your views without restraint."

A retainer named Mutō raised a hand. "If I may," he said.

"Speak."

"I wholeheartedly support the chief councilor's position. It is vital that we proceed with caution."

Another raised his hand.

"Speak."

"I agree. To put it plainly, the enemy is two thousand strong, while we are fewer than a hundred. And to make matters worse, none of us is equipped for battle. We left our quivers and muskets and such back at the castle, which is already going up in flames. Our spears and armor are at home, but it sounds like those homes are also likely to have been destroyed. Thank goodness our families managed to get out in time and escape to the western border post. You're sure about that, aren't you, Kakari?"

"Yes, indications are that nearly everyone got out safely," he lied, hoping to head off any questions of responsibility.

"In any case, as I say, we are weaponless. Under the circumstances it's imperative that we await further news and proceed with utmost caution."

"I also urge caution."

"Hear hear."

"Absolutely."

The men who'd been sounding the drumbeats of war only a short time before were suddenly urging a wait-and-see approach, one and all. Even before hearing Jūnoshin's account, they'd seen what the Bellyshakers had done to Manabe Gosenrō, the most accomplished fighter they knew, and it had struck fear in their hearts.

It was quite the sorry spectacle for men who drew regular stipends in exchange for a pledge to put their lives on the line in wartime.

One of them was sufficiently discomfited to raise a different point.

"Councilor, if I may?"

"Go ahead."

"What I'd like to know is how the situation was allowed to get so out of hand. And since I believe you were the one officially in charge of dealing with the Bellyshaker threat, I can't help feeling that much of the responsibility falls directly on your shoulders. In fact, when it comes right down to it, our present predicament would seem to be entirely your fault. Have you given any thought to committing hara-kiri."

"Wh–what kind of question is that? This is no time for pointing fingers. We should be concentrating on how best to overcome the enemy. Isn't that right, my lord?"

"Actually, I was asking myself the same thing. You gave me to believe, in no uncertain terms, that the situation was being taken care of. So why didn't that happen? When I'm told something will happen and then it doesn't, it means something's definitely wrong, and I need to know what the problem was."

Naitō became flustered. "W-w-well, that is, it's this man Kakari Jūnoshin who's the actual expert in these matters, and I was relying entirely on him, so he'll need to be the one to give you the particulars," he said, attempting to shift the blame onto the ronin.

Jūnoshin had seen this coming a long way off, and was ready with his response. "That is correct, my lord," he said without the slightest hesitation. "I am the expert on these matters. At Councilor Naitō's request, I have been doing everything in my power to prevent the Bellyshakers from gaining a foothold, right down to this very day. But my best efforts have now proved to be in vain. I therefore met with Bellyshaker leader Chayama Hanrō and ordered him to bring an end to the lawlessness. Unfortunately, he refused. The only explanation I can offer is that I came up short."

"You messed up."

"I messed up," Jūnoshin said crisply.

"I see. So, basically, the error was in who we chose for the job."

Lord Kuroae appeared satisfied that he had gotten his explanation, but a vociferous debate promptly erupted among the retainers about holding the person who hired such an incompetent contractor accountable. Those belonging to the former Ōura faction took the hardest line.

"Does this not call for Councilor Naitō to commit hara-kiri, my lord?"

"You must order him to slit his belly!"

Lord Naohito raised his voice over the clamor. "Quiet! Settle down! It's fine for us to have spent a few moments pursuing the question of responsibility, but before that, this room was filled with voices of caution—*we must be careful, we must be patient.* So what I want somebody to tell me now is: just how long are we supposed to wait? If we cool our heels here, are the heavens going to open up and shower us with weapons? What exactly is the plan? Who can tell me how we're going to take this bull by the horns?"

The retainers were all at a loss, and the room fell silent as everybody stared at the floor. Then a deep voice came from near the entrance.

"If I might be permitted to speak."

All eyes turned. A monkey sat in a formal position, just inside the door. It was Deusu Nobu'uzu.

Without taking his eyes off of the monkey, Lord Naohito said, "Ōura?"

"Yes, my lord."

"What is the meaning of this? I need an explanation."

"Deepest apologies, my lord. I'm sorry you've been subjected to such an unseemly display." He turned to the monkey and hissed, "This won't do, Deusu. We're in the great lord's presence and you're being rude. Begone now, begone. Do you hear me? Begone."

But the monkey didn't move. He simply sat there with a cheeky grin on his face, ignoring his master's exhortations.

In consternation, Ōura and Shume leapt to their feet and grabbed him from both sides to hustle him away, but Deusu let his whole body go limp and flopped heavily about, refusing to cooperate. His thick fur compounded the difficulty of getting a good grip, and they were still trying to gain control when the lord called out.

"Never mind, never mind. It's not a question of anything unseemly. I only wanted to know why I heard this monkey speak."

He seemed entirely unruffled, and spoke with the calm composure befitting a man of his station. The same could not be said for his retainers, however, nearly all of whom were frozen in shock, unable to move; some had even wet themselves.

Ōura released his hold on Deusu and prostrated himself. "I'm terribly, terribly sorry, my lord."

"There's no need to apologize. Just answer my question. How is it that this monkey can speak?"

"Indeed, my lord. I'm afraid I do not know."

"You don't know? And you think you can leave it at that? A monkey is uttering words just like you and me!"

"Indeed, my lord, I found it exceedingly curious as well and looked into it at some length, but to no avail."

"How can you call yourself monkey commissioner? Enough. I'll talk to the creature myself. Tell him to come forward."

"But that would be beyond all—"

"I said enough!"

"Very well, my lord. Deusu, you heard what the great lord said. He wishes you to approach."

"Yes, sir," the monkey replied, before moving forward to prostrate himself in front of Naohito.

"I can't see your face. Sit up."

"Yes, sir." Deusu did as he was told.

"Uh-huh. You're a monkey all right—no doubt about that. Do you have a name? You needn't worry about protocol. You may address me directly."

"My name is Deusu Nobu'uzu."

"Where are you from?"

"The mountains of Dewa."

"So, tell me, then. Why is it that you can speak?"

"I fear the answer to that question eludes even me. To a degree, any monkey can understand what people say to them. But normally, they're not actually conscious of language. They're only conscious of themselves and the world around them. In my case, though, I became aware at some point that my head was swimming with words. I then realized that these words represented a third entity besides myself and the world—and that they in fact opened up a whole new world besides the one I'd been living in all my life. I saw as well that the two worlds were skewered together by a sort of spit, and that this spit was none other than the processes of thought that were the inevitable result of gaining the power of speech. Which is to say, the world of words was skewered to the real world by means of something else derived from the words. It's a rather odd relationship, really. That's probably why nobody ever notices it. People don't, I mean—at least not normally. I happened to notice it because I was a speechless monkey. I think the true explanation most likely lies either in that cogitational spit itself, or in some other conceptual function emanating from it. In that sense, asking how I came about my power of speech is like trying to capture a mirage—no matter how you try to explain it, you just keep going in circles."

"I see. So there's no point in pursuing the question?"

"Exactly."

"That's quite profound. But the power of speech in a monkey is no idle business. I can't just ignore it."

"What do you intend to do?"

"A monkey talking for no good reason is a threat to the public order."

"So it's off with my head?"

"That's right."

"I see. Well, that's certainly your prerogative. But I need to warn you that executing me will pose an even greater threat to the public order," Deusu said with an insolent smirk.

Naohito vs. Deusu. The curious sight of their liege lord matching wits with a talking monkey set off a buzz of whispers among the retainers.

"He's certainly an articulate little devil."

"No kidding. It's mind-blowing. What's Ōura gotten us into?"

"Yeah, good question. But look at him. Even with all the big words he throws around, he's still at root a monkey. He doesn't have the first clue how to be polite, and he sits there scratching his butt right in front of the lord."

Naohito hurled his usual straight, fast ball. "Go on. Tell me how," he said, without cracking a smile.

"That's exactly what I wanted to do a while ago."

"You mean when you asked if you could speak? Fine. I'm listening."

"It relates to the subject of this meeting, which is to say, suppressing the Bellyshakers."

"What could a monkey possibly know about that?"

"There are some things only a monkey can know."

"Very well. Let's hear it."

"All right. As I was listening a while ago, I heard considerable concern about the limited size of your fighting force, and I thought in that case I might be able to help."

"What're you trying to say? That you have a vast army of foot soldiers at your beck and call?"

Deusu smiled. "Not in the sense you mean—that would be asking a bit much. After all, though I may be able to talk, I'm still only a monkey. But you're actually not too far off. I do have some reinforcements I could put at your service—if you should so desire."

"What sort of reinforcements?" Naitō broke in impatiently.

"Monkey troops. A monkey strike force."

"And where exactly will these monkey troops be coming from?" This time it was Ōura who wanted to know.

"Right here."

"Here?" Ōura said, pointing at the floor.

"Yes, here," Deusu nodded, also pointing at the floor. "The roughly fifty monkeys living in this compound are all highly trained fighters. I've been secretly putting them through drills myself. With their help, you can defeat the Bellyshakers. Without them, as has been made all too clear, you're woefully short of men—which is to say, if you kill me, you'll never be able to put the Bellyshakers to rest. The danger this group poses to the public order has already been demonstrated beyond any doubt, and it's far greater than any hypothetical threat a talking monkey might present. To execute me would be to permit their outrages to go on unchecked."

"I see. That does seem to make sense," Naitō said. "But can monkeys really be any use in battle?"

"We might not be as effective as you humans on an open battlefield, but you're hardly our match when it comes to guerilla warfare in the wooded mountains or street fighting in populated urban areas. The reasons should be quite obvious. You folks are limited to advancing on the ground, but we can swing through trees and clamber over rooftops to get the drop on the enemy when they least expect it. In other words, arrows and muskets are useless against us. Spears? Swords? *Hah hah hah hah.* What good are they when you've got a monkey wrapped around your head scratching your eyes out? You seem unaware of just how sharp our nails are."

Deusu yanked his nails against the tatami. The mat tore open to expose the subfloor below.

"Indeed. And how many monkeys are under your command?"

"About fifty at present."

Naitō let out a long, contemplative grunt. "So against an enemy of two thousand, we could have as many as seventy men and fifty monkeys? Will it even be a contest?"

"Not to worry," Deusu said lightly. "The enemy is a ragtag rabble without the slightest discipline. The only organized resistance will likely come from the two hundred or so men guarding Chayama himself. The rest are more like the bunch who attacked the fellow lying over there, roving about in groups of four or five that we can pick off separately. Besides which, I may have only fifty monkeys now, but I can multipy that number many times over in practically no time at all."

"Explain."

"I have reserves all over Japan under my command. The minute I send out runners, they'll start making their way through the mountains to gather here. I can easily have a thousand troops at the ready overnight."

"It'll be a romp," somebody said.

"Ah, but we must not become overconfident. Chayama is a formidable opponent. He has a tremendous personal magnetism— the remarkable ability to win people over. That means we have to be prepared for the number of Bellyshakers to continue to swell. He may be able to rally legions of airheads and nutcases from around the country in the same way I can summon my monkey troops."

"So we have a battle between airheads and monkeys shaping up," Naitō muttered.

As he listened to Deusu's pronouncements, Jūnoshin was experiencing persistent doubts about his own sanity.

Have I gone totally out of my mind? That Deusu character can't really be a monkey, can he? Surely he has to be a samurai actually, and I just think he looks like a monkey for some reason. But then how do I explain the comments other people are making about monkey smells and monkeys needing to know their place, as if they're seeing the same thing I am? Even Lord Naohito referred to him as a monkey. Which means what? That he's not actually talking, just going oo oo ah ah like the rest of his kind? But that wouldn't make for much of a conversation, and there's no way he'd be at the center of attention in a war council. So what's really going on? Is it all just in my head, a hallucination—no actual monkey or war council to begin with? And the pungent smell wafting this way from the guy who peed himself next to me is a figment of my imagination, too? But if I'd gotten that far off my rocker, you'd think I'd be totally incoherent, yet I seem to be able to talk with the people around me just fine. Except maybe that's an illusion, too, and from their perspective I'm a drooling, raging lunatic. In other words, everything I'm seeing is in my own private fantasy world. But that would imply the world itself is crazy, in which case does feeling like I've gone bonkers in a world that's crazy mean I'm actually quite sane? Man, my head hurts.

Meanwhile, buoyed by the promise of Deusu's reinforcements, the deliberations of the war council proceeded apace. Now that they could expect the monkeys to do the bulk of the fighting, the retainers who'd joined in a chorus for caution following Jūnoshin's report were enthusiastically beating the drums of war again. They seemed to have quite a flair for the flip-flop.

It was decided that the full contingent of samurai and monkeys would march from the Bureau of Monkey Affairs before dawn and muster once at Sondai-ji Temple on the edge of town before hitting Bellyshaker headquarters at daybreak. After quickly neutralizing the main enemy base by capturing or killing Chayama, they would track down smaller elements scattered throughout town and destroy them one by one. The most important thing now was for everybody to get some rest.

"If that takes care of things here," said Deusu, "I'll go fill my fighters in on what's happening and get those runners on their way." Giving a little wave, he headed for the monkey house.

A bed was prepared for Lord Naohito, and his retainers all turned in—though most were now so fired up for battle that they had difficulty falling asleep.

At around that same time, Konji could have been seen tearing at breakneck speed down a dark country road.

He was trying desperately to shake off the crushing sense of devastation that filled his chest.

"*Noooooooooooo!*" he cried at the top of his lungs as he ran.

And what might be the source of his great distress?

Perhaps an hour earlier, shortly after he withdrew to the monkey house and around the time Lord Naohito was calling Deusu forward, he had suddenly felt as if his soul were on fire. Until that moment, his foray into the heart of Bellyshaker territory and serving as stretcher-bearer for the wounded swordsman had kept his mind on other things, but once he was relaxing quietly indoors with Ron sitting close at hand, his burning love for her had risen to the forefront of his consciousness.

Osamu was at the far end of the room, playing with some monkeys. A hint of a smile flickered on Ron's lips from time to time as she watched their antics.

Too dazzled by Ron's beauty to look her in the face, Konji dropped his gaze to the white ankles protruding beneath the hem of her kimono. Then, after shifting his eyes nervously back and forth between her feet and the monkeys for several moments, he burst out, "Miss Ron?"

"Yes?"

When she turned to look at him, he was so overwhelmed by her beauty that he thought his heart would be crushed. But he had already opened his mouth; he couldn't lose his nerve now. With his heart leaping into his throat, he somehow found the strength to squeeze out, "Miss Ron, I'd like to ask you to be my wife."

"Not a chance," she answered without the slightest pause.

Tweeeeeeee. Konji turned the whites of his eyes and let out a strange, high-pitched note, as from a flute. But then he quickly pulled himself together.

"I understand completely," he said with a remarkable show of equanimity. "My apologies for coming at you out of left field like that. Now if you'll please excuse me, I need go outside and pass some wind," he added, perhaps intending it to be a joke, though it was hard to really say. Then he very deliberately rose to his feet and made his way outside, before breaking into a blind run the moment he closed the door behind him.

Although he had no memory of the ground he'd covered in his mad dash, he eventually found himself back on the Takeda Highway near the home of Manabe Gosenrō. He brought his steps to a halt.

Dense groves of bamboo pressed close to the road on both sides. He could hear the rush of a river in the distance, and a bright moon lit up the ground.

A jumble of severed arms and legs littered the road—Manabe Gosenrō's handiwork. As Konji stood studying the limbs in the moonlight, he was struck by their marvelous shapes. And in that moment it came to him that he wanted to go on living.

Yeah, I definitely want to live on, he said to himself, breaking into a smile. He spun on his heels and started walking back the way he'd come. At that moment, a sharp pain shot through his side, as if he'd been stabbed with a red-hot poker. Turning in surprise, he heard a *shinnng* and a *fsshhhhh*, then saw the silvery glint of what looked like a large ax swinging at him through the air before the entire world went black.

Hee hee hee hee. Hyuk hyuk hyuk hyuk.

Laughter was followed by the wild beat of a gong, as a band of heedless youths, obviously of ill-bred stock and soft in the head, began shaking their bellies. All of them sported wide gaps where their front teeth should have been.

They were quite plainly cut from the same cloth as the men who'd attacked Manabe earlier. Like those men, they had let themselves into Manabe's home and laid further waste to the structure and furnishings before coming back outside to find Konji standing in the middle of the road. Unanimously agreeing they should make him a Spew Saint, they first impaled him with a spear scavenged from inside the house, then relieved him of his head with a sword.

Hee hee hee hee. Hyuk hyuk hyuk hyuk.

Still whooping and hollering, the troop of youths started back down the road toward town.

From where it had come to a rest on the ground, Konji's severed head appeared to be staring up at the moon and asking: *Why?*

At the appointed hour before dawn, the fifty stout warriors in Lord Naohito's retinue and fifty crack fighters under Deusu's command marched forth to battle from the Bureau of Monkey Affairs.

But they did not appear anywhere near as formidable as this might make them sound. With neither spears nor muskets in hand and only the lord himself on horseback, the column looked more like a gaggle of retirees on the way to their regular *go* club meeting. It was difficult for anyone to get into the fighting spirit when they lacked the proper equipage for battle.

And most embarrassing of all were the purple hoods the men wore over their heads—in accordance with the instructions Deusu had given during the war council the night before.

"If I may have everybody's attention for a moment," he had said, "you will all be issued a purple hood before we depart tomorrow morning. I must ask you to don these hoods and keep them on at all times during the operation."

The members of the assembly exchanged uncomfortable looks. Performing monkeys traditionally wore purple hoods, and nobody liked being told they had to do likewise—especially by a monkey.

"Why should we have to do that?" demanded the clan's biggest grumbler, showing his usual colors.

"My fighters are trained to pounce on people's heads when I give the order, but they need a way to distinguish between friend and foe, so I've drummed into them that they should never attack anyone who's wearing a purple hood. In other words, without the hood, you're likely to end up with your eyes scratched out and your nose bitten off."

"Well, in that case," said the fellow, begrudgingly backing down.

Arrangements had been made for Ron to stay with a farm family nearby. She helped coordinate an effort by all the village women to gather fabric and get the requisite number of hoods sewn together overnight.

When she came to deliver the completed hoods prior to the troops' departure, Jūnoshin said, "The villagers have been told that you and Osamu were working as moles inside the Bellyshaker organization. The two of you can safely hide out here in Hedaka for the time being. I'll come back for you after the battle is over.

Ron silently looked up at him and nodded.

Perfect, thought Jūnoshin to himself. Osamu had been pretty much constantly on his tail—with orders to kill him if he made any missteps—ever since they first set out for Ushichiku to find Chayama. It would be a relief to finally be freed of that threat.

At the same time, he was a little surprised to realize that he'd already made up his mind to return to Hedaka after the fighting ended. He was developing a genuine soft spot for Ron, who also seemed to be sweet on him.

"I'll be seeing you, then," he said.

"Bye-bye. You be careful now."

She walked away between the tiers of theater seating. He watched her go from in front of the longhouses, willing her to turn and look his way one last time. But she never did.

Manabe Gosenrō joined the column of troops as well. Even though he'd received only the most rudimentary first-aid, he had made a remarkable recovery overnight. No doubt this, too, could be attributed to his conditioning as a superhuman swordsman.

But his injuries did have certain lasting effects. The man feared far and wide as a high-handed, stiff-necked killing machine who cut people down in cold blood, had turned unassertive to the point of obsequiousness. He spoke in a timid voice, his eyes downcast, apologizing between phrases, *I'm sorry, so terribly sorry*, stammering endlessly as he tried to get his sentence out, *Um, I mean, that is*, and then apologizing some more while on the verge of tears, *So sorry, my fault*.

Since they were accustomed to regarding him with fear, people assumed at first that he must have something up his sleeve, and that eventually he'd be lashing out with his sword again, screeching, *Are you dissing me?* But when that didn't happen and they realized it never would, they let out deep, pitying sighs.

"It's such a shame. The great Manabe, reduced to this."

Besides bringing about a dramatic change in his character, the injuries took a lasting toll on his body as well. The heavy blow to his head had apparently damaged his brain, leaving him paralyzed below the waist—though quite possibly this impairment, too, was psychological in origin.

Despite these conditions, Manabe had begged to join the campaign. Naitō flatly dismissed the idea, saying he would only be an encumbrance, but Deusu took a different view.

"Why not?" he said. "It'll be fine. Let him come."

In the end, Lord Naohito gave his permission, and Manabe donned a purple hood with the rest. The fact that he could no longer walk presented a problem, but a baby buggy used in performances was retrieved from the prop room for him to ride in, and the lord's palanquin bearers were assigned to push it.

Although the palanquin had delivered Lord Naohito to Hedaka most admirably, it was hardly appropriate for conveying him into battle. Fortunately, the Bureau of Monkey Affairs had a lone workhorse, which could be pressed into service as his mount.

The remainder of the men were on foot as the joint force set out for Sondai-ji in the predawn darkness. The missing Egere no Konji was presumed to have gotten cold feet in the face of battle and fled. A constant *swish swish* could be heard among the branches on either side of the road as the monkey troops swung from tree to tree. Deusu himself accompanied Naohito's men on the ground, toddling along at about the middle of the column.

There was an eerie cast to the weather that seemed to hold both gloom and brightness. Weather: the humor of the heavens; the humor of heaven.

It was daybreak. Inside the tent, Chayama looked nervously about after letting out a fart. He was worried it might undermine his authority if people realized their divine leader passed gas just like everybody else.

Nearest at hand was Jōji, munching noisily on some dried persimmons he'd lifted somewhere.

"Let me ask you something, Jōji," Chayama said. "Do you know what 'cut the *chi*' means?"

"Uh-uh," he grunted as he tore off another bite with his teeth and resumed his noisy chewing.

Chayama was incensed. Would it hurt so much to stop feeding his face for half a second? This was the big cheese addressing him—you'd think he could sit up and pay a little attention, give the question some serious thought. But no, he just mechanically grunts *uh-uh* without the slightest pause. It was pure intellectual laziness—that's what it was.

He imagined the response would have been at least a little different if it had been Ron standing there instead of Jōji, and he wished he hadn't let her go to Hedaka.

Bunch of idiots, he thought, as he looked morosely around the tent. Then suddenly feeling like he was no more than a bystander, he found himself asking, *What the hell am I even doing here?*

Damn good question. How the blazes did all this happen? It's a total mishmash. To begin with, why did I ever agree to start this thing? Four dumb idiots showed up on my doorstep talking about some cockamamie idea they had, and I thought I might play along and have a bit of fun with them, only to have it turn into this big stinking hullabaloo. And I'm probably gonna end up getting killed for my trouble. Somehow or other I've got every halfwit and nutcase from around the domain swarming like ants to sugar, like moths to a flame. In mindboggling numbers. And they just keep coming. They're too stupid even to comprehend what death is, and their brains are so fried on the tokijiku *nuts I handed out that they're jamming firemen's hooks into the sides of their heads or ripping their bellies open and winding their bowels around their necks. The hundred or so samurai this puny little clan can muster don't stand a chance against a mob who'll do stuff like that, so maybe I don't have to worry about getting killed right away. But if this thing drags on and neighboring domains or the central government get worried about it spreading, they'll send in thousands and tens of thousands of their best troops to put it down, and then I'll be dead meat for sure. I should have known it from the start, of course, which brings me back to why I ever let myself get suckered into this thing in the first place. If I'd just gone on living quietly in Ushichiku, I'd have been home free. That's what I sold Sudō out for, after all. So why did I ever let myself get pulled back in? Was it some kind of survivor's guilt? Except, in all honesty, I can't recall ever feeling the tiniest twinge of that. Why then? And for that matter, it's a mystery how it managed to blow up into such a gigantic free-for-all. I couldn't be the one who did that, could I? It has to be somebody else. Like maybe there's some hidden monster living inside me, separate from the person who's thinking these thoughts right now, and he's the one who made it all happen. Does having thoughts like that mean I've gone totally out of my gourd? But if I've lost my mind, it should be only my problem; it shouldn't affect anybody else. And yet just look at what's going on here. A frenzied beat pounding through the air. Blood, mayhem, and death everywhere. Apparently all from my words being turned to action. It's terrifying. All those towers popping up like weeds, too.*

Towers had indeed been springing up all over town. "You must build the party!" he had said to the believers gathered round him. "The party is your tower of strength, so to build the party means to build towers. They need not all be phallic towers. It would be good to have some yonic towers, too."

How this word had spread among the Bellyshaker masses, he had no idea, but by the next morning the ravaged town was thick with new towers.

As he thought back over all that had taken place—from the movement's wildfire growth, to the towers, to everything else—Chayama could only be amazed at the utter ease with which every idea he came up with turned into reality.

Of course, the towers that sprouted overnight could hardly be called proper structures. Most reached only ten feet or so in height at best, and were little more than piles of lumber, grave markers, stone Buddhas, and other scrap items salvaged from merchant houses that had been torn apart or torched. In most cases it was a matter of leaning several long timbers together at the top, and filling the resulting cone with whatever rubble and junk happened to be at hand. A few notable exceptions were clearly the handiwork of people who brought a special passion to the task—rising as high as fifty feet from the ground, or plastered over with mud and sculpted into spectacularly life-like penises.

The town was in ruins, but in many other ways besides these towers, it did not look simply as if it had been burned and pillaged by an invading army.

Streets that otherwise appeared perfectly normal were suddenly blocked by a newly erected wall of rocks or a great mountain of trash.

Nearly all of the big merchant houses along the main thoroughfares had been ransacked, but the looters had not merely rifled the rooms for valuables and made off with what they pleased; they left behind a variety of bizarre and inexplicable calling cards as well: a thick layer of dirt on the tatami; a gravestone erected in the middle of a storefront; a severed head hanging from the lintel.

You might come upon a large vat sitting in some conspicuous place and open the lid to find it filled with nothing but human noses.

Large quantities of fresh graffiti had appeared all over town. Colorful pictures of plants and birds, animals and people, now decorated every plaster fence, stone wall, and temple roof, as well as any other convenient surface. A diversity of artistic styles showed that they had come from many different hands, but the creators had invariably favored wildly garish colors. The effect was nearly enough to send even the most levelheaded folks to the funny farm—especially when helped by the fevered beat still pounding through the air.

For some reason, oil-paper umbrellas had been propped open atop many of the fences and roofs still standing, and these, too, were splashed with gaudy colors.

Hot food vendors had set up shop at many a street crossing. Here was someone offering bowls of soup out of a large stewpot; over there was someone grilling skewered game on cast-iron farm implements and serving it with a dipping sauce of soy, *mirin*, sesame, honey, wild onion, and chives, and calling it *yakiniku*. Both men wore straw hats pulled down low over shifty eyes, with sidekicks beating on drums next to them.

Customers wolfed the food down with gusto, exclaiming to each other how tasty it was.

The shady-looking vendors demanded a hundred *mon* in coppers per serving, which the diners were happily coughing up, but it was in fact a meaningless exchange. With the vaults at merchant houses and the castle broken open, all the copper and gold anybody could want was now free for the taking. The vendors simply dropped the coins at their feet, and nobody could be bothered to pick them up. Money no longer had any real value.

Laughing hilariously as if they thought it was the funniest thing in the world, one group of men went from shop to shop loading strongboxes onto a large push cart. When the cart was full they proceeded to the middle of Genga Bridge and dumped everything over the railing into the Yōrei River.

An upstream dam held the river to only about a foot deep along this stretch. The growing pile of gold pieces gleamed brightly in the morning sun.

The Kuroae-Deusu Joint Strike Force reached Sondai-ji shortly after six in the morning.

Founded in the third year of Keiwa by the venerable priest Sūden, who is also remembered as Grand Master of the Three Disciplines, Sondai-ji was the most prominent temple in all of Kuroae, and its extensive grounds were laid out at an elevation of about one hundred feet on the side of Mt. Maeno, a gently sloping eminence of feminine contour, situated to the northeast of the castle at the tip of the Hagegemo Range, which extends to Mt. Tokugo in the distance. A platform built out over a bluff on the south side of the main hall offered a commanding view of the entire castle town.

The Bellyshakers had not yet come up the mountain, but the monks had been concerned, and they greeted the arrival of the troops with great relief.

The Kuroae retainers caught their breath as they gathered on the platform and saw how horribly changed the town was. They gazed in shock at the extent of the devastation.

The formerly neat rows of houses were in shambles, many of them burned to the ground. The roofs that remained intact had been painted in outlandish colors, and in what surely must have been some kind of practical joke, umbrellas stood open on top of them. The umbrellas, too, had bizarre pictures drawn on them. Streets were blocked by barricades or other obstacles without rhyme or reason, while the unobstructed sections were filled with wriggling black figures—Bellyshakers doing their weird dance. On the breeze came the distant sound of gongs and drums, pounding out a energetic rhythm.

The castle itself was an even sorrier sight. Though relatively small as castles go, it had once been a beautiful structure. Now, set ablaze by Chayama, it had gone up in smoke. The stone ramparts and a smoldering heap of blackened timbers were all that remained. It was like a scar upon the earth. The Kuroae ranks stood in stunned silence.

Deusu strutted about cock-a-hoop, his back arched and jaw thrust forward with confidence, the breeze ruffling his fur. In the absence of any new orders, the monkeys under his command were entertaining themselves in the treetops.

Jūnoshin noticed a bright gleaming light under the Genga Bridge and wondered what it could be. It certainly wasn't normal for the bottom of the river to shine like that, so it seemed to be yet another anomaly to add to all the strangeness of late. "But you know what?" he murmured softly. "I think that light down there might just be a ray of hope." What could he have had in mind to say such a thing?

Lord Kuroae was livid. *How dare they burn my castle down!* he raged. *It's unforgivable. I'll kill them. I'll kill them with my own two hands.* He turned to his chief councilor, who was standing next to him.

"Naitō," he said.

"Yes, my lord?"

"Order the attack at once. All units."

"Yes, my lord."

"Good. Let's get moving."

"Yes, my lord."

"You keep saying that and bowing, but I'm not seeing any action. Get on the stick and order the attack."

"If I may be so bold, my lord."

"What is it? Speak, and be quick about it. I'm angry. I want them all wiped from the face of the earth, pronto."

"I'm afraid we lack the necessary equipment."

"I thought we discussed that back in Hedaka."

"We did, my lord, but there's a limit to what we can accomplish by simply charging in with our swords bared and fighting hand-to-hand. We will be able to operate far more effectively if we equip ourselves with spears, arrows, muskets, and the proper battle gear before we make our attack."

"But the castle has been burned to the ground."

"Indeed it has, my lord, but it appears from this vantage point that the samurai district remains mercifully unscathed, so the men should still be able to retrieve any weapons they keep stored at home. It would be well to do that before we launch our attack."

"Aha, I see. Excellent idea. Let it be so."

Naitō relayed the order for a weapons run to the men. For fear of what might happen if they encountered the enemy en route, they decided to advance in close formation as they descended the mountain and made their way into town. Sure enough, the moment they reached the samurai district, a roving band of Bellyshakers leapt out of a side street with a stolen lance and speared one of the men in the stomach.

"*Urgghh,*" he groaned as he doubled over in pain.

Deusu didn't miss a beat. "*Geshi geshi,*" he shouted, and a swarm of fierce young monkeys swooped down from nearby roofs, flashing wide red mouths and screeching at the top of their lungs. They tore at the Bellyshakers' eyes and noses with razor sharp nails, ripping their faces to shreds.

"*Aaaack!*" Even for the lunatic Bellyshakers this was too much. They crumpled to the ground in a chorus of screams, and the troops fell on them with their swords, slicing them up like sushi. As several of the attackers met their bloody demise, the others hastily took to their heels.

Fending off a second and third attack in the same way, the troops made a circuit of the samurai district, gathering up spears and muskets, bows and quivers, armor and helmets, footgear and surcoats. They still weren't equipped to normal battle standards, but as they tied back their coat sleeves and knotted their headbands, they were finally beginning to look like a proper fighting force.

"Now we're talking," somebody said. "It's hard to get into the spirit without my gear."

"You said it," came the reply.

Morale had risen dramatically. The only lingering sour note came from the purple hoods they all still had to wear, which looked as embarrassing as ever.

The monkey troops needed nothing new. They were as ape-naked as always, and had been fired up from the start.

Lord Naohito raised his voice. "The enemy is gathered in the riverbed. They must be punished for their vile deeds. Raise the battle cry!"

"*Ha-ooh!*"

It was a ragged and feeble shout, not likely to strike fear in anyone's heart, but it was the best they could do with only fifty-odd men. Being mixed with monkey screeches didn't exactly help.

The time was about eight when Chayama took his first bite of the croque monsieur he'd made himself for breakfast. *Blech*, he thought, making a face. It just wasn't the same without gruyère.

At that moment Jōji hurried into the tent with a dozen or so men in tow.

"Hanrō!"

"Now, now, Jōji. You know I can't have you addressing me casually by my given name like that."

"The clan is making its move. They're on their way here even as we speak. They've already killed at least ten of our men in the samurai district."

So the moment of truth has come, thought Chayama. But he felt ebullient.

"Shake your bellies," he said with a smile. "Are we to have another darkening of the light? Is that what you want? All you need to do is shake your bellies. But you may also find it useful to pick up a stone now and then. A stone can be a valuable weapon.

Are violets the only flower? Are there not hibiscus and buttercups, too? One lone flower must not be allowed to push two of lower stature aside from the more exalted. Use your stone to send the enemy to Spewdom. That's their destiny anyway. Do not claim the role of Spew Saint only for yourselves."

As always, Chayama marveled at how effortlessly the words rolled off his tongue. Where were they all coming from?

Unaware of Chayama's own bemusement, Jōji shouted "Got it!" and rushed out of the tent with his men. Moments later there was a noticeable rise in the cacophony of gongs and drums and cries and shouts coming from outside.

How did this happen? Chayama wondered again, sitting alone in the dusty tent. He wanted to weep but could summon no tears, so he tucked into the rest of his croque monsieur with his eyes dry.

What had possessed him to make such a thing for his breakfast? he wondered.

It was almost as great a mystery to him as how he had come to be in this tent commanding an uprising of four thousand people.

Entering town by way of the Takeda Highway to the east, the Kuroae forces had come up with a total of four muskets and four longbows in their tour of the samurai district. Now they proceeded to the great bend in the Yōrei River, where its southward flow turned to the west, and crept up the back of the embankment near the Genga Bridge, taking care not to be detected by the crowds milling about the riverbed below. The game plan said that a volley of musket shots and arrows from here would promptly send the rabble of commoners scattering in terror.

Deusu's monkey corps lay low in the grasses on the overgrown embankment, looking out for enemy elements approaching from the west across the bridge, from the north along the levee, or by way of the Takeda Highway behind them. The fifty intrepid monkeys had proved their mettle beyond any doubt on the way here, easily overwhelming the bands of five and ten Bellyshakers who'd tried to stand in their way.

All of a sudden the crowd in the riverbed seemed to become aware of the Kuroae presence. Their heads turned as one toward the levee as the drums went on beating.

A distance of about eighty feet separated the two sides.

Naitō believed the key to victory was in striking first. "Fire!" he bellowed.

Ka-boom! The muskets roared and bowstrings snapped.

A man went down at the foot of one of the scaffolds, and another near one of the tents. Naitō broke into a triumphant smile, but at that very instant, *chunk*, a flying rock blasted him square in the nose and sent him tumbling to the ground. Before he knew it, a thick hailstorm of stones came pelting down on the entire company, and cries of distress rose in every direction. *Aiii! Oof! Ouch!* The archers and musketmen were helpless to notch another arrow or get off a second shot.

With his nose throbbing fiercely, Naitō shouted, "Take cover behind the levee!" and rolled down the back of the embankment to lead the way. When he opened his eyes after coming to a rest, he could still see stones whizzing by overhead. *Damn*, he thought. *Look at 'em go. I never was much good at the martial stuff.*

But a samurai couldn't be making excuses in the middle of a battle. Lord Naohito was waiting for him at the bottom of the levee.

"What're you doing down here, Naitō?" he scolded. "Why aren't you up there charging into enemy ranks?"

"We were thrown back by a barrage of flying rocks, my lord. You can see for yourself what it's done."

The Kuroae forces were indeed a pitiful sight.

Some five hundred hurlers in the riverbed had loosed their stones in a single volley. With five hundred stones from five hundred fists flying at only fifty men, the targeted troops hardly stood a chance. The least fortunate among them got clobbered with ten or more hits at once and lay knocked out cold. A man could be heard bellowing that he'd taken it in both eyes and couldn't see a thing. A fellow gushing blood from a gash on his head was bawling like a baby.

I have an army of softies, thought Naohito.

"You're all a disgrace!" he shouted in a rage. "Fine, fine. I get the picture. I'll just have to lead the way myself."

"That's out of the question, my lord."

"Why should it be out of the question? What good is a warlord if he doesn't lead the way?"

"It would violate all conventions of war."

"Convention be damned. What choice do I have when my men act like such wimps?"

"Perhaps this is a time to call on the monkey troops."

"The monkey troops?"

"Yes, my lord. They've demonstrated remarkable strength this morning. Send them in first to soften the enemy up, and then the rest of us can go in to capture or kill Chayama. Yes, yes, I believe that is our best course."

Naitō hurried away to speak with Deusu and found him gazing off toward the Takeda Highway, lost in thought.

"Deusu," he called out as he approached.

The monkey turned. "What is it, Naitō."

"I realize this is rather sudden, but we've decided we'd like your troops to lead the assault."

"All right."

"Great. Like right now?"

"Sure, we can go now—on one condition."

"And what might that be? Money? Bananas?"

"No, no, nothing of that sort. But see this terrain? It's a riverbed. A wide open space with unobstructed visibility. As I said before, leading the way across open ground isn't really our strong suit. Once we actually engage and we're fighting at close quarters, we should do just fine, but we have to charge head-on into their barrage of stones to get there, so we're bound to take some casualties. And meanwhile, what? You and your men are just watching the show from the safety of the levee?"

"Not just watching. We'll be laying down supporting fire."

"Will you really?"

"And in any case, as a matter of principle, it only makes sense that monkeys would take a bullet or two for their masters."

He realized his mistake as soon as the words were out of his mouth. Deusu's facility with the language had lulled him into the sense that he was speaking to another man. But he was, after all, a monkey, and he responded in the way Naitō instantly knew he would.

"See. What'd I tell you?"

"No, no, no, I didn't mean it that way."

"That's okay. I'm quite aware what you're thinking. So I might as well be direct about what I want, too. On our day of victory, you agree to grant me samurai status."

Naitō's eyes popped wide. "Samurai status?"

"That's right."

"Well, now, I don't know about that. Samurai status for a monkey would be most unusual."

"Are you saying it can't be done?"

"I really don't believe—"

"Fine. Then count us out. We'll head on back to Hedaka."

"Oh, no, no, I can't let you do that."

"Then you'll have to make me a samurai."

"Well, *hmm*... The thing is... I really don't have the discretion to... *Hmm*... But on the other hand, we can't afford to have you pull out at this point either... *Hmm*... All right. You leave me with no choice. I'll see what I can do. My first concern right now has to be breaking this impasse. You have my word. I will put you in for promotion to samurai. If anybody tries to object, I can say you're actually one of us, you just happen to look like a monkey, or something of the sort."

"Much obliged." A wry smile spread across his face.

"So, then, how about you get started."

"Actually, I have one more condition."

"Now, wait a minute."

"If you don't like it, I can just take my fighters on back to Hedaka."

"Fine. Let's hear it," Naitō snapped impatiently, casting an anxious glance toward Naohito for fear that the lengthening delay might put it into his head to charge off on his own.

But Deusu was in no hurry. "As I said before, we monkeys are at a disadvantage in open field situations, and riverbeds are no different. Since that's exactly where you're sending us, I in fact have to assume our casualties will be substantial. Now, you may shrug and say, 'What's a dead monkey or two?' But these are fighters I trained under my wing, and every one of them is near and dear to my heart."

"I understand completely."

"Of course you don't. And I don't expect you to. But…"

"But what?"

"I need you to step up to the plate, too."

"Meaning?"

"You and your men go in with us."

"We go in with you?"

"Exactly. I'm not talking about Lord Naohito himself, of course. But doing the dirty work while you sit back on high and watch the show doesn't really wash with me. I mean, you're all samurai. When there's a war, you're supposed to put yourselves out there on the line. Calmly look death in the eye. That's why you get to be top dog and strut about like big shots even in ordinary times. But now, when the fateful day arrives, you want us monkeys to take the heat for you. That hardly seems fair. In fact, it's pretty embarrassing."

"Well, yes, but—"

When Naitō started to reply, a booming voice cut him off from behind.

"You're absolutely right."

It was Lord Naohito, who'd strode up just in time to hear the monkey general's last remarks. He'd grown tired of waiting as Naitō's exchange with Deusu dragged on.

"It's for times like this that the samurai receives his stipend," he said, turning to Naitō. "Are you really going to let a bunch of monkeys steal your thunder? Muster the men and get moving. And if I see anybody holding back," he added as he slid his sword from its scabbard, "I'll cut him down myself."

"As you wish, my lord," Naitō said. He turned to face the men laid out in the grass along the embankment. "Attention all troops!"

he shouted. "We will be commencing the attack momentarily. Prepare to advance!"

With slow, cloddish movements, the men began hauling themselves to their feet.

The men were now crouched in the grass near the top of the levee, spears gripped under their arms, bare swords propped against their shoulders, breathing tensely. The enemy remained alert in the riverbed with stones in hand, ready to throw on sight.

"*Cha-a-a-arge!*" thundered Naitō.

"*Geshi geshi!*" called Deusu.

"*Wah-ohhhh!*" roared the men

"*Yeep yeep yeeeep!*" screeched the monkeys.

A wave of men and monkeys raced down the embankment into a thick shower of river rocks. *Thwack, thwack, thwack, thwack.* The projectiles found targets one after the other, but this time the men were too pumped up to feel the sting.

"Keep moving! Don't stop!" Naitō shouted, and the men pressed forward.

The monkeys distinguished themselves again by being first to reach the enemy. A few sharp yelps went up as those hit by particularly large rocks limped off toward the bridge, doubled over in pain, but the vast majority made it across the divide to begin tearing at Bellyshaker faces and eyes with their sharp nails.

"*Aiiii!*" screeched the stricken, as they fell to the ground or squirmed to break free.

Remarkably, the first samurai to bloody his sword was the paraplegic Manabe Gosenrō. Hot for revenge against the kind who'd put him in a monkey's baby carriage, he was snorting like a racehorse from the moment he reached the top of the levee, but the porters who'd pushed him there wanted only to get out of harms way. To Naitō's cry of *Cha-a-arge!* they gave the carriage one last push, and made off for the bridge as fast as their legs would carry them.

"We got you this far. Now you're on your own!" they shouted over their shoulders as they went.

The carriage trundled down the embankment toward the enemy, tipping precariously from time to time but somehow managing to remain upright. Stones flew in its direction one after another, but Manabe had anticipated this and crouched low inside the carriage to avoid being struck. Only after reaching enemy ranks did he lift his head and begin swinging his sword to the right and left. *Mwa hah hah hah hah hah hah hah!* he laughed, as the carriage rolled on and he mowed down every Bellyshaker in his path. In no time at all there were thirty bodies piled up behind him—a feat that came to be remembered as "Manabe's thirty-man slice and dice." He was a fearsome swordsman indeed to have wreaked so much carnage from a violently bouncing baby carriage.

But it could last only so long as the cart sustained its forward progress. Once his ride rolled to a halt, the legless Manabe was like a sitting duck. The enemy was instantly upon him, kicking over his carriage. As he struggled to crawl from the wreckage, they ran him through with a spear and carved him up with his own sword into dozens of tiny pieces.

It was a gruesome yet fitting end for a cold-blooded hit man who'd sent so many to their graves without the slightest twinge of emotion.

As the Bellyshakers regrouped from the assault of the monkeys and Manabe's slice-and-dice, a banner was raised and a voice rang out over the din.

"Keep together! Rally to the flag!"

It was Deusu. Waving his banner high, he issued another sharp "*Geshi geshi!*" to the monkey corps and raced for the scaffold that was closest to the bridge. "Rally to the flag! Rally to the flag!" he repeated as he went.

As Bellyshakers attacked from all sides with staves and spears, the Kuroae men jabbed, jostled, and cut their way to the foot of the scaffold. From there they began advancing as a unit toward the second scaffold and tents to the south, repeatedly spreading out to strike and then falling back into formation as Deusu barked instructions.

"Eat this, shit-for-brains!" shouted a spearman named Kataoka Sahei as he impaled anyone who stepped in his path. A young blood who looked to be under twenty swung at him with a stanchion, *whoosh!* Kataoka ducked in time to spare his head but took a glancing blow to his shoulder, *thok*, and a dull pain gripped the spot. Turning with a fierce glare, he found the man looking at him with a silly grin on his face. It ignited Kataoka's fury, which flared even higher when he caught sight of a long, squiggly hair growing from a wart next to the guy's eyebrow. Stoked jointly by the pain and the silly grin, a primal rage exploded within him.

"*Aaaaaaaarrgh!*"

He let out an ear-splitting cry as he brought his spear about and smashed it into the side of his opponent's head, *whammmm!* The man reeled unsteadily from the brain-damaging force of the blow.

"Stagger all you want, you'll get no sympathy from me!" Kataoka roared as he drew the spear back and thrust it deep into his adversary's stomach. *Ha-yahh yahh yahh yahh yahh*, he shouted as he strode several steps forward with his victim skewered on his spear tip. The man dropped the club he held as he stumbled back two steps, three steps, then fell limp. His color had turned a deathly shade of blue. He was the eighteen-year-old son of a subsistence farmer, a good-for-nothing fellow who spent his time drinking and gambling instead of helping in the fields. When he heard about the new movement in town, he'd turned a deaf ear to his parents' entreaties. "It's the dawn of a new age!" he'd declared jubilantly as he set out to join the excitement—only to meet this sad demise.

"Serves you right, asshole," Kataoka said as he yanked on his spear to free it. It failed to release, so he set his foot to the corpse for better leverage, but just then, *thwump*, somebody bashed him hard from behind.

"Damn it all!" he cried, as something inside him seemed to snap. "What's everybody ganging up on me for? What'd I ever do to you? Why me? Why me?"

He turned and started after the assailant with his bare hands, when *wham!* A rock came flying and smashed him squarely in the side of the head, sending him head over heels to the ground and knocking him out cold. He had suffered a severe brain contusion and never regained consciousness.

Kataoka Sahei was dead at thirty-four. He had been a mild-mannered man in life, not at all given to fits of rage.

His intemperate behavior on this occasion could be attributed to a kind of temporary derangement that came from being thrust onto the battlefield without enough time to prepare himself mentally for what he would face.

Meanwhile, Nagaoka Shume had been lurching one way and another about the riverbed without taking down a single enemy.

To begin with, he had escaped being struck by so much as a single flying rock on his way across the divide.

When he realized his good fortune, he was staring at a wild tangle of hair belonging to somebody looking the other way. "*Ha-yahh!*" he cried, and raised his sword to strike, but the man spun round to face him, so he beat a quick retreat, "*Ai-yi-yi-yi!*" Bumping immediately into another fellow, he set his face with a ferocious scowl and moved again to strike, but at that very moment a monkey leapt out of nowhere to pounce on his intended victim and gouge his eyes out. Unmanned by the gruesome sight, he let out another "*Ai-yi-yi-yi!*" and turned hastily away. He was bouncing from one such encounter to another when he heard a voice behind him shouting, "Rally to the flag! Rally to the flag!" and looked over his shoulder to see Deusu waving his banner for the troops to gather at the foot of the northern tower.

Ahh, what a relief! he thought.

He'd been floundering about without the first idea what he was doing. Now that the two sides had joined battle, his mission was to slaughter as many enemy as he could, yet somehow, time and again, he kept coming up short. Seeing somebody with half his jaw torn off and moving in to finish him off, only to chicken out at the last moment and scuttle away with a nervous titter hardly seemed very soldierly. It was just pure flailing amidst the blindness of battle.

Which was why Deusu's rallying cry fell so sweetly on his ears. He would no longer have to stumble around in a fog all by himself. He turned to look at the scene by the tower. Deusu had thrust the pole of his banner down the back of his tunic and was shouting orders with his sword in the air. A cloud of dust hovered over the battlefield.

That is one amazing monkey, Shume thought. *I can count myself lucky to be under his command. I wonder if the monkeys I trained ever felt that way about me. No matter how insignificant or incompetent a man may be considered elsewhere, once he returns home he is the master of his domain. If he has a wife who waits on him as her one and only master, he will surely be filled with a boundless love for her. But just to be clear, I do feel a little embarrassed about being reduced to doing a monkey's bidding. Wait a minute. Who do I think I'm talking to?*

After briefly lifting his eyes to the sky, Shume started for the scaffolding at a light trot. Somebody behind him swung a spear. The shaft flew harmlessly past his head, but as it spun on around the butt end caught a corner of Shume's purple hood and tossed it into the air.

"*Geshi geshi.*"

His field of vision turned red. Then black. A searing pain shot through his body. He thought he would go mad. "*Aaaaaaaagh!*" he screamed, and crumpled to the ground.

No one fell on him to deliver a coup de grace, but the trampling feet of the surging crowd ruptured his organs, crushed his ribs, and brought his life to an end. He was forty-eight.

Despite a handful of such casualties, the Kuroae forces had the upper hand. The Bellyshakers waved spears and clubs about and made a great deal of noise, but with nothing but threadbare kimonos to protect them and many of them on wobbly legs as well, they were easy pickings for the retainers' flashing swords.

It had also become clear that few of the Bellyshakers had any desire to fight. Only the two hundred or so left in the area between the towers were making any serious effort. The throng gathered near the tents beyond were mostly content to be spectators, standing with big grins on their faces as they took in the action. Men atop the southern tower continued to pound on the drums, and some of those on the ground were still shaking to the beat. Others milled about the field kitchen, slurping up bowls of rice gruel.

The closest these Bellyshakers came to joining in the battle was when, by whatever impulse, someone bent down to pick up a stone and hurled it off. The half-hearted throw would invariably fall far short of the Kuroae men.

But the crowd by the tents was also a much larger group, numbering perhaps eight hundred to a thousand already, with many more in sight along the levee farther south, coming this way to join them. A group from the riverbed could be seen climbing the embankment as if to welcome the new arrivals.

Remembering that they'd left Lord Naohito at this end of that same levee, Naitō turned to the monkey general.

"Deusu," he said.

"What is it?"

"We need to pull back to the embankment."

"Why do you say that?"

"Lord Naohito's there."

"That's no reason."

"But—"

"If you're so worried, we can bring him down here," he said, then raised his voice to shout, "Somebody go find Lord Naohito and escort him to the tower!" He sliced an assailant in two with a single, clean stroke even as he spoke. It was a spectacular display of prowess, especially for a monkey.

"I'll go," volunteered Jūnoshin.

"Good. See to it," Deusu said.

"B-b-but we're badly outnumbered," sputtered Naitō in protest. "We'll do better retreating to the embankment once to regroup."

"That makes no sense. If we fall back now, what was the point of charging down here to begin with? Why should we give up our hard-earned ground?"

"But down here it's like fighting with our backs to the wall. Up there we'll have a path of escape."

"Is that all you can think of—getting away? Why don't you think a little more about dying?"

"I don't have that option. As chief councilor, I'm accountable for the safety of my men. If you won't call for retreat, I'll order it myself."

"And let certain victory slip through our fingers?"

"Certain victory? When we're outnumbered more than ten to one? That's monkey-brained claptrap!" Naitō screeched, finally losing his temper.

Deusu just stood there grinning. "Take a look behind you," he said.

Naitō turned around, and his eyes went wide.

Beyond the northern tower, Genga Bridge was jammed to overflowing with hundreds and thousands of monkeys who looked like they were spoiling for a fight.

"Wh–where did *they* all come from?"

"Didn't I tell you I could get monkeys here from all over the country in a single night? Still think I'm talking monkey-brained claptrap?"

"Oh, not a bit, I didn't mean it that way. I never doubted you for a moment."

"It's rather late to be saying that now," Deusu said. He swung his arms over his head and leapt into the air. As he touched down again, he let loose at the top of his lungs, "*Geshi geshi!*"

Yeep yeep yeep yeep!

With an ear-piercing cacophony of screeches, thousands of monkeys clambered over the railings, slid down the girders, and scampered up the riverbed, ignoring the purple-hooded samurai while swarming all over the fighting Bellyshakers. The doughty men wielding spears and staves went down in howls of agony as the monkeys tore at their faces.

Not satisfied with having neutralized the front line, the monkeys pressed on, carrying the attack to the spectators watching the action from the rear. The vicinity of the southern tower and tents quickly descended into pandemonium as screaming Bellyshakers tried to flee.

"*Bwah hah hah hah hah hah hah!* What a riot!" Naitō exclaimed, just as Lord Naohito arrived.

"You seem in good spirits, Naitō," he said.

"Indeed, my lord."

"How goes the fighting?"

"We clearly have the advantage. It should be only a matter of time before the enemy has been crushed," Naitō said, sounding terrifically pleased with himself.

"I wouldn't be so sure," Deusu put in from the side.

"Oh? Whyever not? Just look. Your troops are rolling right over the enemy. My lord, can you believe the size of this monkey army?

Never in my life have I seen so many of these creatures in one place."

"Nor have I."

"There you go, Deusu. Even the great lord agrees."

"But we cannot allow ourselves to become overconfident. See the levee? There are more of these idiots arriving all the time."

"And the operative word is idiots. Every one of them has the brains of a wooden puppet. I say bring 'em on. A few thousand fools like that can't hurt us."

"Ah, but you trifle with fools at your peril. Get enough of them in one place and they can be a dangerous force—beyond your control no matter how smart you think you are."

"Hmph, I have no idea what you could be talking about," said Naitō, cocking his head skeptically. But in the end, Deusu turned out to be right.

"I must have been dreaming," said Chayama when he heard Jōji calling his name. Then even though he hadn't been asked, he began recounting the dream, almost as if to himself. "I was eating something called a croque monsieur, except it didn't taste very good, so I decided it really didn't cut it without gruyère, when suddenly you rushed in to tell me we're surrounded by Kuroae troops. I was upset, and I wanted to cry, but the tears wouldn't come. Talk about a weird dream."

"It wasn't a dream, sir. We really are surrounded by Kuroae forces. And most of them are vicious fighting monkeys."

As Chayama listened to Jōji's droning voice, he became aware of a certain familiar feeling coming back over him.

"*A hah hah hah hah.* So they're trying to quash us, are they? Ever since getting these tattoos in Gifu, it's been hard for me to separate dream from reality. I suppose it was to be expected. They want to rain on Egubo's wedding parade. In any case, Jōji, I imagine you came back for a reason. What is it?"

"Osamu's here."

"Very well. Show him in."

He went to lift the tent flap and Osamu entered. He had on a purple hood and was covered in a thick layer of dust.

"I, I, I, um, um, I, I, I just got b-b-back."

"Is Ron with you?"

"On, on the way, um, um… a l-leak… I, I, I had to take a l-l-l-leak, s-s-see—"

"Are you trying to say she gave you the slip while you were taking a leak?"

"S-s-sorry."

"That's okay. Don't worry about it. But tell me this, Jōji," he said, turning back to the other man. "Are the monkeys killing many of our people?"

"Quite a few, yes. But it doesn't matter. The north side of Takeda Highway is teeming with monkeys. There must be millions of them—the whole area's packed solid. They've completely overwhelmed the Kuroae men. But south of the road is jammed with our people, every one of whom's itching to be divine shit, and most would happily settle for getting spewed. They have no idea of themselves or what they have to live for, they're just mindless bodies throwing themselves at the monkeys."

"Excellent, excellent. That's exactly what we want to see. When it's not real, when it's just a picture in their minds, they might clamor to be shat or puked, but the true test comes at the moment of death, when the devastating anguish and terror of that moment comes crashing down on them. Decades' worth of realities come to a boil in that instant. And the heat has a purging effect. Excellent, excellent. Except, if that's the end of it, then it's just another darkening of the light. We had a small breakdown in Ushichiku, and now we have a great big breakdown in Kuroae. I do wonder why it's never a middling breakdown. That's my fundamental question. At any rate, Osamu, do you think you can make it from here to the southern tower?"

"I, I, I, um, yes, I, I, I have a p-p-p-purple hood, so I, I, I, I'm safe."

"If you have a purple hood, the monkeys don't bother you?"

"D-D-Deusu said so."

"Interesting. Well, all right, then. I now pronounce you Saint Osamu. Climb to the top of the tower, and when you see anybody approaching this tent, lift them into the air and blow them to pieces—all of them, whether people or monkeys. I hereby name

Ron a saint as well. As for myself, I will remain plain old Chayama Hanrō. Now, be on your way."

Osamu pointed to himself and stammered in surprise, "M-m-m-me?" but Jōji grabbed him by the arm and dragged him out of the tent.

The northern half of the riverbed had become a solid brown carpet of monkeys. The southern half was chockablock with the multitudes of fools previously seen arriving. It was a showdown between monkeys and fools.

But the fighting could hardly have been more one-sided. The monkeys had come primed for battle, and they swarmed over the enemy with their deadly nails bared, ripping faces to shreds right and left. The fools hardly knew what hit them. They'd come as curiosity seekers out for a good time, casually asking each other, *What's up? What's going on?* only to find themselves under vicious attack. Squirm as they might in terror and pain, it was all too late. Nearly to a man they were maimed for life or killed.

Osamu reached the top of the southern tower and looked down over the riverbed. *That's one hell of a lot of monkeys*, he thought, and then felt an annoying sensation come into his head, like a heavy rain pounding down inside it. Trying to shake the feeling off, he swung his arms up in front of him, palms down, first to chest level, then on above his head.

Several hundred monkeys at the foot of the tower rose into the air like a single undulating blanket.

Their eyes darted about in bewilderment as they realized they were hanging in midair.

Osamu drew the tips of his fingers together, then snapped them out again as if flicking away droplets of water.

It was a horrific sight. The blanket of levitated monkeys exploded all at once. A dull, muffled *ka-thoom* was followed by a shower of blood, guts, and body parts falling to the ground. Most were monkey parts, but there were human heads and limbs, too, for the mingling of the two armies in close combat meant there'd been a good many men around the foot of the tower as well.

Helped by the wind, some of the bloody shrapnel was carried all the way to the northern tower, which was now the Kuroae command post, and a fleshy object landed on Sugawara's cheek with a *splat!*

"*Ew ew ew ew eww*," he cried, jumping into the air as he brushed the thing off.

"What's the matter?" Naitō asked.

"Something disgusting landed on my face."

"Looks like it might be somebody's nose. But I need you tell me, Sugawara—what the blazes did my lying eyes see just now?"

Naitō waited in silence for an answer.

Nobody spoke. Nobody could.

Which need certainly be no surprise. Tens of thousands of monkeys had overrun the riverbed from this direction, while tens of thousands of plainly brainless, mindless, witless, useful-thoughtless human refuse came pressing in droves from the other. The two armies had collided between the two towers in a chaotic sea of pushing and pulling, quickly melting into one great mass of bodies with no telling monkey from man. And then, like a bad dream turning even worse, a great big swatch of the melee had all of a sudden lifted into the air and blown to smithereens.

No normal understanding of the world could explain what had taken place, and even the normally imperturbable Naohito was struck dumb by the sight.

Then a second explosion occurred. Several hundred more monkeys burst in midair. Fine droplets of blood spread in a cloud of red mist.

A third explosion soon followed, and a fourth. With explosions coming one after the other, the riverbed became a veritable scene from hell, piled high with the torn body parts of both man and ape. Even the dauntless monkey troops faltered in their advance as fear entered their hearts. On the other side, the vanguard of arriving fools stopped short; caught unawares by the abrupt halt in front, those who happened to be descending the side of the embankment toppled like dominos, and a hundred of them went to their deaths.

The dominos fell quietly. The whole battlefield had grown still. Only the low moans of the wounded could be heard.

"It's Osamu," Jūnoshin said. "He's turned against us."

"What?" snapped Naitō. "Osamu?"

"That's right, your lordship. That's who you see there on the other tower. In the purple hood."

"Sugawara! You said Osamu feels obliged to you and will do anything you say. Go tell him to stop this nonsense."

"It won't do any good," said Jūnoshin.

"Why not?"

"Because he's a simpleton. He's only loyal to his most recent benefactor. First it was Konji, then it was Master Sugawara, and now it's Chayama."

"Really? How do you know?"

"Well, if truth be told, when Konji and I were here yesterday, we ordered Osamu to kill Chayama, and he wouldn't do it. He just hemmed and hawed about how Chayama had been good to him. Talk about pissing me off. I mean, why should the likes of Osamu get puffed up about obligations all of a sudden? But what could I do? Chayama's the only one he listens to now."

"That bastard," fumed Sugawara.

"Call him whatever you want, but you have only yourselves to blame. Think about it. You gave an all-important role to a halfwit, and then figured you could sit back and put your feet up because the fool was going to take care of everything. Well, this is the bill coming due. You'd have done better to take the whole thing a lot more seriously from the start, not to mention, be willing to get your own hands a little bit messy. Instead, you got up on your high horse and insisted that all that sort of menial stuff wasn't for you, you had loftier things to do, so you dumped all the dirty work on me and Konji and Osamu and the monkeys—which is how you ended up in this fix."

"You'd better watch your tongue, young man!"

"This is hardly the time for niceties. The clan is crumbling before your very eyes. What exactly do you intend to do about it?"

"Well, hmm... Under the circumstances... hmm... I suppose we'll have to see what Deusu can do for us."

"Putting all your stock in a monkey again?"

"Silence! Deusu is no ordinary monkey!" Naitō bellowed, and at that very moment another explosion took place. *Ka-thoom!*

"Deusu!" shouted Naitō.

The monkey general was standing to one side atop the tower, quietly watching the action with his arms folded across his chest.

"Ah, there you are, Deusu. Have you been standing there all along?"

"As a matter of fact."

"What is your counsel here?"

"It should be easy enough to put a stop to the explosions."

"How?"

"Simply call in your archers or musketeers and shoot the man down."

"Of course," said Naitō, pounding a fist into his hand. He quickly descended the tower.

But after he was gone, Deusu muttered quietly to himself, "Not that killing that one fellow is likely to resolve much of anything. When a man is capable of blowing things up like that, and a monkey can stand here jabbering like a person, and untold thousands of monkeys and men are warring meaninglessly on this improbable riverbed, you've got much bigger problems to deal with before you can hope to achieve anything. But these people never see beyond what's staring them in the face right now."

"Bwa hah hah hah hah hah hah!"

Osamu burst into peals of laughter each time another swatch of bodies exploded. He had been ridiculed and picked on all his life, ever since he was a little boy, and he'd gotten used to blaming it on "my dumb brains" and accepting it as his lot. His sole consolation came from being able to lift things into the air and blow them up, but his stepmother had deprived him of even that pleasure, forbidding it in such strong terms that he continued to think it was taboo long after she'd been run over and killed, and to this day, any time he broke down and snuck off into the mountains to move boulders and such around, he experienced terrible pangs of guilt afterwards. Now, for the first time in his life, he'd been given license to use his power openly, and on a scale he'd never even dreamed of before, so he was riding on cloud nine. He had blown up nearly three thousand men and monkeys already.

"*Bwa hah hah hah hah hah hah!*" he roared, and raised his arms again. Just as he was about to flick his fingers, *fwoooosh*, an arrow came flying from near the northern tower and, *thonk*, pierced Osamu's neck. At almost the same moment, *chonk, chonk*, two musket balls tore into his chest and stomach.

Something hot gurgled up his throat, and then a sudden chill spread through his body. As the world began fading to gray, he mustered the last of his strength to whip his arms downward. The several hundred men and monkeys dangling in midair were slammed violently to the ground and sustained massive injuries.

His mind flashed orange for an instant, then went completely black as he collapsed to the platform on top of the southern tower.

My happiest days were when I drove a packhorse and was making my own way, he thought in his waning consciousness. It made me mad when customers called me stupid and refused to pay, but that was still the best time of my life.

With these thoughts, he slipped quietly into oblivion. He was thirty-five.

Chayama was standing in front of the tent watching Osamu blow up multitudes of monkeys when he saw him fall to sniper fire.

"Excellent!" he said. "Most excellent indeed! The tapeworm squirms. At this rate, absent the support of the lira, the masses will soon have the aspired trots. Magnificent! All these exposed innards tell us the world is turning inside out. It's been a very long time since I've seen such spectacular spewing. Do dogs have Buddha nature? Can monkeys attain Spewdom? Such silly questions. The tapeworm squirms. I feel embarrassed, now, for burning the castle down. But there's nothing to be ashamed of in what I see here. I saw the castle as a symbol, and I thought burning it down would make the tapeworm squirm so we could all become turdheads. That's why I did it. But when I gaze across this scene of destruction, I realize that fixating on the castle just goes to show that I'd long since been defeated by reality. Or taken in. Now we must wallow in this shame and shame ourselves even more. The tapeworm squirms. Burning down a castle means nothing. We have to stake our whole being on denying our whole being. More and more and more. More and more and more and more. Very soon. Without any support of that kind for our hearts. The tapeworm squirms."

He turned to Jōji standing beside him.

"Strike the gong," he said. "Beat the drum. We must shake our bellies. Mix it up with everything from Dorothy's merengues to Lyubi's erotico-musical airs in a gentle four-four beat."

Jōji ducked into the tent to get a marching drum and began beating on it. *Rat tat tat. Rat tat tat. Rat tat tat.* Chayama promptly hauled back and belted him hard in the face.

"Didn't I tell you four-four time?" he snarled. "What're you doing triple-time for?"

Jōji got back to his feet with blood trickling from his nose and began drumming again. *Rat tat tat tat. Rat tat tat tat.*

"Excellent, excellent. The tapeworm squirms. Even that little miscue is all to the good. Get it wrong first, then put it to rights. That's the formula, and it's vital to have a formula. We can simply repeat it again and again. Excellent, excellent. Now, then, I suppose I should get to it myself," he said, sounding very pleased indeed.

Bending to the ground, he gathered up some entrails—whether they belonged to man or monkey, no one could have said—and deftly piled them atop his head as if arranging a fancy do. Then, shifting one foot slightly forward and the other slightly back, with elbows tucked against his sides and hands loosely balled in front, he eased his midsection into motion.

"*Pee-yew,*" he said. "Boy does that stink! But it's all to the good. These entrails on the head are the best part. Shaking it up with a crown of guts in the middle of a battle—have you ever seen anything so stupid? It's got to be a first and last. But come on, folks, don't let me outdo you. I got these tattoos in Gifu. Down a bowl of gruel to build up your strength. And if you feel your spirits sagging, just chew on some *tokijiku* nuts. Do you know the name literally means "time thusly suffers"? That is how time suffers. Or you might try a head replacement. See all the dead monkey parts lying around you? Just scrape one of those heads out with a spatula, and pull the empty skin down over your own sorry block. *Voilà!* You're a cross between man and ape. Then again, you could give a dead monkey the head of a man. The squirming tapeworm egests divine shit to the sound of Lydian chromatics. A solemn cadence rising out of utter decay."

First to pick up the beat were other nearby drums.

The area around the southern tower and tents had fallen silent in the face of the monkeys' ruthless assault and Osamu's mass explosions, but now Joji's strong and steady beat emboldened the musicians to resume their lively playing. As if in response, the distant and disjointed sound of gongs and drums coming from among the fools streaming this way on the embankment gained new strength as well, quickly matching time with Jōji's beat and swelling into a single, massive, pulsating rhythm.

"*Ohh hoh hoh hoh hoh!* Shake your bellies, everybody. Shake, shake your bellies!"

But Chayama's prodding was hardly necessary. The fools who'd flocked to the riverbed were like automatons programmed to blindly follow the crowd at every turn. They were the sort who promptly joined any queue, never mind what it was for, and when they heard something was selling like hot cakes, they always had to have one, too. They thought the events they witnessed on stage were the gods' honest truth, and they idolized their celebrities even as they scorned them. None could ever be bothered to think for themselves, yet they never questioned their own personal uniqueness.

In other words, they weren't constitutionally capable of holding themselves still when a pulsating beat filled the air. All ten thousand had begun rotating their torsos the moment the drumming resumed, creating a spectacle of comic proportions to warm Chayama's heart.

But it was a hideously grotesque spectacle as well.

A thick layer of blood and guts painted the ground seamlessly, and heads, limbs, and torsos were scattered everywhere. Many of the fools had begun mimicking Chayama to fashion headdresses of entrails, or donning monkey heads to turn themselves into bellyshaking ape-men.

The Kuroae contingent gazed at the scene in horror.

"What could possibly be the sense?"

"This isn't just a battle anymore."

"It's end times."

"We should be afraid. Very afraid."

Trembling in fear, they stood frozen to the spot, unable to move.

But the monkey troops were taking it even harder than the men. The source of their distress was in the ape-head masks.

Monkeys are highly intelligent, and they're not easily fooled by the likes of scarecrows or deer-startlers. But what does spook them is the sight of their own dead. One village plagued by thieving monkeys tried every means they could think of to ward them off without success—until they killed one of the pests and hung its corpse by the roadside, and the unwanted visits stopped. Given this peculiarity of their species, the sight of men wearing dead monkey heads was enough to drive Deusu's troops to distraction. They scurried wildly in circles trying to get away, or turned violently ill and began throwing up, or clung to each other in terror while screeching at the top of their lungs.

Atop the northern tower, Deusu stood with folded arms, contemplating the scene.

"Interesting," he finally said. "They're literally mixing men and monkey parts. And here I thought that by joining the ruling elite as a monkey, I could bring down the status quo, but at the same time claim a place for myself in it and ultimately, at a more fundamental level, save the world. But that's actually the idea most revolutionary regimes have; it's hardly anything new. In other words, my cause is lost. I am defeated."

And with that, the monkey general abandoned the human posture and mannerisms he had previously assumed, and shinnied down one of the tower supports like any other monkey. When he reached the ground, he raced to a position roughly halfway between the two towers and let loose an ear-piercing *Yeeeeeeeep!*

There was a note of tearfulness in it.

As he screeched, he spread his arms wide and began turning his body around and around, picking up speed at an astonishing rate.

Then a strange thing happened. The spinning monkey began to stretch taller and skinnier. *Yeeeeeeep!* He continued to screech as he spun. Before long, the monkey as chunky as a rice mortar had slimmed to the width of the tower uprights and gained nearly the same height. The pitch of his voice had risen, too, and his *Yeeeeeeep!* was now like the excruciating screech of metal on metal. Everybody within range hurried to cover their ears.

As the moments went by, his girth dwindled further, to the thickness of a rope—a thin brown cord stretching up into the sky. The pitch of his voice rose beyond the range of the human ear.

But his fellow monkeys still heard the message loud and clear, and they responded by moving to the foot of the rope, taking hold of it, and climbing toward the sky one by one.

Bwonnng. Bwonnng. Bwonnng.

Suddenly, three resounding chords that blended notes from all up and down the scale rang out overhead, and as each chord sounded, thousands of brown ropes dropped from above like a driving rain. Monkeys everywhere reached for the nearest rope and began shinnying skyward.

"They're beating a retreat to heaven," someone murmured.

That was exactly what they were doing. There was something sublime in the sight of thousands of monkeys ascending into the sky on ropes dangling from above.

But Lord Naohito and his men could not afford to stand there gaping at the extraordinary sight. The pulsating music continued unabated, and the bellyshaking with it.

Naitō was the first to find his tongue. "Once the monkeys are gone, we won't stand a chance," he cried in alarm. "We must pull back, my lord! You must order a retreat!"

"*Hrumph.* With such an absurdly surreal scene unfolding in front of me, even *I* find it hard to object. But I still think some careful deliberation is in order. For example, what to do about all these unsightly dangly things? We can't cut them down because they're attached at the top, but is there perhaps some way to yank them free? How do I find out? Just order my burliest retainers to see what they can do? Or do I need to call in some professional strongmen? And what about cleaning up this riverbed? There are a great many practical matters like that to consider one by one. Or rather, if I don't concentrate on practical matters like that, I think I'll go out of my mind. Unless maybe I already have. Is that why I'm seeing such crazy things? Damn it all. Hell if I know. Well, whatever. I shall approve the retreat."

"You heard him, men!" shouted Naitō. "Retreat!"

"There's just one problem," Ōura said.

"A problem?"

"How do you propose we go about it?"

"What kind of question is that? By putting one foot in front of the other."

"That's not what I meant. Have you seen the bridge lately?"

Naitō turned to look. The span once filled from end to end with monkey troops was now jammed with Bellyshakers, and the throng stretched on down the road toward the Takeda Highway with everybody gyrating to the beat of the music. Untold numbers of brown ropes hung down in this direction as well.

"We're surrounded?"

"You said it."

"Curses! That leaves us no choice," he muttered, then turned to Lord Naohito. "We're surrounded on all sides, my lord. You must ride the horse to safety and find your way to Sondai-ji. The rest of us will join you there as soon as we can."

"Very well," said Naohito, and wasted no time climbing astride the horse tied to the base of the tower. He whipped his mount into a brisk trot toward the embankment, but he hadn't even made it fifty yards before a spear from one of the Bellyshakers, resurgent now with the monkeys gone, plunged into the horses rump. The animal reared, throwing Naohito to the ground and out of sight.

"I was afraid of that," said Naitō, who saw it all from the foot of the tower.

"They wouldn't actually kill him, I don't imagine," Ōura said. "But how the blazes did this happen?"

"Beats me. At any rate, I figure I'll head for Sondai-ji. What're your plans?"

"I don't know. Go back to Hedaka maybe."

"Might make sense. Well, I suppose I'll see you if I see you."

"Right. The only question is," Ōura chuckled, "in what world?"

At that moment, a wave of jostling Bellyshakers swarmed over their position, pulling them in opposite directions. The Kuroae forces scattered every which way in a maelstrom of blood and entrails, hair-raising ape-men and kooky music.

Retainer Yahoso Genba, who earned a stipend of thirty *koku* as one of Lord Naohito's regular escorts, was a man highly versed in the way of poetry. Never once, however, had he shown anyone his work. Since his poems did not adhere to the usual conventions of form, he feared outrage from his superiors and potentially negative repercussions on his career if he were to make them public. Now, as he was being pushed to and fro by jostling Bellyshakers, he marveled at the mystery and wonder of poesy.

Some months before this, he had been inspired to compose a poem that went as follows:

Countless strings dangling
Countless apes ascending
Countless pigs rooting
Countless dogs chasing
Behold the motley mix
Behold the disarray
Ape melding with swine
Swine vying with canine
What was it the great monkey said
Before he quit to heaven?

It had struck him at the time as an exceedingly strange poem. He could not fathom what it was about. At a loss how such a verse had ever come to mind, he tossed it on his discard pile.

It described this very scene! he now realized, in a mixture of wonder and bewilderment. He tried to sort out what it could imply as he stumbled among the press of bodies.

His chain of thought went something like this:

I am an obscure poet. But however obscure I may be, I composed a remarkable poem that foretold future events. It can only have been a revelation from heaven. That is to say, although I remain unsung by my contemporaries for my genius, the gods recognized my talent and saw fit to put that poem into my head. As a matter of fact, carrying this a step further, could the poem perhaps be not just prophetic but creative? In other words, the gods didn't merely give me the power to foretell the future with my poetry, they gave me the power to actually shape it.

And with that, the man who'd been floundering about in an absolute panic, his face streaked with tears, felt a delicious sense of calm settling gently over his consciousness. It had suddenly dawned on him that if he was the one who created this scene, he should also be able to alter it in any way he chose.

A Bellyshaker beside him was *hyuk-hyuking* like a clueless imbecile as he danced. Yahoso flashed him a smile.

It's the power of my poem that's making you do that, and I love you all for it. But I have certain responsibilities as the creator. Time's a-wasting.

Climbing to the top of the northern tower, he plopped himself down in the middle of the platform and took out the notebook and portable writing case he always carried with him. He liked to be prepared for whenever inspiration might strike.

"Let's see, now, some saké…is too much to ask, I suppose," he mumbled to himself. "I have such a hard time getting the words to flow without a drop or two of lubrication."

It was out of the question, of course, but he turned to his notebook without seeming to be especially disappointed. The truth was, he didn't really need alcohol to get his creative juices flowing; he'd only said it to console himself.

"Now then," he said, as he poised his brush over the paper with a self-important air. His usual approach to writing was actually quite arbitrary: he simply jotted down whatever words popped into his head, one after another, without any regard for the rules of composition. But in this case he came to the task with a specific objective—to bring an end to the turmoil all around him—so he paid somewhat closer attention to the coherence of what he was setting down.

The strings disappeared
The Bellyshakers fizzled
The castle rose again

The old order was restored.
Peace enfolded everyone.
Peace prevailed everywhere.

The parallelism at the end is perfect, he thought with satisfaction when he had finished. *I certainly do have a way with words, don't I?*

He took a look around. Nothing had changed.

That's strange, he thought, and then it came to him. *Of course, of course. It's been several months since I wrote the poem that brought about today's events. There must be a time-lag before the poem comes true. Which means I need to get more of the future mapped out right away.*

He promptly started in on another poem to sketch out subsequent events.

In the early stanzas, he described the economic prosperity that followed successful cropland expansion, irrigation, and flood control projects; sustained harmony between lord and subject; and people throughout the land leading lives of unprecedented happiness. But the character of the poem underwent a change when he wrote of himself rising to be lord of Kuroae Domain. He surrounded himself with beautiful waiting ladies and held sumptuous banquets featuring the rarest delicacies of land and sea. Before long he was lopping off the heads of anyone who incurred his wrath and living as profligately as he pleased. When such deeds began to weigh on his conscience, he added lines claiming he was acting in the best interest of his subjects, or that a beheading was justified because the victim had shown he was evil to the core, and so forth, and the poem degenerated into a string of lame rationalizations.

It was the sort of thing that happens when an ordinary man of no particular talents gets it into his head that he's an unprecedented genius who's been chosen by the gods.

He continued to work on his poem atop the tower for quite some time, mumbling to himself as he wrote.

And Yahoso was showered with glory,
His praises sung throughout the domain…

He had just set down these words and smiled in satisfaction, when a rock came hurtling through the air and hit him square in the head. He toppled to the platform and died. He was forty-six.

About that same time, in the shadow of the very tower where Yahoso met his demise, a figure that looked like a chrysanthemum monkey at a garden show was jerking his head up, down, right, and left, and shaking his belly harder than anybody else around. A man in a monkey mask had plastered himself with hundreds of chrysanthemum blossoms above the waist and slathered his lower parts with green paint.

It was Makubo Magobei.

The Bellyshaker movement had brought him an exhilarating liberation, freeing him from all duty and obligation, easing all his pains and torments.

Just by shaking his belly, he could lose himself in a cloud of euphoria.

But this was not to say that he had attained perfect peace.

If he happened to interrupt his movements, a powerful sense of emptiness would descend over him. Or sometimes it would be of feeling of terror. He would hastily chew on a *tokijiku* nut, but the terror would not recede right away.

So he'd become convinced not only that he could never stop shaking for even a moment, but that he needed to keep taking his antics to new levels. That was how he'd ended up in a monkey mask and chrysanthemum coat. But he worried about what he could come up with next that was even crazier.

Still, all the wackiness brought him joy. His ludicrous costume was a distinct part of the liberation he felt, since once he'd done something that absurd, was there any doubt he could go even farther off the deep end? The bellyshaking itself, with its throbbing beat and rhythmic movements, added a more purely physical sense of freedom.

"*Ah! Ah!*"

Low moans of ecstasy escaped his lips as he swiveled his torso about.

Then he noticed a sensation of warmth spreading across his lower belly.

It felt as if a monkey clinging to his stomach had peed on him.

Except, of course, there was no such monkey.

This is weird, he thought, without interrupting his movements. But the temperature began to rise and kept getting hotter and hotter. When it became too hot to bear, he finally stopped shaking and cried out, "My belly's burning! My belly's burning!"

The intensity of the heat made him wonder if his stomach might actually be on fire. He frantically tore at the blossoms plastered to his torso, but no flames leapt forth. What he found instead was a deep brown patch above his navel that continued to feel blazing hot.

"My belly's burning! My belly's burning!" he wailed again and again.

Then another strange thing happened. Through no will of his own, the brown spot began thrusting forward, pulling his belly behind it. But his head and his feet remained anchored in place and didn't move, so he soon looked as if he'd been put in a Boston crab hold. The torturous position on top of the already unbearable burning raised his pain to new heights.

"*Eeeahhgggh!*" he shrieked.

The others nearby went on dancing, oblivious to his cries.

Even after his body was bent as far back as it could go—farther than anybody knew a body could bend—the brown spot kept pulling. Then *crack!* His hipbones snapped.

"*Ai yi yi yi yi yi yi yi!*"

He shrieked louder still as the shattering pain pulsed through him. He was now folded completely in two, backwards, with his hair touching his heels. Yet, somehow, his stomach and the brown disk remained at the same height. His whole doubled-over body hovered about three feet off the ground.

The dancers around him finally began to notice what was happening. They ceased their movements and gathered about in a circle.

Just as the circle was closing, Chayama arrived with Jōji in tow. He quickly stepped forward into the ring.

"If I may have your attention," he called to the crowd, "this is no time to stop your bellyshaking. It's time to shake all the more! Pound your drums all the harder! I don't know this man's name, but whoever he is, he is about to become divine shit. He is on the verge of joining the shit stream of the tapeworm that swallowed this world. It's a wonderful thing, a wonderful thing, a truly wonderful thing! The best way to help him on his way is by shaking your bellies with everything you've got. Rejoice!"

The crowd let out a roar.

One of their members was on the threshold of his deliverance.

The circle of onlookers began shaking again, now more vigorously than ever.

At first there was no change, as Magobei remained suspended in midair, crying out in pain. But then it happened.

Beginning at the fold in his stomach, his body began to disappear.

And not simply by dissolving into thin air, but, bizarrely, as if being sucked bit by bit through some kind of a hole, *thwurp*, *thwurp*, *thwurp*. Except, of course, there was no actual hole. Those standing opposite Magobei's head could see only a black circle about a foot across hovering at the point where the fold in his stomach had disappeared. Those on either side saw him sliding steadily toward that spot and vanishing instead of moving on past, leaving less and less of his remaining body to see.

Perhaps sensing what was going on, Magobei cried out with renewed anguish. "*Aaaaghh!* It feels squiggly! I can't stand it! It's like rubber pounding on my belly. *Aaaaghh!* I feel squiggly all over!"

His cries continued as more and more of his body was sucked into the hole.

"Excellent! Most excellent, indeed!" said Chayama again. "He has now become divine shit up to his chest. You're down to the last stretch, good sir. I wish you all the best! Let's have it, folks! Pour on the craziest things you can think of!"

"Please, somebody-y-y-y!" Magobei cried out, as if prompted by Chayama's voice. "He-e-elp!"

But no one stepped forward. They all simply went on shaking.

Glorp. His head and feet went through, and the cries abruptly ceased. His two hands remained for several more moments, hanging limply over the rim of the black hole, but just as someone started to reach for them, they, too, were pulled on through with a final *glorrrp*. The black circle hanging in midair quickly shrank to a point and disappeared.

"Our brother has become divine shit," declared Chayama, and when the crowd went into a frenzy, he hastened to add, "But you should not yet be rejoicing. You should be sad, for the man is now all alone in the void. Have you any idea how it feels to be cast out into the emptiness as a solitary turdhead? Shake your bellies, my friends. Shake your bellies harder. Follow him down the path he has just trod. Join him in becoming turdheads, one and all. That was not the only sphincter. Every person in the world has an opening for his bowels. His own separate orifice. And every person in the world becomes a turdhead in his own way, in her own way. Every one of you is different, and it's all good."

A fresh roar went up from the crowd and the bellyshaking resumed. Someone barreled about among the dancers swinging a dead monkey. Others shinnied a few feet up the sky-ropes and dropped onto the crowd below, shaking their torsos as they fell through the air. As the antics grew wilder and wilder, a woman who'd been doing a slow swivel on the levee let out a sudden cry.

"My belly's burning! My belly's burning!"

As with Magobei, when the temperature had become too hot to bear, her stomach jutted forward in a series of unstoppable thrusts, until *crack!* her hip joints gave way and she was folded completely in two.

"*Eeyaaagghh!*" she screamed madly.

Hovering in midair, her body quickly began vanishing into another invisible hole. At the end, several tangled tresses of hair dangled over the edge for several moments before finally slipping on through. Perhaps a woman's long locks were somehow difficult to pass.

Now similar cries began rising in every direction. The crowd was turning into divine shit all up and down the riverbed and embankment.

The sun stood directly overhead, unmoving, as if stuck permanently at high noon.

The sky was a mind-blowing blue. A stark-raving-mad blue.

Only at this juncture did it occur to many of those present that they did not really care to be expelled from this world as shit.

Abruptly abandoning their shaking, they turned to flee the lunatic riverbed, but it was no use. One after another they were halted in their tracks, folded in two, and dragged excruciatingly through invisible holes into the unseen beyond.

Those who were left could but run helplessly in circles with tears streaming down their faces.

No one remained in the riverbed. The sun was still perched high overhead, going nowhere. From one end of the sky to the other was pure, unblemished blue.

Then far in the distance, a strange white form appeared—long and slender, with a hollow in the middle. The immense object flexed and rippled as it moved through the sky, until all at once it swooped down and scooped the whole of Mt. Tokugo right out of the landscape, altering the ridgeline of the mountain range in the blink of an eye. Moments later, a gale-force wind arrived, blowing the sky-ropes sideways and lifting swirls of gravel from the riverbed.

The wind blew on and on without letting up, then abruptly rose even higher. This was no mere wind, it was a fearsome pneumatic force.

The absurdly gigantic scooper that had fluttered across the sky to lift an entire mountain from its footing was carried off somewhere by this powerful blast, and a short while later there came what had to be described as a crash—though it was certainly no ordinary *Crash!* It was the kind of *CRAAASHH!* you might hear if every dish in the world was smashed, every bell in the world was rung, every window in the world was shattered, and every piano in the world was dropped to the street below, all in the same instant; a *CRAAASHH!* so ear-splittingly loud that if there'd been anyone left to hear it, they'd have been rendered profoundly and irrevocably deaf.

At least half of the sky-ropes whipped sideways were torn off and blown away by the wind, which arrived in three sustained blasts with short rests between. The last was the most violent of all, and it blew so hard that it peeled a layer of earth right off the ground and stood it on end, raising the Yōrei River with it like a waterfall. But this lasted for only a moment before the upraised swatch of earth, too, was torn off and blown away like a tattered rag.

Beneath where it had been there now appeared a deep cone-shaped pit, with shiny white walls like a porcelain rice bowl. At the bottom of this smooth white bowl was a single black dot that looked no bigger than a tiny poppy seed.

It was Chayama Hanrō.

He was shaking uncontrollably.

He could make no sense of where he was.

In a full circle around him, all he could see was a plain white surface sloping upward. Nothing marred its immaculate expanse.

The only contrast discernible anywhere was far, far above, where the white rim of the bowl met the cerulean sky.

He could hear nothing.

He had attempted to climb the slope, hoping to escape the oppressive white. But the surface was slick, with no holds to grab, and the distance to the top much too great. He slid back down after gaining only a few meters.

The result was the same every time, but he kept on trying, again and again and again. He had nothing else to do.

Eventually, though, he gave it up. He had exhausted both his strength and his will. He sat in a daze at the bottom of the bowl, wondering what in the world had happened to him.

Had he become divine shit, too?

Was this the "true world outside" that he'd been talking about?

But how could that be, when so many others had disappeared in midair, and not one of them was here?

Plus the sky above was exactly like the sky over the riverbed. He couldn't recall ever having pictured a blue sky outside the tapeworm's gut; he'd had more the image of a dark void. Didn't that have to mean he was still in the same world as before, and that the top of the white slope up there was the riverbed?

But why this? Why should he be the only one left? Even if it was all made-up, even if he'd only been selling a bill of goods, the whole idea of escaping the tapeworm's gut had been his. So why should he, of all people, end up as the only one left in some totally white place he'd never uttered a single word about?

At any rate, here he was, staring at this crazy white world all by himself, the only one here. A world no one but he could see was a world that existed only inside his own head. So could he change the world by bashing his head open?

As Chayama was still pondering these things, something in the distance high above caught his eye. Beyond the rim of the bowl to one side, a flat, shiny object like a huge wall panel was descending, ascending, then descending again, over and over. It immediately came to him that it was a blade.

And just as quickly, he understood: a giant kitchen knife was chopping something up next to the bowl.

In which case the bottom of this white cone might well be the safest place to be.

The thought revived his spirits a little, and he decided to try shaking his belly again.

The operative principle remained a mystery to him, but since it was by shaking his belly that he'd gotten into this fix, perhaps shaking his belly some more would at least serve to move things along. Even if it turned out to make matters worse, anything seemed better at the moment than remaining forever trapped in this confoundedly white world and quietly going insane.

He stood up and began moving his belly.

Nothing happened.

Who am I kidding? he thought, and promptly gave it up.

The top of the bowl was hopelessly far away, and the vast white slope seemed to bear down on him with crushing force.

The knife continued to slice up and down next to the bowl.

I should get some sleep, he thought. *Maybe this'll all turn out to have been a dream.*

He lay down on the bottom of the bowl. The surface was pleasantly cool to the touch, and he hoped this might help him drift off, but the oppressive whiteness infiltrated behind his closed eyelids and kept him from sleep.

I'll wait until the sun sets, he thought, and sat back up.

The sun never set.

Kakari Jūnoshin was walking through the ravaged town. Flattened houses, tipped rain barrels, piles of rubble—it was a scene of utter devastation.

But all was now quiet. Not a sound could be heard, and not a soul could be seen anywhere. Not even a cat or dog.

Where is everybody? he wondered. They couldn't have gone much farther than this by now.

He had only a vague memory of how he himself had gotten here. He remembered fighting his way out of the riverbed, cutting down anybody who crossed his path. Gosenrō had taken thirty men with him on his way to death, but many more than that had fallen in Jūnoshin's wake. He killed in order to live. *Chok!* A hand flew off. *Chok!* A head tumbled to the ground. When he realized his sword had become bent, he tossed it aside. His hands were sticky with blood, and he wanted to wash them, but every rain barrel he passed was lying overturned.

Finally, he spotted a large earthenware jar standing upright just inside the door of an eatery that appeared to be largely spared from damage.

It was the tavern he'd come to with Gosenrō.

The jar was filled with water, and it was untainted. There was even a dipper.

First Jūnoshin cleaned his hands. Then he took a drink.

The water was delicious, and he filled the dipper again and again. With his thirst slaked, a thought came to him, and he started for the back. He wondered if he might be able to turn up some rice and saké.

The kitchen appeared largely untouched as well. He looked in every jar and container, but found only the likes of soy sauce and salt, no saké or rice.

Out of luck, he returned to the front of the shop.

I should probably head on back to Sondai-ji to see what I can find out, he thought, and started for the door. Just then a shadow fell across the opening from outside.

"Who goes?" he shouted, jumping back and reaching for the short sword still in his belt.

But then he recognized Ron and let out a sigh of relief.

"I thought I saw someone moving around in here," she said as she entered.

"It's you!" exclaimed Jūnoshin, suddenly on cloud nine. "When did you get back to town?"

"An hour ago, maybe. What exactly happened here?"

"I wish I knew. It's just a total mess. A lot of people died, but I can't explain any of it. Everything was going perfectly fine at first. But then Osamu went nuts and started blowing everybody up. Until he got picked off, too. And there was this incredible horde of monkeys. I started swinging my sword blindly to get away, and somehow found my way here."

"I can't make head or tail of what you're saying."

"That makes two of us. To be honest, nobody was willing say so out loud, but there's been way too much strange stuff going on. I definitely think something's gotten seriously out of whack with the world."

Ron let out a cackle.

Jūnoshin was taken aback. He'd let down his guard with her and candidly expressed how he felt. He hadn't expected to be ridiculed for it.

"What's so funny?" he said.

"Oh, I'm sorry. But if you don't mind my asking, what makes you think something's so seriously out of whack?"

"Do you really have to ask? It's been one weird thing after another lately. Osamu, for starters. How could he do that stuff? There's just no way to explain it. And then there's Deusu Nobu'uzu."

"Ah, yes, the monkey."

"That's right, the monkey. The monkey who could talk just like us. And commanded his monkey army like a master tactician to boot. I can't explain him either. Nor the multitudes of monkeys who showed up out of nowhere to join the battle—did they spring from the earth, or fall from heaven? More likely the latter, I suppose, since that's where they fled in the end, up thousands of brown ropes dangling from the sky. But how is that even possible—ropes dangling from the sky? What're they attached to? It makes no sense. It's just too weird. There's too much I can't explain."

"Then do you mind if I ask you something?"

"What?"

"Are you implying you *can* explain everything else?"

"What're you getting at?"

"You're so silly," she giggled. "For example, take a look out there," she said, gesturing toward the doorway.

At first glance, he saw nothing unusual. Apart from the town being in ruins, it looked like any ordinary day outside.

But then he noticed something quite impossible.

Hovering on its side at about eye level was a foot-long lightning bolt of brilliant white light, periodically throwing out fiery sparks.

"That doesn't normally happen in the natural world, yet there it is," she said. "Which just goes to show that Master Chayama is right: the reality we see around us is purely an illusion."

Hearing her speak of Chayama this way set off alarm bells for Jūnoshin. He'd been a little uneasy about Ron from the moment she first walked in. Compared to when they were en route to Hedaka, or when he'd said goodbye to her there, he sensed a certain coolness in the way she regarded him.

"You actually believe what Chayama says?" he asked.

"Yes, I do. Accepting it makes the most sense to me."

"So you're on your way back to him now?" he said, his heart pounding.

"Why would you think that?"

"Well, I mean, if you believe in him…"

"I never said I believed in him. I believe the truth of what he teaches. I…" she started to say, but broke off.

"You what?" Jūnoshin said

She looked him straight in the eye. "I want to go with you."

His heart leapt. Her directness thrilled him to the core.

"Ron," he said, "Chayama could be right when he says this world's an illusion. In fact, I'll grant that he probably is. But as you can see, I'm still alive and kicking. I've made my way through life by my own power, without attaching myself to any particular organization. And that's how I intend to go on living. It's the only way I know how. If the Kuroae folks found out that the world's nothing but an illusion, I doubt they could go on living at all. But that's not me. I'm not one to question the fundamental nature of the world. Why should I care? I intend to go on living no matter what the world is—an illusion or a total fiction or whatever. Because I'm a punk samurai. That's what I am, Ron," he said, returning her gaze. "Are you sure you want to come with a man like that?"

She simply nodded, without saying anything.

He smiled sheepishly. "Shall we go then?" he said, and stepped out the door ahead of her.

The ruins outside were unchanged, as was the position of the bright midday sun. There was still no one else to be seen, but the white bar of lightning continued to throw sparks, and the atmosphere was displaying fits of madness. The blue sky was now partly torn, leaving blank patches here and there.

"I don't care," he spat out, then turned toward Ron to suggest they head for Ushichiku.

At that moment, Ron stabbed him with a bamboo spatula.

The spatula had a sharp, pointed tip that plunged into his liver.

Surprised by a sudden heavy sensation in his side, Jūnoshin instinctively put his hands to the spot. He felt the blood and realized he'd been stabbed.

"What was that for?" he said, as he fell to a knee.

Ron stepped around to face him, gazing down at him.

"You still don't recognize me, do you?" she said. "You killed my father in front of a wayside teahouse on the edge of town. This is my revenge. Master Chayama took me in after that, and he fixed my eyes so I could see again. The only reason I pretended to be attracted to you was so I could get close and kill you with my own hands. *Hah!* That'll teach you, Kakari Jūnoshin!"

Thud. Thud. Thud. Thud. Between the violent bolts of pain that shot through him with each pulse, Jūnoshin barely managed to squeeze out a reply.

"You're right. That was my bad. But you just got done telling me you believe the world's an illusion. If that's really true, what's the point of mounting a vendetta against your father's killer? If it's all an illusion anyway, why should you get so hung up on retribution? That's the part I don't follow. If it's all arbitrary, wouldn't it be a whole lot easier to just forget it and move on? Why do you insist on cause bringing effect even when the world isn't ruled by cause and effect?"

"Because it makes me mad! And besides…"

"Besides what?"

"It's exactly because the world's that way that I can't let some things go."

Jūnoshin could not reply. A sudden chill had come over him and his teeth were chattering too hard for him to speak.

Hugging himself tightly with his arms, he fell forward onto his face, thinking, *I'm going to die like a dog from being stabbed in the liver with a bamboo kitchen utensil, all in a world of illusion.* He ached for one last glimpse of Ron's beautiful countenance, but he had no strength to lift his head, and even with his eyes open he could no longer see.

Ron watched the life ebb from Jūnoshin's body, then spun on her heels and walked away without a second glance. After taking several steps, she stopped, turned her head back, and exhaled blue sky into the air.

The sky was make-believe beautiful. So beautiful, it was pure make-believe.